TOAST

Hells Mission

BOOK 5

Rick Allen

First published 2025 by Rick Allen

Copyright © Rick Allen 2025

This novel is entirely a work of fiction. The incidents and some of the characters portrayed in it are the work of the author's imagination.

A catalogue record for this book is available from the National Library of Australia

Publisher:
Inspiring Publishers
P.O. Box 159, Calwell, ACT Australia 2905
Email: publishaspg@gmail.com
http://www.inspiringpublishers.com

National Library of Australia Prepublication Data Service

Author: Allen, Rick

Title: **BOOK FIVE: TOAST – Hells Mission/*Rick Allen***

ISBN: 978-1-923449-38-1 (print)
ISBN: 978-1-923449-39-8 (ePub2)

The Author

Rick Allen lives in Woodsdale, Tasmania, with his wife Lesley. Rick is a 'born and bred' Tasmanian (b1956) with a keen interest in naval history, military horses and saddlery, long equestrian journeys and the history of his profession; that of a saddler. He started his education at Cosgrove High School, and with his father a merchant seaman and professional fisherman, his grandfather, a master mariner tug skipper in London, and his great-grandfather, a master mariner, Thames barge sailing captain, it was a natural progression for Rick to join the Navy at the age of 15 and complete his education at HMAS Leeuwin in Western Australia.

Rick was assigned to the Electronic Technical Weapons branch of the Navy and served on many ships and support depots. Upon discharge from the permanent Navy, Rick served another eight years in the Naval Reserves on a patrol boat. Some of the hats that Rick has worn since those Navy days include those of qualified electrical fitter, workplace trainer and assessor, ship's master, marine engine driver, saddler, and horseback tour guide, just to mention a few.

Rick's passion to write comes from a desire to pass knowledge and stories on to others.

Table of Contents

Dedications

I dedicate this book to my mate Buck

Ex-Navy JR, Paul Rogers

Acknowledgements

COVER DESIGN

Photos of HMAS Fremantle by
LSETP/ POETP Gary Haigh

Other photos used in this book were copied
by me from my photographs

"No copyright infringement is intended"

Statistics, where appropriate by Wikipedia

**Those people in my life who inspired
the main characters in this book**

Even though this book is fiction, it is based on real life
characters. Their names have been changed to protect their
privacy, and I would like to formally acknowledge them here.

MY EDITING TEAM

I would like to formally recognise
the other half of my editing team,

Lesley Allen. Thank you for your many
long hours of dedicated work.

Cast of Main Characters

TWADDLE ORIGINALS

Richard (Dick) Mann Ex-navy chief petty officer clearance diver, weapons specialist and demolition expert. Started his navy career at HMAS Leeuwin as a junior recruit, then a weapons mechanic before becoming a CD. Sometimes appears grumpy and has a huge "bite" if provoked; but is really a gentle giant. Six-foot-five in stature. Balding with a grey beard.

Beth (Patch) Mann Formally Beth McFarlane of Western Australia. Expert in all things IT. Married to Dick on 23rd March 1979. Has five children with him. A woman with a heart of gold who would do anything to "make it all right".

Jack Smouch Ex-navy petty officer clearance diver, specialist sniper, and member of the 'Mile" club and world record with a confirmed kill at 2815 metres. Started his navy career in the Marine Technical Propulsion (Stoker) branch. Deep down, he just wants to help his mates and would bend over backwards to do so.

April Smouch Married to Jack. French sustainability expert. Previously worked for the French Government. Has one child with an abusive ex-husband. Met Jack whilst he was on a holiday after his first tour of Afghanistan. A gentle unassuming woman of great resolve.

Wayne (Sarge) Michaels Ex-army sapper. Expert in small arms, explosives and demolition. Adept with his hands in more ways than one can imagine. Would do anything for his mates.

Annie Palmer Expert Horsewoman. Partner to Sarge. Treated like a daughter by Dick and Patch. Just loves everyone; especially animals... well, mainly horses!

KINGS TOWN HOSPITAL

Dr Roger (Doc) Johns Mate of Dick and Patch. Ex-Royal Australian Navy Reserve Captain. Keen sailor. Prominent ear nose and throat (ENT) specialist. Has one daughter from a failed marriage. A mild-mannered doctor at heart.

Nari Kim South Korean triage nurse on a working holiday at Kings Town Hospital and Doc's girlfriend. A passionate woman who would die for her man.

Dr Phil Brown Surgeon.

Dr Ted Green Anaesthetist.

Dr Les Solomon Cardiology expert.

Dr Helen Smith Diagnostic imaging specialist. Not really a doctor; but posing as one after a suggestion by Doc to save her life.

Dr Henry Swain ENT specialist. The only doctor older than Doc. Respected by everyone.

Dr Alex Wallace Endoscopy specialist. Escapes on his yacht Rumble.

Dr Rob Simpson Gynaecologist. 55 years old. Moved to Benoa.

Dr David Benson Haematology specialist.

Dr Lynda Browne Nephrology expert.

Dr Bruce Charles Oncology specialist.

Dr Bob Silver Orthopaedic surgeon.

Dr Patricia Collins Radiotherapist

Dr Dave Reddy Renal specialist

Dr Reginald Miles Urologist.

Dr Julie Smith Paediatrician.

Dr Michael Bane Gynaecologist.

Dr Christine Simmons Haematologist.

Dr Ian Walters Intensive Care Specialist

HIGH HEAD ORIGINALS

Ernie Flood Ex-army reservist, crane driver working at the Bull Bay terminal for Gary Town Cranes. Lives in the High Head Lighthouse. Good friend of Patch and Dick. Would give you the shirt off his back if asked.

Belle Flood Housewife, good friend of Patch and Dick, married to Ernie, one daughter (Nic). Lives in the High Head Lighthouse.

Nic Walt Ernie and Belle's daughter, pilot station museum curator, mother of Gaz and Boz. A wild child in her youth, calmed somewhat by the robustly handsome Smokey.

Smokey Walt Chief river pilot in charge of the Ramat River pilot station. Ex-navy coxswain, married to Nic. A 'take no prisoners' kind of guy.

Gaz and Boz Walt Sons of Smokey and Nic. Trainee river pilots under their father. Both ex-army reservists.

Charlotte Platt Gary Town senior constable. Married to Henry

Henry Platt Gary Town senior constable. Married to Charlotte.

Kylie Wiggins University student. Orphaned when the alliance killed her parents.

Claudia Smith Local girl found hiding from the alliance at Cimitiere Creek. Sister of Chris Smith. Usually a loaner. Became friends with Bill after the Holocaust.

Chris Smith Local boy found hiding from the alliance at Cimitiere Creek. Brother of Claudia Smith. Ex-army reservist. Worked for the Hydro Electric Commission in Lawn.

Bill Gates Local lad found hiding from the alliance at Cimitiere Creek. Ex-army reservist. Worked at the Gary Town fish and chip shop.

NORTH KOREAN ALLIANCE

General Jun Lee Sung North Korean general in charge of the whole invasion. A proud career army man. Ecstatic to be picked by the President to lead the invasion force at the age of sixty.

Captain Li Chun Second in charge under the general. A career army man who took his position very seriously.

INDONESIAN ALLIANCE

Admiral Adi Atmadja Captain of the super tanker - Indo Maersk. Overall commander of all Indonesian Alliance. Due to retire as soon as the nationals have been placed, and a suitable replacement can be found.

Nurul Atmadja The admiral's wife. A doting woman who gave up her own career to serve her husband and raise her children.

Huje Samira Major.

Raja Atmadja Captain. The admiral's nephew.

Lieutenant Colonel Raj Sumatro Indonesian Alliance commander at Benoa, east coast. Proud to be chosen to lead the Indonesians. A likely candidate to replace the admiral as supreme commander.

Adina Sumatro Wife of Raj.

Ambar Mother of Adina.

Kevin and Indah Sumatro Raj's parents

Wayan Raj's grandfather. An ex-military man who is proud that his grandson made it on to the list to invade Taswegia, sealing his longevity.

PATROL BOAT WARRNAMBOOL

Commander Suprapto Commander and career navy man. Quite short in stature. Chosen because of his humanitarian manner.

Lieutenant Joko Executive officer. Second-in-command.

Chief Ade Engineer.

STRONG FORT BAY ORIGINALS

John Badman Julia Bay farmer. Reluctant leader.

Helen Badman Wife of John Badman.

Trish and Billy Badman John and Helen's children.

James Smythe Julia Bay architect.

Miriam Smythe Wife of James. Retired schoolteacher.

Robert Crawfield Dentist.

Gina Crawfield Wife of Robert. Dental receptionist.

Sid Crawfield Son of Robert and Gina. Ex-railway worker.

Ellen Crawfield Wife of Sid.

Helen and Craig Crawfield Children of Ellen and Sid.

Cedric Bilton Retired shipping agent.

Aileen Bilton Wife of Cedric. Self-employed hairdresser.

Mick Jones Farmer.

Sarah Jones Wife of Mick.

Roger, Jimmy, Shelly and Michael Jones Children of Mick and Sarah.

Graham Walton Courier driver.

Bentley Frank Chartered accountant

Barbara Frank Wife of Bentley.

Josh, Jill, Blythe and Anna Frank Children of Bentley and Barbara

Tony Oglio Retired concreter and pizza expert.

Mary Oglio Wife of Tony. Retired bank worker.

BENOA ORIGINALS

George Black Schoolteacher.
Wendy Black Nursing sister.
Kelly and Rob Black Children of George and Wendy.
Mick Swab Barman.
Peter Howe Retired fisherman.
Brian Smith Service station attendant.
Yvonne Smith Wife of Brian. Medical receptionist.
Hilary Smith Daughter of Brian and Yvonne.
Jack Davis Retired fisherman.
Joan Davis Retired schoolteacher.
David Numa Benoa Motel staff member.
Eleanore Fame David Numa's partner. Self-employed hairdresser.
Clinton Ramon Invalid pensioner and ex-butcher.

William Green Wildlife attendant.
Helga Sven Swedish exchange student and wildlife attendant.
Dr Margaret Bones General practitioner.

FISHERMEN-BLACK INK

Harold Patmore Skipper
Riley Patmore Nephew deckhand
Fishermen- Christa Leanne
Harry Montgomery Skipper
Gary Montgomery Deckhand

FISHERMEN-CARNIVORE

Len Roberts 39 Carnivore skipper
Bart Wooley 26 Carnivore deckhand
William Dart Ex Yimbala skipper

EX MARY ISLAND

Paul Gray Mary Island head ranger
Gregory Price Mary Island ranger
Shaz Horsewoman

STRAWBERRY BAY ORIGINALS

Brian Green Real estate agent
Jill Green Daughter of Brian and Gwen
Gwen Green Wife of Brian
Alf Grood Unemployed
Samuel Roberts Landscaper
Liz Smith College student
Max House Builder's labourer
Nikki Boon Nine-year-old daughter of Sheryn and Rob
Rob Boon Butcher
Sheryn Boon Fruit and veg manager

Riff Hans Retired carpenter
Gertie Hans Ex-smallgoods factory worker
Simon Hans 14-year-old son of Gertie and Riff
Fran Gonzalez Vineyard worker
Roberto Gonzalez Concreter

STRINE TEAM

Lou Parry Horse trekking business owner and friend to Dick and Patch

Doug Harris Police sergeant
Tom O'Grady Strine mayor
Dennis Parry Lou's father and fire chief
Bill Mallard Publican
Denis Crawfield Skipper of the St Bernadett
John Crawfield Deckhand and son of skipper
Dr Phil Hyland General practitioner

TELLER TEAM

Nevile Post Farmer ex-trail riding operator

Val Post Farmer ex-trail riding operator and wife of Nevile

WATTLE TEAM

Chris (Santa) West Petty officer ex-clearance diver Junior recruit Joined with Dick

Pat West Wife of Chris

Barry (Baz) Cole Petty officer ex-clearance diver Junior recruit Joined with Dick

Lyn Cole Wife of Barry

Brian (Buck) Williams Officer ex-clearance diver Junior recruit Joined with Dick

SUE WILLIAMS WIFE OF BRIAN

Mike (Blue) Bone Sargeant Special Air Service (SAS) served with Dick in Gulf War trained together in 84

Anita Crisp Partner to Mike
Griz Wattle local

LORD BARRON TEAM

Denis Brown Farmer
Diane Brown Farmer wife of Denis
Noel Chambers Worker
Nettie Crumb 18yo Worker
Palana Boss Island Team
Henry Allen Fisherman
Celia Allen Wife of Henry
James Wiggins Fisherman
Trish Wiggins Wife of James
Black Mark Team
Bobby Williams Mechanic
St Anne's Rebels Team
Rose Whyat Part-time barmaid
Barry Crosin Builder
Nick Millhouse Apprentice builder
Trent Millhouse Apprentice panel beater

STRATH TEAM

Nigel (Nobby) Clark Trail ride owner
Brenda Clark Wife and guide
Nick Wooley Guide
Michelle Good Nick's partner and guide
Dave Charmers Salmon farm worker on ride
Linda Ward Salmon farm worker on ride

Christine Bell Salmon farm worker on ride
Shane Briars Salmon farm worker on ride
Nugget Rolands Gunsmith. Mate of Jack

CHOOK HOLE LAKE TEAM

Pete Shot South Bay Hotel manager
Delilah Shot South Bay Hotel manager
Matilda Grundig South Bay Hotel waitress
Willy Stodding Fisherman
Margaret Stodding Willly's wife
Linda Stodding Doctor. Daughter of Willy and Margaret.
Rachael Smith Teacher's aid
Shayne Books Apple orchard worker
Don Smart Apple doctor
Brian Graves Wooden boat shed manager

BOLLARDS BEACH MOB

Helen Waters Camper
Chris Waters Camper
Billy Frees Camper. Grandson of Helen and Chris.
Lauri Tern Camper
May Tern Camper
Chris Tern Camper
Vert Frey Camper

LITTLE DUCKPORT MOB

Paul Constance House painter Kings Town
Mal Turnish Real estate agent from Devon

CHINAMAN BEACH TEAM

Wendy Lord Benoa schoolteacher

Bill Lord Benoa plumber

FROG ISLAND LOCALS

Fun Bay
Pat Bisch Lighthouse keeper
Steve Bisch Lighthouse keeper
Ivan Schwartz Shack owner from Kings Town. Accountant
Cindy Bennet Kings Town retired army mechanical engineer
Julie Sweet Shack owner from Kings Town
Rod Sweet Son of Julie
Julia Sweet Daughter of Julie
Ron Barr Local winemaker
Debra Barr Sister of Ron. Vineyard worker

DENIS POINT TEAM

Gladys Ponder Housewife
Bill Ponder Retired government employee
Phillip Grange Publican
Elizabeth Grange Publican
Shakira Grange Barmaid
Mervin Watt Retired. Airforce maintenance fitter

TASWEGIA II CREW

John Williams First officer
Bradley Scott - Captain
Helen Williams Third officer
Maurice Stone Bosun
Tegan Collins Medical officer
Gary Sweet Second officer
Brian Cooper Hospitality officer
Jillian Bryant Purser
Kenny Samson Deck rating
Helga Miob Gaming supervisor

Jock Page Second engineer
Wallace Bellows Engineer
Terri Graham Chef
Liz McDonald Kitchenhand
Lesley Bruning Housekeeping superintendent
Marie Browning Housekeeping
Mr and Mrs Bristol Passengers
Paul Gabon Passenger

FOUR HUMMOCK ISLAND TEAM

Lauren Wilson Tour operator. Children were at school when E1 hit

Thomas Wilson Ex-regimental sergeant major (RSM). Father and groundsman

GRASS TEAM

Reg Gowen Ex- Royal Australian Regiment (RAR) sniper
Rusty Gowen Ex-RAR
Grant Youl Professional shooter
Britteny Munn Professional shooter

THE RESISTANCE FRONT (TRF) ELITE SQUAD

Dick Trainer
Jack Trainer
Thomas Wilson Ex-RSM
Sarge Trainer
Tom Cooper Ex-RAR corporal
Reg Gowen Ex--RAR sniper
Rusty Gowen Ex RAR
Grant Youl Professional shooter
Britteny Munn Professional shooter

Bird Island Team
John Hammer 48 Farmer and owner
Chris Hammer 54 Brother
Kayleen Hammer 50 John's wife
Billy Short 29 Stockman
Tracey Webster 26 Billy's girlfriend
Murray Mills 49 Shooter

BROWNSVILLE/ WYNN TEAM

John Webster 56 RAR SGT still serving but at home awaiting medical discharge

Ester Webster 57 John's new wife
Robbo 46 Radio operator ex-ham radio buff
Queen Island Team
Gill Barmaid
Kelly Barmaid
Graham Farmer
Vlademir Cheesemaker

Prologue

IN 2000, a long-debated international law was passed to help combat climate change. All vehicles manufactured from that point on were to have the E1 (Engine 1) modification – a device that reduced emissions to less than 1 per cent. To assist with emission reduction, every country worldwide agreed to get rid of all pre-2000 vehicles. Vehicle owners were given two years to decide to either sell their pre-2000 vehicle to their government for pittance, or to choose to have them modified.

The world was a different place after the events of 9/11 and the consequent 'War on Terror'.

While the rest of the western world was thoroughly engaged with the 'War on Terror', some nations focused their efforts on planning their revenge against the major powers. North Korea, Indonesia, India, Pakistan, Turkey and Iraq banded together to form the Alliance.

In mid-2014 a united push against ISIS took place, with all non-Alliance nations agreeing to deploy 95-100 per cent of their military forces.

Tensions reached boiling point on 17th December 2014 when North Korea pushed the button to unleash its nuclear arsenal on Central Europe and the United States.

Swift retaliation came within thirty minutes.

A small number of countries within the Alliance had predicted this retaliation, with North Korea, Indonesia and India secretly forming a pact to identify a safe haven where they could start again if the world was obliterated.

They agreed that the only two safe havens were New Haka and Taswegia, and within a few weeks of the first strike, the new Alliance invaded Taswegia with a mandate to annihilate every citizen, to make way for their own people. Knowing that their own medical staff would not arrive until the landing of the third convoy, they realised they would need to keep the native doctors alive for now.

The invasion date was Friday 2nd January 2015. The new Alliance arrived in 20 purpose-built super tankers, powered by old steam and fuel oil engines, which had been filled with members of the invading force - some six weeks before the button was pushed. The invasion had begun.

Two Taswegian former navy clearance divers, best mates Dick, and Jack, along with their mate Sarge, an ex-army sapper, and their partners Patch, April and Annie quickly realised that their only hope was to contact other survivors who might be able to help them rid their land of the Alliance.

A danger-fraught week of travel began, with Dick and Jack travelling by road and sea, and with Sarge, Patch, April and Annie on horseback. Along the way both groups encountered Alliance troops more than once, narrowly escaping with their lives. Eventually they managed to reach the relative safety of Hell's Beach. Here, they set up camp, thinking they were well out of reach of the Alliance at last.

However, their reprieve from danger was brief, awakening one morning to see a Fremantle class patrol boat had appeared at the entrance to the bay. Realising they were about to be discovered; Dick and the others worked together feverishly to overpower the Alliance crew and take control of the patrol boat. However, the skirmish left Jack's wife April seriously injured, and in urgent need of medical help.

After rescuing Dr Roger 'Doc' Johns and his girlfriend Nari, a South Korean triage nurse, the adventure continued with the torpedoing of an Alliance super tanker, resulting in a small victory for the resistance fighters. After an emergency operation on April, the team rescued the survivors from Benoa and trained them to retaliate. Now it was time to regain possession of their home, starting with the Peninsular!

Rescuing survivors from around the southeast, Dick and his band of resistance fighters establish a base at Strong Fort Bay and train the ex-farmers and the rest of the group into the T.R.F. (Taswegian Resistance Force). With the power of the ex-Royal Australian Navy Patrol Boat *HMAS Fremantle*, they wreak havoc with the Alliance forces and gain control of the Peninsular....

... With a wild plan to re-power pre-2000 vessels the TRF gains strength, liberates the Strine locals and trains them to defend the West Coast from the Alliance that had not yet invaded them. Bolstering the Peninsular and Mary Island, they head north to team up with a bunch of rebels at High Head. Whilst in convoy with *Dementia* and *Nancy Kay*, the *Fremantle* is side tracked to rescue the *Spirit of Taswegia II* - adrift since the E1.

TRF Vessel FCPB Fremantle 147-foot ex- RAN and
Indonesian Patrol Boat Twin 3200 HP MTUs

Chapter 1
Frog Island

Sunday 1ˢᵗ March 2015 Black Ink, Denis Point

0800 hours, Harold could hear the voices from below, he had risen early and checked a few things in the engine room, smiling to himself, he thought of the younger ones on board, it didn't take Alf long to cuddle up to Shakira, and Shayne to Debra. He had taken a few days off, so to speak, honing the newcomer's weapons skills, and partially to wait for the *Retaliator*.

The ex-air force fitter Mervin was next up, helping himself to a coffee. The sixty-eight-year-old RAAF fitter started his career servicing Iroquois helicopters in Vietnam around October 1968. He and Harold spent quite a bit of time getting to know each other over the last few days.

Shayne and Alf were next to appear, both looked like they had swallowed the cat, Alf asked, "How did you go with Johnny the other day, Skipper?" The thirty-year-old ex-fisherman answered "Great, we should see the *Retaliator* by the time we get to Legs. Riley and a relief team from Lewis will give us a couple of days, because after that we get a new vessel, coming down from Strine, one of the ones that Harry, Gary and Jill have been working on with the locals, but I'll keep you all posted."

1200 hours and the skipper held a meeting in the wheelhouse, Harold asked.

"What are your thoughts on us mounting a raid on Kettle? We might be able to sneak in amongst the marina vessels unnoticed, clear a few homes, then back here for the night. I'd suggest a night raid, but I reckon the marina would be a minefield of ropes, sunken boats etc."

Shayne stated "Might be a great intro to the new recruits, wet their whistle so to speak." Alf agreed.

"We could lead two groups; one takes the old ferry terminal and the other the hlotel." Harold drew up the plan, called everyone to the wheelhouse then informed them.

"Short raid this afternoon, team one will be led by Shayne, with Brian, Pat, Steve, Ivan, Cindy and Debra. Team two will be led by Alf, with Peter, Samuel, Christine, Ron, Mervin and Shakira, which leaves *Black Ink* crew as Me, the Doc and the Sweets. If there is too much trouble, come back to the boat, if we get into trouble, we will stand off and wait for your signal. Now both team leaders will have a portable UHF on channel 19, only use it, when necessary, not sure that the Alliance haven't infiltrated the system." There was an air of half excitement amongst the group, some disappointed, like the fifteen-year-old Sweet twins who obviously wanted in on the action.

1400 hours, the *Black Ink* silently made its way into Kettle Bay, at three knots it wasn't making any wake. The old Kettle to Frog ferry was still attached to the terminal while various small yachts sunk on their moorings, the farthest finger of the Marina jutted out from the tlerminal building. This was the one that Harold slid alongside, bringing the eighty-five-foot ex-slquid boat's black hull to a gentle stop on the huge fenders. The only noise was a small squeak as the air-filled fenders rubbed against the marina pontoon.

Twenty minutes later, with mooring lines attached, weapons and ammo issued, a fully loaded team one climbed up onto the timber and concrete pontoon. Shayne turned and whispered to the team,

"Safety's off, follow my lead." With this, he led them to the terminal building. with its restaurant, ticket office and café, marine brokerage business and couple of upstairs flats. These were certainly worth looking at. Sneaking up the stairs, Shayne changed to his Type 54 with suppressor, suggesting the others do the same. At the top of the stairs he could smell cooking, this meant that either someone was home, or they were out and could come back at any time.

Slowly, opening the door, one National was revealed, sitting with their back to the door. TNhe ex-orchard worker took no chances and fired from the doorway.

"Dooff." The 9mm round hit the National fair square in the middle of his back, the hollow point entering midway, taking out his backbone and exiting through the sternum leaving a hole larger than a tennis ball, making him slump forward. Shayne and Brian entered the room, they could hear voices coming from another room and waited either side of the door. Quite confused, the rest of the team entered, not hearing the voices, thinking the first two had cleared it.

When the NK National woman stepped into the doorway, she was confronted by six TRF members armed to the teeth. Looking at the male slumped forward in his chair, she screamed! Steve points his Type 68 at her but can't get a clear shot, this was because Brian had the woman in a headlock, until Shayne managed to shoot her with his pistol. Shayne whispered

"Check all the other rooms, use your pistols." Now, he knew that not everyone had suppressors, but their Type 54sd would be quieter than the 68s.

1500 hours, Alf's tleam two had scampered past the tlerminal building. Keeping to the marina pontoons, they passed hundreds of vessels, some sunk on their moorings, frying their electronics, their main engines, along with their bilge pumps after the E1 hit. Sometimes this would blow a hole in the bottom of the boat, depending on where the engine device was located. Alf could have easily stayed and looked at the boats all day, he just loved them.

The Kettle Hotel overlooked the bay and the marina, self-conscious of being seen was always on the eighteen-year-old's mind, and this time was for a good reason, 100 metres from the marina office they were bought under fire from the hotel balcony.

"Boom...Boom...Boom."

The Type 68 assault rifles familiar sound, the rounds splintering the pontoon around them. Quickly hiding behind a cruiser, Alf and Peter returned fire; the shooter was not prepared for this and disappeared back into the hotel. On the run again to the office they were out of the firing arc, under the hotel balcony. Alf motioned to Peter, Ron and Mervyn to enter there, while he took the rest of them to the end doorway.

The trio climbed the internal stairs to the main entry of the hotel, at the same time Alf and crew came in from the end doorway. They found themselves behind the Alliance trooper taking cover behind a counter, Alf quickly dealt with him.

"Dooff," also in the room were six more Nationals, running away from Alf, they ran into Peter, Ron and Mervyn. This time all three opened up killing the six quickly. Meeting in the middle, Alf and Debra teamed up to clear the lower wing bedrooms, while the others split into teams of two to go over the rest of the building.

1600 hours, Shayne and team one had successfully cleared the terminal building along with the two flats upstairs and the two closest homes to the terminal. On their way back to the *Black Ink,* they could hear gunshots coming from the hotel, Brian commented.

"Hope the others are all ok"?

1700 hours, Alf gathered them all in the hotel's dining room, Mervyn collected the trooper's weapon and ammo, Shakira made a beeline for the toilets and collected toilet rolls and sanitary items. Ron gestures for the group to be quiet, he could hear a vehicle pulling up outside, Alf quickly got the group to split in two, either side of the front doors to the dining room.

Peering out of the side panel - a piece of glass about two inches wide, Alf saw not a jeep but a truck, 'damn' he thought. Knocking off for the day, it was obvious, the truck full of troopers were staying at the hotel. Alf and the team had probably killed the operating staff of cooks, waiters and house staff.

Conversation flowed pretty fast between the troops, Alf was trying to make out their numbers, he held up both hands showing eight digits and waited, the outer doors opened into a foyer of sorts, maybe a place to take off a heavy coat and hat in days gone by.

The inner doors opened inward, blocking the TRF members from their foe, the doors flipped back on their door closers. Alf fired all eight rounds from his supressed type 54 pistol in quick concession, dropping all eight. Mervin was looking at the front door, lucky he was, because what the group didn't count on, was the driver, a bit slow maybe getting out of the truck or simply wanted a quick cigarette before coming inside.

The driver pushed the double doors partially open, blocked by a body on the floor, to be confronted by a scene of mayhem in front of him - eight fellow troopers lying dead. The man was in the process of drawing his pistol to shoot any of the five enemy in front of him, but was so engrossed, he failed to see the sixty-eight-year-old retired air-fitter bring down the butt of his Type 68 Assault Rifle, on his head, 'Crack'.

Alf turned to see the grinning Mervin standing over the trooper, still sporting the 68 ready for another belt, Alf remarked.

"Fuck, that was close, I owe you Mervin." The sixty-eight-year-old replied,

"He's probably not dead Alf." whilst dropping the empty clip out of the pistol and inserting a full one.

"Dooff."

"He is now, mate!" Looking around the room, he was proud of these newbies, his gaze finally landed on Shakira who was smiling, the eighteen-year-old deckhand put his arm around her waist.

"Especially proud of you girl."

Peter and Samuel checked out the car park, while Ron and Mervin removed all the troopers' pistols and webbing. Peter discovered all their type 68 assault rifles on the back of the truck. Shakira reached up and kissed the eighteen-year-old long and hard, her tongue finding its way into his mouth, Peter and Samuel suggesting the pair get a room.

1800 hours, they made their way back down the marina finger towards the *Black Ink,* Peter, pulling a marina trolly loaded to the brim with weapons and ammo, Samuel, Ron and Mervin were leading the way, Shakira next and Alf bringing up the rear.

About halfway down, the deckhand recognised a vessel on an adjacent arm of the marina, telling the others to go on ahead, he said

"Tell the Skipper I'm checking out one of his old vessels, I'll only be another fifteen minutes." A thumbs up from Peter, and Alf made his way along to the *Tangara*. – a fifty-six-foot Huon Pine fishing vessel. This, he knew was Harold's father's boat, it started out as a Crayfishing boat, then ended up long lining, might have even done some shark fishing, he stepped on board only to see Shakira following him,

"Crikey woman, you should be with the others."

The twenty-year-old ex-barmaid just wrapped her arms around his neck and kissed him saying.

"I just want to be with you Alf, all the time; I haven't felt like this with anyone else before." Alf smiled, saying.

"Did you let anyone know where you would be?" She replied.

"Peter and Sam know, oh and old Mervin, anyway what's so special about this boat?" Alf grabbed her hand and led her down to the engine room, leaving the hatch open for light so he could see what he was looking for.

"This, my dear, is an L8 Gardner, an 851 cubic inch, 170 brake horsepower, Diesel Marine Engine but more to the point it's pre-2000!" Shakira was no dummy, she got it straight away.

"You mean it's still working?"

Grabbing the twenty-year-old more passionately now, he rammed his tongue down her throat, grabbing hold of her arse cheeks, they parted, he could already feel the movement down below, she ground herself onto his manhood, which felt like he was going to blow a zip, back to earth he continued.

"You wait till tonight girl; there's room in my bunk for you." Shakira looked sheepishly at the deckhand.

"And what will your cabin mate think of that?" Leading her up on deck he winked.

"Don't have one!"

1835 hours and the pair ran along the extreme finger, then slipping the short amidships mooring line, they leapt aboard. Harold quickly went astern, turned the vessel and gently steamed out of the bay, the same way they entered, looking at Alf with one of those 'what have you been up to' looks, he said.

"Peter and the crew report a good outcome in the hotel, bagged a few weapons etc. What was your take on it Alf, did they work well together?" The eighteen-year-old gave them all a good rapport, especially Mervin saving their bacon. Setting the auto pilot, Harold continued.

"Getting on well with Shakira mate? And what was with the covert stuff on the way back?"

Alf filled the skipper in with what he had seen, Harold was all ears, the thought of seeing his father's vessel again nearly brought tears to his eyes, but when Alf told him about the L8 Gardner he chuckled.

"You reckon she still goes mate?" Alf, in love with all things 'Gardner', reckoned you couldn't kill them with a grenade and suggested that it would make a great vessel to service the island. Harold liked the idea and suggested they do a raid in the next night or two, to see if it was possible to get the old girl going.

2030 hours and with the anchor dropped and the evening meal out of the way, the mood was cheerful enough with everyone interested in the *Tangara* and what it could do potentially for Frog Island. Kept at Denis Point, this vessel could be used for fishing, transporting locals from one end to the other, servicing Legs and maybe if they found any ex-locals, be used to bring them back; anyway, the final ok would have to come from Dick or maybe Doc.

2200 hours, the wind was up, Shayne had the first watch, followed by Samuel taking the guts, and Alf the morning. The noises on board gradually subsided, as various members took it in turn to shower and prepare for bed. Alf, having a last discussion with Harold and Samuel about the *Tangara,* was second last to shower behind Harold.

Entering his Cabin, the eighteen-year-old was not that surprised to see Shakira already tucked up in bed, her flaming red hair, normally tied back, now fanned out across the pillow.

Stripping off, Alf climbed in alongside of the twenty-year-old, they locked mouths immediately, the redhead pinned him to the bed, taking the upper hand. This was a first for Alf, he usually had control. He eventually went wild, he couldn't just lie there, the deckhand grabbed her hips and met her violent down wood thrusts. For what seemed like an hour (more like 4 minutes) they grunted in ecstasy. A similar action-packed adventure was going to be played out after the first watchmen finished his watch.

Monday 2nd March 2015 Black Ink at anchor, Denis Point

0900 hours, after another raid ashore to collect some of Mervin's veggies and a couple of bunnies he had hanging, Harold was watching the weather, the wind had picked up, blowing in from the Northwest. He was not sure whether to risk the run over to Kettle; the thirty-year-old decided to give the crew a lay day. It would be wise after they stirred up the hornet's nest yesterday.

Most just lounged around, some fished off the deck, Ron and Christine decided to go for a bike ride. Ron suggested they venture down to the old ferry terminal, Frog Island end, well it was not really a terminal, just a shed that used to be a shop, although Ron knew of an old salmon farm close to the terminal, and thought they might try their luck for some salmon.

1600 hours and with most of Alf and Shakira's day spent in bed, the eighteen-year-old was beginning to think the flaming red head was a nymphomaniac.

Finally surfacing because of hunger, they were in time to see Ron and Christine pull up alongside in the dinghy, Shakira, yelling out to the pair, "Get any Ron"? Christine answered,

"Yep, got six and not bad sizes either." Passing up the fish to Alf and Shakira while they secured the dinghy properly. Ron suggested they cook half of them for tea; this was gratefully accepted by all, so Alf helped Ron clean and fillet the fish.

Tuesday 3rd March 2015 Black Ink, Kettle Marina

0500 hours, it was decided not to stay at the Kettle marina, Harold thought it best they drop off a selected few to try and get the *Tangara* going, *Black Ink* would steam over at 0400 hours, dropping the party off shortly after. Harold was pretty sure he would be ok going in the dark. The armed party was made up of Alf, Peter, Mervin and Shakira, they were trying to sort out the team when the bold red head stood and said she would like to go as well, the skipper knew why but thought it wouldn't hurt.

0600 hours, the *Black Ink* was on its way back to Denis Point. The raiding party were aboard the *Tangara* with everyone down in the engine room except Mervin, who was keeping guard from the wheelhouse. Alf set up some portable fluorescent lights and checked the old girl's fuel status; he had come prepared with a twenty-five-litre drum full.

First job was to crack all the injectors and then manually pump diesel from the fuel pump, well the good news was the boat's fuel tanks were quarter full; bad news was they probably had condensation and rust in them, having not been used for a while.

0900 hours, injectors cleaned, meanwhile Peter had discovered the fuel tanks were stainless steel, which was a huge bonus, although the fuel would be old. The group had brought a spare battery with them and hoped this would be enough to start the eight-cylinder engine.

Alf suggested Shakira investigate the rest of the vessel, to see what was still on board. With the battery hooked up, the engine was barred over manually, seacocks opened; he got Mervin to turn the key

"Whirr...Whirr...Whirr...Stop mate!" Alf and Peter checked all their connections, then realised they had the gearbox in gear.

"This should mean it will turn over quicker Alf." Yelling to Mervin to try again, they sat and waited. Sticking his head out of the engine room hatch he could see Mervin staring intently along the pontoon, placing his finger to his lips, Alf knew this meant company.

The trooper was probably just inquisitive, or he might have been doing his rounds, but it didn't matter, he was trouble, walking past the boat he only had two more then turn around. Shakira snuck up behind Alf and was about to open her mouth when the eighteen-year-old clamped his hand over her lips, she realised what was happening and looked out at the trooper merrily heading off the way he came.

"You didn't want to kill him Luv?" she asked.

"No, not sure how many there are, so best to keep it quiet," she replied.

"It's not going to be quiet when she starts Luv." He hadn't realised that fact, or even the time it would take to drop all the mooring lines and skedaddle.

1030 hours and Mervin did a reccy along the pontoon finger, declaring it all clear, Shakira untied most of the lines leaving just one. Back on board with Shakira and Mervin in the wheelhouse Alf called out.

"Try that again Merv." He turned the key.

"Whirr…Whirr…Whirr…Chugg…Chugg…Chugggggggggg," she fired, Alf brought the rack back to idle, Shakira yelled out.

"Shit luv there's a lot of black smoke; they'll see us for sure."

Emerging from the engine room, the eighteen-year-old, gave the signal to drop the last line and he went astern out of the *Tangara's* berth, far enough out he then turned hard to port and gunned the throttle, narrowly missing the end of the pontoon with her stern as she swung around.

"Boom…Boom…Boom…Phoot Phoot Phoot." Taking fire from the hard ground by the hotel, the 7.62 mm rounds were entering the water as the seventy-year-old vessel gathered speed, heading away from the danger, noises behind were dissipating when the engine stopped dead.

"Shit shit, what the fuck!" Alf ducked below to find Peter trying to stop the fuel leak, looking up he yelled.

"Lines are that old mate, that one's shit itself." Looking around the eighteen-year-old grabs a garden hose and a couple of hose clamps. Mervin started yelling.

"Mate, we've got company." Shakira said to Alf.

"Troops running towards the last pontoon, where they will be able to just about jump on board." Alf yells back.

"Luv, just steer away from the pontoon and keep your head down." Climbing back into the wheelhouse the red head swings the ornate timber spoked wheel to the left, not realising you didn't have to have the motor going to do so.

Mervin was already setting up with his Type 68, with a lot more clearance to the pontoon they still had to contend with the gunfire.

"Boom...Boom...Boom...Boom." The Alliance rounds were coming quick and accurate, splintering the seventy-year-old vessel, this was quickly returned by the sixty-eight-year-old ex-airman, making the Alliance shooter pull his head in for a minute or so.

"Boom...Boom...Boom...Boom...Boom...Boom..." Alf had taken off the unserviceable fuel line and squeezed the green reinforced garden hose over the bayonet fitting, 'shit forgot to put the hose clamp on first', he hated working under pressure and boy this was pressure! Slipping the stainless-steel clamps on from the other end, he left Peter to do these up, while he did his. Manually pumping the fuel through the line, he called out for Shakira to turn the key.

"Whirr...Chugg...Chugg...Chugggggggggg." They were off, Shakira beside herself yelling.

"Which way do I go Alf?"

Alf finally stuck his head out and made the dash to the wheelhouse, all the time Mervin was pumping round after round into the little shed where the threat was coming from. This was a fuel shed on the end of the main pontoon. Standing behind the red head and helping her steer the fifty-six-footer, was sort of surreal. Like a scene from a movie, here he was with the heroine and a wild gun battle continuing around the pair, bullets ricocheting off the near flat water.

"I could get used to this Alf," as she wiggled her backside into his groin.

"What, you mean all this fucking shooting?"

With 200 metres between the Alliance gunmen and the *Tangara* Alf was happy, making four knots, he decides to turn to starboard and head across in front of the old ferry, still at the terminal.

"Where are you going Luv?" Asked the red head, even Mervin turned to look at the deckhand. Ten minutes later, with Peter back, looking a lot like Alf, drowned in diesel, the eighteen-year-old says,

"Standby starboard side, we are going to steal some fuel." Peter looks at his mate.

"Of course, the old rowing sheds, they have a gravity feed system. Merv you might like to keep a watchful eye, as we refuel."

Thumbs up from the sixty-eight-year-old, he was kind of enjoying it, smiling at the antics going on between the red head and the young deckhand, wishing he was forty years younger, he thought, 'ah well let them have all the fun, who knows how long we could be around for'.

Bringing the seventy-year-old boat to a stop then quickly astern, Alf managed to get it close to the fuel outlet, he reckoned that the Alliance probably didn't even know it existed; it just looks like a box on the jetty where the rowing club launched the racing shells.

"Just the two tanks Peter, yep here's the spanner,"

Shakira was holding the hose while Alf ran up to the rowing shed, found the stop cock and turned it on. Merv was all eyes on the ferry terminal some 500 metres away, 'so far so good' he thought.

1300 hours, a gurgling sound coming from the starboard filler was the sign to stop, the red head then transferred the gun to the port filler and pulled the trigger. Peter screwed the cap back in and nipping it up with the spanner. Alf was hiding behind a dumpster waiting to turn the valve off.

1330 hours, with tanks full, and all on board, the sixty-eight-year-old nods toward the ferry, yep Alliance, then it started again although at maximum range they still tried.

"Boom…Boom…Boom…." With the shots falling short, the *Tangara* turned to port and headed back across the channel. Alf hugged Shakira grinning,

"Well, the bastards will know we have a vessel now."

Wednesday 4t^h March 2015 Sixty-five-foot Conquest Retaliator, Frog Channel

0900 hours, upon entering the Frog Channel, Riley and Crew were glad to see some new scenery. Looking at the Chart Plotter, Legs was about halfway down on the port side, looking at the radar, the twenty-year-old declared,

"Looks like the *Black Ink* just in front of us, about five miles, pulling out of Denis Point, and what have we here, another fishing boat." dialling Harold's number he asked.

"Mate, the fishing boat looks nice, what gives?" Harold replies.

"Hi Riley, just something that Alf dragged home yesterday, tell you the full story over a beer tonight at Legs." The twenty-year-old continued,

"Lead the way mate!"

Chapter 2

High Head Three Prong Lawn Raid

Friday 6th March 2015 TRF Convoy, Bull Bay, Ramat River

2030 hours and jeep one, with Dick, Patch, Ernie, Belle plus another six TRF members were clearing the first lot of homes on the Gary Town highway at Duck Point. Jeep two with Jack, April, Nic, Boz, Claudia plus six ex-Spirit members. Close behind them were the two trucks, with Henry, Boz, Kylie plus twenty TRF Members and Chris, Bill and another twenty TRF members in the second truck.

Spread out in a fan they swept across the homes at Duck Point. Sarge had issued each lead vehicle with a couple of Type 54 Pistol suppressors; the mix of experience was awesome. Clearing NK Nationals from these homes was quick and efficient. Dick pulled the four vehicles together as he laid out the next part.

"Next lot of homes is the start of Lawn City, one jeep and one truck to work as a team, so one will do the left-hand side of the highway and next team will do the right-hand side, we will meet at the Ramat Marina and gather reinforcements from *Dementia*."

2300 hours, most of the homes so far had no troopers, this was out of character with other raids Dick and the TRF had seen. Jack wondered if this was part of a re-group, he thought maybe they had withdrawn the home guard for a major push somewhere else. Some 600 homes cleared so far with only two casualties, one ex-Spirit member was knifed by an enthusiastic female, and one ex-Spirit passenger was pushed off the second story during a raid, unfortunately he died from his injuries.

Friday 6th March 2015 Dementia, Ramat River

2200 hours and Smokey was back in his element; Buck thought it easier if the ex-river pilot took control of the fifty-five-footer. Buck was issuing weapons and ammo, the plan was that May, Laurie and Chris would babysit the boat while alongside. Sue asked Smokey.

"Where are we on the river Smokey?" He pointed ahead and to the chart.

"See that point jutting out, that's Duck Point, the lights of those vehicles would be TRF I reckon." Sue could see the intermittent vehicle lights, she commented.

"Not much noise, I thought we should be able to hear gunshots." Her husband waded in on the conversation.

"Suppressors honey." Travelling alongside the main wharf area, slipping facilities, all redundant now, one more corner and the marina opened up in front of them, the river was running quite fast, at times up to five knots, Smokey called out to Buck.

"Mate where did you want to put her? We can land on one of the extreme fingers, but that's a long way from the hotel or I can put her right in front of the Ramat River Hotel." Buck pondered for a moment.

"Is anyone likely to be at the hotel mate?" The ex-river pilot didn't know,

"Maybe we berth her somewhere in between and then move closer after the hotel is cleared."

"Roger that, Buck."

2345 hours and bringing the *Dementia* alongside the middle pontoon as quietly as possible, Laurie ran down the turbos and shut off the main engine. Gathering the troops, Buck was led by Smokey to the ground floor of the Ramat River Hotel.

Friday 6th March 2015 Nancy Kay, Ugly Point, Ramat River

2200 hours, Santa could just make out the jeep lights coming along the wharf, and turned to Vert,

"You two ok with the babysitting, any danger, retaliate or last resort, flash her up and move out into the middle of the river." Vert looked at the skipper, then to Rose.

"Not a problem, you just take it easy, don't do anything stupid." Bringing the sixty-five-footer alongside the Ugly Point wharf, they were met by two jeeps. jeep one with Sarge, Annie, Josh and six other members and jeep two with Henry, Josie, Grant and another six members. It didn't take long for the twenty odd members to hop off the *Nancy*, then split up and pile into both vehicles best way they could. Santa commented to Sarge.

"Looks like the first order of business is to acquire another couple of vehicles," Sarge replied.

"Spot on Santa, now Henry you're the local boy, you lead the way." leaving the *Nancy Kay*, the ex-G-Town senior constable led the two vehicles up onto the road. Splitting up, Sarge and Annie's jeep would cover everything right, this was about 200 homes all the way to the point, while Henry's jeep would turn left covering everything between there and the Ugly Point Maritime College.

"Right Sarge, we will meet you at the college say around 0300."

Henry and team hit the first street and on the fourth home struck it lucky with an Alliance jeep parked out front. Trying to clear homes with no or little noise and for everyone to get some experience meant they shared the Type 54 with suppressor fitted, having two of them sure helped.

Saturday 7th March 2015 North Ugly Point

0015 hours, Sarge and Annie relished in the clearing, so much so after nine homes the ex-Sapper had to force himself to share the suppressed pistol and train others to do the clearing. Josh was a natural, the twenty-six-year-old ex-Service Station attendant was quick and with no hesitation. Annie commented,

"You're a natural mate." Sarge put Josh in charge of a team of his own looking after six members; he gave them a street to clear. Sarge also had a couple of the Spirit's crew, Tegan and Gary along with eight other ex-passengers, split into four teams of four, this made the little groups more manageable, one problem was with only two suppressors this meant some clearings were noisy.

Saturday 7th March 2015 South Ugly Point

0015 hours, Henry and two others belted on the door of the home sporting an Alliance jeep, the door opened by a sleepy female, quickly dealt with by the ex-police Senior Constable. Entering the hallway, he motioned to the others to fan out. Josie and Grant together found the trooper, using the Type 54 pistol for the first time Josie cringed at the noise it made, she hesitated. She shot the jeep driver in the shoulder, stirring him up like a hornet's nest; he catapulted out of bed and was on to the twenty-five-year-old medical student in a rage. Trying to strangle the girl with the only good arm created a problem. Grant couldn't get a clear shot so jumped on the pair, starting to club the man with his pistol butt.

Eventually after many blows to the head, the trooper collapsed to the floor.

By now Henry had cleared the rest of the home and came to see what all the fuss was about. Quickly shooting the man in the head, they rifled around to find the jeep keys.

"So, what happened Josie?" The twenty-four-year-old explained about her wild shot, the ensuing fight then being saved by Grant. Henry replied.

"Well at least you weren't hurt or killed."

Saturday 7ᵗʰ March 2015 Ugly Point Maritime College

0320 hours, Henry and the two jeeps were waiting at the entrance to the Maritime College, pointing he said.

"Looks like jeep lights coming now." Sarge, unlike Henry, had managed to collect another jeep and a truck. This now had Gary driving and Tegan passenger, the fifteen or so members divided up amongst the three vehicles.

The Ugly Point Maritime College consisted of various classrooms including Survival Centre, Marine Fire-fighting Training Centre, Damage Control Unit, Fast Rescue Boat Training, as well as Rope Work and Navigation. On top of that there was accommodation for up to one hundred, this, they suspected was home to Alliance Troops and was what Henry wanted to clear. Sarge asked.

"How do you see this working mate?" Henry pointed to the plan prominently situated on the sign out the front.

"Mate if you and your group can clear from the dining room north, we will do the south side, not sure whether they are even using the place." Sarge relayed that to his team, and they spread out, the ex-Sapper reminded them that because of the rooms being close together, stealth was of the essence.

0400 hours, Henry was showing his team how to use the pillow at point blank to muffle the blast. The problem with some of the rooms were that they were locked, tapping on some worked, the inhabitant sleepily opening the door to have a Type 54 Pistol barrel jabbed into their chest, the first three units revealed a very different result. Henry points out.

"They all seem to be troops Grant, so when we are finished, I'll get some of our team to collect the weapons and ammo."

0420 hours and Sarge hit the jackpot, clearing the last room on the end of a covered walkway; he had a quick look around the corner just to make sure there weren't any more rooms and wow! Pointing around the corner his team found twelve Alliance vehicles in the back car park.

0530 hours, with a meeting back at the main entrance, Sarge and Henry compared notes, Henry started.

"Sarge, we cleared fifty-six rooms, six were empty, fifty troops in the other rooms and a fully operational kitchen and dining room." Sarge smiled and reported,

"Not quite as many as you, fifty rooms, four empty so only forty-six troops, but we hit the jackpot by discovering twelve vehicles in the back car park.

All we have to do now is find the keys." Henry was happy now; he was starting to think the troops were transported from somewhere else.

0615 hours, Annie and four team members were bringing out the last of the weapons and keys, Josh and four others were trying to match keys with vehicles.

Henry's team were doing a similar activity, relieving the rooms of their weapons and ammo.

Fifteen minutes later, with all weapons loaded up, the final tally was eight jeeps and four trucks, with all keys found except one, Henry suggested,

"We'll take all the vehicles back to the Ugly Point Wharf and the *Nancy Kay* where they would rest until the afternoon, redistribute the teams into the vehicles for the next raid."

Saturday 7ᵗʰ March 2015 Ramat River Hotel

0030 hours, Dick, Patch, Ernie and Belle started on the bottom floor of the hotel while Jack, April, Nic, Boz and Claudia went to the top. The brief was the same, try and make this as stealth as possible! Nic and one of the Spirit crew sourced the master key from the hotel office, this was going to make the clearing fast.

Dick and Ernie decided to breach the rooms while Patch and Belle covered their backs, Type 54 pistols only and suppressors or point-blank range only. Reaching the top floor, Jack was totally stuffed, poor April was still a floor below, the first thing the ex-CD Sniper realised.

"How come there are only four doors on this floor?"

Belle explained, "These are the luxury suites Jack, each taking up a quarter of the top floor excluding the lift and stairwell." Finally getting their breath back, Jack tried the master key that Nic provided, opening the door, he gave the key back to Nic and she quickly opened the other three, they would go in one at a time and use the suppressed 54.

The first suite door opened into a foyer, through to a kitchen, ceramic tiles on the floor, huge dining and lounge rooms, this one had two bedrooms, and the place was ornately furnished. Jack was wondering 'how much would this set you back a night.'

Entering the first bedroom, the ex-CD Sniper found two in bed, 'Dooff, Dooff' quickly dealt with. Noticing the uniform on the hanger in front of the wardrobe he thought 'high ranking officer.'

Boz and Claudia were clearing the second bedroom, it was empty. Finishing the rest of the rooms, they met in the stairwell where Jack was carrying a uniform tunic. Boz asked.

"What have you got there, Jack?" The ex-CD replied.

"Not sure, but Dick will want to know about it." They proceeded to the next level down, a more standard layout with ten rooms; half of which were empty all the rest were junior officers.

0300 hours, Dick and team were starting level 4 when Jack met them on the stairs.

"All clear mate, a few of the troops are bringing the weapons down as we speak, oh and you might want to look at this uniform." Jack produced the tunic and the name tag that went with it.

"Great work mate, I wonder who Lieutenant Colonel Lee Bowe was?"

Contacting the two trucks that had been clearing east of the town, everything was working out, Patch and April took it upon themselves to keep tally of the Alliance troopers killed, this would also help with weapon distribution.

0500 hours, Boz jumped out of the last truck into the Ramat Marina car park, reporting to Ernie and Dick.

"Four casualties' guys, unfortunately two dead and two wounded, not serious."

The sixty-four-year-old ex-crane driver asked.

"What happened mate?" His nephew answered.

"Too much noise at one home, the other home next door had a trooper and when Brian entered the trooper shot him, Bill was quick enough to get him before he re-aimed."

With all the TRF members in one spot the question was, what to do now, they had cleared over half the homes in Lawn, they could wait at the marina till dark then continue on south or withdraw to Gary Town and re-group. Dick could see the pain on Ernie's face, still hurting from the injury. He suggested.

"Why don't we strategically withdraw to Bull Bay, catch up with the others and re-think the next attack." With nods all round, the four vehicles headed off back up the highway while the *Dementia* let go all lines and proceeded back down river.

Buck was first to comment.

"Smokey, what happened to the water, not bloody much left at low tide." The forty-eight-year-old river pilot smiled.

"Welcome to my river."

Saturday 7th March 2015 Nancy Kay, Ugly Point Wharf

1400 hours, the four vehicles drove over to Ugly Point after six hours sleep, what they found as they rounded the corner was a mass of captured Alliance Vehicles. Most of the team was resting; Sarge had put a perimeter guard on the driveway to the wharf. They met the very diligent Josh, Josie and Barry keeping an eye on the vehicles when they arrived. Dick opened discussion.

"Looks like you had a profitable night Sarge, any casualties mate?" The ex-sapper reported.

"Only two Dick, one dead and one wounded but we scored a shit load of vehicles as you can see. We have cleared all the way north from the Maritime College as far as you can go; we also have a rough tally on the night. Amongst the six individual teams our score is 316 Alliance Troops and 403 Nationals, weapons accordingly." Doc was really impressed with their efforts, Dick and Ernie looked at Patch, who reported on their raid.

"Well rough count goes like this, four casualties, two dead and two wounded, both have been looked at by Doc and Nari.

Alliance troops number close to 200 including one Lieutenant Colonel. NK nationals' number 4000; shit when you say it like that it's scary." Doc asked.

"What was the Colonel's name?" Jack still had his name tag.

"Lieutenant Colonel Lee Bowe, he was living on the top floor of the Ramat River Hotel, quite a posh place, only four rooms on the top floor." Nari adds

"Lieutenant Colonel Lee Bowe was the Commander of the Lawn Alliance; I have heard his name many times in Kings Town." Doc commented.

"Well, that's really bloodied their nose"!

Chapter 3
Kings Bridge West Coast

Sunday 22nd February 2015 West of Kings Bridge TRF Outpost

1600 hours, Blue and Anita, standing with their backs to the fire, were getting a warm from the huge open fire the boys had lit at the BBQ shelter. Baz and Lyn just returned with twelve men from a reconnaissance towards Kings Bridge reporting

"No sign of them Blue, I don't know whether it's the weather, or the fact we scared the shit out of them, what's our next move mate?" The fifty-six-year-old ex-SAS Sergeant looked at the sky, pulled out a map of the surrounding area and suggested,

"I reckon we sit tight till morning, then at sunup, we move as far as we think is possible towards the Kings Bridge Hotel. If I was the Alliance, I would use the hotel and the caravan park to house my troops. We only have one side road between here and the hotel and that's to Lake Clara. The road's about twelve kilometres long and ends at a wilderness lodge, accommodation, restaurant, etc. what do you reckon mate?" The ex-CD smiled.

"You're the specialist at this shit mate, but it sounds good to me, where would you hold them off if we can advance tomorrow morning?"

"The hotel, its past the turnoff and still 400 metres from the shop then the caravan park then on to 'The Wall'" The ex-CD replied.

"What's 'The Wall'?"

"Some huge carving, all out of Huon Pine, supposed to be fantastic, the bloke's been doing it for about twelve years, its 100 metres long, three metres high and double sided."

1930 hours. With twenty men on forward lookout, the rest were bunkered down in tents and vehicles close to the BBQ area. Wood gathering parties to collect more wood, although it would take them a week to burn through what was already there. Blue thought it would keep the men active and warmer than standing around.

Feeding 100 men in the wilderness, on a freezing cold night is not everyone's cup of tea, but Anita and Lyn managed to pull it off with help from three men; a BBQ was the only answer. The last truck to leave Queens was loaded up with a full lamb cut into chops along with twenty kilos of sausages; these would help to go with the twenty dozen eggs and twenty kilos of bacon for breakfast.

Sunday 22nd February 2015 Strine Hospital

0900 hours and the fifty-nine-year-old doctor was going over the charts of the hospital's patients, life had been brisk since he was first introduced to the only aging medical man in the town. Dr Phil Hyland, who ever since, had been later and later in getting to work. It seemed the good doctor didn't really want to be there.

Alex had enrolled the aid of his other yachty mates who escaped the Kings Town Alliance. Dr Ted Green Anaesthetist, and Dr Bob Silver Orthopaedics were a great addition to the Strine Hospital. Ted and his new girlfriend Hazel were working as a team, the twenty-nine-year-old Hazel made a pretty good nurse, and Bob had previously hooked up with Gill while in Donkey Bay.

"Looks like Phil is AWOL again this morning Alex" He replied.

"Well, I don't think his heart was really in it mate, after all he was past retiring age, I think all he wanted to do was potter in his garden and go fishing from time to time." Bob with Gill, her daughter Margo and grandson Hugo set up house in one of the shacks, now empty around the other side of the bay. This suited Bob, a self-confessed fitness fanatic, as he liked to walk to work.

1500 hours, Alex had got into the habit of knocking off at this time; he had thought he would move from Lou's house, but ever since that Wednesday morning episode he was hooked on the woman. The sex was fast and furious between them, he was revived, nothing like his wife, who had been horrifically killed by the Alliance, there was no holds barred with Lou, he was smiling just thinking about the buxom blonde.

0900 hours and Lou was smiling after yet another early morning session with the doctor, ever since the *Fremantle* arrived, she secretly thought, her lifestyle had changed dramatically for the better. She now had some purpose to life, with daily checks on the lads re-instating the pre 2000 engines into a newly acquired fleet of ex commercial vessels and looking after her new man.

Through the support and guidance from her old friends Dick and Patch, the buxom blonde felt fantastic, she would run supplies and reinforcements up to the front lines, so to speak at Doonah and Kings Bridge, arrange to bring back Alliance vehicles, enabling life to move forward at Strine. Her first job this morning was to check on the engine progress on the following vessels:

The *St Bernadette* was a sixty-foot steel ex fishing boat, this was nearly completed, and when everything was ticked off, she would be joining the fight up north with the *Christa Leanne*, Harry Jill and Gary were in charge of this job.

The *Specialist* was a sixty-five-foot steel ex-cray boat, it would also go north with the *St Bernadette* and eventually be based at Queens.

The *Wind Spirit*, a forty-foot glass sailing cat would stay at Strine.

The *Cougar Anne*, a fifty-foot steel ex-cray boat would be deployed to Port Apples and assist with the liberation of the Channel towns. She would be leaving in a few days to make the journey, hopefully getting there by the fifth of March. Dick had asked his old mate Baz Cole, the ex-clearance diver and his wife Lyn, alongside local TRF boys Sid and Craig, original deckhands on the boat, the owner had moved back to Devon before the E1 hit.

1100 hours, as Lou sauntered up the gangway of the *Cougar Anne* calling out,

"You about Harry, Jill or Gary?" A head popped up from below. It was Sid, he smiled at the blonde reporting.

"I think they are over on the *Specialist* Lou, all finished here. Craig and I are just cleaning up." Lou smiled and proceeded towards the sixty-five-footer, where she witnessed the last of the mounting bolts being done up on the huge L8 Gardner engine.

"Looking good guys, how long before the *Cougar Anne* is ready to sail?"

Harry replied.

"I reckon a couple of days Lou, might pay to go and get the new skipper tomorrow, so he can be involved with the work up trials."

Lou added.

"Nice work, I'll pick Baz and Lyn up tomorrow, they need re-supplying anyway."

Monday 23rd February 2015 West of Kings Bridge TRF Outpost

0700 hours. "First reccy group heading off now Blue." The ex-SAS Sergeant and Anita were warm in their double swag, when the TRF member shook them.

Waking his mate Baz in the other swag he asked,

"You are heading back today mate?" The ex-CD opening his eyes to see steam coming out of Blue's mouth, answering.

"I reckon so mate, that's if Lou doesn't forget us, how's the push going?" Blue replied, "Should know in about thirty minutes, they have already left, it takes about ten minutes to get to the turnoff, a couple more to the hotel and return. Oh! breakfast is on." Packing the pair's clothes and possessions together, Lyn asked her husband,

"Are you looking forward to the next bit luv?" Baz smiled to himself.

"What more can a man ask for, but to go into battle alongside his wife and some great mates, and you know what, this type of battle here on the ground is not the same as being at sea, question is luv, do you like the thought of being at sea with me?"

Lyn was used to the pushing and pulling of being a naval wife, she had been a nursing sister for forty odd years, she didn't mind boats, as long as it wasn't too rough, a bit like Dick's missus Patch, she did admire Patch, wondering where they all were right now.

1200 hours, "looks like a jeep approaching Baz," one of the rear guards yelled out. Lyn had their entire kit ready, and with help from Lou, loaded it onto the ex-Alliance jeep. Baz wandered off to find his mate.

100 metres down the road, Blue was just finalising the troops for the official move to the Hotel. Sending one truck and twenty

men to Lake Clara while the reccy jeep reported no one at the hotel. Blue was anticipating an ambush, so had thirty men stop short and flank the Hotel, while another group would come up behind it, the reccy team saw no evidence that anyone was living there.

"We're off Blue, Lou has just delivered a weeks' worth of tucker and four more recruits. Lyn and I have said our goodbyes to Anita, mate you take care, see you at the piss up at the end." Laughing the ex-SAS Sergeant exclaimed.

"Fuck mate is that all you Pussers think of?"

Wednesday 25th February 2015 TRF Vessel Cougar Anne

0800 hours and Baz, Lyne, Sid and Craig were loading the last of the supplies to last the boat a couple of weeks. Lou, Bill, Tom and Alex were wharf side to wave them goodbye. Alex yelled out,

"When you see the Doc next, tell him everything is perfect here in Strine."

Lou hugged the good doctor hoping she was the reason he was happy; Alex knew she would be thinking that and leaned down and kissed her, this was the first time affection had been shown in public.

Hitting the starter on the fifty-footer, they all heard the huge GM engine start, Sid and Craig retrieved all lines and the ex-CD eased the vessel away from the wharf. Pushing the throttle forward to twelve knots, he set the auto pilot for the heads. With everyone in the wheelhouse he asked.

"Everyone happy with the sleeping arrangements?" Craig and Sid had the luxury of a cabin each, while Baz and Lyn were in the skipper's cabin at the rear of the wheelhouse. Both boys answered in the affirmative while Lyn just snuggled into Baz's arm.

"I'll be alright if the weather stays like this, and I get to share a bunk with you."

Craig asked. "How long till we get to Port Apples skipper?"

Baz replied. "Weather dependant, about four days mate, if it gets too rough, we will lay over somewhere." The boys said there were quite a few spots down the coast, remembering when they fished with old George, the boat's original owner.

Wednesday 25th February 2015 TRF Doonah Outpost

1200 hours. The group had seen no Alliance since Baz and Blue had left and were very happy with their position; the weather had eased, so no snow and quite warm days, which they knew eventually would spell trouble.

"Just changing the guard Boss." The TRF member originally from Wattle was happy, he now felt like he had some purpose in life, the drag since the E1 was terrible, nothing to do, nowhere to go, the ex-Wattle barman was whistling as he and three of his mates wandered up the track towards the cutting overlooking the Devon to Pram Mountain road.

He stopped, held out his arm as if to warn the others, pointing and squatting he whispered.

"Something moving in the scrub to the right, it could be Alliance trying to flank the lookout post." He and his mate moved off to the right while the other two continued on as if nothing was wrong. Yep, he was right, crawling up a slight mound, the pair could see six troops crouching down doing a weapons check.

They were only twenty metres from the post, what happened next was in a split second, the pair running at the six, Type 54 pistols drawn, had to cover the 100 metres before they would be able to guarantee a kill shot. The ex-Wattle barman caught something out of the corner of his eye, he did a double take, what he was seeing was the main part of the Alliance raiding party, from what his brain digested this was around 100 men.

At fifty metres, one of the six turned around first, the barman's mate levelled his pistol to fire, but missed, the split second it took for him to re-pull the trigger, and he was impaled on the trooper's bayonet. The six shots out of the barman's 54 doing its job, he now had the main force coming up the slight bank as he ran down to the path to alert the others. With the original four guards now alerted, plus the two coming to relieve them, they had seven to fight off 100. Yelling at the top of his voice to warn them of the impending attack gave the guards time to radio to base and send for help.

1300 hours, "Yep that's right boss, sounds like a large advance, Mike reckons a hundred, yep correct, we have cover for now, shit incoming fire, Ping...Ping...Ping...yep rounds ricocheting off the boulders, Boom...Boom...Boom...Boom..., yep, we're alright fuck, Mike has just scored a couple of hits, hang on Boss it looks like an RPG. Trooper has stood up to take aim, fuckwit, Boom... he's dead, right you're going to come up behind them great, don't be long." He relays the news to his mates the battle goes quiet after five minutes.

"Don't like the sound of this guys, oh I see him, stupid bastard thinks he can flank us, no shit-face, it's too close to the cutting, Boom.... Boom....Boom....bye bye, how are you guys going over there?" Three were behind another huge rock, yelling back.

"All good so far, hang on Boom...Boom...Boom...Boom...Boom, sounds like the cavalry has arrived, Boom...Boom...Boom...Boom... Boom... Yep it's them alright." They could hear screams as the Alliance raiding party came under attack from the full force of the Doonah TRF contingent, looking to his right the barman sees the boss.

"Right men that was a close one, we have the couple that are left on the run, with any luck they will lead us straight to their vehicles, Boom...Boom...Boom... well sounds like they found them." The men changed guard; two were detailed to remove the bodies down to the main HQ, then dispose of the Alliance bodies in an appropriate spot.

The reccy squad appeared driving the three trucks and a jeep up the road, the boss asks.

"How far down the road were they?"

First driver answered. "About five kilometres, they left one trooper to guard the four vehicles, he didn't hear us coming."

The trucks were met by four of the relieved guards lugging the weapons and ammo from the Alliance attackers. Mike reported.

"Tally was eighty-nine troops and two officers, so we got a shit load of weapons, but you know what's funny, none of the buggers had any more that twenty rounds on them, opposed to the normal 100." The Boss added.

"Might let Dick know about that revelation, and by the way guys great outcome even if we lost one man, could have been much worse if you hadn't seen them." The ex-barman smiled and said

"So does this mean you're shouting the piss tonight?"

Chapter 4
Alliance Update

Monday 2nd March 2015 Alliance HQ Kings Town

1200 hours, after the bleak start to the day, General Jun Lee was trying to think of things that made him happy, he might go out to the In-Cat business and check on the progress there, some of his engineers had mentioned that they could possibly fit a pre-2000 engine into the large catamaran that was nearly completed. Calling the captain to get the jeep ready, he thought they might enjoy lunch at the hospital on the way out.

"Captain, I wish to see the huge catamaran's progress but, on the way, we will enjoy lunch at the hospital." The forty-year-old nodded in approval.

Arriving at the hospital some fifteen minutes later, the pair made their way to the canteen. While eating, the captain had a runner deliver a note, turning to the general he reported.

"Sir reports in from Kettle and Bronze, some troopers report a vessel was moved from the Kettle Marina to another jetty, then left the area. Troopers engaged the rebels with rifle fire, and they sustained a few casualties, not sure about the rebels! Also, NK Nationals reported a fast rubber boat at Julia Beach."

The general took it all in, he knew this moment would come, he was just hoping it was after they had power over the seas, he chose to change the subject.

"Good food Captain." The general did enjoy his food, catching sight of one of the young nurse aides, he enquired whether she was still enjoying the work, and how they were being treated by the Taswegian doctors. After the girl had left, Li remarked,

"I have information about one of the doctors getting too close to one of the young girls." The general had heard this before.

"Yes, the one we sent to Soothe, wasn't it, and then brought him back when we were down on numbers, what was his name, Ruddy or something. The Captain corrected the general.

"Doctor Dave Reddy sir, and the girl Mi-kyong. They seem to be spending quite a lot of time together; she is quite young and the daughter of a market gardener."

The general pondered over the problem.

"Is this really a problem Li, has the man done anything bad to the girl, beat her or abused her?"

"No sir, as a matter of a fact the head nurse tells me that he is quite generous with the girl."

"So, Captain we will just watch and see, shall we?"

1400 hours, pulling up outside the In-Cat's huge sheds at their Prince Bay workshops, they climbed over the huge railway tracks that the cradle was sitting on. Jun Lee admired the huge eighty-five metre catamaran. This one was originally destined for Japan, the generall smiled to himself thinking 'the Japan scum didn't deserve the vessel anyway'.

This hull was almost complete when the E1 hit, rendering the four huge Caterpillar C280-16 marine diesel engines unserviceable. They were rated at 5650kw each and drove huge Wartsila Water Jets.

NK Catamaran 'Gin Gum Kim'

The captain read out the specs on the huge cat as he and the general looked around its plush interior.

"Capacity sir of 692 persons (passengers and crew) in three lounges, 151 car spaces @ 4.5m long x 2.3m wide (755 car lane metres) or 330 truck lane metres @ 4.6m clear height plus 300 sqm @ minimum 4.0 clear height. Vehicle Decks: Truck Deck - Axle load of 13 tonne (single axle, dual wheel) from Transom to Frame 45. 2.0 tonne (single axle, single wheel) from Frame 45 forward. Mezzanine Decks hoist able decks, 0.8 tonnes (single axle, single wheel) Four Caterpillar C9 diesel generators rated at 250eKw each, 440V 60 HZ, 3 phase, four wire distribution with neutral earth allowing 256 V single phase and transformers to supply 100V domestic appliances."

"Wow Captain this is certainly some vessel, now where are my engineers and what have they done to get this in the water, we need to have firepower on the ocean!"

The captain scurried off to find the 'engineer' although he was nowhere near the calibre of the engineers arriving on the third convoy, just a mere retired motor mechanic. Finding Guhn Kuhn, the seventy-eight-year-old trying to get the endless chain operational, he marched the man to the General.

"So Guhn Kuhn how far have you got with re-powering this vessel with a pre- 2000 engine?" The old man was not really suited to this kind of pressure and only agreed to assist, unfortunately he had no one to assist, or that matter to assist him.

"Ah General, I have only just found an engine of pre-2000 type, I am still trying to work out a way to get old unserviceable motors out of boat, I have no assistants sir." Jun Lee was not happy.

"Captain, you will get this man whatever he needs, this I make number one priority, with the rebels active on the seas we need this vessel in the water ASAP." Li quizzed the man as to what he needed, and promised the general he would see to it.

Calling into a NK National's home at Bridge, the pair would be picking up, then delivering two young girls to assist at the Lakeside Hospital. This would also give the generall a look over the facilities.

Driving back to the general's office the captainl decided the time was right to tell him about his great idea.

"Ah! General, I have some good news," Looking sideways at the captain, Jun Lee smiled 'Oh great another failure from the captainl' he thought.

"Well out with it man, don't keep me in suspense."

"You know General how we have been at a loss to search the particularly dense sections of the Taswegian forest areas. I have been working on an idea for the last two weeks and I think I may just have solved the problem." The captain hesitated then continued.

"I have formed a horse troop!"

The general didn't know what to say and then blurted out.

"How was this possible without my knowledge Captain, where did you get the troopers from and the horses. I didn't know we had any riders?" Li was afraid the general was not happy and thought he was in trouble.

"Do you not like my idea General?"

"On the contrary Li, I think it is bloody fantastic, when do I get to meet these horse troops?"

"If we weren't going to Lakeside tomorrow General, it would be then, but let's say first up on Tuesday."

Monday 2nd March 2015 Lakeside Medical Centre

0900 hours. A normal day in the life of Urology Specialist, Doctor Reginald Miles - first Kings Town, then the forty-six-year-old was sent to Dove, then recalled to Kings Town and now whisked away to Lakeside.

Having to do everything himself was now getting a regular way of life, the Alliance were giving him no helpers, but he did hear that today he was getting two of the general's new assistant nurses, from a group of volunteer girls, but he would believe it when he saw them.

1600 hours. "Come doctor, you come now, wife having a baby!" Reg could hear the distraught voice of one of the troopers trying to get his wife to the door of the hospital. Assisting the man with his wife, Reg finally placed her onto the delivery table, checked her vital signs and ushered the man outside. Taking the times between each contraction, the urologist was normally dealing with urinary, prostate, bladder, kidney & cancer problems, this would be his first childbirth.

The woman's blood pressure was low, and he was watching it. The contractions were coming regularly now and closer together.

1730 hours and fully dilated, Reg was doing his best to deliver the child, and after what seemed like a really long time, the six pound baby boy arrived. Cleaning up mother and son, Reg allowed the distraught father to see them both, he heard a jeep pull up outside, 'shit not another customer' he thought.

"Doctor, come and meet your new nurse assistants!" Yelled the captain.

Reg opened the door and was greeted by the captain; the general and two young girls, Reg bowed slightly.

"Pleased to meet you all." The girls were introduced to the forty-six-year-old and given aprons, one was shown into the delivery room where the proud parents enjoyed the newborn.

The general and the captain were presented to the couple, smiles all round, then Jun Lee wanted a look at the facilities and was halfway around the forty-eight-bed hospital when they heard.

"Come doctor, quick, my wife she is a bleeding, down there."

Reg opened the door to see the husband pointing at the woman's vagina, the assistant nurse was in hysterics, a little too much for the young girl on her first day. Reg did everything in his power to save the woman, but she had lost too much blood, this unfortunately was the most common cause of postpartum haemorrhage, it is when the uterus does not contract enough after delivery, death occurs through loss of blood.

An hour later, walking out of the delivery room, Reg was met by the captain, the general and the distraught husband, he reported.

"Sorry, I couldn't save her, too much blood loss, but the baby is doing fine." Jun Lee commented.

"Ah so sorry for your loss, these are sad times, trooper what are you doing, put the pistol away, Captain, order this man to put down his weapon."

The captain was too far away from the man to physically stop him, he was really angry, ranting.

"You kill my wife, you pay, you kill my wife, you pay." With tears running down his face the young man levelled the Type 54 pistol at Reg and pulled the trigger.

"Bang!" The 9mm round entered the doctor's body just above the breastbone slightly off centre to the right. The general got to the man first, grabbing his arm.

"Lower the weapon trooper, that's an order, Captain check the doctor please." Li checked the doctor's pulse and found him still alive.

"He needs to go to Kings Town immediately General."

Quickly asking the two assistant nurses to help with a pad bandage, they stemmed the flow of blood. By now Li had the jeep backed up to the entrance, the trooper was handed over to the Lakeside Commander till later. With Reg safely loaded onto the Willy's knock-off jeep, they left.

Tuesday 3rd March 2015 East Kingstown Horse Stables 0900 hours

Entering the Kings Town Horse stables, the general was in awe of the activity. The old racing stables currently housed around forty horses; Jun Lee could see the round yards, the exercise track and the multiples of individual paddocks, segregated with white sighter wires and battery powered electric fences.

"Most impressive Captain!"

Entering the tack room, the general was confronted with a wall of saddles, variants from English all-purpose to western, with their ornate carvings and roping horns. Enquiring as to which style of saddle was preferred, the horse troop sergeant replied.

"Well General, most of us like the Australian Stock Saddle, whether this is traditional, or the new half-breed hybrid design of fender saddle. We find it the most reliable in the extreme hilly country, where we are going to be searching."

"When are you going to be ready to be deployed Sergeant, have you had practice in these extreme conditions and to what area?" The sergeant looked at the captain for some sort of guidance with the answer.

"Well sir we thought that the dense bush out the back of Apples would be a great place to start, especially around the Judd area. We know there are rebels in that area and suspect they are holding up in the mountains. The horse troops have been on exercises behind us in the bush, conveniently on our doorstep."

"And transport Captain, how do you propose to get the horses to the areas?"

"This is the easy one General, every third Taswegian home has a double horse float in its back yard, and we simply tow them with our jeeps. The horse troops are made up of troopers from across the state with the suitable riding ability, they have been re-assigned here. We board them at the old International Motel near the old Kings Town airport. They train every day; we also have blacksmiths on hand to keep the horses well shod. The breeds are mixed, even though we are situated at the racing stables, not many of them are in actual fact, racehorses."

The general and Captain Li watched as the first troop of twenty riders, tacked up the immaculately groomed horses. In ten minutes, they were all mounted and formed up, their Type 68 Assault Rifles slung over their shoulders, webbing belts housing the type 54 pistols and ammo.

Tuesday 3rd March 2015 General's Headquarters, Kingstown 1200 hours

"Very impressive indeed Captain, but why did you not inform me of this idea?" The captain answered.

"Simply sir, I was not sure it would come together, we only received the last twenty riders three days ago, making up the numbers to forty." Jun Lee was smiling, he loved the idea, but he thought 'it won't hurt the good captain to think he is in trouble'.

"Keep me posted Captain; I want to know how these horse troopers fair in the Taswegian bush."

Chapter 5
Dove Blockade

Friday 27th February 2015 TRF Barricade Glen Highway Glen

1300 hours and it's change of watch, the first week's TRF watch keepers were back. Just dropped off by Nobby, the outgoing team reported only a few activities during the last seven days but nothing substantial. Nobby helps unload the groceries.

"Great job guys and girls, I will be back each day, so if anything is needed just tell me tomorrow."

The previous team had reported two attempts to breach the barricade, one was Monday, they heard a truck approach, screech to a halt, a number of Alliance troopers tried to attach a rope to the tree, while some of them tried to flank the outpost. The Bren Gun made short work of the group at the truck, while two members cut off the flankers. Nobby was part of the team and suggested moving the tree enough to allow the truck and the previous jeep stored in the apple shed to come to their side, adding to their fleet of vehicles.

The last time was yesterday, when, with no warning they heard troops advancing across the paddock behind the outpost. These too were dealt with.

"Delilah and I will take the afternoon watch, Rachael and Shane can do the dogs, Matilda if you're happy to cook and do the day shift." The thirty-five-year-old waitress didn't mind the day shift.

"Sounds good to me guys, as long as you still like the food." Shane and Rachael decided to investigate the back entrance, so to speak, the ex-salmon farmhand had wanted to set up some sort of early warning system, so they didn't get caught with their pants down, but now because the Alliance tried this approach last week all the more reason to rig something up.

1430 hours. "Might do a bit of a reccy Pete, Rach and I will be gone a couple of hours, I want to investigate the next part of the road and maybe sight the next barricade site." The ex-hotel manager agreed.

"Good idea you two, take your weapons and be safe."

Shane and Rachael disappeared out of sight at the edge of the paddock, choosing to follow a small animal track through the dense bushland. After a kilometre the pair emerged out onto the main highway about three kilometres from the outpost. Shane pointed,

"Looks like another large apple shed, house looks empty, the makings of a roadside stall area, you keen to go further luv?" The ex-teachers aid had become quite smitten with the twenty-five-year-old, eventually sleeping with him while they were off watch. She was now quite open about the affair, it made it easier with the sleeping arrangements.

"No problems Shags, we have only been gone fifteen minutes." The ex-farmhand smirking a little about his boyhood nickname being used again.

1510 hours and the pair crept up to the top of the hill overlooking the Port Apples marina, on the way, they had passed about six old farms, all empty, Shane commented

"One farm, then the Geeves football ground, if you are up for it, I think I have found our next outpost." She beats him to the punch line.

"I reckon you're going to say the Port Apples Hotel, opposite the marina because it is a natural blockade, road and ground are only 20 metres wide between the hotel and the water." Shane was impressed.

"Smart cookie luv, you're spot on, just need to check the hotel for Alliance, then we might go on the old road through Geeves, there is likely to be NK Nationals residing in the homes there."

Making it to the hotel car park in record time, they noticed first of all there were no vehicles present, and no smoke from the chimney. Scouting around the back they peered into the kitchen, no signs of life, entering the back door it felt eerie. Rachael checked the main bar area, saw no one, Shane the dining room, same there, they both mounted the stairs and checked the dozen accommodation rooms upstairs, all were empty, with no sign of the Alliance at all.

1545 hours and back at the turnoff to Geeves, they approached the first home, empty, the next three were the same. The main street had half a dozen shops, all closed, the next house on the right, had smoke coming from the Chimney. They elected to go bush and pass the next ten homes from the safety of the bush, this was pretty much the same, until they got back to the old apple orchard where they started.

1640 hours, the pair emerged out onto the paddock behind their outpost, Pete yelling out.

"Only bloody just made it, you're both late for the watch but do tell what you've found out."

The pair went on to describe the afternoons reccy, the unusual findings of empty homes and the hotel. From this the group, over dinner, discussed the next phase of their occupation. Shane suggested.

"I reckon a midnight raid up the old Geeves Road, what, there is only about twenty homes, a lot of them were empty, we could clear all of them in one night, then take up residence at the hotel, work out how we were going to barricade the road and move the whole shebang to there." The ex-hotel manager like the idea, adding.

"I like it, we could also take over the old salmon farm grounds on the right just before the hotel,I you know out on the point." Rachael laughed and spoke.

"Not only that, but there is a huge fuel depot there now, we put it in just before the E1, it was to service all of our Well Boats, it's massive, three huge tanks each holding forty thousand litres, you know the sort, they look like shipping containers. Each one has a partition separating the diesel from the petrol."

Sunday 1ˢᵗ March 2015 Geeves Back Road

0030 and having moved the tree after dinner the night before, they mounted the two jeeps and snuck along to the first occupied house on the old Geeves back road. Pete, Delilah and Matilda in the first jeep while Shane and Rachael were in the second. Pete took the first on the right while Shane took the left, both TRF members trying the front door first then the back, neither party came across a locked door.

Shane opening the front door, his supressed type 54 pistol in hand, Rachael just about hugging the twenty-five-year-old. First bedroom yielded a couple of occupants.

"Dooff...Dooff." Second bedroom same.

"Dooff... Dooff." Third bedroom three kids.

"Dooff...Dooff...Dooff." Rachael whispered.

"All clear." Exiting they can see Pete across the road doing the same; in the moonlight they give him the thumbs up signal.

Third home for Shane and Rachael was the first to sport a trooper, this meant a weapon and some ammo would be acquired. Rachael was already busy collecting sanitary products.

0340 hours, the last home for Shane and Rachael, one more trooper. The nineteen-year-old whispered.

"It's too easy Shags; we had more resistance in Dove, what gives?" Shane met up with Pete, they had the same concerns, both mounting up it was a short drive to the hotel, in the moonlight they could easily recognise the marina, the hotel and ground in between.

After checking the hotell, Pete and Delilah stayed, giving some thought to what to use as a barricade. Shane and Rachael moved down the dirt road to the salmon farm compound and eventually the fuel depot. Shane asked.

"How come there are no boats at the jetty Rach?"

"All the Well Boats would have been in the channel tied up to a leases Shags, this depot is really only used to re-fuel and offload nets."

He was impressed with the storage. While in the yard they discovered a huge boom, well made, out of steel, it even had drop-down wheels, who knows what it was originally intended for, Shane smiles.

"Looks like I've found our barricade."

Pete and Shane were able to attach the huge boom to the back of a jeep and tow it into place, finally letting it drop from the back of the jeep, removing its wheels, Pete declares.

"No bastard will be able to move it without a vehicle mate."

The group set up the Bren gun on the second-floor balcony, with clear vision all the way to the shop, some two kilometres away, and one kilometre back towards Geeves. The bedrooms were on the same level, with the kitchen below. The girls had managed to go back to Glen and retrieve all of their possessions.

1150 hours, afternoon watch keepers Shane and Rachael were waking up, having slept from 0600 hours. Matilda cooked breakfast for Pete and Delilah then crashed herself. After the move, Pete and Delilah were keen to get some sleep. Shane asked.

"Have we phoned Nobby yet, to let him know we're not home?" Pete gasped "Shit no, I clean forgot mate, too fucking tired, can you fill him in please?."

Rachael set up the Brick phone with battery and solar charger.

"Shit it hasn't been charging for a while, Brrr...Brrr...Brrr... oh Gooday, is that Nobby, yeah, it's Rachael and Shags, no all good, but we have moved, yes that's right the whole outpost. We cleared Geeves last night after a reccy Shags and I did, yep new outpost is Port Apples Hotel. We have secured the fuel depot, no sign of the Alliance and not many troopers last night. I think it was only, how many Shags, right Nobby he says only two."

The Dove TRF Commander liked the report.

"Shit guys, that is fantastic news, you guys are awesome, and I can add to that, we will, or now I can say, you will be seeing the *Cougar Anne* very soon. She's entering the Apples Riveru as we speak, was going to come here and wait till we had cleared Port Apples, but now she can come through to re-fuel, whilst waiting for the *Retaliator* and *Black Ink*, before commencing raids on Maggot and Kettle. I'll give you Baz's brick phone number, you can lead him in. I'll see you tomorrow for a stores run."

1600 hours, Matilda was up to cook the evening meal, Rachael and Shane had touched base with the skipper of the *Cougar Anne*, they were only one mile away from the jetty, Shane suggests.

"Are you right for half an hour Matilda, Rach and I will go help Baz tie her up, if there's any trouble wake Pete and Delilah, but otherwise let them sleep, a big day for them last night."

Standing on the Jetty both could see the fifty foot blue steel ex-cray boat round the point, its white bridge clearly visible with the afternoon sun shining off it. Before long Baz had her alongside, so after introductions all round, they suggested going back to the hotel for dinner, Rach had forewarned Matilda to expect four extra guests.

1800 hours and with everyone sitting in the huge dining room overlooking the marina, they could just see the fifty-footer alongside the wharf, out on the point. Delilah enquired.

"How was the trip down Lyn?" The fifty-nine-year-old pulled a face.

"Oh, I suppose some of it was ok, I'm not the sailor!" Baz added.

"She didn't like the worst of what the west coast dished up." Baz remarks

"Had a call from Harry yesterday, it seems we will be meeting them and the

Retaliator on Wednesday at Legs. It will take about ten hours to get there, back out of the river and then continue up the channel." Shane asked.

"So, what's on the agenda for you guys, between now and Tuesday?" Baz replied.

"Refuel tomorrow, then whatever you had in mind, till say midnight Tuesday."

Pete looked at Shane.

"Are you thinking the same as me mate?"

Monday 2ⁿᵈ March 2015 Port Apples TRF Outpost

1200 hours and Baz, Lyn, Sid and Craig pulled up in an Alliance jeep; courtesy of one that was captured last week.

"Great feed Matilda, I don't know how you do it." Declares Lyn. With nods all around Pete suggested a quick meeting to go over the night's attack.

"Baz, if you can slip lines at midnight and cruise over to the main Port Apples Wharf, we will meet you there, first we will have cleared the half a dozen homes between the shop and the wharfl, re-grouping from there, to work our way around the point. At the same time Shane, Matilda and Rach will clear up over the top road, between the shop and the other side of the point. Our objective is to put another barricade where the road is at its narrowest just before President, effectively cutting off the channel."

Tuesday 3ʳᵈ March 2015 Port Apples Wharf

0020 hours, the three jeeps met, exchanged greetings, Baz, Lyn and Sid in one jeep, Shane, Rachael and Matilda in the second, with Pete, Delilah and Craig in the third. Shane's jeep had the least homes to clear and soon found them on top of the hill overlooking the town.

"Only got four more to do girls, surprised we haven't seen any troopers."

Matilda had a theory

"Maybe they are short, Shane, you know we keep killing them, they have to run out eventually."

"Could be, let's see how many the rest find."

0425 hours, "I see them coming now girls." The two pull up together, Shane asks.

"How many troopers did you come across; we had none!" Pete adds,

"One here." To which the ex-CD ads.

"A couple here also, what gives, maybe they are running out, or more likely pulling them back for a major offensive."

With Rach, Matilda and Delilah, making the new outpost cosy, the others returned to tow the boom around, deciding to take the short cut over the hill, instead of right the way around the river.

The new outpost was a large weatherboard home right on the road, with huge bay windows giving full view around the river to President. Bottom windows could be opened to accommodate the Bren gun, Baz commented.

"Shit I haven't seen one of the old model Bren Guns for ages, I bet Dick had this hidden away." Pete replied.

"How did you guess, and what makes it an old model?" The ex-CD asked.

"Early ones were British, and ran .303 rounds, the new modification made them 7.62mm to bring them into line with everything else they were using, bloody fantastic weapon." said Shane.

"Yep, I love shooting it."

2300 hours, Pete and Delilah drove back the five kilometres to the main wharf not so much to slip the *Cougar Anne's* lines, but to retrieve the jeep, yelling out to the crew as she went astern from the wharf.

"See you further up the channel, keep your heads down and stay safe."

"Brrr, Brrr, Brrr, yes mate, Hi Harold."

TRF Vessel Cougar Anne

Chapter 6
Barracouta

Sat 28th February 2015 Honey Town, Mary Island

0900 hours and only twenty-four hours since the *Fremantle* had left, the group had settled in very well, looking up to Len as their leader. This made him smile, by his reckoning he was still very much a beginner at this killing stuff. Standing at the window, looking down at the jetty and the forty foot RHIB *Mary*, his mind was wandering back to when he was fishing, occasionally the *Carnivore* would visit the Island in-between cray shots.

He would stand and look at her alongside the jetty, the Mary Island Ferry would usually occupy the main side of the jetty and in slack periods, the RHIB would be used instead of the twenty-two-metre ferry to save fuel costs. He was miles away when he heard a voice, Len....

"Len here's your drink." It was Liz handing the skipper his coffee, and the seventeen-year-old gave him a hug, thinking his thoughts were back with his family.

"Shit, sorry luv, I was back fishing."

Accommodation at the ex-ranger's home was easy, it had four double rooms and a bunk room sleeping six, so it only stood to reason Helen and Chris took one double, Len and Jill another, Josh and Billy shared the bunk room. Being a tad old fashioned, Helen was not happy about the thirty-nine-year-old skipper sharing his bed with the seventeen-year-old girl, and on many occasions made it quite clear. Chris on the other hand was quite alright about it, maybe even a little jealous. Len called them all together with his next leg of the plan.

"Well, I suppose you are all wondering what happens next, now the Mary is up and running, first thing is to give her a test run, probably this afternoon, thought we might explore north of Bollards Beach, Round Bay, all the way to Little Duckport, and if time permits, over to Rifle Island and the camp site at Chinaman Beach." Chris asked.

"Who's going Len?"

"Well Chris, you, Jill, Josh if the leg is up to it and me, but I'm not trying to exclude anyone, Helen, you and Billy are more that welcome to come if you wish, we will be armed, and I can't guarantee not running into trouble."

The skipper left the room on purpose to go to the toilet; he knew they would debate it while he was away. Back in the room, Helen approached him.

"If it's alright with you Len, Billy and I would like to come." Len smiled.

"Great stuff, we will leave at eleven, Jill, could you help Helen and Josh to get some food and drinks together? Chris, if you could give me a hand to make sure both fuel tanks *are* full?" Len was making his way down to the RHIB, next thing he knows Jill is jumping on his back.

"Chris said he would help Helen, if I wanted to come and help you." Len was not sure that wasn't the way it went down, but he felt happy Liz was with him, in a strange sort of a way, he had fallen madly in love with the well-put-together seventeen-year-old.

The purpose-built tour vessel is the only one of its kind in Taswegia. *MV Mary* is a twelve metre RHIB, powered by triple 300hp Mercury Verado outboards. Offering all of the fun and adventure of similar tour boats, without the cold, wind and spray. They called it champagne cruising on an adventure boat! The *Mary* is legally surveyed for thirty passengers.

It is large and spacious and allows guests to move freely between two viewing decks. These decks provide remarkable viewing, when deep inside giant sea caves underneath spring-fed waterfalls, or when at rest having lunch. The top deck gives a wind-in-the-hair experience and a total 360-degree view of Mary Island's stunning coastline. The bottom deck provides shelter from the summer sun and also the wind and spray.

The bottom deck is very unique and unlike no other tour boat. It combines the comfort of a fully protected sun lounge at the bow with an open rear section for getting up close to nature. The aft (rear) seats of the lower deck can also be protected by a large drop-down window that is often used to protect the boat on the windward side.

It also has a full sized, locking and flushing toilet with views that every other toilet can only dream of having! There is plenty of room in the bathroom for changing into swim wear. It is private and very comfortable. The centre Helmsman's position was raised and sat three seats back from the bow giving the skipper plenty of forward vision, aft were stairs to the elevated viewing section a small sink, fridge, food preparation areas and gas stove. Len yelled out.

"Yep, that'll do luv you can turn the electric drum pump off?" Topping the triple fuel tanks up out of the 200 litre drums on the jetty gave the thirty-nine-year-old satisfaction he would not run out of fuel; with a capacity of 1500 litres this would be a test for fuel consumption, not knowing how thirsty these 300HP outboards would be.

1100 hours, and with everyone on board, food, drinks weapons and ammunition were issued. Type 54 pistols for everyone except young Billy and a number of Type 68 assault rifles. Dropping all lines, Len backed the *Mary* away from the jetty, turning to port, he headed for Bollards Beach. Giving the outboards time to get to operating temperature he tested maximum speed. The RHIB responded to the 900HP reaching nearly fifty knots.

With a slight easterly swell, the vessel left the water on a few occasions, Len brought the sticks back to half throttle and a more sedate twenty-five knots.

Bollards Beach came and went very quickly; Chris was sitting next to the skipper and comments.

"A lot quicker this time Len." he smiles.

"Yes, I think we'll head to Round Bay mate and give the shore a good going over; actually, can you ask Josh and Jill to hoist that Red Ensign please, we might as well show the colours to hopefully some more survivors." Jill and Josh found the Red Ensign in the little flag locker on the top deck, clipped it to the flag halyard and pulled it to the top.

1230 hours, the skipper pulled the sticks back, the forty-footer came off the plane to about eight knots, Len announced.

"This is Round Beach, anyone know why it's called that, because it certainly isn't round. Jill and Chris were watching for movement ashore, nothing spotted. Len increased speed to twenty knots and headed to Little Duckport Lagoon. He knew this was a great duck hunter's hangout and hoped that somehow there was a few hiding out.

1330 hours, turning to port, the RHIB rounded the point, and into the entrance to Little Duckport, dead in front was Sheep Island and little Sheep Island, the evidence of duck hides were everywhere.

"Got to watch the depth in here, gets pretty shallow at low tide, but it's high tide at the moment so hopefully it shouldn't present any problems." With all eyes scouting the shore it was little Billy who spoke first.

"Somebody in there, Mum, by that duck hide." Helen pointed to where she thought her son was looking, Chris and Jill also peering through the binoculars, Jill confirms the sighting.

"Yep, got him, male about thirty, armed, moving slowly left to right across the front of that duck hide." Young Billy was ecstatic, being the first to see someone.

Len killed the engines while Chris yelled out to the man.

"Hey mate, we are on your side, how many of you are there?" Nothing but silence, Len started the engines and headed in shore constantly watching the depth, four metres, three metres, two metres, trimming the outboards up a little, one point three metres, he was hesitant to go any further. Eventually they could see the bloke levelling his weapon at the RHIB, Josh yelled out.

"He's going to shoot at us!" The thirty-nine-year-old skipper commented.

"No, I don't think so mate, he's just using the scope to get a closer look at us, but just to be certain, Chris can you get him in your sights up on the bow please."

For fifteen minutes they all sat there, Len, then fed up with it all yelled out! "Mate if you don't want to join us fine, we'll piss off, you've got five minutes."

With this he started the triple donks, then asked Helen to put a cuppa on, saying.

"Well, if he doesn't move by the time it's poured, we're off."

1400 hours, "looks like you won skipper, the bloke's waving to us, yes it looks like he's saying it's deeper around the other side of the island." Len motored the RHIB around Sheep Island, and found the channel that took them close to the shore; he warned.

"Weapons drawn guys; this could be an Alliance trap."

Nudging the forty-footer into the bank, they were greeted by two duck hunters who quickly handed their possessions aboard and followed it onto the RHIB. Extending his hand the first one introduced himself,

"G'day I'm Paul Constance and this is my mate Mal Turnish.Boy, are we glad to see you." Helen commented.

"You didn't look that keen fifteen minutes ago," The forty-eight-year-old ex- house painter sheepishly replied.

"Yeah, sorry about that, we had to make sure you weren't the bad guys."

So, as Len doubled back on his course out to open sea, the two new boys were brought up to speed as to what had happened to their world. The hardest part was when they learnt that both Kings Town and Devon werewere now in the Alliance's hands, so the likelihood of their families being alive was just about zero.

Over a feed and a hot drink, the pair described how they usually camped together each year, when the E1 hit they didn't realise, till about ten days later, when they ran out of beer. They couldn't start their four-wheel drive so went to the nearest farm for help, it was there they learned of the E1 incident and pending nuclear holocaust. Going back to the farmer's family a couple of times, they had be-friended them. Swapping fish and ducks for veggies and grog, they were reasonably happy, thinking that at some time, someone would come to their rescue. This went on for a couple of weeks, then, one time whilst visiting, they witnessed the Alliance Death Squad pull up outside.

The family's eldest child was pushing a mower around their tiny front yard 'Boom, Boom' they heard the shots; Paul was first to see what was going on, in a split second he realised the jeep was not friendly. The farmer returned shots, which only seemed to irritate the squad, Paul and Mal had left their weapons back at camp so could offer no assistance. The family wouldn't leave, Paul and Mal exited the back of the farm just as the farmer was shot. As they crept along in the long grass, they could hear the ungodly screams coming from the farmer's wife, then the Boom, Boom, Boom from their weapons. Scared and not knowing anything else, they laid low for a week, re-appearing back at the farm to see no bodies but NK nationals moving in, it was then that the penny dropped.

1500 hours and on approach to the western side of Rifle Island, the skipper brought the *Mary* back to ten knots then rounds the point to Chinaman Beach, educating the crew.

"Chinaman Creek and Beach were great spots for campers over the Christmas holidays, they used to get a lift from Duck Cruises who offered the pickup service from Duck to the beach three times a week." With no waves affecting the small sandy beach, they nudged the *Mary* onto the sand. It was agreed that Josh, Chris and the newest TRF members Paul and Mal should split up and search the two likely camping spots. Mal and Chris go right while Paul and Chris do the other end of the beach.

Trying not to look too menacing, the group went with pistols only, Liz and Helen lending the newbies theirs. At the right-hand side of the beach was a small track leading some 300 metres to a nice, secluded campsite. The pair walked in on two people sitting around a campfire, surprised to see armed people, it startled the pair, the male spoke.

"Christ you scared the shits out of us, who the fuck are you anyway?" Josh and Mal filled the pair in quickly suggesting they join the TRF, waving back to Len to bring the *Mary* back into the sand.

Meeting Paul and Chris, who reported nothing they all re-joined the vessel. With introductions all-round the skipper soon had the RHIB dancing along at twenty-five knots; by the time the Mary Island jetty came into view everyone was well acquainted.

1950 hours and back in the ex-ranger's house, evening meal done and dusted. Most couples had moved off to bed, the burning question on the newcomers' lips was the same, is there a possibility that their families would still be alive? Paul, Mal, Len and Jill were the last standing, enjoying a glass of port out of Ranger Paul's secret barrel, Paul asked again.

"So, Len you reckon everyone is dead in Kings Town?" Len could hear the desperation in the man's voice, this was hard, because he knew there was no hope, all he could do was tell Doc and Nari's story or what he knew of it.

Sun 1ˢᵗ March 2015 Honey Town, Ranger's Residence

0800 hours, Len stood up from the breakfast table.

"Weapons training in one hour at the old quarry." The air was full of excitement, the foursome was still trying to come to terms with the reality of it all, and separately had asked everyone else whether it was all real or not. An hour later, Len, Josh and Jill had set up the targets and weapons, Jill counting out the ammo. Paul was first to find the quarry and he commented,

"Aren't the targets a bit close mate?" Directing his query to the thirty-nine-year-old skipper. Len laughed.

"Mate you've got to get up real close to kill these bastards."

The usual, instruction with the Alliance weapons and ammo, starting with the Type 68 then finishing with the 54, it was easy to see Paul and Mal were no slouches when it came to shooting, and they were, well a little bit cocky, making faces when the Benoa schoolteacher had her go, the same with her plumber husband.

Jill thought 'wait till this pair get into the real stuff, then we will see what they are made of' the seventeen-year-old reported what she saw to Len, he wasn't surprised.

1300 hours, Len called a team meeting, he had detected that Paul and Mal thought the whole TRF thing was a bit over the top, 'who made him boss' was overheard between the pair, Len started.

"Tonight's raid, two prongs so groups are- Josh, Chris, and Mal, while I lead Jill, Wendy, Paul and Bill. Mal asked

"How can the first team be led by Josh, he's just a kid." Before Len could answer, Jill replied

"Because he is the most experienced out of the three of you, he's done more raids, killed more and has been injured." There was silence, Paul followed.

"What is a raid, are we supposed to steal food or something?"

Len could see his feisty girlfriend was about to speak but he put his arm on Jill's shoulders,

"The raid is as follows, team one takes the northern end of town, clears as many homes as possible, get a vehicle if you can, team two, we will grab Dick's old Hi-Lux and go towards Oxford, the word is, they haven't replaced Nationals there, our goal is to block the supply line at Oxford, where the road is closest to the river. The thirty-nine-year-old could see the question arising in Paul so pre-empted,

"Clearing, Paul, Mal, Wendy and Bill, means kill everyone in the house and no it doesn't mean steal food, you kill everyone, take the trooper's weapon and ammo, if there is one and relieve them of their sanitary items." The air was full of nothing; Len turned towards Jill, gave her a wink and finished off,

"We leave at 2100 hours, that's 9 O'clock, any questions?" Wendy asked the usual

"When you say kill everyone, you don't mean women and children as well do you?" Jill answered

"Yep, that's exactly what we mean."

Jill and Len retired to their bedroom for some rest before the raid.

1930 hours, "Great meal Helen and Wendy, really appreciate it." The fifty-five-year-old ex- vegetable planter replied

"Our pleasure Len, and thanks for letting me stay behind with young Billy, really appreciate that."

2300 hours, the skipper slides the forty-foot RHIB in alongside the jetty where Dick and Jack had acquired the CJ. Dicks 1998 Hi-Lux still parked where they left it. After all, nobody would realise it still worked, Jill and Josh attach the mooring lines, Josh gathered his crew and walks off towards the town centre. Len and his team climb aboard the Hi-lux and head out of town towards Oxford.

2345 hours, team two, Wendy asks,
"How come we don't see any bad guys, Len?" He went on to explain that the TRF had hit the town hard, and the Alliance hadn't got round to replacing the Nationals.

Sarge and Annie had annihilated the whole forty strong Garrison, and it had only been replaced by six; they also decimated the town of Oxford. Driving past the service station, now in ruins, and the Oxford Motel, they were pretty sure no NK

Nationals were present, over the bridge, all the homes on the approach were empty.

They doubled back towards the Willy Town Road, and it took another three kilometres before they saw an occupied home. Len suggested

"I'll take this one with Bill and Jill, that leaves you Wendy, to cover the vehicle, remember if anyone approaches you, shoot to kill." The ex-schoolteacher was not all that confident whether she could actually do that, Jill gave her a hug suggesting she would be alright.

The knocking at the front door brought an elderly man to open it, armed with the suppressed 54 pistol 'Dooff' was all it took. Bill helped the body to the floor and coming to terms with what they had just done, followed the skipper into the first bedroom. Len helped Bill drive the pistol barrel hard against the woman's chest then pulling the trigger, a slightly louder 'DOOFF' as his was not supressed. In a dream state, the ex-plumber followed Jill and Len throughout the house shooting another five people, three of which were children.

By the seventeenth home at Sprung Beach, even Wendy had pulled the trigger on a couple. To the pair of Benoa locals, it all seemed a little bit surreal. Driving back towards the bridge, Len was looking for something to block the highway with; passing the council yard he stopped and backed up.

"That's it, we need that huge water pipe, it's got to be a metre round and six metres long, even got feet so it can't be rolled." Bill reckoned the aging Hi-Lux in low range would probably tow the pipe to where they wanted it.

Monday 2ⁿᵈ March 2015 Oxford Highway Oxford

0400 hours and with some of the team on the tray, Len and Jill in the cab, the aging Hi-lux was straining in low range to pull the massive pipe. Once they had momentum, it eased. Dragging the water pipe to the required location, Bill then released the towing chains that Jill had miraculously found behind the driver's seat, in a blue plastic box. Not quite in position, they hooked onto the pipe at the top and managed to turn it over onto the legs, they were like skids making it just about impossible to move it.

Len was happy, he addressed the group.

"Well, that's great, now the pipe has been put in place, we find out that team one, has had a win, and what comes next, yes Wendy?" The thirty-four-year-old schoolteacher was quick to pick up what was coming next,

"We need to guard both entries and exits, don't we Len?" Smiling he replies

"Yep, you got that, first time, so we go and help the others, all the while, working out who's watching what. We are not as isolated as you might think, if we have cleared all of Barracouta, we will move house to there, so to speak. With no enemy from the sea, the only way in, is through here, or the Indonesians coming back down the highway, from the northern end."

Sun 1ˢᵗ March 2015 Barracouta Garrison HQ

2345 hours, Team one approaching the Alliance Garrison HQ. Josh whispers

"Right, there should only be about six of them inside, and by the looks of it, one jeep and one truck in the parking lot. I'll lead, Chris behind me and Mal you cover our arses, Type 54s only, I have the suppressor."

The seventeen-year-old felt his leg, trying not to worry about the throbbing pain. The front door was open, the guard non-existent, they quickly found the sleeping quarters, single bunks after all, they had plenty of space left. 'Dooff' next room

Josh handed the supressed 54 to Chris, 'Dooff' then the next one to Mal, 'Dooff' no one hesitated and the last three provided no problem.

Finding the keys, provided more drama than killing them, after going through each room twice, Mal ran out to the car park yelling,

"Fucking keys were left in the fucking vehicles." The ex-real-estate agent holds them up like a trophy. Josh suggests they leave the truck for later on and take the jeep. Clearing all the homes between the Garrison HQ and the old service station at the northern end of town, one house behind it, then the Semi-Trailer manufacturer, 'Barracouta Trailers' famous Log-Jinker builders.

The house was full, Josh got Chris to lead, he went second and Mal back-up. Halfway through they changed, and Mal led, Chris second and Josh back-up, this went well on that home, the one the other side of the trailer builders was not so good, all went well until Mal was confronted by two teenage girls. the forty-seven-year-old had daughters the same age, and just had a meltdown. The first girl screamed, and attacked him clawing his face, in the ruckus the second girl tried to run, Chris had no alternative but to shoot her on the run, with a very loud BANG.

Monday 2ⁿᵈ March 2015 Benoa Highway North of Barracouta

0240 hours and the last house before the huge property 'Bill Roger' was full. No less that fourteen NK Nationals and one trooper. Josh tried to kill all of them with the silenced 54 pistol, the same as before, he gave each member a turn with the silent weapon. It was Chris's turn to clear when it came to the trooper's room, Josh whispered

"Mate you go in, use the suppressed 54, I'll cover you." Chris opened the door, but what he was confronted with was a very awake trooper reaching for his 68-assault rifle. Two shots caught the man in his right shoulder and hip, this failed to slow him down, he managed to get the assault rifle to bear on Chris and squeeze the trigger, the 7.62mm Nato round shot from the hip was close to its mark, the 39mm long round hit the retired plumber in the side, a clean through shot. Josh following Chris into the bedroom, quickly despatched the irate trooper yelling.

"Mal got a man down!"

0500 hours and back at the trailer manufacturer, they met Len's team, applying first aid to Chris's wound. Josh told the skipper, the only thing they had to do was drag something across the road at the pipeline. Len suggested a couple of the boats on trailers, outside the panel beaters, this was quickly done.

Len and Bill found a twenty-five-foot Bertram on a triple axel trailer, this filled the gap nicely.

0900 hours, Helen met the *Mary* at the jetty, satisfied they had done as good a job as possible, Len reported in to Dick.

"Brrr … Brrr … Brrr … yeah G'day Dick, it's Len, yep, all good although we have got one casualty, yep, it's Chris through and through no, his side. We have blocked the highway north and south, yep just below the property, 'Bill Roger' and at the river south end, yep, we'll set up watch keepers next, no south of the bridge, we found a great six metre length of water pipe, one metre diameter, shit didn't think of that Dick, good idea, we'll go back and change it to the bridge." Len got off the phone, shaking his head,

"I'm a fucking dickhead, forgot the road to Willy Town, which means we have to move the pipe to the northern side of the bridge, who's up for a return trip?" Mal asked.

The roster for guard duty was three people at each end of town, fully armed, if trouble presented itself, one would round up the four off duty.

"First watch keeping guards are Jill, Mal and I, southern end with Josh, Wendy and Bill northern end. Helen, Chris, Paul and Billy take a rest; we will do three hours on, and then change ends, then three hours there, then three off sort of rotate. Now Chris if that wound plays up, you just rest, we'll cover you some other way." Helen, Chris and Billy decided to bunk down in the Barracouta Motel manager's residence, right on the highway. Wendy and Bill, the police residence and Paul and Mal moved into the waterfront pub.

1230 hours, with Mal on watch, Jill and Len were taking it easy when the thirty-nine-year-old thought he would phone Dick again with the good news.

"Brrr ... Brrr ... Brrr ... Yep Dick, its Len again, mate we did move that pipe, good call, and guess what, while we were there, a truck came from Willy Town ... no we had already put the pipe up, ... yep shot them both and guess what was in the back, ... no guns ... a shit load of food supplies, oh I reckon enough to keep a small town going, haven't finished counting it, but Jill reckons 600kg of rice in twenty kg bags ... yep set up now, moved this morning, re-located two teams of three each ... Yep righto and good luck."

"Brrr ... Brrr ... Hello, yep Len here Dick, oh I see..." Len turned to the group,

"That truck is different to the NK Alliance because it's an Indonesian Truck; a M35A3 with a Caterpillar 3116 Diesel engine. Dick reckons it was going to Benoa, and we get a big well done!"

TRF Vessel MV *Mary*, forty-foot RHIB

Chapter 7
Battle at Bronze

Thursday 5ᵗʰ March 2015 Sand Alley Hotel

0800 hours, a crew meeting, most of the off watch TRF members were asked to attend. Johnny chaired the meeting and asking Vince and Laurel to take part, he explained that Riley and the *Retaliator* were working the Frog Channel area at the moment until the *Cougar Anne* arrives then the *Retaliator* was required back at Sand Alley. In the meantime, to do the watch changeovers at Lewis they would use jeeps.

"Thanks for making it team, as you know we are working off a major plan put together by Dick, Sarge and Doc. This has been going fantastically, but we have reached the next stage, that is to push the Alliance all the way back to Soothe. This will mean two prongs, first will be nighttime clearings, from Sand Alley to Bronze and from Lewis to just outside Soothe. Then it is all the way to Soothe eventually barricading the highway at Mid-Point. The clearing of Soothe itself will be huge; stats tell us if every home is occupied it means some 300 homes." Vince asked

"How many jeeps Johnny, and how many to a jeep?" The ex-farmer thought this was a little out of his depth and was not sure he knew the answer. "What would you do Vince or Laurel, after all, you're both military."

"Strategy is not one of my high points Johnny, more the likes of Dick and Jack who have both served as covert operatives, and they are into all the covert shit, but I think I know what they would say. Three to a jeep, three jeeps or more on each front, so that's a minimum of six jeeps and eighteen personnel, it's what worked well clearing the Peninsular."

"I like it Vince, draw up the rosters, best way you see fit."

Vince and Laurel sat down with the crew list, taking into consideration the wounded, and who was away with the *Retaliator*, then started.

- Sand Alley
  - Jeep one Vince, Laurel and William Dart
  - Jeep two Will, David and Eleanor
  - Jeep three Brian, Mick J and Bentley
- Lewis
  - Jeep one Paul, Jack and Rob
  - Jeep two Riff, Clinton and George
  - Jeep three Johnny, Cedric and Tony
- Back-ups to be Max, Graham, James and Brian Green

1450 hours, Vince found Johnny inspecting the pump that the ex-navy technician had developed for getting the fuel out of the service stations.

"Great work with this, Vince, this will be a great help, how did you go with the rosters"?

"All good mate, suggest we check weapons and go tonight, simultaneously start at 2100 hours." The ex-farmer smiled "Let's make it happen."

2100 hours, at north Sand Alley the three jeeps were waiting for the start, when Vince gave them his go speech,

"All weapons checked, make sure you have enough ammo, those that have suppressors make sure you have plenty of 9mm, I think if all goes well you will be doing the most killing, but feel free to share the weapons around."

First home on the right was about ten kilometres up the road, then one kilometre to the next on the left, this is the sequence they took, the third jeep took the Julia Bay back road, this had around fourteen homes, the goal was to meet up at Bronze.

2300 hours and jeep one was nearing the Bronze Alliance HQ, this home was an old dairy. Vince knocked on the front door, a small woman answered wearing a towel, this put the ex-navy technician off his guard, hesitating just for a minute. She seemed not to realise the danger she was in, she spoke, bringing Vince out of his trance, he pulled the trigger "Dooff."

William was his back up and Laurel drove the jeep, next room empty, third room down the hall, William shot his first pair of Nationals, he liked the suppressor, yelling enthusiastically,

"All clear."

Vince hadn't checked the bathroom, and on his way up the hallway, the bathroom door opened smacking him in the nose. The female could see William, but not Vince who was behind her, sporting a rather sore nose. The twenty something National made out the towel clad woman on the floor, then screamed. William turned but couldn't shoot because of Vince in his line of sight, she came at the ex-fisherman like a train, fists thrashing like lightning.

Vince, tackling her to the floor, eventually got the girl in a headlock, shutting off the air supply and then 'crack' breaking her neck. William commented.

"Christ, mate is it always like this?" Vince collapsed on the floor with the woman firmly in the headlock position.

"I fucking hope not, William!"

2300 hours, jeep three, Brian and Mick were clearing a group of homes close together, Bentley was driving. They had reached the Julia Beach shacks, these had been cleared by Dick before, it looked like the Alliance were not game to re-fill these homes, so they had a clear run right up to the outskirts of Bronze.

2315 hours and jeep two pulled up alongside Vince in jeep one, Will asked.

"When do you want to do this mate, looks like a couple of jeeps and a truck at the old backpackers." Vince had done the sums; he could also remember what Dick had said about the café with the old Hydro single man's quarters out the back.

"Mate I reckon I do the quarters with the suppressor, then we hit the café together. I can't really see anyone up at this time but keep an eye out for jeep three. Will, if you and David could start the couple of homes on the other side of the road, El, can you drive?"

Fourteen troopers Vince shot at close range with the suppressed 54 pistol, he remembered Dick saying the rooms were not locked and this was certainly a bonus.

Laurel chose to load all the weapons and ammo while the boys checked the café, nah empty. Hearing a couple of muffled shots coming from the home over the road, David and Will exiting just in time to meet jeep three. Vince spoke to the three teams

"Ok only about three homes between here and the timber mill, a lot of ground to cover, so we might take one each, then stop at the mill, then only one home there on top of the hill."

Friday 6th March 2015 Lewis to Soothe Road

0130 hours, jeep three, Johnny had signalled them to stop, the three jeeps were making excellent time, something to do with 50% of the homes they entered, being empty. They now sat on the main highway to Bronze, three kilometres from Soothe. Johnny whispered.

"One home on the right, attached to the whisky distillery, then two more a kilometre from here. One road at Rusty Creek on the right, this probably has five homes, then one on the left over the creek. The fruit and veg place on the right, and then we are knocking on Soothe's door."

Paul, Jack and Rob decided to move forward and clear the Rusty Creek Road, Riff, Clinton and George would do the in-between homes leaving Johnny, Cedric and Tony to do the whiskey distillery and the one on the left before the Rusty Creek Bridge. Cedric commented

"Hope we can get some samples?"

0300 hours and with the distillery cleared, samples gathered, Johnny pulled the jeep up just over the Rusty Creek Bridge. A few moments later, Clinton and Jack stopped. The seventy-year-old retired fisherman whispered.

"Mate, not many troopers, only got a couple of sets of weapons and they weren't sporting much ammo either." Johnny had a theory,

"I reckon they're short, proof will be in the pudding at Soothe. The old barracks will be where the bulk of the troopers will be housed. One of us will clear that, the other two will take the left-hand side of the town, and Vince's lot, 'yep here they come now' will take the right-hand side."

The sight of the three jeeps coming down the hill, across the bridge was a warming sight for everyone concerned. The six jeeps now took a few moments to report and catch their breath. All were in agreement, they didn't find many troopers, well apart from the fourteen Vince killed at Bronze.

0330 hours and Vince volunteered to take out the Red Bottle Inn, the suspected Alliance accommodation-come HQ, well positioned, plenty of beds, the only problem was it was two stories high.

Laurel pulled the General M151 Diesel variant jeep up around the corner from the front door. Vince and William opted to split up, William would hop the fence and enter via the back door, while the ex-navy technician would just walk in the front door, this was always open, due to the varied times troopers would return.

The front two rooms had been converted to small dining rooms; a hallway connected these to the remainder of the lower floor. Passing a steep stairway on the right, Vince was soon looking at William, who had observed the kitchen and utility rooms. The stairs were old and creaky, the sound they made sent shivers up the pair's spines, the musky smell was a combination of old carpet, smoke and Asian cooking smells.

The top floor consisted of twenty bedrooms, all small, but adequate. Vince started on the first room, while William remained at the door,

"Dooff" William gave Vince a little smirk as he entered the second room, "Dooff" and so it continued all the way along to the end room. Room five was different, larger with an ensuite, quite possibly it was the host or owners in its day. William wanted a go, so they swapped, and the ex-fisherman entered.

"Dooff" Dooff." With a huge smile, he continued down the other side, William clearing the next ten rooms, five of which were empty.

0500 hours, with the beginning of the dawn, the sun creeping above the hilltop, due east of Soothe, troops were stirring. Vince entered the seventeenth room just as a trooper opened the door on room twenty. William slipped inside the doorway touching Vince on the arm, as to warn him as the man walked past, still half-awake to the bathroom. He spoke, obviously thinking that someone was coming out of Vince's room. He stopped and turning towards Vince, probably about to continue the early morning chit chat. Vince had no option but to shoot the man before he came too close to William.

"Dooff." The trooper fell heavily making a huge noise, falling headfirst into a potted plant on a tall stand. It was bedlam, noises from the other couple of rooms probably complaining about the noise. Vince broke the record of how fast to clear each room.

With a 'devil may care' attitude, the forty-seven-year-old ex-pusser, shot them from the doorway, standing, out of breath he said.

"Fuck mate, that was close, we should get a move on with collecting the weapons before it gets too much lighter." William was already starting to carry the 68's down the stairs, Vince whistled to Laurel who backed the jeep up over the curb right up to the front door. With fifteen type 68 assault rifles, 130 rounds of 7.62 ammo, three type 54 pistols and 100 rounds of 9mm ammo Laurel whispered,

"Great haul, any trouble?" William described the near miss and subsequent noise, Laurel saying she heard it down on the street.

0530 hours, at the start of the causeway, Vince, William and Laurel waited for the other jeeps. They had the greater number of homes to clear, but between the five teams, this would only amount to

45 homes each, and with a large percentage unoccupied, could be done within the time allotted. Laurel points,

"Looks like one coming now Luv, it looks like El driving." Pulling up alongside Will, David gave the thumbs up signal, next jeep was Johnny's. The ex-farmer reports,

"One casualty, Paul has been shot in the foot, not sure whether it was user error, or a trooper did it." Vince recommended they stop at the causeway, because to clear Mid-Point during daylight would be suicide. Johnny agreed, all they had to do was decide on what to block the road with.

0600 hours and with all teams present, Laurel had a look at Paul's foot. Not too bad, she dressed it on the spot, while the others found something suitable to block the road.

Adjacent to the start of the causeway was a rural supply business, and before long they found the huge 988 Cat Front End Loader. This was used to load gravel and mulch, and with some effort, could be towed to the road and with a substantial crash barrier on either side nothing could pass. Vince asked

"What's the weapons tally?" Each jeep replied-

- Will's jeep, ten 68's and two 54's
- Brian's jeep acquired six 68's and one 54
- Paul's jeep acquired fifteen 68's and three 54's
- Riff's jeep acquired nine 68's and no 54's
- Johnny's jeep acquired eleven 68's and two 54's
- Laurel reported fifteen 68's and four 54's

Giving the night a total of sixty-six, Type 68 assault rifles and twelve Type 54 Pistols, the ammo was a bit on the short side with only 310 x 7.62 rounds and 69 x 9mm rounds.

"How far did you get up the highway towards Mead Stead"? Brian replied,

"Until there were no more homes mate, but I reckon we will have to put a guard on the outskirts of town, you know in case they discover the back road into the place." Johnny realising they would have to now man this blockade, as well as the one north which was calling for volunteers and it didn't take long for the old Sand Alley crew to put their hands up, along with Riff, Clinton and George.

Leaving Will, Eleanor, David and the welcome addition of Mick and the other three, the four jeeps headed back to Sand Alley to arrange the clean-up squads. Watching them go Mick commented.

"I think I would rather be here, than picking up dead bodies." El added

"Yep, by my recollection the count must be over 4000 NK Nationals and about 100 troops." Will decided the best place to snipe from was the top floor room above the plant nursery, this was overlooking the road. They had clear vision to Mid-Point and in the other direction past the chook farm to the town entrance. Two would be on watch at all times, the other pair sleeping or doing roving patrols around Soothe.

The northern blockade would be at the end of the straight, at an old tourist coach depot. Discussion was had as to whether they would actually block the road or not, George decided they should, and suggested an old tourist coach, neatly fitting cross the bitumen road.

"At least that will slow them down," added Riff and Clinton.

"Yep and am I happy we loaded up with all those RPG's we found in that jeep at the B&B, we counted twelve so split them with Will's crew."

1800 hours, Sand Alley, after some well-earned sleep, Johnny dialled Dick's number

Brrr ... Brrr ...

Chapter 8
Alliance Worried

Monday 9th March 2015 Alliance HQ Kings Town

0830 hours and pondering over the events of the last week, General Jun Lee thought it was only yesterday, but it was nearly a week since that fateful night he and the captain transported Doctor Reginald Miles from Lakeside to Kings Town Hospital after he was shot by the distraught trooper whose wife died giving birth.

Such a terrible affair, Jun Lee and the captain tossed it about for ages, if they locked up the trooper, who would care for the baby, in the end they decided to de-mote the trooper back to the lowest grade possible. Waiting, as he usually does on report day, he heard a knock on the door,

"Come in Captain; tell me, how are the reports coming in?" The forty-year-old captain looked worried,

"No reports from Soothe, Bronze or Barracouta yet sir?" The General looked puzzled

"What about our northern members and the Indonesians?"

"No nothing from them either, sir." Jun Lee sent the Captain to follow up.

0910 hours "Where are my reports, Captain Li Chun?" Hearing nothing, Jun Lee rose and searched the entire building, eventually questioning a clerk, to the reply, the captain left ten minutes ago, didn't say where he was going.

1050 hours, after what seemed forever, the captain appeared.

"Sorry sir, I had to get a driver to check personally on the situation at Soothe." The general was a little peeved but inwardly commended the captain for his resourcefulness.

"So, what was the verdict Captain, he must have been driving very fast to make there and back." The forty-year-old hated giving his superior bad news, but lately that is all there was.

"He didn't make it to Soothe sir, there seemed to be a roadblock at the Soothe end of the causeway." The general was again puzzled.

"Seemed to be Captain, what do you mean, seemed to be!" The captain ran his finger around his collar feeling the heat.

"The driver passed Mid-Point and entered the last causeway, as he approached the end, he could see a huge earthmoving machine parked across the road, approaching, he was fired upon, the passenger sustained mortal wounds, he had to back the jeep up the whole causeway. His assumption was that rebel forces have taken Soothe." Jun Lee was turning a dark crimson, shaking his head he blurted,

"You know what this means Li?" The forty-year-old captain shook his head in the negative, not really sure where the general was going with the question.

"This means that these rebels have control of not only Soothe, but Lewis, Purple Sands, Bronze, Sand Alley and the Peninsular, God only knows what our losses are." Li added

"We have a messenger just in from the channel sir." The general rose out of his chair, looked out the window at the

Kings Town Harbour, always peaceful 'oh how he wished it was all over'.

"Li, make sure that we have a 100 men stationed at Mid-Point, and get me a plan to flank the rebels. Now let's get some good news from down the channel."

The Maggot messenger was ushered into the office where Captain Li Chun read the report.

"The Dove messenger did not return, and when another was sent to replace him, he didn't return either, a small squad was sent to investigate, and they were fired upon just the other side of President." Jun Lee asked the messenger whether he was part of the squad investigating, he nodded in the affirmative.

"So, in your own words Corporal, was this a large force or a well-trained small ambush party?" The corporal replied

"Well sir in my opinion they were certainly well trained, two shots hit our jeep, this sustained two kills, both head shots. The position was well elevated with clear line of sight and could be successfully defended with a handful of men." The general asked how he had survived,

"The driver and passenger were killed when we stopped to make out the barricade, myself and four others removed the dead and pushed the jeep backwards for 100 metres or so, then I started the motor and turned it around, collected my comrades to drive back to Apples." Jun Lee enquired

"And all of this whilst you were under fire, I must truly commend you Corporal."

Dismissing the messenger, Jun Lee turned to the captain,

"That man deserves a medal Captain, see to it. Now it seems that these rebel scums are military, and we think we know how they are moving around, by sea, with a rubber boat at Julia Beach and an old wooden fishing boat at Kettle. We must get that Catamaran on the water so we can fight back; check on its progress Li. We need to withdraw some troops and mount a full offensive at President, how many troops do we have in the area captain?" Consulting his paperwork he replied,

"400 at Apples, 200 working home attachments, 100 at Maggot and another 200 at Queens plus 250 attached to homes in the area, we also have 1000 men on standby here at Kings Town."

"Right Captain, work out a plan, consult the area commanders at Apples, Maggot and Queens along with our top strategists here in town, also look at Soothe, whether we can re-secure the town. Oh, and how did your horse troopers go at Judd, did they rouse out any rebels?"

"They searched the whole area, found nine rebels and killed them sir, nearly got another two driving around in one of our jeeps but couldn't quite keep up with it. We were thinking of dispersing both units up above Mead Stead, in the Red Mountain area."

1400 hours, the general's jeep pulled up outside the Kings Town International Catamaran's Building Prince Bay, where he found the retired mechanic, Guhn, Kuhn and four others pulling the engine out of the eighty-five metre Cat.

"How are you going Guhn?" The seventy-eight-year-old bowed to the general, "Last one out now sir, we should have the engine secured by tomorrow."

Jun Lee smiled

"Great news Guhn, you and your team are doing exceptional work under the circumstances."

Wednesday 11th March 2015 Alliance HQ Kings Town

1000 hours, "come in Captain, now what news do you have surrounding our offensive at President and Soothe?" Captain Li Chun, involved with all the top strategy soldiers was halfway there,

"Well, it seems until we can get a boat operational, the rebels have the upper hand down the channel sir, and it would be suicide to attack their well-fortified position without sea support. Soothe on the other hand has a back door, a road exists between Mid-Point around the lagoon and joins the Soothe to Oxford highway, this we can mount a full attack and out flank them."

"How many men do they have at Soothe Captain?" The forty-year-old didn't know the answer and he didn't really want to tell the general.

"Err not really sure sir; we have not been able to get reconnaissance into the area."

"So, Captain, it seems these rebels have the upper hand again, we have an alternative route but are unsure of how many we are facing, I must say not a great scenario we find ourselves in, is it Captain?"

"No sir, our top people are saying they couldn't possibly have more than a hundred men at Soothe, so we are working on that number."

"You have the order to mount the offensive, with whatever number of men you and your strategistsdelete see fit to accomplish the mission and as soon as possible, these rebels are not standing still for long."

Thursday 12th March 2015 Back Halfway Point to Soothe Road

0700 hours, Senior Lieutenant Lum Si Gow, a forty-year-old veteran soldier with twenty-three years' service in the army, was given command of the forces to be known as *hwanan jimseung* or 'The Angry Beast'.

They had gathered from 0400 hours, the twenty trucks and three jeeps now parked on the side of the dirt road. Lum called his only junior officer, and senior non-commissioned ranks to go over the plan.

"We will strike out at 0730 hours in three waves; the first six trucks will join the highway north of Soothe and strike towards the town. This will be backed up by the next six trucks half an hour later, and the last eight trucks half hour after that. Each wave will be led by a senior NCO, we want to get inside the town and disperse either side of the main road eventually taking the Barricade. As soon as this has been removed the other section at Mid-Point will move east into the town."

0750 hours and approaching the northern end of Soothe, the first truck driver slowed down, he could see the little dirt road on his right that the second wave would be coming down, there were half a dozen homes on the right-hand side and what looked like a huge bus parked across the road. The senior corporal decided to gently ram one end of the bus to move it enough to drive past; he motioned to the second truck to assist. He figured with the combined 280 HP and low range the KM450 Light Cargo Trucks would have no problems.

They were hard against the huge white bus, engaging low range then they started, wheels squealed, the smell of burning rubber, the passenger in the first truck spoke, but never quite got the words out, but if possible, he would have said.

"Incoming RPG, back up!" Unfortunately, he never got the words out, the type

69 Rocket Propelled Grenade, with an effective range of 200 metres and the outpost only 100 metres away couldn't miss. The 85mm grenade shattered the first truck's side window, missing the passenger by millimetres, exiting the open driver's window and hitting the second truck's main pillar behind the passenger's door.

"Whoosh, Boom."

The explosion was massive; the blast was powerful enough to lift the second truck off the ground, throwing it to the right, the first truck exploding in a fireball rolling it to the left. Senior Lieutenant Lum Si Gow ordered the next two trucks to dismount and return fire, this they did; the outpost was taking fire now from the two trucks when the second wave emerged from the dirt road. They turned towards the burnt-out wreck of the second truck, didn't quite dismount quick enough as a second RPG was fired, hitting the truck's rear canopy.

"Boom", and it too exploded in a fireball. Lum was pushing his ground forces

to flank the outpost, and some of them had even managed to secure a hold at the back of the property.

0820 hours. Whilst trying to sneak to the back door they were seen and fired upon, the remaining two troopers withdrew to the safety of the fence, the scene was set, three trucks blown to smithereens, and nine trucks blocking the main road, with another wave to come soon. Troops had started to work their way through back yards on the other side of the main road or to the right of the bus barricade. Unbeknown to them, the noise of the two RPG attacks had drawn the attention to the other rebel outpost, who flanked and engaged the men on foot roaming the back yards. All this with a clear shot of the mass gathering of trucks, they let loose with another RPG.

"Whoosh". This 40mm x 85mm rocket snaked its way towards the second wave's second truck,

"Boom." The explosion not only took out that truck, but the two others alongside.

0840 hours and Lum gave the order to pull back out of sight, he now had five trucks destroyed and some 100 troops dead.

Taking a moment to gather his thoughts, he yelled to his second in command,

"Take fifty men and continue to flank to the left, and another fifty flanking to the right." The team on the right had to get over the normal wooden paling fence about 1.5 metres high, this alone was causing trouble, each time one of them managed to get halfway over they would simply fall back, they heard no noise but clearly, they had all been hit in the head by a sniper.

'Bloody sniper's rifle', thought the Senior Lieutenant, and a good one, losing nineteen men they tried to bash the palings enough to make a hole at the bottom of the fence. This was successful and the thirty-one troopers found their way to the back of the nearest home. The sniper's fire was coming from the next home along, or so they thought. Sending three across the street at a time proved fruitless. The bark of the type 68's a constant reminder that they were facing their own weapons. Not wanting to lose any more, meant the sergeant dug in at the house, he was down to twenty-one men, ordering three to go right, he thought they eventually got around the sniper while he waited, small arms fire echoed out, he had no way of knowing whether they made it or not.

0950 hours, Lum was trying to get a truck over the curb and around the back of the tourist coach depot, he was taking fire and eventually came to a halt, the men exiting were cut to pieces by the barking Type 68's. For two hours they exchanged fire, then with only 194 troops left, all spread out across the 300-metre front, eighteen men pinned down behind a home near the sniper, it was reported that their ammunition supplies were getting very low, some of the troops were down to their last magazine. This he thought was ludicrous, but looking at his own 9mm supply it was rammed home, he only had one spare magazine for his own pistol.

Ordering a retreat was one of the hardest things that the senior lieutenant had ever done, and it was going to be a messy withdrawal. As the forward troops returned, they were cut to pieces. For the last wave of trucks to turn around, they had to expose themselves, this was fatal, as the RPG operators had a field day. Another five trucks were blown up, thankfully not full of troops; they were on the ground scampering away from the vicious fire fight. Lum waited till all that was left of the first and second wave retreated back up the main highway, his driver bringing up the rear, this was also a fatal mistake, the driver, looking in the rear vision mirror could see the rebel running out onto the road and shouldering the RPG, not knowing how far away they were, the driver hoped it was far enough.

"Whoosh Boom" it wasn't.

NK Alliance KM450 Light Cargo Truck

Chapter 9
Fremantle to Queen Island

Monday 9ᵗʰ March 2015 FCPB Bull Bay, Ramat River

0745 hours, the previous day Dick had suggested that a roving patrol do a daylight run, clearing anything they had missed the night before, volunteers were sought and the following volunteered,

Ugly Jeep two- with Henry, Josie, Grant, PLUS six TRF members

Lawn Truck one- with Boz, Kylie PLUS ten members

0800 hours and Doc orders.

"Single up all lines, main engines please Chief." Patch was on the quarterdeck with Ernie, Belle, Nic, Smokey, Boz and Gaz. Boz just back from the roving patrol when Patch declared.

"Geez it was great to see you guys, so glad you're all-in-one piece." She was sad to say goodbye, only just catching up with them all. Dick joined the group and with hugs all round he said.

"Better get off now or you might just come with us." Grinning Ernie asks, "Where to now mate, and when do you think we can all sit down and have a beer in peace?"

The ex-CD looked at his wife and friends.

"Well, we're off to Queen Island to hopefully raise an army to raid the Northwest and as to when it will all be over, sorry, can't answer that one, not yet anyway. We'll think of you as we sail past in a week or so on our way back down the coast, remember the good news, we have control from Soothe, south and President south, the whole west coast and now it seems High Head to Lawn, east to Scott."

0810 hours, Doc orders.

"Slow astern port, slow ahead starboard, fend off that wharf, slow astern together." Picking up the VHF microphone Dick radios the other two vessels.

"*Dementia* and *Nancy Kaye*, good luck with supporting here, and when you take the Boss Island members back home, start the recruiting for the St Anne attack, call if you want us, *Fremantle* out." Going astern, away from the Bull Bay Wharf, Doc spanned the FCPB in her own length and headed out into the river to sea, picking up the mic, Dick broadcasted.

"Full crew meeting in one hour." Turning to Doc, he asked.

"Want a brew mate?"

1000 hours "Brrr ... Brrr ... Brrr ... Yep who have I got, right hi Len, how's it going?" After the call Dick went over the next part of the plan.

"Destination Grass on Queen Island, distance around 150 nautical miles, at present speed ten hours, ETA 2000 hours tonight, although bad weather may slow us down. We plan to engage the locals and recruit an army, hopefully with a better result than Boss Island, train them for a couple of days, then on Thursday head for Bird Island where we will contact the Hammer family. Hopefully then, conduct raids across the northwest down as far as Alfred River and west to Sheepnorth, hopefully even clearing down as far as Devon. Now it's over to Sarge." Sarge started,

"Weapons and ammo audit ready, we are sitting pretty, still nearly 300 Type 68 Assault rifles and nearly 30,000 7.62 rounds. Type 54 Pistols are down to 120 and 12,000 9 mm rounds.

We have acquired thirty-seven Type 69 Rocket Propelled Grenades (RPG's) and a varied assortment of weapons the Alliance had taken off Taswegians. You know, .22 rifles, some 308's, .223 and .224, numerous shotguns and plenty of ammo to go with them. Based on what Dick just said, we should be aiming for around a 200 strong army, although we won't issue everyone a pistol, I think that just about sums it up." Jack commented.

"Same training as before, we will offer it to all able-bodied personnel, over the age of sixteen, short range targets and hopefully we can get close to 200." Nari asks,

"We can't fit all those people on the *Fremantle*, can we?" Doc put his arm around her smiling.

"Sorry, forgot to tell you that the *Christa Leanne*, *St Bernadette* and *Specialist* will be joining us there, they will take over as transport after we have set everything up." Dick followed

"You all know the *Christa Leanne*, with Harry, Jill and Gary on board, what you don't know are the others.

St Bernadette is a sixty-foot steel, and the *Specialist* is a sixty-five foot, both ex-fishing boats, crews will be:

- *Specialist:* Skipper will be Dr Ted Green, a mate of Doc's and Hazel Hemmingway his decky, these will be joined by a couple of Strine local fishermen off the boat
- *St Bernadette:* Skipper will be Denis Crawfield and his son John Crawfield

These vessels will be paramount in overtaking the Alliance in the Northwest and hopefully we might find another one on Queen Island to re-power."

The rest of the day was pretty eventful; sea state was kind to the patrol boat and its crew.

1200 hours, lunch was cold meat and salads, some fresh bread and handmade cheese. The bread was a frozen dough, re-constituted, the salad from Belle's gatherings and the hand-made cheese compliments of Nic.

With Jack and April on watch, while Annie swapped for engine room duties, everyone else was having a well-earned rest. Dick and Patch cuddling in their bunk, Doc and Nari snoring, well at least one of them was, Nettie was sound asleep in the radio shack and Sarge in the senior sailor's mess.

1600 hours, change of watch, Dick and Patch took over, both electing to pilot the FCPB from the flying bridge, Patch asked,

"What's that land in the distance Luv, is that Taswegia?"

"That, I reckon will be Four Hummock Island." It was then they both heard a radio call.

"Anyone receiving on VHF channel 16, over?" Dick was curious; the voice was definitely female and sounded really worn out.

"Might give them a call, I don't think it was fake, or a trap, anyway they can't hurt us out here, grabbing the Mike he transmitted,

"Delta Echo, Delta Echo, receiving you five out of twenty, say again your last over." The pair waited and listened, then with much more bravado, the female transmitted.

"Oh, thank God someone is there, can you hear me, we are marooned on Four Hummock Island and need your help over." Dick looked at Patch

"Better wake the Doc Chook."

1625 hours both Doc and Nari were on the Bridge with Dick and Patch, Doc transmitted.

"Four Hummock Island, this is the Patrol Boat *Fremantle* what is your status, how many and where on the Island are you over?"

There was a small pause then,

"There are four of us, well not really, only two here now, but my children will be back soon and we're at the Homestead at Chimney Point, the western most tip." Dick was setting the course for that point, marking it on the chart saying, "It will probably add six hours to our journey Skipper." The sixty-five-year-old declared.

"What can we do, can't just leave them there, alter course to land at Chimney Point." Turning to port, the FCPB rounded the northern tip and started down the coast.

1730 hours. "Well, that my friends is Chimney Point, small sandy beach, let me know the depth please Nari."

"Seventeen metres my man, thirteen metres my man, nine metres," Doc called for anchor stations, throttling back, to all stop. Sarge and Annie manned the windlass, the chain rattling down the hawse pipe, and with the anchor settling on the bottom, Doc went slow astern then all stop.

"Deploy the RHIB Dick, take Patch and Nettie with you, oh and side arms, take no chances, but before you go, what do we know about this place?" Patch found some info in a tourist paper she picked up in High Head, she read.

"For many centuries, the island was a summer hunting ground for Aboriginal people of the Northwest tribe, who reached the island by swimming across five kilometres of open water from nearby Shooter Island.

Its European discoverers were Boss and Flounders, who named the island in 1798. More explorers, shipwrecked mariners and sailors followed.

In 1978 the majority of the 7,400 hectares was declared a nature reserve; and in 2001 a state reserve.

From 1932 until 1951, the island was run as a farm by Cissie and Bill Nichols until John and Eleanor Alliston took over with their four children, Venetia, Robert, Warwick and Ingrid. The family maintained a presence on the island until 2006.

Eleanor Alliston is the author of "Escape to an Island" and "An Island Affair", which tells of her family's adventurous years living on Four Hummock.

Originally built in 1910 and then renovated, the Homestead is situated against a group of mighty trees, overlooking an open field grazed by native kangaroos and Cape Barren Geese. Step out onto your large deck area and enjoy your morning cuppa with the wildlife, watching a colourful Three Hummock Island sunrise.

Take a picnic or bottle of wine down to Home Beach, which stretches completely uninhabited as far as your eyes can see. Bird enthusiasts can walk the shoreline and catch a pair of sea eagles soaring gallantly overhead.

The Homestead is incredibly comfortable and adaptive to your needs - a warm haven after a long day of bush walking adventures, or a cosy place to escape and catch up on some reading. Wherever you are, you'll be rewarded with the sound of soft waves in the background, lapping at the island's stunning granite coast.

With a fully equipped kitchen, the Homestead allows you to be completely independent. Request some organic greens and herbs from the garden and cook yourself up something flavoursome to enjoy at your outdoor table while the sun goes down.

All linen is provided during your stay. There is a large collection of books to enjoy while here, as well a television, and a number of DVDs.

Four Hummock Island is Eco accommodation. All power is provided through renewable sources such as wind and solar. There are no high-drawing appliances such as electric kettles or hair dryers on the island. All water is provided through rainwater tanks and a nearby spring. We politely ask that you enjoy these resources but refrain from overindulging. All guests are asked to take their rubbish with them. Sounds like a really nice place to have a holiday"

1800 hours and Dick helps his wife and Nettie on board the twenty-two-foot navy RHIB, hitting the keys, he quickly brings the twin 150 HP Yamahas to life. Patch slipped the bow line while Nettie slipped the stern line holding them alongside the patrol boat, with both women seated up forward he punched the throttles forward, the RHIB jumped like a cat about to pounce on an unsuspecting bird. The breeze had dropped but the first thing that hit them was the air quality, it was pristine, and the beach looked so perfect.

As the RHIB approached the sand, the trio could see a couple of people on the beach; Patch and Nettie were preoccupied looking over the side.

"Look at the water it's so clear". Dick nudged the RHIB up to the small jetty then killed the motors. Nettie climbed up onto the reasonably constructed timber jetty holding the painter, from his position behind the centre consul the ex-CD smiled to himself, both women looked like a pair of Palestinian freedom fighters, both Patch and Nettie in shorts, runners, heavy cotton blouses and floppy hats complete with webbing belt and holster, spare magazine pouches. Dick must have portrayed that 'Navy' look in his navy-blue cargo pants, leg bands, black boots, and navy Woolley Pulley, webbing belt and holster. Jumping up and securing the stern line, they were met by a woman in her thirties and a male, who turned out to be her father.

1845 hours, "Hello I'm Lauren Wilson and this is my father Thomas Wilson, we are so glad to see you, what has happened to the world? No boat from Tassie to re-supply us, my kids should have been home from boarding school before Christmas, no phone just the VHF radio but there have been no ships until now." The ex-navy clearance diver shook their hands, all the time thinking 'how do you tell someone that the world you knew four months ago doesn't exist anymore. Patch and Nettie turned to the sixty-one-year-old ex-CD, not really knowing what to say. Patch finally said,

"I'm Patch, this is Nettie and to answer your question I think it's better if my husband Dick starts." Both were looking intently to the ex-Diver for guidance.

Dick started from the beginning, not knowing if they knew anything about the nuclear holocaust and the subsequent EI satellite collapse, this would answer why there has been no boats or phone contact since then. The next bit didn't go well, after learning about the invasion and what they were doing to our fellow Taswegians it obviously hit home that their relatives were by all probability dead.

Lauren broke down and was consoled by Patch and Nettie, the pair walking the distraught woman back up to the homestead, Dick stood looking at Thomas for a few minutes until the man spoke,

"Terrible times it seems my boy! And where do you fit into all of this, from what you have alluded to, you're the main reason we are fighting back, how have you stopped going insane?"

"Thomas, I have some great friends and a wonderful wife, it is also because most of us that started this fight are ex-military and have the knowledge to outsmart them, and by God kill them, but looking at you here now, you seem quite calm after I have laid it out in front of you, you know if I were a betting man I would say that you're ex-military, am I correct sir?" The seventy-two-year-old replied

"Well spotted, Dick, wasn't it? I was in the army, made it to the rank of Regimental Seargent Major or RSM if you like. I did thirty-five years for the country, even did a stint in the SAS so I know a little about you CD's." Dick shook Thomas's hand.

"Welcome aboard RSM, good to meet you, now let's get your things together and get you off this island." Dick and Thomas were met at the front door of the homestead with the girls carrying Lauren's belongings, the ex-CD had just enough time to get a quick peek at the luxurious building.

1930 hours and with the guests being shown to their quarters, Jack and April assisted with stowing the RHIB with Dick and Jack operating the windlass and April hosed off the dirt as the chain came aboard. Doc ordered.

"Slow astern both, spin her around Dick, course *345 degrees* all hands to the bridge." The guests entered the bridge followed by all the crew, some moved to the flying bridge due to the cramped space. Dick introduced everyone, April and Patch had made sure they were given their bunks; Thomas would be in the Junior Sailor's Mess while Lauren would be berthed in the radio shack with Nettie.

After a late supper, the next three hours was spent learning how the pair survived on what they had in the pantry, power was still operating through the solar system, although it took them till early January to realise no one was coming to rescue them. Every day Lauren transmitted on the VHF radio, when the protein ran out, Thomas caught mutton birds and snared a rabbit now and again.

The ex-RSM explained,

"Bloody lucky you turned up when you did, I hadn't had any luck for nearly a week, all we had left to eat was some rice and spices, water was not a problem though, as the rainwater tanks had plenty with only the two of us."

Tuesday 10th March 2015 FCPB Entering Grass Harbour

0130 hours, with Dick and Patch on watch, Jack in the engine room and April just up keeping everyone company, Dick consulted the radar, visibility of the harbour was not that great, so his decision was to not go alongside till first light, who knows what debris is scattered around the little harbour. Jack emerged from down the hole,

"You want me to wake the Doc mate?" Dick replied,

"Nah, I think we can anchor her without disturbing their sleep." This drew a smiling comment from the sixty-one-year-old French woman,

"Didn't sound like much sleep was going on when Patch and I passed their door bringing the brews up." Both women giggled

"Jack, can you and April man the windlass, Chook the depth sounder." Patch read out the soundings.

"19 metres ... 16 metres ... 10 metres ... 6 metres ..." Dick came back to neutral then a touch astern to take the way off, while he broadcasted.

"Drop anchor Chief." The anchor fell away dragging the chain to the bottom six metres below, touching astern to set the anchor. When Dick was happy with the swing he ordered.

"Finished with main engines Chief, you and April get your heads down, Patch and I will keep the watch till 0400."

0800 hours, Dick emerged on the bridge having devoured SCRAN, he was met by Doc.

"Thanks for letting Nari and I sleep last night mate, glad you decided not to take her into the wharf." The sixty-five-year-old was pointing to the rusting wreck right in front of the entrance. Nari was on the flying bridge binoculars in hand scouring the shore. Dick asked,

"Any sign of life Nari?" The ex-triage nurse grinned.

"Two people about ten minutes ago, then they ran away."

"Brrr ... Brrr ... Brrr ... Hello, Patch speaking, who's this? Oh right, he's here, Luv it's for you, its Ted Green on the *Specialist*."

"*G'day* Ted, how are you travelling, right that close, looks like you made good time, is *St Bernadette* with you? Great, we anchored in the outer harbour last night and are now about to go alongside, watch out for the sunken vessel right in front of the wharf." Hanging up the brick phone, Dick relayed,

"Both vessels will be here today, they are currently only thirty miles away."

Doc and Dick decided to get alongside ASAP then take it easy till late afternoon, by then the other two would be here, one can berth outboard of the *Fremantle* the other on the shallower side inside the wharf. Doc manoeuvred the 137-foot patrol boat stern in on the wharf starboard side too, with all mooring lines set he ordered,

"Finished with main engines Chief, can you give me our fuel and water status, double up all lines?"

1100 hours. "Skipper, those stats you asked for, fuel 65% water 75% but I have spied a fuel outlet on the wharf, just got to check we have hoses long enough, it appears someone had cut the line making it a tad short. Water should not create a problem, tap right there, and what looks like water tanks ashore, should be enough gravity feed." Doc could see where the chief was pointing towards the water tap,

"Great Chief, I'll leave it up to you then?" Jack acknowledged and said that he would get some help to scrounge a hose long enough to do the fuel but in the meantime the water tank was filling.

Leaving April to turn off the tap when the filler overflowed, then top up the port tank, the ex-CD sniper and Dick rummage around on shore looking for a fuel hose. There was plenty of old buildings to choose from, including what looked like an old fish factory, maintenance sheds, a mine office, conveyor belts etc. Working out they were short about fifteen metres there wasn't much to choose from, electing to come back after SCRAN the pair returned back on board.

1230 hours and with everyone up and seated in the mess, Nari, Patch and April with help from Lauren put on a mixture of help yourself sangers, tinned spaghetti or baked beans on toast, cold meat, Spam, cheese, fresh tomatoes. April reported,

"Both freshwater tanks are full, caps back on, not like the last time you asked me to do it, I forgot to screw the caps back on, boy was Jack peeved, lucky for me they got stuck at the scupper and didn't end up overboard." Thomas asked,

"How are you going with finding that hose? I can help after lunch if you want a hand." With a thumbs up from both CD's stuffing their face with a Sanger, Lauren, tongue in cheek, asked,

"What happens to us now? Do we drive around with you forever; or do we get put ashore here to fend for ourselves?" Doc, not sure she was for real, answered

"Good point Lauren, usually the people we rescue join our cause and help fight the Alliance, but I suppose in your case if you have family here on Queen Island you can get ashore and stay with them, if not you could join us in the fight. Now I know you have admitted to me you couldn't see yourself actually killing anyone, but one answer is, help in other ways, like you told me, you started off as a nurse many years ago, so you could join the medical branch if you like. Thomas, with your skills and experience we could use you with training, actually Dick, Sarge and Jack have hatched a plan and might run it past you later."

1400 hours, the trio were fossicking around the shore buildings.

"Haven't been in this shed Dick?" Thomas and Dick joined Jack in the maintenance shed attached to the mine.

"Right, this looks like it's the right diameter and probably length as well, let's get it out in the open, it's been coiled up that long we'll have to run it out and let it settle, that will give us time to find a joiner pipe and some hose clamps."

Pulling the coil out to the wharf, Jack motioned to Dick they had company, the ex-CD turned to face a male, armed with a hunting rifle, he didn't look that friendly waving the barrel in front of the ex-navy diver the man gruffly asked.

"Who the fuck are you, and what are you doing on our island, stealing stuff."

Now Dick could see that Thomas was coming up behind the bloke but didn't like the chance of the weapon discharging if the ex RSM grabbed him. The ex-CD pushed the barrel up with one hand, pulling his Type 54 pistol out of its holster with the other, ramming it up under the man's chin saying.

"Now, that's not very nice, you ought to be friendlier when you have visitors." Another voice spoke,

"And you ought to be smarter!" The voice came from another local sporting a hunting rifle, the first bloke smiled, Dick just said.

"Fuck me, not another one." He then nodded to Thomas who had his pistol drawn and planted well and truly in the second man's back. The pair were relieved of their weapons by Jack then Dick started.

"Now let's introduce ourselves first, I'm Dick, this is Jack and Thomas, we are members of the TRF or Taswegian Resistance Fighters and you are?"

"Reg Gowen and this is my little brother Rusty, who are you guys, are you Navy or something? Bloody nice warship."

1730 hours, Dick had filled the boys in with the way of the world to date, it seems they were good lads and ex-army to boot. Dick, Jack and Thomas extended an invitation for the pair back on board at 1800 hours and if they could bring others with the same experience, the TRF had a proposition to put to them. Doc asked the pair,

"So, tell us your idea Dick and Jack and I reckon Sarge has a hand in it as well." Dick replied

"No let's wait till our guests arrive then we will unravel it." April, from the lookout's chair yelled,

"Coming down the wharf now guys, looks like there are five of them."

"Welcome on board the FCPB *Fremantle*, this is the Captain, Doc, Nari covers medical, Jack's the engineer, Annie the assistant engineer, Sarge weapons, April and Patch and Lauren watch keepers and provisions, Nettie is the trainee and Thomas." Reg started

"I'm Reg, my brother Rusty, Tom, Grant and Brittney, but you forgot someone, what's his name, Dick what do you do." Doc spoke for the ex-CD.

"Well, yes Dick, he's just Dick, you could say he is my executive officer, first mate, but he's everything." Dick opened the meeting when,

"Brrr ... Brrr ... Brrr ... I'll get it," yelled Jack.

"It's for you Dick, it's Len." Dick excused himself for a few minutes, returning he continued

"Now you have all had something to eat and the Queen Island residents have all been briefed on the world as we know it, I would like to run an idea that the chief, sarge and I have been playing with.

We think there is a place for an elite squad to be trained with all of our expertise and be the arrowhead for the TRF. Launching raids against the northern Alliance, first job will be to contact the Hammers on Bird Island, from there strike at Monty and right through to Brownsville. With 100 volunteers manning the *Specialist* and *St Bernadette* striking at Devon, we should be able to take control of the Northwest." Tom Cooper asked

"What are the *Specialist* and *St Bernadette?*" Doc continued.

"These along with the *Christa Leanne* are TRF vessels which will be based in this area to continue the fight when the *Fremantle* leaves, as a matter of a fact they are entering the harbour as we speak, so we might break for 20 minutes and get them tied up."

2000 hours, all three crews had joined the meeting, introductions sorted, Dick had been getting the background details off the locals when he continued.

"Initially we think the elite squad will be made up of the following volunteers, oh and feel free to put your hand up if you decline the invitation.

- Sarge Michaels, Sarge is an ex-sapper with all the relevant skills that go with that tag, he will be one of the trainers
- Thomas Wilson, Tom is an ex RSM and SAS soldier, he will assist Sarge with the training
- Jack Smouch, ex-navy CD sniper he will be one of the trainers

- Tom Cooper ex RAR corporal
- Reg Gowen ex RAR sniper
- Rusty Gowen ex RAR
- Grant Youl professional shooter
- Brittney Munn professional shooter
- Dick Mann, ex-navy CD specialist, he will also assist in the training

This training will be held on Four Hummock Island, the *Christa Leanne* will be stationed there. When we think you are ready you will join the *Fremantle*, we will deposit you ashore on Bird Island, one problem is, the rebels there do not know you are coming and we have no way of warning them, so let's hope you are good enough to infiltrate their ranks without anyone getting killed, I'll take questions now."

Brittney puts up her hand,

"It's all sort of exciting and killing people is certainly new to me, but I'm keen to be trained, you boys seem to know what you are doing, how long do you see the training going for?" Dick answered.

"Hope to be finished by Sunday Brittney." That brought a hush over the room.

Patch questioned.

"Who is going to train the 100 locals if we can recruit them?" Now she already knew the answer but wanted to make sure it was bought up. Jack answered.

"While we are on Four Hummock Island, that training will be conducted by the other TRF members with experience, such as-Harry, Jill, Gary, Patch, Nari, Doc, Annie and April, the *Fremantle* will return here to facilitate that. Remember all of these members have had extensive front-line experience, when you think they are ready, the three vessels will transport them to the various hotspots, but Dick and Jack will be back to supervise this part of the invasion." Rusty asked.

"When do we start?" Doc answered.

"Go home now and get your stuff together, we sail at 0800 hours tomorrow. In the meantime, if you can talk any of your neighbours into joining, bring them along as well, the rest of the team is itching to start, and the *Fremantle* will be back tomorrow afternoon."

Dick called them all together to discuss the phone call from Len, gathering on the bridge were, Doc, Nari, Jack, April and Patch.

"Decision time team, Len, Vince and crews have successfully changed the pre 2000 donk back into the *Waubs Bay*, we have to decide where this vessel would be better utilised." Jack asked.

"How big is she Dick?"

"Seventy-foot steel ex-cray boat, it now has an L6 Gardner driving her." Doc suggested.

"What about bringing her up to Bass Island, filling her with troops and getting her to run the raid on St Anne along with the *Nancy Kay*. Should be able to split sixty troops between them, she's going to be better getting across the bar, and we know the *Nancy* can do it." Dick added,

"If the *Fremantle* could carry another forty troops, we could run them ashore north of St Anne and get Ernie and his team to come in from Scott. Maybe in a week or as soon as we have finished here, in the meantime if both boats could get to Blackmark and start training."

All present liked the idea, Dick finished by saying.

"I'll call him back Brrr ... Brrr ... Brrr ... Hi Jill is it? yeah Dick here, is the skipper around, oh in the shower, no probs, Vince and Laurel there, yep put him on, hi mate, yep if the *Waubs Bay* can steam to Blackmark and help Santa, Pat and crew to train the locals, well we need about 100, yep that's right, sixty split between the *Nancy* and *Waubs Bay* with forty on board with us, no we can't get over the bar, so we'll put them ashore north of St Anne, thanks mate, keep me posted."

Wednesday 11ᵗʰ March 2015 FCPB Fremantle Grass Harbour

0750 hours, Dick turned to Thomas.

"Hope you don't mind me volunteering you for the gig mate."

"Glad you did, look forward to it, and it's not like I don't know the Island, ah looks like a crowd is gathering." Doc ordered.

"Single up all lines, main engines please Chief." They could already detect the *Christ Leanne*, moving away from the *Fremantle's* port side waiting for her to leave. Doc continued.

"There's our five with kit, looks like another twenty-five or so, well that's a great start, drop all lines slow ahead port Dick, slow ahead both cleared the wharf, hard to starboard half ahead both." Dick picked up the VHF Microphone,

"Harry, Ted and Denis, see you all tomorrow night, *Fremantle* out."

Chapter 10
Push to Benoa

Saturday 7ᵗʰ March 2015 TRF Barracouta HQ

1200 hours. "Brrr ... Brrr ... Brrr ... Yep Len here, oh great Vince, you and Laurel had a good trip up, yep we're at Barracouta, no the Marina, you'll see the *Mary* as you approach, yep look forward to it" Jill asks

"Who's going on the raid luv?"

"Well, I reckon, it'll be Vince, Laurel, Josh, Paul and You and I, that's if you want to come Hon?" The perky seventeen-year-old punched him in the arm playfully,

"Wouldn't miss it for the world."

Len and Jill took the jeep back to the marina, and standing alongside of the forty-foot RHIB *Mary*, the pair could see the ex-navy RHIB making its way into the channel, Len caught the bowline, Jill caught the stern line, soon the group were on their way to the southern outpost, introductions, a brew then off to the northern outpost.

"Had much activity over the last few days?" Vince asked. The thirty-nine-year-old ex-fisherman told the story.

"We have had the first truck that I told Dick about, full of Indonesian food supplies, two days ago we had a jeep try to move the pipe, we shot them and confiscated the jeep, another one stopped the other side of the bridge, not game to come any closer. From the north, one jeep yesterday, we shot them but another one behind them only snuck its nose around the corner then retreated, apart from that all quiet." Vince asks.

"So, what's the plan of attack mate?"

Len laid out his idea. "The next property is 'Bill Roger' its homestead on the left; there are only half a dozen homes till Little Duckport and only a couple to Rocky Bay then Scallop Bay, my intention is to push the Indonesians all the way to Quiet Bay, there are some huge wine making properties on the way like Devils Beach but not many houses. I suggest we go tonight at 2100 hours, hit 'Bill Roger' first then keep going." Laurel asked.

"Where do you see the next blockade, Len?"

"I would like to see it just before Benoa, there is a tip on the right-hand side, just before that, a home overlooks the road both ways, it belonged to my aunty, we could successfully hold the road from there.

2100 hours, two jeeps, re-fuelled were at the northern outpost, Vince, Laurel and Josh in one and Len, Paul and Jill in the second. Type 54 pistols with suppressors for Len and Vince the rest just pistols, although they carried a Type 68 in each jeep and Vince brought along a couple of surprises, two RPG's.

2110 hours, Vince turned the General M151 Diesel Variant jeep into the long driveway curling up to the homestead. With deer fencing evident, and still 100 sheep running in the front paddock, this was one of the premier properties on the east coast.

Dick and Patch told Len how they used to pick up repairs from the place a few years ago, the couple had two small children. They didn't know what to expect so just drove straight into the house yard onto the concrete driveway. The ex-navy technician and Josh made it to the door at the same time someone must have seen the jeep lights, a small child opened up, probably expecting to see their father, Josh hesitated, the child spoke, Vince shot the kid "Dooff".

Entering into a lobby full of boots, jackets and kid's toys, they found themselves in an open plan kitchen, dining come lounge. The lady of the house was sitting on the couch with another elderly couple,

"Dooff...Dooff...Dooff." A child yelled out from a bedroom, Josh went to investigate, shooting the ten-year-old through a pillow.

. Vince cleared all the other rooms. Stopping at the main bedroom, the forty-seven-year-old reached over and picked up an officers Tunic, name tag *Major Raja Atmadja*.

"Wonder where the good major is?" Said Vince out loud; Josh appeared as if to say who are you talking to.

"All clear mate, just another kid."

2120 hours Len, Paul and Jill were clearing the small weatherboard house right on the highway. Len had always liked the property, now he had mixed feelings, clearing the home in eight minutes the thirty-nine-year-old showed no mercy, falling in love with the suppressed Type 54 pistol he was like a man possessed.

An hour and a half later, the township of Duck and its 120 homes, this is where they had to get it down pat, front doors only, if locked, knock and go in from there, most of them had two troopers with them. The Indonesian weapons were different, the Pindad P2 Semi-automatic pistol and the SS1-R5 Raider assault rifle were the standard issue weapons, the 9mm pistol rounds were compatible with the NK Alliance, but the 5.56·45mm Nato round for the Raider was different, it was smaller but certainly packed a bigger punch.

At the edge of town, Vince pulled up first, Laurel counted the haul.

"Thirty-two Pistols, 65 Raider Assault Rifles and a shit load of ammo." They could hear Len's jeep coming, he reported a similar haul. Both jeeps travelled together for the next piece, then split. There were five homes each, on opposite sides of the road, they continued like this all the way to Rocky Bay which overlooked Scallop Bay, this property sported a jeep parked outside.

"Looks like another officer here, be on your toes!" Vince and Laurel tested the front door, 'damn' thought Laurel it was shut, back door open, they entered what looked like four bedrooms. Laurel took one Vince the other, the ex-navy Communicator used the pillow to muffle the blast when she shot the elderly couple.

Vince could already smell trouble when he pushed the creaky door open, the officer awoke, levelling his pistol at the forty-seven-year-old. Vince dropped to the floor, rolling over, then shooting up.

"Dooff" "Dooff." The two rounds caught the man in the groin and stomach, but enough noise to wake his wife, who must have put her hand on her husband's stomach, only to feel it oozing with blood, she screamed loudly.

"Dooff!" By the time Vince had checked both bodies his wife called out.

"All clear" The uniform tunic revealed *Lieutenant Colonel Huje Samira*. Vince thought 'getting higher in rank, way to go, might keep hold of the name tags for Dick'.

Joining his team at the jeep they had a bit of a drive to the next place.

Sunday 8th March 2015 Just south of Benoa

0200 hours and Len's jeep drives down the long driveway to the property 'Devils Beach'. This was a remarkable property, a premier vineyard, famous for their award-winning Pinot. Overlooking the coast, the property even had a retail outlet near the highway, a full wine making plant and a wonderful home complete with boat sheds. The courtyard caught their eye, it had a jeep under the carport.

Knocking on the front door brought a young girl to answer, the thirty something opened it to Len pointing the Type 54 at her chest, she turned to run, but the 9 mm round found her back, right between the shoulder blades.

This was a very elegant home; one of culture, thought the ex-fisherman closely followed by Paul while Jill was covering the front door. The first bedroom was obviously the girls, possibly a maid, second one was occupied by another older woman, and

"Dooff." Len quickly disposed of her. The master bedroom was easy to detect, pride of place overlooking the bay, with the vines between them and the water, a boatshed could be detected in the moonlight.

Len eased the door open; Paul was backing him up when.

"Bang!" The sound of the unsuppressed Pindad P2 Semi-automatic Pistol going off was deafening, then Len fired two rounds.

"Dooff...Dooff." In quick succession, the first finding the female's body but the second missed the male; he gathered composure and fired again.

"Bang, bang!" Another two shots, by this time Len was at the foot of the bed, He fired again.

"Dooff", The male slumped over.

"Fuck, Paul was that close, or what?" Realising Paul wasn't standing behind him sent the ex-fisherman into a spin, stepping back he tripped on the forty-eight-year-old duck shooter's body, 'fuck, fuck, fuck' he said to himself, yelling to Jill.

"Jill quick, Paul's taken a hit." The seventeen-year-old came to his aid, but between them the light was bad.

Dragging the six-foot five-inch 120 KG duck shooter was difficult, with the lights of the jeep they could see that he had been hit twice, both kill shots to the chest. Kneeling down in front of the NK Alliance jeep, Jill grabbed Len's arm.

"Len someone is at the door." Straight away he thought, shit we didn't finish clearing the rest of the home, swinging the suppressed 54 pistol at the figure he pulled the trigger.

"Dooff!" The man fell to the floor. Jill checked him, then finally secured the rest of the home.

"All clear luv, I reckon he must have been the gardener or something. Shit with a maid, a cook and a gardener, this guy must have been someone real important." The pair re-entered the home, looking for a uniform tunic, nothing to be found, then tucked away in the wardrobe was a naval officer's tunic. Len held it up to the light, the name tag said *Admiral Adi Atmadja*.

0400 hours arriving at the home of Len's aunty, Vince and Laurel had already cleared it.

Chapter 11
Peninsular in Trouble

Sunday 8th March 2015 Crayfish

0900 hours, Max liked Sundays, it was when the twenty-four-year-old delivered his smoked and fresh salmon to his neighbouring TRF members. Starting at Crayfish and ending up at Sand Alley. There was a small percentage that didn't want his products, but this didn't worry the salmon farm manager as it was the Mansfield's who were out of the way at Calmly - the arduous journey created more trouble than it was worth.

What he had been looking forward to all week was seeing Helen Crawfield again, he was smitten with the seventeen-year-old, and over the past weeks had sort of asked Helen's parents if he could officially court the girl. Surprisingly last Sunday, Sid and Ellen had given in and allowed it from this Sunday.

Max had been pretty busy, and now with the push to Soothe, the twenty-four-year-old was keen to catch up with the latest news when he delivered fish to the outlying areas. He decided that he would take Helen with him on the last part of his deliveries to the Sand Alley outpost.

1100 hours, Max had covered all the properties that had asked for salmon and leaving Cedric and Aileen Bilton's Falcons Neck Vineyard, was driving back down the Do-Town road when he noticed his heart was doing a little flutter in anticipation of seeing Helen again. Over the neck and turning left, there was only the Crawfield's property on this road.

An hour later, pulling into the cattle property's driveway, he as usual was met by the bubbly seventeen-year-old who reached in and kissed Max, before he had time to stop the jeep. Passing over the box of fresh and smoked salmon to Ellen, and after getting the rundown of TRF movements in Soothe, he and Helen headed off. The first stop was the chook farm right on top, overlooking the bay, then on to Starlight and the Oyster farm with David and El. He knew they were manning the Soothe outpost and as previously arranged he put the order in the cool room.

1300 hours, pulling up outside the Sand Alley Hotel only to find it too was empty, decided to leave it in the Hotel's cool room and a note on the door. Helen leant over and kissed him, this time she was bolder pushing her tongue into his mouth, he could smell the cleanliness, the toothpaste, perfume and soap, boy was he lightheaded.

1340 hours and driving back towards Falcons Neck he had one hell of an erection. He was finding it hard to disguise, Helen was jammed right up alongside of him, cuddling rubbing her hand across his chest, when he took his eyes off the road, she was just looking up at him with those blue eyes. Coming down the hill towards the Falcons Neck Hotel she leaned over and whispered.

"Let's have a look at the hotel Max; I haven't seen it before."

Turning into the top driveway, the pair were introduced to the early warning system the hotel had in place to warn staff upon the guest's arrival. Pulling up outside the front entrance they proceeded inside, the scented candles still presented a strong perfume. Making their way to the front of the dining room the enormous panorama unfolded in front of them with views all the way to the tip of the Peninsular.

Helen kissed the twenty-four-year-old passionately, allowing her tongue to work her way around his mouth, Max was still trying to resist going all the way with the girl, not wanting to stuff up his relationship with her parents. He found himself lifting her jumper off to reveal two huge breasts fully contained in an ornate frilly bra. With this unhooked, he buried his head between.

"Ooooh, ahhhh, God that feels fantastic Max, don't stop." Pushing the Seventeen- year-old back onto the couch, he kissed her passionately

"Mmmmmmmm, oh." she pulled his face clear.

"I can't take that anymore; it drives me crazy, put it in Max!"

1600 hours and dressing, the pair looked like they had been in a fight, with their clothing creased and after some minutes, Helen asked,

"Was it good for you Max?" the twenty-four-year-old was flabbergasted, all he could get out was "Better."

1700 hours, dropping the seventeen-year-old at the front gate Max felt a little ashamed not saying hello to her parents, he felt guilty for having sex with the girl, his mind was going one hundred miles an hour, 'was she a virgin, he felt no hymen, was she on the pill, didn't really want to get the girl pregnant, crikey she almost raped me' not that he minded she was a good sort and couldn't wait till next Sunday.

Monday 9th March 2015 Crayfish Salmon Farm

Later, Max was out at one of the pens when the Willy's knock off jeep entered the farm car park. the twenty-four-year-old could make out three men approaching the wharf, signalling Max to come in, he wondered what the problem was. He knew he was on standby to relieve at the outposts, 'maybe that's what they want'. Pulling in his oars and tying up the work punt, he stepped onto the wharf, confronting him were Johnny, Graham and Roberto.

"Hi guys what's the problem?" The forty-seven-year-old ex-farmer spoke,

"Max, there's been an incident, and we have a few questions, where were you last night?" Max had no idea where this was going, saying,

"Home like every other night mate." Graham asked.

"What time did you get home mate?"

"About 1800, dropped Helen off around 1700, you can verify that with her or her parents, what's all this about?"

Max was getting agitated, smelling a rat, he was thinking he was going to be stitched up for something. Johnny continued.

"Young Helen didn't make it home last night mate, do you know anything about that?" Max was gobsmacked, his brain going over the last time he saw her.

"That's bullshit, I dropped her at the front gate around 1700." He was now getting angry.

"Where the fuck is she if she didn't make it home?" Graham finished

"That's what we are trying to piece together; Sid and Ellen have been looking for her all night apparently you were the last one to see her yesterday, where did you take her Max?" The twenty-four-year-old not wanting to hear anymore, tried to get to his jeep, Roberto grabbed him saying.

"Mate we need you to calm down and tell us the truth."

Well Max just exploded, smacked the ex-concreter in the jaw, kicked out at Johnny and tackled Graham to the ground. But the ex-courier driver was no light weight, and soon had Max subdued.

"Tell me what's going on you bastards." Finally getting the truth out of the twenty-four-year-old they tried to piece it together, Graham surmised.

"So in-between, you dropping the girl off at the front gate around 1700 and her not getting to the homestead something happened, did you turn around and pick her up again, did she run down the road chasing you, come on mate tell us the truth?" Max took a long breath.

"It's as I said, dropped her off around 1700 and came home." Johnny pushed a little more

"We have witnesses that you left Sand Alley just after 1300, it doesn't take that long to drive her home."

Max knew he was in trouble for not being able to fill in those extra two hours they here shagging at the Falcons Neck Hotel, but he sure couldn't tell them that.

"We stopped at the lookout then again at Chequered Pavements, Helen hadn't seen them." Graham held Max by the arm saying,

"I think you should come with us until it's all worked out."

He didn't go quietly, but he did go, dropping the twenty-four-year-old off at the Crayfish police lock ups, they left to a stream of abuse coming from him. The two made their way back to the Crawfield's property, after first dropping Roberto off at home. Johnny asked,

"Well mate what do you think?" Graham answered

"It's a bit thin on the ground Johnny; I think he is lying, couldn't look us in the eye."

"I'm not convinced he is guilty, hell we don't even know what happened to the girl and until we do it's just a missing child."

Turning into the beef property the pair stopped at a distraught Ellen on her knees sobbing, Johnny got out and comforted the woman,

"What's wrong Ellen, where is Sid?"

The thirty-seven-year-old just points to the bush on the other side of the paddock. Graham drove the jeep to where Ellen was pointing, he found Sid on his hands and knees with his daughter's body, it had been partially covered by leaves, getting out Graham yells.

"Mate, are you alright, wholly fuck, mate let go, you don't need to see any more." He physically had to remove the ex-railway worker away from the carnage in front of him.

With Sid sitting in the jeep, Johnny comforting Ellen, Graham drove the jeep back to where his wife was, she was going bonkers wanting to have a look at her daughter, all Graham said was,

"No, not yet Ellen, let me take a blanket to wrap her up in." Leaving the pair with Johnny, he started back to the body. Carrying the old blanket, he brushed the leaves away revealing a naked body with blood coming out of every orifice, signs of recent sex, semen, her throat had been cut, that's probably what ended the girl's life but not before she was tortured.

Graham lifted the girl neatly wrapped in the blanket and placed her onto the back of the jeep. The sixty-eight-year-old had daughters and plenty of nieces of his own. As he drove back towards the house he was thinking 'I hope for your sake Max, you are innocent because at the moment it does not look good for you!'

Chapter 12
Stand at Duck Point

Wednesday 11th March 2015 Lawn HQ

0900 hours, Sergeant Co Lum pulled his jeep up outside the Lawn Town Hall, he was nervous, constantly surveying the area, ever since the caning they received two days ago and the death of their commander, everyone was worried. The rebels had mounted a full-on attack, by sea in an old fishing boat and by land, witnesses say they had over a 1000 men.

The thirty-four-year-old career soldier was based at South Lawn, and had been called back by the second in command, Major Pin Lim Ho.

"Come in Sergeant, take a seat." The clerk had shown Co to the major's office, sitting in what was once the mayor's office, Co marvelled at the ornate Taswegia timbers used in the building. The major was sifting through some paperwork and filing it into personnel folders. Shaking the sergeant's hand,

"Glad to finally meet you in person Co, I can call you Co can't I, let's be less formal in these unusual times, well you are probably wondering why I have called you in this morning?" Co answered

"Well sir I presume it has something to do with two nights ago?"

"Call me Pin, and yes, the facts are, the rebels attacked in force by sea at the Ramat River Marina, by land down the eastern side of the river, taking out everything from High Head, Bull Bay, Ugly Point on the western side and the surrounding suburbs east of the marina.

Losses were huge, 258 troopers and officers including Lieutenant Colonel Lee Bowe and as far as we can estimate over 5000 NK Nationals, a sorry state of affairs Co.

Our main concern now is how to manage this; we have only 740 troops left, 200 of those were stationed in the city centre and the rest down your way in South Lawn. I have officially taken command and sorry to land you in the mess, you are now promoted to Lieutenant and my 2IC."

Co was shocked and it showed on his face. "Thank you, sir, I'm a bit overwhelmed but happy at the same time, what are your orders sir?"

"Good question Co, normally we would mount an offensive against these rebels, but with their three-pronged attack we simply don't have the numbers to do this, apart from the fact we do not have any force on the sea. I had thought of sending 200 men on each side of the river to test their numbers, but that leaves us open from them coming upriver behind us. The other more worrying fact is our ammunition levels, what are your troops carrying?"

"I too am worried about this and did bring it up with lieutenant colonel hoping he would re-supply our ammunition from Kings Town, but this did not eventuate. My men only have an average of sixty rounds each of 7.62mm rounds for the Type 68 Assault rifles and those that have type 54 pistols, only ten rounds each. The main concern is, I have no reserves to issue, none whatsoever." The first lieutenant was shocked,

"I'm surprised but not, my troops in the city have even less than that, not a good sign if we are to mount an offensive."

The second lieutenant offered a suggestion.

"Maybe if not an offensive, we could set up roadblocks at Duck Point as a lookout on the river and one on the highway on the western side of the river at Ex.

We could hold these with around 50 men in each site; maybe bolster their ammunition back up to regulation."

"Good idea Co but I fear if we use all our ammunition in one basket so to speak, we become weaker elsewhere."

The pair was interrupted by the Kings Town messenger; Pin Lim Ho read the communiqué, smiled and handed it to Co.

"Request for ammunition denied at this time, you are to make do with supplies in hand. Promotions Senior Lieutenant Pin Lim Ho to Major, Congratulations sir and commiserations re the ammo, I'm not sure what to say."

"Maybe we should take a drive Co and investigate your recommended sites." The lieutenant suggested some back-up, along the lines of twenty men in a truck.

1230 hours, "this site looks good Co, I think we should send in our *'bundae leul jeongli'* squads to clean up the bodies, then follow with a truck and squad to keep an eye on the highway." The lieutenant was in agreeance.

Looking over Duck Point the pair could see it was right on the water's edge and would not take much to set up a listening post, in one of the many now empty homes that backed onto the river. Co asked,

"Are you going to re-distribute Nationals into these homes sir?"

"Don't have any more to house Co."

1500 hours, "a great spot here at Ex sir, once again right on the river and the highway, when do you want to start this action?"

"First thing tomorrow Co, fifty men here, fifty men at Duck Point on the highway with a truck and a jeep and ten men at the Duck Point riverside with a jeep."

Thursday 12ᵗʰ March 2015 Duck Point Highway Outpost

1000 hours, "sounds like a vehicle Corporal, coming from there," the trooper was pointing up the highway north of their position. The group had arrived at 0800 that morning and set up in the large weatherboard home right on the road. They managed to push a couple of vehicles damaged by the E1 across the road to form a barricade, with snipers on both side of the road they waited while the vehicle noise got louder and louder.

"I see it Corporal, it's a truck, one of ours, stopped on the hill, maybe it's our troops."

"Don't be a bloody fool Trooper, it's the rebels, why else would they stop just out of range."

1000 hours, Ex outpost, they too had set up that morning in the Ex-bakery, good vision of the river and the highway. Lieutenant Co had decided to oversee this outpost himself, and he elected not to barricade the road but to ambush any vehicles that came down the highway.

"Vehicle coming sir" Co looked back up the main street of Ex towards the hotel, yep there it was, a truck was approaching.

"Wait till they are level with the hairdresser over the road men, then open fire." The group waited while the KM450 light cargo truck slowly made its way south,

"Level now sir, open fire men."

"Boom...Boom...Boom...Boom...Boom." The sporadic fire from the men's Type 68 assault rifles was deafening, coming in from both sides of the highway, the 7.62 mm rounds tore the truck's cab to bits, it swerved into the guttering and came to a halt.

It was obvious to Co, the truck's driver and offsiders were dead, his men attacked the back of the truck spraying rounds through the canvas canopy.

"Three in the cab sir and eight in the back, all of them are dead." The newly promoted officer smiled thinking to himself 'yes this is the way to fight back'

"Well done men a great victory over these rebel scum, clear the truck and bodies." It was then they came under fire from the north.

"Boom…Boom…Boom…Boom." The accuracy was perfect, four shots and four kills, it took the troops a number of seconds to work out which way the fire was coming, Co yelled to the corporal.

"It's coming from the IGA supermarket!"

The rest of the troops from over the road finally made it to cover and returned fire; only two shots came their way, prompting the troopers to return fire once again. Five minutes later they thought it was over when they received another two shots, one of the men thought he had a lead on the rebels and emptied his magazine into the spot, two more troopers hit. The thirty-four-year-old had worked out what was happening, gathering his NCO's around.

"Bastards are making us use the ammunition supplies, check your ammo and give me a report." looking back at the IGA the career soldier thought to himself 'I bet you have already left'.

1025 hours, Duck Point river lookout, the men had set up in a colour bond home between the road and the river, the home had at one time, four horses in the paddocks behind it, and these had been moved to another property closer to the highway. The men were split into three teams of three, and one floater; the three on watch were situated in the upstairs bedroom overlooking the river.

All were enjoying a hot tea when one trooper saw something with his peripheral sight, almost choking on his tea, he blurted,

"A boat Corp, a boat!"

The trio yelled to their comrades and with two of them running to the river's edge they engaged with their assault rifles on auto.

"Boom...Boom...Boom...Boom...Boom...Boom...Boom." Not knowing if they were on target didn't seem to matter, as the white boat accelerated it was out of sight within a minute.

1040 hours, Duck Point Highway outpost.

"The rebel truck is still there, Corporal, it's been forty minutes." The Corporal was looking intently through his high-powered binoculars at the vehicle; he couldn't see any men, he thought 'what are they up to' he called the squad's best sniper.

"Have a shot at the vehicle, trooper and let's see if we can drag out a response." The soldier set up a rest for his Type 68 with telescopic sights and looked long and hard at the truck agreeing with the corporal,

"Boom." With the vehicle at the extreme edge of the weapons range, he saw the round hit the truck's bumper bar, this drew no response, the sniper took three more shots in slow time, adjusting the sights off their scale, the Corporal standing behind the man observing with his binoculars.

"Boom...Boom...Boom...Boom...Boom...Boom...Boom." Intense fire was coming from their flank, so intent with the sniper's action the troops failed to see the rebels outflank them and with everyone looking up the highway towards High Head they were caught off guard.

With massive casualties, it was only two men left standing at the end of the barrage, the first made it to the jeep parked behind the stables and as the driveway was now compromised, he drove off across the paddock, heavy fire followed him but managing to crash through the wire fence he made it out on to the road. The second trooper tried to run down the Duck Point road but was cut down in the process.

1205 hours, Lawn Alliance HQ, the major's clerk tapped on the door.

"Come in Lance Corporal." The aging soldier bowing in apology enters to tell the major there is news from the Duck Point outpost. Ushering the trooper in, the major asks what he had to report,

"Sir we have come under attack, and I fear we have become overrun."

The major couldn't believe his ears.

"What are our casualties, and have they breached the barricade?" Slowly getting his breath back

"All lost sir, last I witnessed one trooper running down the Duck Point Road."

"How did you manage to escape?" The major wanted to know whether there was any sign of cowardice with the trooper leaving before the fire fight.

"I managed to run to the jeep but couldn't get past the ambush so drove across the paddock managing to smash through the wire fence sir, at that point everyone else was dead." The major called his clerk in and ordered.

"Lance Corporal, get a replacement truck, twenty men and follow the trooper back, re-take the outpost at all costs, see if you can hunt down an RPG and get it to them."

1830 hours, Alliance HQ, Major Pin Lim Ho, still trying to sort out messages to be delivered to Kings Town requesting reinforcements and sourcing some more troops from South Lawn, was about to go home to his wife and children. The forty-two-year-old was living in a small unit above the library; he had sent his clerk home earlier, exiting the building he could make out gunfire coming from the marina.

Chapter 13
TRF Elite Squad

Thursday 12th March 2015 FCPB Fremantle at anchor Chimney Point, Four Hummock Island

0800 hours, Having anchored the night before, the *Fremantle* was slowly coming to life, Dick and Patch were liaising with April and Nari, sorting out food for the team whilst they were on the Island.

"We have nine plus whoever I can coerce into cooking for us." The ex-navy CD was hoping Patch would stay and to help her, April or even Annie although Annie was not renowned for cooking. Patch looked at April and got the nod.

"Alright you win April, I will stay."

Loading the meat and dry provisions into the RHIB, along with whatever fresh veggies they could spare, Doc was pretty sure they would be able to source these on Queen Island. Dick broadcast.

"First run ashore in 5 minutes." The RHIB was filled with seven of the team plus provisions and clothing; it made the trip and unloaded at the jetty. Thomas would show the team members to their quarters and the pantry-come cool room to keep the meat etc.

Dick and Jack were on the bridge going over the finer details with the next bit of the plan, then joining Sarge and April in the RHIB they waved goodbye to Doc and the crew. Sarge asked.

"When does the *Christa Leanne* arrive Dick?"

"Tonight, mate, well I think that's about right."

1300 hours Dick, Thomas and Jack had sorted out a spot to carry out weapons training, similar to Strine they set up various ranges from 10 to 100 metres, targets were twenty litre drums. It seems the Island used to get their cooking oil in these and never threw anything away, the range was set with six lanes, one for each of the Elite Squad and one for the instructor.

While this was being organised, Sarge was unpacking all the weapons and ammo, as this was going to be a stealth unit the Type 54 Pistol with Muzzle Suppressors was imperative.

Dick, Sarge and Jack had come up with the idea that each squad member would be issued with two Type 54's, one on each hip with six spare magazines, this would speed up the rate of fire, not having to change the magazines over potentially gave the member sixteen rounds instead of the usual eight. Going through all the webbing holsters they had in stock Dick had noticed the Alliance must have yielded to left handers and issued LH holsters to them, this is what gave the trio the idea in the beginning. Cutting the ends out of each, to accommodate the suppressors was first on the agenda.

Sarge was finishing with the left-handed holsters on the belts, when Dick and Jack appeared at the homestead. Calling the group together Dick said.

"Right is everyone happy with their quarters, we will start in thirty minutes, Patch are you and April ok with the victualling, oh is there any questions?"

"Dinner tonight is BBQ lamb chops, new potatoes and salad." It was Brittany who put her hand up.

"Thanks Chook, yes Brittany, is it?"

"Yeah, thanks Dick just asking if Grant and I can have a double room, Thomas has us billeted in singles." Dick looked at Thomas who was smiling, the ex-SAS answered

"No one said anything, so I'm not a mind reader and I would never assume"

1400 hours Dick, Jack and Sarge stood in front of the TRF Elite Squad as they were now known. Dick went through the specs of the Type 68 Assault Rifle, getting them to strip the weapon, clean and load. Sarge took them through the same on the RPG-7 a weapon Sarge had used whilst in the Army, but now it was the weapon of choice with the Alliance, probably the easiest to use and the cheapest on the market. It is best used up to 200 metres range, the manual boasts a maximum range of 920 metres where the grenade explodes. It fires a 40mm grenade and was primarily designed to take out armoured vehicles.

Jack finished off the session with the suppressed Type 54 Pistols, this was going to be the weapon of choice, the Type 68's was just in case.

1500 hours, with drums set at 100 metres, the five members fired five rounds standing, then sitting and last the prone position, lying down. Sarge had set all of these 68's up with telescopic sights and was keen to see what sort of shots they all were.

With weapons on the ground, they all went forward to check the groupings, Dick commented.

"Tom Cooper, nice group mate 112mm at 100 metres, Reg Gowen same mate excellent grouping 54mm at 100 metres, Rusty Gowen 97mm at 100 metres, Grant Youl 70mm at 100 metres and last but certainly no slouch Brittney Munn 65mm at 100 metres, well move your drums out at ten metres and we will repeat the exercise with the Type 54's."

The group were issued with the twin holsters, and the brief was to fire all sixteen rounds in rapid fire. The standout of the group after this exercise was Tom Cooper the ex RAR corporal in a time of eleven seconds and a grouping of 110mm. Because of the expense of the grenades, they would not be firing one till the real thing, they also did not have that many in stock (32 to be precise).

1700 hours, Jack remained behind with Reg Gowen who would be the designated sniper for the group, Dick recommended.

"Wrap it up for the day, go over your weapons, clean them and clean-up for SCRAN." The ex-CD found Patch and April up to their necks making salads, hard boiling eggs and scrubbing potatoes. Patch looked up to see Dick and suggested,

"Oh, look April, it's Dick come to give us a hand to get the BBQ going." Smiling he said.

"No problem, I'll just clean up first" Cleaning the hot plates he was joined by Jack.

"How did you go with our sniper mate?"

"Well ran the drums out to 600 metres, that's about all we could stretch, ten shots with a group of 204 mm."

"Not bad for someone who is new to the weapon Jack, your thoughts?"

"Yep, I agree and after all 200mm is inside a body perimeter."

"Got anyone else in mind for some, one on one tutoring?" The ex-navy sniper pondered the question for a moment.

"Yep, I reckon the girl, Brittney she has potential, might give her a lesson tomorrow night." Dick continued to clean the steel BBQ plates then someone yelled out.

"Boat coming into the bay Dick."

Christa Leanne was dropping anchor just as the meat was brought out of the kitchen, Dick suggested,

"Might pay to wait thirty minutes and offer these guys some tucker as well, if we have enough to go around?" Patch smiled and nodded in the affirmative. Jill and Gary already swinging the boats tender overboard, twenty minutes later the trio were introducing themselves to everyone again in the homestead's large dining room. Harry was telling Dick that the *Fremantle* would be back the next night.

1930 hours and with the meal over, Patch and April returned to the kitchen to clean up, Brittany offered to help, but was required in the dining room, Dick stood to run out the next part of the plan "Tomorrow morning will be the same as this afternoon, weapons practice; Sarge will take you all on a cross-country trek, firing your weapons at all different targets already set up by Thomas and Sarge, with the exception of Brittany who will be mentored by Jack on sniper tactics. Thomas and I will be at each location to supervise the shoot. The main thing we want you to get accustomed to is carrying all the weapons and ammo over rough ground, sort of like an obstacle course with guns." Dick continued.

"After lunch we will go over the first part of the operation to Bird Island, the *Fremantle* will be back around 1830, you get a night off tomorrow night, then Harry and crew will transport you to Bird Island, eta approximately 1400 hours and the *Fremantle* will transport the Queen Island TRF members to assist in contacting the Hammers."

Friday 13th March 2015 Four Hummock Island

0930 hours, the first route march saw Sarge, Tom, Reg, Rusty and Grant crawl up over a huge sand dune for the first shoot. Dick and Thomas had concealed the first lot of targets, so they were partially exposed; each member had to identify and shoot each drum. The range was forty-five metres with Dick giving all clear, the ex-CD and the ex-SAS soldier watched as the four shooters slowly identified and shot, with the exception of Grant, he was having trouble finding the fourth drum, this was automatically rectified when someone else fired and moved the target. Thomas commented.

"Not bad Dick, well with the exception of Grant, who needed a little persuasion as to where it was." Dick agreed with Thomas and the pair moved on to the next scene. This was a close-up, Thomas had led Sarge the day before to an old shed, down on the rocks on the other side of the Island, the pair had set this scene up so the shooter entered one end, then because it was dark inside, the drum targets were set at random distances, the goal was to shoot all seven drums as quick as possible, they would enter one at a time. Dick pointed.

"Looks like them now, crikey he's probably run them a bit, and it's Reg first."

The ex RAR sniper was slightly out of breath when he entered the end of the shed. The observers could hear the familiar 'Dooff' as he executed each drum, completing the run in fifteen seconds; Thomas went inside to score him.

"Seven out of seven Dick." Next was Tom, the ex RAR corporal, as trained, he used the Type 54 pistols one in each hand, Thomas smiled.

"Ambidextrous, that's a novel approach Dick."

With a time of eleven seconds, four faster than Reg, Thomas scored the man "Same mate seven out of seven." Next up was Rusty, eighteen seconds and a score of six out of seven, the seventy-two-year-old stood alongside Dick and whispered.

"Missed the second last one mate." Last into the building was Grant, the professional shooter, not really accustomed to pistols, he felt a little out of his depth.

"Time of twenty-eight seconds Dick but still scored seven out of seven."

1200 hours and with the group finished the training, back at the first 100 metre range where Jack was finishing up with Brittany, the ex-sniper enquired.

"How did they go guys?" Dick answered.

"Pretty good, all in all, mate, what about our new sniper?" Jack smiled,

"She's a fast learner mate, and maybe could be a little better than Reg." This comment brought a grin to both Brittany and Reg. Thomas added.

"Looks like some healthy competition." Harry and crew came ashore for SCRAN having completed some maintenance on board ready for the briefing that afternoon.

1400 hours and Dick addressed the group.

"Great results team, you all pass with flying colours, so now onto the next bit. The *Fremantle* will be back tonight with the Queen Island TRF, so a night off tonight, one last range practice tomorrow morning then *Christa Leanne* leaves at 1100, *Fremantle* leaves at 1200, eta Bird Island 1400. We will be trying to contact them on VHF and UHF but if all else fails just show up. The RHIB will put you ashore where we hope to team up with the island's inhabitants, any questions?" Brittany asked,

"Where do we go from there Dick?"

"Depends a bit on the Hammers, but I would say first job would be to take back their farm and slowly clear back towards Monty. At the same time the *Fremantle* will mount the main assault at Brownsville, our first objective is to take control of the entire Northwest down as far as Tomma." Grant asked.

"Do we have to carry both weapons and that much ammo?" The thirty-nine-year-old professional shooter was feeling the strain of carrying that much weight.

"Well Grant you could lose a bit of ammo and run the risk of being able to replenish it from your enemy, I will leave that up to you."

1900 hours, *Fremantle* drops anchor and the RHIB makes its way to the Chimney Point Beach jetty, Nari and Nettie in control of the twenty-two-footer, Nari waved to Dick.

"Doc wants a meeting tonight, are you up for it?" Dick was soon joined with Sarge, Jack and Thomas leaving Patch and April relaxing in the lounge room.

2000 hours. "Welcome to the new members of the TRF, I hope that weapons training went well yesterday, and you are all pumped for this next phase." The ex-navy CD looked around the room at the thirty-nine men and women seated in front of him, ages ranged from seventeen through to sixty five. Dick laid out that range practice was tomorrow morning then what the next bit would be, a lot of these members all had relatives on mainland Taswegia and were keen to kill any Alliance they came across.

Saturday 14ᵗʰ March 2015 TRF Vessels Fremantle and Christa Leanne on approach to Bird Island

1430 hours, "Bird Island, Bird Island this is Patrol Boat *Fremantle*, Patrol Boat *Fremantle* transmitting on VHF channel 16 over……. nothing heard Skipper, trying UHF."

"Bird Island, Bird Island this is Patrol Boat *Fremantle*, Patrol Boat *Fremantle* transmitting on channel 1 over, still nothing heard." The FCPB was standing off Bird Island one nautical mile, *Christa Leanne* was close by, Sarge had deployed the RHIB and was standing by with the five members of the Elite Squad, Dick picked up the UHF microphone again.

"Bird Island, this is *Fremantle* on channel 40 over." There was static coming in, Doc was just about to give the signal to send the squad ashore, when

"*Fremantle* this is John Hammer on channel 40 do you copy?"

"Loud and clear John, are you up for some visitors mate?"

"Tides too high for you to come across," Doc looked at Dick then realised they thought we were coming in via Monty.

"Bird Island, suggest you look to the north over."

"Well fuck me, looks like you have brought the Navy! How do you intend to come ashore over?"

"RHIB coming in now, we will come in and anchor over." Dick, Sarge, Thomas and the five members of the squad make the forty-knot trip to a sandy beach on the northern side of the Island. Running the bow into the sand; they were met by the Hammers, Dick first ashore holding out his hand,

"Hi, I'm Dick Mann; this is Sarge, Thomas, Reg, Grant, Brittany, Tom and Rusty." John Hammer smiled,

"Boy you guys are all dressed up with nowhere to go, I'm John Hammer, this is my brother Chris Hammer, my wife Kayleen Hammer, Stockman Billy Short, his girlfriend Tracey Webster and our game controller Murray Mills."

"We yes we might be a tad over dressed for a BBQ tonight, but a little birdy tells me you're having trouble with the Alliance, we were in the neighbourhood, thought we might lend a hand." John was really smiling.

"Mate I like the way you think, let's get a drink and tell stories for a while."

1600 hours. The next hour and a half brought the Hammers up to speed on the TRF and the rest of them with the Alliance.

"The buggers have tried a few times to get out to us but can't, we have done a few sorties ashore but just lately they have finally put a squad at the boat ramp keeping tabs on our every move, but I reckon you have guessed that, because you came ashore where they couldn't see you on the other side of the island." Sarge and Dick laid out their plan to stealth ashore at the boat ramp, kill the observers, then clear the Hammers family home, re-group and go on from there. Chris asked.

"How many men have you got; I take it you're not going to stop at Monty?"

"Yeah, you're right Chris, the Fremantle has another thirty-nine TRF members trained up to land at Brownsville, if this squad, along with any of you who wish to join us advances on Brownsville from this direction, we hope to clear all the homes in-between." Kayleen looked puzzled.

"Err Dick, that's a lot of homes, what do you intend to do with all the occupants?' Now Dick figured John's wife had not worked it out.

"Maybe I should reiterate what we have been doing over the two and a half months, we have been systematically killing our enemy, so far we have sank two Super Tankers with 550,000 dead, probably over 100,000 NK Nationals or more dead and I have lost count of how many troops we have killed." This he could see was not sinking in. She said, with an elevated tone.

"You talk about the numbers like they are nothing Dick, was there no other way?" Sarge started telling the story from the beginning with the fifty-year-old woman silently listening. John and the others took it all in with a look of horror on their faces, finally the shooter commented.

"Boy, sounds like you guys have been at war since the beginning and what you go around in the middle of the night and shoot these people in their sleep, what about the noise?" Sarge and Dick and all the members of the squad just drew their type 54's showing the suppressors. Dick finished up.

"They are not people, they are our enemy, they have not hesitated to annihilate all of us, what do you think happens to all the people they take the homes off? What do you think they were going to do to you, if they caught you?"

2300 hours, Dick had brought the RHIB around the back of Bird Island and was heading to the left of the boat ramp, on board were the Elite Squad members, Sarge, Thomas, John, Chris, Billy and Murray. Sarge and Dick both had NVG's and exited the boat first, making their way to where John had told them the Alliance Outpost was situated.

"Dooff...Dooff...Dooff...Dooff...Dooff." By the time John and the rest had got there it was all over.

"Shit, you didn't waste any time guys." The four members shooting one trooper each, Brittany voiced her opinion,

"What's this guy's shit." John apologised thinking to himself 'shit I just assumed they were all male' but looking closer he smiled,

"Sorry luv, what now Dick, Sarge?" Sarge pointed in the homestead's direction,

"Well one of you can lead us in the least exposed way and we will clear the home for you." He pointed to the four elite members and seeing Chris had put up his hand.

"You lot on me." They disappeared into the blackness; John had suggested that the little caravan his brother used could be occupied." The ex-CD replied.

"Not for long, lead the way."

Sunday 15ᵗʰ March 2015 TRF Elite Squad Hammers Farm Monty

0050 hours, John, Billy and Murray led Dick and Thomas through the thick bush Tea Tree, emerging out onto a concreted area sporting a huge machinery shed and the caravan on one side. It looked like someone was using the van because of the fire drum outside; the ex-CD put his hand on the fire pit.

"Still warm, you lot stay here, Thomas back me up." Dick gently tried the door handle, locked; Thomas gave Dick a look and shrugged his shoulders. Dick banged on the door with the butt of his Type 54, this scared the rest of them, it was loud in the silence that surrounded them, the trees were protecting them from the constant wind that seemed to pester everyone in this area.

They could hear stirrings, a man spoke, Dick replied, "mwoga munje ya!" meaning what's wrong, a minute later the little man opened the caravan door, not all the way, just enough to see who was there.

"Dooff." Dick shot him in the head, more noises from inside, a female's voice, Dick said, "neoneun mueos-eul wonhani," meaning what do you want; this seemed to calm down the woman. Dragging the man's body outside, he entered the van, with NVG's on if didn't take the sixty-one-year-old time in finishing the job.

"Dooff." John was impressed at the speed Dick worked, and it was about now Sarge called out from the house some 200 metres away. Dick pointed.

"Looks like the house is clear as well." John and the others couldn't believe the speed, by the time they got there, Sarge had turned around both jeeps, found the keys and had them idling.

0200 hours, jeep one had Dick driving, John, Billy, Murray, Thomas and Brittany. The second jeep had Sarge driving with Tom, Rusty, Grant, Reg and Chris.

Speeding off towards Monty, Dick and Sarge educated the newcomers in clearing TRF style.

First home, Dick took Murray to back him up, with Brittany to go second, clearing the first bedroom, the ex-CD nodded to Brittany to clear the second. Hesitating just a little, she achieved the kill, at the last bedroom, Dick pointed Murray into the room, two shots and it was all over. Stopping, the pair, pointing out they were to take the troopers weapons and ammo along with any sanitary items they found. This continued for the next two hours with each jeep gaining experience.

0400 hours. The two jeeps made their way into Brownsville after doubling back to do the six properties north of the town. With the first homes coming up, John asked.

"When do we stop, daylight?" The ex-CD replied.

"When we meet the rest of our troops." John was surprised, not knowing that the *Fremantle* had unloaded troops at Brownsville and were at this time heading north to meet Dick and Sarge. Third house in, Dick pulled up, letting Sarge's lot clear the little yellow weatherboard home. Dick was pointing to three sets of headlights coming towards the group. Jack was driving the first, and pulling up alongside Dick, introductions all round.

"How's it been mate"? The ex-Sniper replied.

"Mate all good, fast learners although we have one wounded, trooper got to his weapon before the kid could shoot. I think he hesitated because of the nude girl with the trooper, you know how it goes, what about you?"

"Yep, cleared all the way north to Monty and the Hammer's farm, I guess all we have to do now is the town itself and South Brownsville." Annie pulled up next, jumped out and gave Sarge a huge hug as he exited the home. Jack pointed a thumb towards the twenty-nine-year-old horsewoman.

"Annie and crew have done the town centre, and Nettie took a jeep south."

0600 hours, dawn and the five jeeps part company, the next charge was down the west coast to Alfred River clearing as they went through Marr. Annie swapped with Brittany who took over as driver. Dick swapped with John, and Sarge swapped with Tom.

Four jeeps restocked ammunition, and headed out towards Marr, Dick, Sarge, Billy, Jack and Annie taking one jeep back to the RHIB at the Hammer's boat ramp. They would pick up John's wife and Billy's girlfriend, leaving them to clean out the Hammer farm. With the group safely in John's farm, Dick made sure they all had a good supply of Type 68's and few Type 54's, weapons and ammo.

Twenty two foot Rigid Hull Inflatable Boat (RHIB)

1000 hours, the RHIB was skimming along at twenty-five knots on its way into Duck Bay and onto Brownsville Harbour to join the *Fremantle*. Sarge asked Dick.

"How did it go mate; are you please with the result?" The ex-CD ponders what his mate asked, in amongst all the engine noise of the twin 150's, he yells.

"I think you asked if it went well. Not bad, considering they were all green, but we will tell, when they return in a day or two, we will see how they have gone."

1300 hours and the twenty-two foot RHIB was slowing down, approaching the *Fremantle's* starboard side, Doc and Nari glad to see the crew back, quickly tied it up, wanting to know all the gossip over a cuppa. Doc was really happy Annie and Nettie had gone the extra mile, clearing the majority of the town. Annie holds up an Alliance uniform shirt, Dick comments.

"Looks like a Senior Lieutenant, Annie, what was his name?" She replies, "Senior Lieutenant Bin Pin, not very old either." Dick was curious whether the

ammo and well, the placing of troops was light on, both Sarge and Annie agreed this was the case, Doc asks.

"Do you reckon we have them on the back foot mate?"

"I think so, but we will see tomorrow night, Sarge and I will take Thomas and Annie, and Jack if he wants a run." Doc asks.

"Where to mate" The ex-CD replies.

"Southwest, Doc towards Welsh Town, there has got to be 200 homes in the surrounding area."

Monday 16th March 2015 TRF Elite Squad Marr Hotel

0600 hours, having cleared all the houses between Brownsville and Marr, the four jeeps eventually crashed at the Marr Hotel, posting sentries just after midnight, the group rested. John was impressed with the Elite Squad, the more they cleared the better they got. Brittany had been keeping the stats.

"Well John, we cleared 148 properties last night, thirty-two were empty, 100 had troopers, 590 NK Nationals were killed, ammo was low, we only collected 500 rounds, that's about five per trooper on average and on the downside, we lost one member yesterday, so with the one the day before we're down two." After breakfast the group gathered outside near the transport. Out of the thirty-nine from Queen Island they had only lost two and with the Elite Squad of five plus John, Murray and Chris gave a total of forty-five men. With the addition of two Alliance trucks acquired yesterday they weren't as squashed in.

The idea today, was to clean up the surrounding properties between Marr and the back road to Sheepnorth; this would include about thirty homes on the back road, then seven dairy farms on the approach to the Sheepnorth property. Reg drew the short straw and would be driving one of the trucks, he would take ten men from Queen, and Chris would drive one of the jeeps with six men. Because this would be a daylight clearing the risks were greater. Tom reminded them.

"Don't forget what Sarge, Dick and Jack taught us, daylight means trouble so fully automatic with our Type 68's." Rusty would drive the second truck with another ten from Queen then, Tom in the next jeep with seven, Grant and Brittany with six and last is John, Murray and seven members.

The roll out would be Chris's jeep and Reg's truck heading off towards Sheepnorth, Tom's jeep would handle the side roads between Marr and Alfred River while the remaining members, Rusty's truck and grant's jeep hit Alfred River full on. John would lead on from Alfred River.

1100 hours, Marr Sheepnorth Road, Chris pulls up at the next driveway, looking at the letterboxes it had three farms along its driveway. whistling Reg to take his crew in, he drove on to the next home, this was right on the white dusty gravel road. He had been issued with a suppressed Type 54 pistol, and he was in love with the weapon, the ultimate in stealth, 'boy wouldn't this have been awesome when I was growing up?'.

Taking three members with him he approached the front door, sending the other three around the back.

"Bang, Bang." The fifty-four-year-old farmer belted on the door then tried the handle, 'its open 'shit should have done that first.' He opened the ornate front door to see a NK National coming down the hallway towards him.

"Dooff" he shot the man in the chest, thinking the three men at his back would have had the sense to check the first room on his left, but no, a trooper emerged from the bedroom to find a group of locals walking down the hallway, a National lying on the floor dead, well, the man did a double take, back into his bedroom to get his rifle then, "Boom...Boom." he shot the last 2 in the back. Chris ducked, span around and shot the man in the upper body.

"Dooff!" Realising two men were down, he grabbed the member next to him and entered the main dining room where they were confronted by five more Nationals.

"Boom...Boom...Dooff...Dooff...Dooff." Two shots with the Type 68 and three with the Type 54. He eventually yelled

"All clear mate, check them out." but feeling for a pulse was fruitless. Driving out onto the road the five of them were met by Reg's truck. The mood was sombre amongst those Queen Island men, all mates to the dead men. Chris yelled.

"Good news is, that was the last on this road, next farm is turn left at the tee junction then five kilometres towards Sheepnorth.

1100 hours, Tom and his seven compatriots took off in front of the main column concentrating on all the side roads, first one three kilometres out, off to the right, driving straight up to the front door they spread out, attacking the house from both sides. Whilst running around the side, Tom could see Nationals inside through the window; the ex-RAR soldier shot two of them through an open window. Hearing the Boom, Boom from a Type 68 coming from the back of the house meant trouble, could be a trooper or his men clearing the place. Rounding the corner, he was happy to see the latter. The home yielded seven Nationals and no trooper.

1210 hours, and they were on their fourth home when the shit hit the fan, they didn't even get close to the building when they were fired upon. Stopping the jeep, they tried to flank the shooter, but he was dug in pretty good. Tom beckoned one of his men.

"Mate, you cover me while I crawl up closer." The member fired.

"Boom...Boom...Boom...Boom...Boom," this was enough time for Tom to get within pistol range.

"Dooff", the group quickly cleared the rest of the home, yielding only the trooper's wife and three children.

1100 hours, John led the way for Rusty's truck and the last jeep with Grant and Brittany stopping, before the last hill that overlooked Alfred River, John and Murray checked the small bungalow on their left.

"All Clear Murray!" This was where Brittany would gain access to a water tower to set up a sniping solution. With the thirty-four-year-old professional shooter climbing the ladder and making herself at home they could see all the way to the hotel, she passed on her finding to Grant who had climbed halfway up.

"Shit luv, looks like twenty or more that I can see." The thirty-nine-year-old smiled.

"Start whenever you want honey." Returning to the three vehicles they slowly made their way over the hill, then pulling over behind the old garage. TRF Members dispersed to the adjoining homes only to find them empty. Rusty whispered.

"The secret here, is how far down the road to the hotel and bridge before being seen, any minute Brittany will open up with her sniper rifle, when they take cover follow me and move forward."

1230 hours, "Boom...Boom...Boom." The sound of the unsuppressed sniper rifle was extremely loud and from her position she could see the first three troops go down, this sent the rest into a flurry, as they tried to work out where it came from. This is the secret to sniping, only fire in bursts of three that way there is not enough fire for them to see the origin.

1600 hours, Brittany had only fired another burst of three and sitting still they waited, the Alliance was silent, it appeared they had no idea which way the rifle fire came from. John and Rusty's team were joined by Tom after his jeep had successfully cleared the side streets. Grant had set up another position to the right of the bridge in the old Tourism building; from the top floor he had a position to oversee the front of the hotel and the bridge access. John whispered to the main body of men.

"I think we will wait till dark."

Tuesday 17th March 2015 Welsh Town

Just after midnight, having started on dusk the *Fremantle* branch of the TRF had cleared all the homes between Brownsville and the entrance to Welsh Town. Sarge was driving with Dick riding shotgun with Jack and Annie in the back. The road had just come over a rise, the one and only dairy farm on the left was empty.

Dick pointed.

"The next farm on the right Sarge and judging by the smoke coming out of the chimney means someone's home." Sarge brought the jeep to a halt just off the road on the right-hand side; Dick and Jack went in while Annie backed them up. Trying the front door, they found it open. The warmth of the fire resinated throughout the house and the difference between the cool night air outside and warm inside was enormous. Dick went left, a bedroom.

"Dooff...Dooff." Jack went right, one trooper.

"Dooff." Annie carefully making her way down the passageway. Dick entered the children's bedroom 'shit' six kids, trying not to think too much about it, he went about the task of ending their lives, with the suppressor it seemed surreal, hardly any sound, one moment they are breathing, next they aren't.

"Clear" whispered Jack as he checks the back of the 1930's farmhouse.

0200 hours found the group at the football oval behind the shop, three homes to go, then round the bend to the right and twelve on the next street and four on the last off to the left. Swapping around with Thomas driving, they decide to split up with Dick and Jack taking the right-hand side of the street and Sarge and Annie the left. Sarge was always trying to speed up the process thought Annie and he would work as fast as he could. The ex-sapper charged into each house not caring how much noise he made just shooting everyone inside, what he missed Annie would finish, the pair got the time down to a couple of minutes flat. Jack whispered.

"Christ Dick, Sarge and Annie have finished that side and disappeared round the next street, poor Thomas doesn't know whether to follow them or wait for us." Dick replied

"Mate, just signal him to follow those two, we will catch up." The ex-sniper waved Thomas around the next street while Dick cleared the last bedroom. Back out on the street Jack leaned the rifles and ammo against the concrete bus shelter.

"I'll pick these up on the way back."

0400 hours, catching up to Thomas after clearing only one home on the street, Jack and Dick were met by Annie and Sarge.

"What! Finished the street already Sarge?" The forty-five-year-old grinning, replied.

"Yep, did the last one in one minute fifty seconds." Looking at the seven lots of weapons and ammo in the jeep, Dick asked Thomas to stop at the bus stop and pick up their remainder. On the way back to the *Fremantle* Annie asked.

"When do we clear the highway south Dick, towards the Rock?" The ex-CD laid out the next bit of the plan.

"Since you have asked Annie, I hope the Elite Squad can finish their area soon, then re-group with us and push on towards Rock, then all the way to Burnside. From there we will hopefully hook up with the outpost at Doonah, combine forces to take Devon then Loraine, then hook up with the High Head TRF and push down the highway to Kings Town." The twenty-eight-year-old looked at Dick.

"Sounds easy enough Dick, but in reality, can we, do It?"

"I think we can, not because we are better trained than them, but simply we are smarter, for instance how many sets of weapons have we collected tonight?" Sarge, sitting alongside Annie in the back seat turned and counted the weapons,

"165 Type 68 and 85 Type 54's."

"And how much ammo is there Sarge?" Digging around the ex-sapper does a rough count,

"About 400 rounds of 7.62 mm and 500 rounds of 9 mm." Dick summed it up.

"I rest my case, when we started this war; we were collecting an average of 100 rounds of 7.62 mm for each trooper, now it's what, around five, so what's happened you may ask? It's easy, they are running out of ammunition because we were smart, collecting everything we could off them to bolster our supplies. The 9 mm ammo works out to be six per weapon, in the beginning they were carrying six spare magazines extra or a total fifty six rounds each. I think as we draw to the end of this war, they will be trying to kill us with their bayonets only because they have no ammo left."

Tuesday 17th March 2015 Sheepnorth

0001 hours. Having cleared all the dairies up till the main Sheepnorth property Chris had decided to wait till the wee hours before clearing the main farm. He was sure that this had around thirty-two people, usually to run the property but now the Alliance had taken over that number could be greater.

"Right guys once inside the front gate, I'll take the manager's residence on the right, Reg if you can disperse your men to take the bunkhouse, when finished with the manager's residence, we'll do the next two homes, if we are right that will be all of them."

0115 hours, Reg entered the bunkhouse, it was made up of six rooms with four bunks in each room, as he was the only one with a suppressor, he would do most of the killing, he brought one other man as back up while the other seven kept a lookout around the outside of the building. With back-up, Reg was in his element, the suppressed Type 54 was a great weapon apart from the small capacity of its magazine, so before he started, he made sure that he had six spare magazines loaded, halfway through, he swapped and let his 2IC have a go. This bunkhouse only had eighteen Nationals with no trooper.

0200 hours, with the jeep replenished they, successfully cleared the manager's house, yielding a couple and four kids, the next home had the troopers and their partners, this yielded three troopers and three women with two kids, weapons and ammo to suit.

0300 hours and the last home on the Sheepnorth property was a large brick and tile dwelling, with a jeep parked in the driveway the group thought a trooper at least, if not an officer. Chris whispered to the ex-sniper.

"Your call mate, how do you want to do this?" Reg checked his Type 54 and ammo.

"I'll lead in the front, you two around the back and you watch my back." Trying the front door to find it open he gingerly entered the home, bedroom on the left, a double bed.

"Dooff...Dooff." He stopped to get his eyes adjusted to the NVG's and the surroundings. The room on the right was accessible via two sliding timber doors; these squeaked loudly as he attempted to open them. With just a foot to peer through, he stuck his head around the door to see what was in the room.

A lounge room, a recliner with what looked like someone sleeping in it, not wanting to create more noise, the ex-sniper took a shot from the opening.

"Dooff...Dooff." The two shots found their mark hitting the recliner squarely, they heard a body fall to the floor so moved onto the next bedroom. Motioning to his back-up to cover the door, Reg entered, a double bed, one occupant 'shit' he thought, a loose man.

"Dooff." He shot the female and scanned the bedroom, an officer's tunic over a chair, looked like a senior lieutenant.

"Bang!" Reg heard his back-up swear and hit the floor outside, the fifty-one-year-old went low and huddled in the corner beside the door, he was hoping the officer would think that the man he shot was the only intruder. The officer called out, and kept calling out as he entered the room, with just one foot inside the doorway, Reg was not taking any risks.

"Dooff." Shooting the man in the upper chest, the 9mm round continued up through the man's neck and exited out of his head. **0500 hours,** so the brief was to meet up with the rest of the squad and get in touch with the rebels south of Alfred River. Rusty was not happy he lost a man, but thinking about the conditions that all three men lost their lives, it was inevitable the untrained men would be a hindrance, but it was not their fault.

Tuesday 17th March 2015 Alfred River

0010 hours and the Elite team's sniper had successfully shot eleven Alliance Troopers up until dusk, they elected to lay low until midnight. Although Tom, Grant and Brittany decided they would do a stealth raid on the hotel around 2300.

Gaining entrance to the old timber hotel, the trio managed to clear all the troopers. The Alliance had posted two guards, one in the foyer to the hotel and one on the veranda to the outside rooms; these were easily disposed of with the suppressed pistols. Brittany and Grant quickly cleared all the rooms outside while Tom started downstairs in the main building.

0300 hours, by the time John and Murray made it to the hotel's entrance, the place had been cleared by the team, John called them together.

"I have heard that there are other Taswegians running around down towards Tomma, we need to make contact with them without them shooting us, any thoughts?" Tom answered,

"We could mount a flagpole to the jeep and fly the Aussie flag."

"Yep, I like it although they might just think it's a trick." Rusty suggested,

"Mate I reckon we leave them, at some time they will come here to give the Alliance another licking, when they find out all of them have been killed, they might try to find us, we could leave them a vehicle, and a note." John smiled.

"Rusty that's the best Idea I've heard to date, lets sleep till 1000, then head back to Brownsville and the *Fremantle*, shit I reckon Dick will be pleased."

Tuesday 17th March 2015 FCPB Brownsville Harbour

1400 hours, Patch was sitting in the sun, devouring a chai latte, the fifty-four-year-old was chatting with April, Lauren and Nari;

the raiders had crawled into their bunks around 0600 hours that morning and slept till midday.

"What was it like growing up with Tom as a father?" Lauren pondered for a moment; Patch thought she probably had been asked that question a thousand times.

"It was great when he was home, which wasn't much, mum and he split up and she basically brought me up. I didn't really get to know him until he retired and started helping me on the island." Nari smiled and decided she would break from her usual persona of not talking about her upbringing.

"I can relate to both of you, I know Patch, your father was an engineer and didn't spend much time at home, I haven't told anyone, but my father was a politician, high up in the South Korean Government, and at one stage was a member of the foreign diplomatic service. My mother refused to go with him on his postings, preferring to stay at home and bring up my brothers and me, she eventually went back to work herself as a matron."

"Is that where you got the direction to become a nurse?"

"Sure was, Lauren, I used to listen to all of my mother's stories when she would come home and couldn't wait to enrol."

Doc, Dick, Sarge and Jack were going over the maps of the surrounding towns and their next move down the coast.

"Vehicles coming in Dick." yelled Patch. The ex-CD looked at the clock on the bridge.

"Shit if that's the Elite Squad, they are way early. Sarge can you man that 50 Cal just in case they are Alliance?" Sarge joined the girls on the flying bridge and cocked the gun, making sure the ammo box's lid was off. The convoy of now six jeeps and four trucks pulled up on the wharf; Sarge stands down the 50 Cal yelling below.

"Looks like they multiplied." John led the group onto the quarterdeck and reported to Dick and Doc.

"First off, I must congratulate you guys in the way you have trained us, it must have been hard under the time constraints, and sorry to say we have lost three men. The good news is we have cleared all the homes in the Northwest down to Alfred River and right up to Sheepnorth." Dick asked.

"How did you go with the rebels at Tomma, you must have been fast?"

"Well Dick we decided not to risk it, after all, coming in Alliance jeeps in that country we would draw their fire for sure, so Rusty suggested leaving a vehicle and a note at the hotel, they are sure to come out at some time, it was quicker for us to do that than risk losing a man or more." Doc looked at Dick, both smiling, Dick responded.

"Sounds like a stirling idea Rusty," good work. Well while you were down at Alfred River, we cleared all homes between here and Welsh Town, so the next move is, yes Brittany?" The professional shooter asked.

"Are you moving the patrol boat or do we just continue by road?"

"We'll be moving the *Fremantle* to Rock next, we will take care of the area, you concentrate in the next area of Wynn, let us know by brick phone when you're ready to move into the town, we will come in by sea. My advice is to take over a hotel or motel and get some sleep till late tonight then strike at the few homes lining the highway towards Wynn."

Wednesday 18th March 2015 FCPB standing off Rock

0005 hours, "launch the RHIB" Doc brought the FCPB to a dead stop, taking all way off. Sarge, issuing weapons to Dick, Thomas, Annie and himself, the four TRF members climbed into the RHIB, Jack and Nari in charge of the boat.

With the twenty-two-footer in the water, Sarge released the lift strop, Dick pressed the starters on the twin 150 Mercury Vedado's and moved forward out of the lee side of *Fremantle*. Doc had lingered on the northwestern side of the Rock allowing the raiding party time to get into the harbour without being seen. Dick yelled above the engine noise.

"When we get around the point, I'll idle back and try to go in as quietly as possible. Thomas, how are you feeling, I must admit I was surprised when you volunteered."

"You know Dick. it gets in your blood; I must say, it's brought me back to life so to speak. I was getting pretty bored with just helping Lauren." Sarge acknowledged the seventy-two-year-old with a nod, he and Annie were standing either side of the centre console hanging on to the handles behind the rear row of seats, with Thomas sitting alongside of Dick.

0130 hours and idling the twenty-two-foot RHIB into the Rock wharf they were super quiet, the sea inside of the breakwater was still, it took on an oily effect. Sarge took the liberty of kitting everyone with suppressed Type 54's and NVG's, six full extra magazines each and two grenades for Sarge and Dick.

"Thomas and I will team up and take the hotel first, if Sarge and Annie can start with the B&B over there." Dick was pointing to the huge house on the waterfront, left hand side of the wharf area.

0200 hours, Dick and Thomas gained entry via the bar area, the front door was locked so the pair investigated all other possibilities, bar area was clear, so was the dining and kitchen areas, all bedrooms were upstairs. the ex-RSM whispered,

"Mate two jeeps in the car park behind the bottle shop." The ex-SAS soldier was pointing just out of Dick's range of vision; the ex-CD gave the thumbs up signal, knowing full well there would be troopers staying here. Dick opens the first room at the top of the stairs, and with one single shot "Dooff." Thomas was already at the opposite door, one single shot from him, "Dooff" this went on till all eight rooms were clear. The pair carried all the weapons and ammo downstairs, Thomas went back to the bathroom, conscious about the sanitary items, he wanted to help, all he was able to secure was a dozen toilet rolls.

0200 hours, the Rock B&B, Sarge climbed through an open window, unlocked the door to let Annie in, shooting two Nationals in bed, then four kids, they found the rest of the bedrooms empty. Quickly moving on to the next set of homes, they were back in their element, changing roles they managed about two minutes from entry to exit. Stopping, Sarge whispered.

"Sounds like a jeep luv, coming from the pub." They stopped for a moment to see Dick and Thomas pulling up alongside the pair.

"There's another one if you can't be bothered walking" Sarge was quick to take up the offer, realising they had about eight kilometres till the last house, he got a lift back to get the jeep then continued on.

Wednesday 18th March 2015 TRF Elite and
Queen Members Wynn Highway

0100 hours and the group of four jeeps and two trucks had worked out a system, where everyone got a go of clearing the homes. Successfully clearing all the homes on the highway, they were about halfway to Wynn. Coming up on some side roads they split. Tom and his jeep would do right while Reg would do left, leaving John and his crew taking the right-hand side of the highway and Rusty doing the left. The other two teams would reccy forward to any large buildings.

0340 hours, they had cleared about fifty kilometres with no troops; it was evident when they came across a house that had already been cleared by the advance teams. The side road crews were kept busy. Tom pulled up alongside Reg back on the highway.

"Crikey Reg, I didn't think there was that many houses in these side roads."

"I agree mate, but they were sure chockers." Driving together down the highway until a side road appeared, Tom could just make out the headlights of some of the vehicles in front of him.

Chapter 14
West Coast

Sunday 1ˢᵗ March 2015 Strine

0700 hours, Alex had been woken an hour ago with the supple caresses of his manhood by the busty fifty-one-year-old; she was licking the insides of his thighs much like the session the night before. There was something special waking up to a throbbing erection. The doctor thought 'what day is it? Oh yeah, it's Sunday. He was doing a stores and reinforcement run with Lou today' not wanting her to have control he quickly slid out from underneath her pinned her head down and entered from behind, this was not one of her favourite situations, smiling the fifty-one-year-old blurted.

"You bastard I'll get you for this." Then the abuse gave way to pleasure and a lot of groaning.

0900 hours, Alex and Lou had loaded the supplies from the store at Strine and were making their way to Queens where they would pick up ten TRF members to relieve the troops out at the Kings Bridge outpost. Alex asked.

"Do you like this, Lou; you know the driving and supply?" The busty blonde replied.

"Yes, I love the fact that I am contributing to the war effort so to speak, it's still a bit surreal, you know the whole Alliance and the killing thing. I would rather be involved than not, I don't really think of the danger, not even when I transport the wounded back to Strine. What about you Alex?" The fifty-nine-year-old thought long and hard about the last three months, the direct contact he had with the Alliance, him escaping, after what seemed like an eternity, he finally answered.

"Well Lou, I am really happy that I am here with you, having lived in the horror of the Alliance for a month or so, seen the terrible things they have done, it's definitely real and I guess I cherish what we have." He placed his hand on her shoulder, gave it a light squeeze then brushed her cheek, he continued.

"I am sure that what Dick, the crew of the *Fremantle* and Doc are doing is the only way forward, it's barbaric to kill them all but I really think we have no alternative and God only knows what our life will be like after we win."

"You mean if we win Alex."

"We can't fail Lou; if we don't win I know we will be all killed."

1030 hours and having picked up the ten replacements from Queens they were starting to negotiate the climb up out of the town, the winding road hugging the cliff face on the driver's side with a sheer drop on the passenger's side, this felt extremely arse about tit to the Taswegians, driving a left-hand drive vehicle. They drove over the crest and down through the little gathering of homes known as Gorm made famous by its gravel football oval.

The weather was picking up, the sun was shining, and Alex was sitting in the middle front seat of the KM450 Light Cargo Truck with one of the Queen's recruits alongside of him, the rest of the ten sitting under the canvas canopy in amongst various food supplies in the side seats. Sitting this close to Lou, he could smell her soap and perfumed body; the ample breasts were trying to escape the light cotton blouse she was wearing, some of the buttons were straining under the pressure. The 139HP Diesel Engine, had struggled to make the climb, the jeep was probably not designed to carry that sort of load.

1120 hours. Arriving at the forward outpost, they pulled the aging jeep up in front of the huge stone BBQ structure that now resembled an army base. The fire was still going, swags and one-man tents adorned the area, a group of men were preparing lunch. Lou could make out Anita and went to make her aware the replacements were there.

"Oh, hi Lou, got a passenger today?" The fifty-year-old winked, maybe suggesting there was some meaning in Lou bringing a passenger, Lou introduced Alex and enquired where Blue was.

"On his way back from Kings Bridge Lou, he's been inspecting the front line, and we are about to move camp into the Kings Bridge Hotel."

"Great Anita, when do you move?"

"Straight after lunch, Blue will be bringing the ten members for you to take back." Alex was chatting to a few of the other members there, when Anita asked,

"Alright Lou, what gives with the passenger, or should I say important person?"

"Lou smiled; well, you're nearly right he is sort of special if you know what I mean?"

1230 hours and Blue's truck appeared from the Kings Bridge direction, the men climbing out of the back, the ex-SAS soldier exits the cab, looking a bit worn out, he smiles and shakes Lou's hand.

"Good to see you Lou, who's your boyfriend?" always straight to the point, shaking hands with Alex with Lou answering

"This is Dr Alex Wallace." Blue was quick to engage the doctor

"Great timing Doc, we have two injured on the truck, and one deceased. "They quickly unloaded the injured for Alex to have a look at, accessing one to be a graze, the other a through and through the thigh, Alex suggested they be swapped out and returned to Strine. The dead was bagged and placed on the truck to be returned to their family.

1400 hours, Lou, Alex and the ten standing down, including the two wounded along with the cadaver said their goodbyes.

"So Blue, see you next time at Kings Bridge in about three days"

"Sure will, we move forward in ten minutes?"

Chapter 15
Indonesian Alliance in trouble

Friday 6th March 2015 Indonesian HQ Benoa

0900 hours and Major General Raj Sumatro had summoned his next in command, the newly promoted Lieutenant Colonel Huje Samira to discuss the current crisis. Having re-grouped after their humiliating defeat at Mander, Raj had made sure that it wasn't going to happen again. The thirty-four-year-old had sent reinforcements to St Anne after reports had come back about the rebels attacking by sea and the consequent rescuing of them out on the point.

"Come in Lieutenant Colonel Samira, shut the door and I think formalities are not needed inside my office. I will get straight to the point, we know the rebels have two vessels and they were used to raid St Anne, a small strike but still a costly one for us and on top of the ambush at Mander, I suspect it has made a huge dent in our numbers?"

"Yes Raj, the raid at St Anne killed around 200 of our troops including six *Corps Marine;* the number of Nationals is a lot higher being around 500. We have posted sentries out on the point near where they have to cross the bar in case they return by sea."

"I have sent my report to the NK General informing him of the sea-power they now have, I think he will find this piece of news very interesting, but on to more pressing matters. Our weekly supply truck did not arrive on Monday; this is not like the supply branch to cock this one up. I have sent a jeep to do a reccy to Barracouta and I expect him back any minute."

"What of the weekly messenger from Kings Town, Raj he should have arrived on Monday as well?"

"Nothing Huje, I fear the rebels have control of Barracouta and you know what that means, no rice supply, no contact or support from the NK Alliance troops, we are cut off. I suspect when we had that trouble at the Gulch, it was the rebels and one of their boats that came in and rescued some of their own, our troop numbers are down and a lot of our nationals have made the move to St Anne because of the sheltered waters of St Anne Bay, what are your thoughts on a mass withdrawal to St Anne?" There was a knock on the door.

"Come in Corporal Nok, is the jeep back from Barracouta?" The Corporal ushered the driver into the general's office.

"Well man what did you find out?" The small senior trooper reported.

"Sir I made it to the outskirts of Barracouta where I observed a barricade across the highway, a large boat on a trailer."

"Were you fired upon?" Raj had that look of concern on his face; he had suspected that one day he would have to make a really difficult decision.

"Yes sir it appeared to be manned by rebels, I turned around and came straight back." Dismissing the driver Raj turned to Huje.

"Your take on that?" The older lieutenant colonel pondered for a moment.

"If I was the rebels Raj, I would be mounting a major offensive against us here, we know they have sea power, and from all the carnage we have heard about the NK garrison being destroyed and most of Oxford and Sprung Beach we can only guess their numbers, I am not sure fighting them here is a good solution." Standing to gaze out of his office window he glanced at his home on the waterfront, he would not like the job of telling his wife they had to move, she would never forgive him'

"I concur Huje, we start moving everyone today, after all, the rebels can't engage us if we are not here."

Saturday 76ᵗʰ March 2015 Indonesian Transport HQ Benoa

0800 hours and the logistics commander had literally moved heaven and earth, in twenty hours he had overseen some eighty trucks move Indonesian Nationals and troops alike, the news did not sit well with some of them to the point that a few would not move, electing to stay behind. Huje could see his commander's jeep pulling up outside.

"Welcome sir, all is going well, I expect to have ninety per cent moved by 1800 hours tonight, so that's 40,000 Nationals from the Benoa area. How did it go down with your family?" Raj shivered at the reminder of telling Adina.

"Ah, not that well Colonel, but eventually they were ready when the truck arrived; I had sent word to the commander in St Anne, hoping a suitable luxurious home could be sought for my family. Great job Huje now you must send someone to the properties near Barracouta and break the bad news to the admiral."

Saturday 7th March 2015 Benoa

2000 hours, Raj stood in his lounge room, he was going to miss this house; he had witnessed the moving of the bulk of his people to St Anne, he was proud of Huje, the logistics commander had done a fantastic job removing all those homes. He placed the last of his belongings into the back of his jeep. "Right Nok ready when you are," The corporal smiled and drove towards the main road.

"Anywhere else before we head north sir?"

"No, I think the Colonel was driving home to Rocky Bay to collect his family, so once more up the main road then we head north." The corporal drove to the entrance to the town, down a couple of side streets around the Gulch and back out onto the main road.

"I'm going to miss this town sir"

"So am I Corporal, so am I".

Chapter 16
Port Apple

Wednesday 4ᵗʰ March 2015 Sixty-five-foot Conquest Retaliator, Legs Anchorage

1800 hours and Harold only just beat Riley into the anchorage in front of the little settlement of Legs, the anchor chain was still rattling down the Hawser pipe when the twenty-year-old brought the sixty-five-footer into the bay.

"*Black Ink, Black Ink,* this is *Retaliator,* do you have a copy?"

"*Retaliator* this is *Black Ink,* receiving, glad you could make it Riley over,"

"Glad to be some assistance Harold, permission to raft up?"

"Permission granted mate, we are sending a party ashore in the Alloy Plate boat to search for survivors, my privilege to have you all aboard for tucker tonight."

Harold had sent Peter, Christine and Ron, who had partially checked the town a few days before along with Pat and Steve Bisch. Watching the alloy plate boat make its way to the little jetty alongside the boat ramp, the remaining crew assisted in catching the *Retaliators* mooring lines.

2100 hours after eating, the shore party had returned empty handed, everyone pretty much turned to Harold to go over the next chapter, the thirty-one-year-old cleared his throat.

"I can report the *Dove* members have now cleared all the way to just below President and have put a barricade across the road. Effectively the TRF have control of everything south of there. The *Cougar Anne* was steaming here in the channel to meet us, but I have asked them to wait in the Apples River until Riley gets there to assist with a raid on President. Then up the river to Apples, liaise with Nobby and his members, they will assist on the ground. Tomorrow we will mount a raid on the small area of Woodsville, and our newest vessel to join the TRF fleet, the *Tangara* will be crewed by Alf as skipper, Shakira, Mervin, Samuel and Brian, they are waiting till tomorrow when they will mount another raid on Kettle.

Thursday 5th March 2015 sixty-five-foot Conquest Retaliator entering the Apples River

0600 hours, Riley had slipped lines at 0500 hours and made his way across the channel to the Apples River, time was of the essence so he had the V12 Caterpillar 1000 HP Turbo engine nearly on the stops, running at near maximum revolutions she was doing twenty eight knots making short work of the thirty nautical miles, passing Apple Island and the many disused salmon pens still moored there. Gard Island came up on their starboard side, the river was flat calm and the twenty-year-old could swear the boat surged ahead another five knots in the ink-like water.

Tannin was evident in the huge river, even this far down. Liz was in her usual place in the navigator's chair, Mick enjoying the rest of breakfast around the table.

"What's that cute bay on our right Riles?" The twenty-year-old skipper replied,

"That's Sausage and Eggs Bay and the point on our Port side is Walloper Point." Mick asked.

"Where do we meet the *Cougar Anne* Skipper?"

"Up at Port Apples mate, we should see her in about an hour just after we round that bend way up in front." Because the river was so flat the crew took the time in preparing for action. The 50 Calibre Machine Gun was uncovered and boxes of ammunition brought up from the engine room, and with the boat on auto pilot Riley was the only one who could remember how to load and cock the weapon, so gave them all a quick refresher. All mooring lines were stowed away so that there were no obstacles on deck.

"Mick, can you give Liz a hand in bringing up the Type 68's and ammo please?"

"How many do you want Skipper?"

"I reckon we better have one each Mick, oh and just bring all the loaded magazines."

0800 hours, off Cairn Bay Liz pointed,

"There she is Riles!" The twenty-year-old skipper reached for the VHF microphone,

"*Cougar Anne, Cougar Anne,* do you have a copy, over?"

"*Retaliator,* this is *Cougar Anne* receiving loud and clear, glad to see you guys, how was the crossing?"

"Flat as mate, we'll come alongside and compare notes for today, do you want to call Nobby on the phone and set up the proceedings?"

"Roger that mate"

Riley throttled back to ten knots as he approached the fifty-foot steel cray boat, stopping the boat to take all way off, he manoeuvred the sixty-five-foot Conquest alongside the port side of the steel boat, a spring was attached and a bow and stern line. The crew of the *Retaliator* was soon joined by Baz, Lyn, Sid and

Craig. The twenty-year-old had heard a lot about Baz from Dick and Jack so was excited to introduce himself and his crew.

"Baz great to finally meet you and Lyn, Dick and Jack can't talk highly enough about you, this is my fiancée Liz and TRF Veteran Mick." The sixty-one-year-old ex-CD introduced his crew,

"Mate, thanks for the kind words, they might have been puling your leg, anyway my wife Lyn, Sid and Craig were former deckhands on the old girl when it worked the west coast. I have spoken to Nobby; his group are waiting just south of President and will move on our go signal. We think the way to go is travel up the inside of Chook Islands and use the 50 Cal on anything that is within range, from what Nobby tells me there are about ten properties from where he is and President itself, but they are all between the road and the river. He will take care of the couple of dirt roads that run off to the other side. President itself, we will berth at the wooden boat jetty and clear all businesses and homes we come across."

0900 hours, the sixty-five-foot *Retaliator* was running really close to the shore, Mick was manning the 50 Cal, a bit bigger than the Ultimax, but he had used the weapon before.

"First home coming up on our port side Mick," The fifty-five-year-old ex-barman pushed the safety forward and swung the weapon to port. Liz was spotting for him.

"Boom...Boom...Boom...Boom...Boom," the half inch rounds escaping the barrel between 450 and 600 rounds per minute and with an effective range of 1800 metres it made short work of the NK Nationals toiling in the garden. Liz pointed to a trooper shouldering his weapon, yelling.

"Incoming fire Mick."

"I'm on it, Luv" as Mick found the pestering rifle fire and concentrated another burst.

"Boom...Boom...Boom...Boom." Riley stopped the boat for a last look and then radioed Baz.

"All yours Baz,"

The Cougar Anne pushed bow first into the small jetty at the rear of the property where Sid and Craig, new to the killing, hunted out any hiding Alliance. They searched the home only to find one National running up the road, trying to get the sights on the man, Sid was a bit slow and then "Boom," out of the corner of his eye he detected a jeep shooting at the man.

1134 hours, *Retaliator* entered the small channel between Chook Islands and the Highway, first property right down on the river obviously had a trooper, there were 7.62 mm rounds dancing off the water, the occasional round finding its mark and hitting the boat, the twenty-year-old skipper yelled.

"Nail that fucker Mick; he's busting up my boat." Mick soon found the trooper and silenced him; he probably got a shock to find the boat was sporting a 50 Cal as well as Type 68's. Baz and the crew of the *Cougar Anne* were making their way behind them clearing up the dregs, at one time Riley thought he could hear rifle fire from the road 'must be Nobby's mob' he thought.

1300 hours and coming in alongside the jetty at the wooden boat yard, Mick was scanning the area, while Liz tied her up, Mick yelled to Liz,

"You stay with the skipper and look after the boat Sis, I will clear anything I see ashore, might pay the skipper to phone Nobby and let him know just in case they shoot at us. Liz nodded in the affirmative.

"Brrr, Brrr, Yeah Nobby, Riley here, we have just tied up at the jetty and put three men ashore clearing homes, yeah right, don't shoot them, no wouldn't be that happy, actually I can see your lead jeep now, opposite the *Cougar Anne* clearing that yellow house, right see you in half an hour." Liz put the kettle on and made Riley and her a cuppa, Riley reported that Nobby and crew would be there in half an hour.

The *Cougar Anne* tied up at the old commercial jetty, all that remained there was the old Passenger ferry *Cartela* Lyn read out some specs on the old ferry, *(the Taswegian Aboriginal name for a bull seal) it was built in 1912 at Chook Point, Kings Town, by Purdon & Featherstone for the Apple Channel and Peninsula Steamship Company Pty. Ltd. She was designed to operate as a cargo and passenger vessel in the coastal and riverine trades south and south-east of the city. Tonnage: 194 long tons (197 t) Length: 123 feet (37 m) Beam: 25 feet (7.6 m) Draught: 8 feet 6 inches (2.59 m) she was Australia's oldest continuously licensed passenger vessel.*

1500 hours and rifle fire was all around the sixty-five-foot *Conquest*. Up in the hills, up and down the road; Riley was manning the 50 Cal when Nobby's jeep pulled up in the car park opposite, Brenda and the wounded Dave accompanied him.

"How goes it Nobby?" The twenty-year-old shook their hands and introduced Liz. He had heard a lot about the ex-trail riding boss; now before him was a battle hardened forty-five-year-old, along with his attractive wife Brenda. The twenty-year-old skipper could almost see the trauma that had been in their life over the past two months. Nobby reported.

"Got four teams in jeeps, scouring the hillside mate, what we have found is this area is light on for Nationals and not many troopers either, I reckon the last jeep in will be Shane, Rachael and Matilda."

Thursday 5th March 2015 fifty-six-foot Huon Pine Cray Boat Tangara approaching Kettle

0700 hours, Alf and crew had weighed anchor at 0600 hours; they were now making their way into the marina at Kettle. Deciding to re-visit the hotel the fifty-six-foot ex-cray boat silently slipped alongside right outside the hotel. Quickly killing the Gardner Engine, Alf and Shakira went to the right of the building, same way they entered last time, while Samuel and Brian went to the left and a couple of nearby homes, Mervin was happy to babysit the boat, propped up in the wheelhouse with his Type 68 assault rifle the sixty-eight-year-old was happy.

0900 hours, "I'll go in first luv." Alf gave Shakira a fast kiss on the lips, then entered the hotel on the bottom floor, with Shakira behind the eighteen-year-old they entered the main floor, opposite the main entrance, where Alf had memories of Mervin saving their bacon. Noises coming from the kitchen, Alf pushed one side of the double swing doors to find two chefs merrily going about their business.

"Dooff, Dooff," all over in a couple of seconds. Alf checked their vitals, then whispered.

"Might have a look at the rooms luv?"

The pair worked their way along the arm that housed the accommodation rooms; inspecting all twelve, they found no-one. Re checking the dining room they found one cleaner, come waitress, but were surprised to see anyone.

Alf thought the girl of about seventeen didn't know who they were, to the point where when she first saw the pair, just kept working. He walked up behind the girl who turned and smiled, he shot her at point blank range in the head.

0930 hours, "That was weird Luv, she didn't think we were danger at all, really weird." The pair exited through the front door and walked to the first home of five that were on that side of the main road.

1100 hours and having cleared the first five homes, and the fourteen on the other side of the road, they were moving forward like a steam train.

Alf entered and fired, Shakira kept count, handed him the magazine when he was getting close to running out and collected the booty. The pair took a break and sat on the front steps overlooking the access road to the ferry terminal. The eighteen-year-old looked at Shakira, this woman he had become attached to, her flaming red hair and rounded face. She was wearing denim jeans, a pale blue sweatshirt over a light green tank top, this, now exposed due to the heat of the day, her ample breasts confined by a black lace bra, scuffed pull on elastic sided boots, the webbing holster and ammo pouches strapped around her waist. She turned and looked at the eighteen-year-old admiring her figure.

"What's that look for Alf?" He leant over and kissed the twenty-year-old hard on the lips.

"Just admiring your fantastic body luv," she was embarrassed, no-one had ever told her that, and she smiled then kissed him.

"Come on, more people to kill." The words kind of rolled off the tongue, and made her double take the moment.

0900 hours, Samuel and Brian crossed the entire marina to clear some homes overlooking the old ferry terminal. Entering the first home from the back door, they found four Nationals sitting around the kitchen table, and before a word was spoken Samuel fired the suppressed 54 pistol.

"Dooff…Dooff…Dooff…Dooff." The ex-wooden boat shed manager checked their vitals as Samuel explored the rest of the home. Finding an elderly couple in their room, the male was sitting on the side of the bed trying to get his leg into a pair of trousers while the female was still lying down, "Dooff…Dooff."

1100 hours, they had cleared twenty-four homes, shot 104 Nationals and only two troopers, with the appropriate stock of supplies the pair made their way back to the *Tangara*. Mervin had clear vision of Brian and Samuel as they made their way among the homes, the sixty-eight-year-old was happy to see the pair finally crossing the road.

Thursday 5th March 2015 Black Ink

0800 hours, Harold and Peter were awake when the *Retaliator* slipped her lines, everyone was up, fed and issued with their weapons and ammo, steaming across the channel to mainland Taswegia Harold stopped the ninety foot ex-squid boat and went astern, he was coming alongside the little Woodsville jetty and boat ramp, they had drawn quite a crowd, most of the NK Nationals coming quite close to witness the huge black boat tie up.

"What do we do Skipper, shoot them from here or step ashore and try to get closer to them?" The thirty-year-old was lost for words, having never come up against this behaviour before. Shayne and Peter jumped onto the old timber jetty and make fast the mooring lines. Showing no aggression to the Nationals, they returned on board, gathered their weapons, they left in three groups.

First was Shayne, Debra, and Ivan, second was Pat, Steve and Cindy third was Christine, Ron and Julie, the Sweet kids and the doctor were to look after the boat with Harold and Peter.

0920 hours, Shayne, Debra and Ivan were the first group to catch-up with the NK Nationals that had been admiring the *Black Ink*. Shayne fired as he walked past the pair "Dooff...Dooff," he could see the next and picking up his speed caught them at the front gate to a lovely little cottage.

"Dooff." They entered the home, found two Nationals cleaning up from breakfast, they must have heard the front door open and assumed it was the family returning, words were spoken. Shayne had swapped with Ivan to give the fifty-two-year-old shack owner a turn using the suppressed 54 pistol. The female turned to run for the back door.

"Dooff...Dooff." The 9mm rounds striking the first female in the back parting her ribs on the left side entering her heart and the second female square in the middle of her chest.

0945 hours, Pat, Steve and Cindy found themselves at the Woodsville Pottery Studio, once the home of local potter Bill Dyson, now home to a large family of Nationals. Front door was always open for customers, so they could gain access freely, Steve was given the suppressed weapon, Pat backed up and Cindy covered the front. The sixty-year-old light housekeeper didn't think too much about what he was doing, he just aimed and fired, the problem with nine Nationals in the home was, Steve only had eight rounds in his magazine.

"Dooff, Dooff, Dooff," next room "Dooff, Dooff, Dooff, Dooff," kitchen out back "Dooff, Click, Click." The last woman attacked the sixty-year-old, wielding a bread knife like a medieval swordsman. The twenty something woman struck Steve on the side of his neck, the thirty centre metre serrated bread knife, slashing open his neck severing main arteries as he fell to the floor. The woman was screaming like a banshee, and while he was down struck again, this time imbedding the blunt edged weapon into his chest. If the bleed out of his neck didn't kill him, the blade into his heart did.

All this happened in the blink of an eye, with Pat only five steps behind him. The sight of her husband being killed stopped Pat in her tracks and the fifty-nine-year-old froze, she couldn't believe her eyes, screaming herself was probably the smartest thing she could have done, because it did two things. First it alerted Cindy to come into the home, secondly it stopped the National from screaming. There was a moment where both women just looked at each other, then the National leapt at Pat but unarmed this time, the force of the young woman knocked the fifty-nine-year-old off balance. They hit the carpeted floor in a fierce fireball of pent-up energy. In the tackle, Pat had lost her weapon, the two women were scratching, biting, smacking and punching each other. Pat managed to get one of her legs in-between the pair and with all her might she pushed up until the girl was in the air then.

"Bang." Cindy had entered the home, tried to shoot but couldn't take the risk for fear of hitting Pat, with the girl airborne finally she took the shot. The ex-army mechanical engineer sat Pat against the wall to get her breath and then entered the kitchen. Checking Steve for vitals with her fingers on, what was left of his carotid artery, she glanced around at the mess, blood was everywhere, the bread knife still imbedded into his chest, Cindy pulled the tablecloth off the table, sending condiments across the floor, still rolling around when she covered his body, 'Pat doesn't need to see this' she thought.

1215 hours, Christine, Ron and Julie, having successfully cleared the four homes they were assigned, met Cindy and Pat outside, Shayne, Ivan and Debra also catching up. With everyone trying to console the fifty-nine-year-old, Shayne asked Pat whether she would like to go back to the ship, wiping her eyes she finally said.

"No, I'm fine, let's just get it over with." Ivan suggested.

"I'll go with Cindy and Pat, Shayne it'll be ok." The ex- orchard worker nodded as they split up.

1400 hours and twenty-one homes later they assembled on the jetty, Shayne suggested a stiff drink for everyone then reported the bad news to Harold. With a couple of whiskies under her belt, Pat was being looked after by Julie, Cindy and Debra. Harold was looking at the next town north on the chart.

Thursday 5ᵗʰ March 2015 sixty-five-foot Conquest Retaliator and Cougar Anne Apples

2100 hours, Riley slowed the sixty-five-footer down as he approached the floating restaurant just before the Apples Bridge; the *Cougar Anne* had pulled alongside the apple shed complex on the southern side of the river. Nobby and his teams continued up the main road and its tributaries towards the bridge. Mick and Riley did final checks on their weapons, then hopped over the side onto the floating restaurant, and then ashore, they found themselves opposite the local pub, sounded like a lot of people were still inside.

"What do you reckon Riley, do we clear the pub or wait till they come out, can't be long to kick-out?" Mick pondered over the suggestion, looked at the home alongside then answered.

"Mate I reckon we clear this home, only one on the road, and then wait for the patrons to emerge from the pub."

2230 hours, "Here they come!" The pair could see the first group of three make their way gingerly down the steps, three paces then.

"Dooff...Dooff...Dooff." Quickly dragging them to the side of the pub they waited for the next lot.

"Dooff...Dooff...Dooff...Dooff," this time there wasn't enough time to move the bodies, the next lot catching Riley in the act, with too much alcohol the would-be defenders were no match for the two TRF members and soon enough there was seven bodies to remove.

2345 hours and entering the hotel they quickly disposed of the barman and family, regrouping in the main bar Riley re assessed the town.

"Right, looks like the main road doesn't have many homes but we can't be sure the businesses don't have accommodation attached, so I suggest we work up this side of the road to the roundabout then check the other side on the way back. I think then, we can make tracks to Veronica Sands to pick up a couple of new recruits."

2115 hours and with the *Cougar Anne's* mooring lines attached, Baz sent out two groups to hopefully clear the 100 odd homes on the southern side of the river, fully aware that Nobby was covering everything south of there. Shane, Matilda and Rachael quickly searched the apple shed, no people but they did find a jeep

"Great find guys, we don't have to walk." The first set of homes were on a side road that ran alongside the main road, this was probably the old main road until they built the new one, there were three homes up on a small rise. The occupants were still up sitting around in the lounge room with a few candles burning, it didn't take the suppressed Type 54 long to do its magic, next home, they came across their first trooper and the third was empty.

2300 hours, Peter, Christine and Ron covered the homes over the road from the side road, Ron was quick on the Type 54, killing everyone inside before Peter and Christine could get their eyes adjusted. With four to go, they swapped, and Peter took over the suppressed Type 54, and on the last one, Christine took over the lead, once again the TRF members found no troopers.

Friday 6th March 2015 Apples

0030 hours, Shane, Rachael and Matilda were approaching the bridge in their acquired jeep; behind them they could just detect gunfire ever so faint in the distance, Shane cocked his ear to the sounds.

"Must be Nobby's lot we can hear, and right on time, Peter, Christine and Ron made their way to the jeep. Peter reported.

"Mate we cleared sixty-one homes, no troops, but a shit load of sanitary items."

"Fifty-nine homes for us and same, no troops, I reckon we catch up with Riley's mob and do the whole town."

With all six in the jeep, they crossed the Apples Bridge and drove to the roundabout. Sighting the *Retaliator* crew on the left as they were halfway there, stopping they consulted their progress.

"We have only two homes to go, then everything this side of the roundabout is done, that only leaves a few sporadic homes in the street behind the main road, how do you want to handle it, Riley?" The twenty-year-old skipper replied.

"I reckon if we split into three teams, one takes the main road, one the road up past the council and the other behind the supermarket. Let's hope we find another couple of jeeps; my legs are killing me oh and we need to get these recruits promised by Harold." Shane, Matilda and Rachael took the main road, moving a lot faster than the rest because of the number of businesses, and by the time they got to the old takeaway shop at the start of the main road they had only cleared four homes.

0245 hours, Peter, Christine and Ron hit the jackpot, a jeep and a trooper, dispatching all the occupants, they revelled in collecting the Type 68 assault rifle and ammo, with Christine collecting the bathroom products. The sound of a jeep behind the trio sent shivers up their spines, then realising it was Nobby's lot of four jeeps, Nobby pulls up alongside the newly acquired jeep.

"To keep out of your way, we will clear out along the Judd road, I have already sent a jeep along the southern side of the river, we should meet at Judd, and you guys are doing a sterling job."

0400 hours, Shane, Matilda and Rachael were approaching the old Apples Motel, two jeeps outside were a dead giveaway.

"Got to be the garrison guys, don't be afraid to shoot first if they wake up." Shane led them in through the front door, Matilda second and Rachael backing up. Shane gave the twenty-one-year-old a kiss on the lips as he left her; she touched his shoulder as if to say 'be careful' he just nodded.

The main hallway sprouted ten rooms; the twenty-three-year-old entered fast. "Dooff," halfway down the hallway, they swapped. Matilda led; Rachael stood

a couple of steps behind, pistol ready. Matilda opened the door to room sixteen, to see the occupant sitting on the side of the bed. Looking at Matilda, the trooper reached for his weapon only to be shot in the arm, the thirty-five-year-old firing wildly, was rattled as the man obviously trying to pick up his weapon with his left hand,

"Dooff...Dooff." finally the trooper slumped onto the floor.

0500 hours. The noise woke the two rooms left; the trio were exposed to three doors opening at once, only one came out with his weapon.

"Bang," the 7.62 mm round caught Matilda in the shoulder, and she hit the floor hard, he didn't see Shane behind the door before the all too familiar sound,

"Dooff...Dooff...and Dooff." All three were accounted for, Rachael got to

Matilda first, in the part light she couldn't see where she was hit. Shane checked all the trooper's vitals, then knelt down at Matilda's side, feeling the blood oozing from her shoulder. Rachael had grabbed a couple of towels to act as a pad, Shane could feel the exit wound and quickly bandaged the two towels into place.

"Better get her back to the *Retaliator* and some first aid."

Driving as fast as he could, the twenty-five-year-old Salmon Farmhand made his way to the Apples Jetty now housing the sixty-five-foot *Conquest*. Riley and Mick were back with the new crew members, Ron and Christine, Liz was on watch and soon administering first aid.

"Bring her in Shane". Rachael and Shane carried the thirty-five-year-old in and placed her on the table in the wheelhouse. Riley thought that Shane and Rachael should go back to finish the job, while he looked after Matilda.

0610 hours, the sun was creeping up over the tree line to the east of Apples, Rachael cuddled into Shane's arm whilst they made their way north to catch up with the rest of the crew.

Just under an hour later, the pair took the left turn heading towards Judd, thinking they heard a lot of gunfire in the distance, they cautiously looked ahead.

"I don't think our lot is this far north luv, might pay us to check it out." Rachael made sure her Type 54 pistol was loaded. The jeep rounded a corner to find them on a dirt track, looking down, the nineteen-year-old teacher's aide said.

"Look Shane, horse tracks." Sure enough, when the ex-salmon farm worker stopped the jeep, he could see not one but many tracks in the muddy gravel road.

"Well, I'll be Rach, must be locals, let's investigate." Driving another three kilometres, Shane stood on the brakes as they were face to face with around twenty riders coming out of the bush, he smiled, saying.

"Great, look at all the locals, holy shit Rach, their fucking NK Troops."

Jamming the gearstick into reverse!

Chapter 17
Raid on Benoa

Sunday 8th March 2015 Just south of Benoa

0700 the sun was well and truly up, the rays piercing through the tree lined hill to the east of Len's aunt's property, only a few kilometres south of Benoa. The two jeeps parked in the driveway; Len gave Vince the bad news about Paul.

"Fuck mate, sad to hear that, he was an ok kind of guy." The five of them were enjoying a brew, looking forward to a few hours rest when Vince looked at Len,

"What's next mate, do we have a plan to go further?" The thirty-year-old Skipper smiled.

"Next we have a go at Benoa, I'm hoping the fishing vessel *Waubs Bay* is still on her mooring, I know where the owner lived, and the original engine is sitting." Vince and Laurel were a bit taken back by the bold statement from Len.

"Len isn't Benoa the HQ for the Indonesian Alliance?"

"Sure is, Vince, my idea is to hit them two ways, one up the road from here and the other by sea. We land at the Gulch and run raids from there."

"Who have we got left to do this mate, a man down today, and Chris is wounded back at Barracouta."

Len nodded in agreeance with the ex-navy technician.

"I'll ask Helen if she and Chris, along with Billy can man the southern barricade at Barracouta that gives us Mal, Wendy and Bill to man a jeep, and if Vince, you, Laurel and Josh can man the other jeep while Jill and I run the *Mary* up to the Gulch. If the two jeeps can get to the Gulch at around the same time as the *Mary* that would be a bonus."

Len and Jill left and made their way back to Barracouta to set up the rest of the Plan, Vince, Laurel and Josh got some well needed sleep, making use of Len's auntie's home. They weren't expecting Mal, Wendy and Bill until later on in the afternoon; Len had given Vince the directions and address of the old owner of the *Waubs Bay.*

1000 hours, Len pulled up at the Barracouta TRF HQ and run his idea past Helen and Chris who were more than happy to oblige, the jeep to join Vince would not have to leave until around 1700, so Jill and Len crashed to catch up on some well needed sleep. Chris, Helen and young Billy had moved to the Oxford Bridge while Mal, Wendy and Bill got some sleep. Mal still trying to come to terms with Paul's death. The thirty-four-year-old was of mixed minds, on one hand he wished they were still camping at the Duck Hide, but then on the other hand, he was proud to be part of the TRF fighting for their freedom, his mind continuing to go back to the days where Paul and he had gone camping and shooting.

1100 hours, Jill was sad over the shooter's death, she hugged the thirty-nine-year-old skipper, whispering.

"Are we going to win Len?" Len cradled her head, kissing her deeply.

"I think we are Luv; I think we are!"

1630 hours and Len turned the keys on the triple 300 HP Mercury Verado Outboards, while Jill was pulling in the mooring lines. Easing the forty-foot RHIB out of her berth he started spinning her around to face the channel, with all lines stowed the seventeen-year-old settled in alongside of Len. They moved out at slow speed until they were level with the last channel marker, pushing the throttles forward the RHIB jumped out of the water to an amazing twenty-five knots. Len had refuelled the vessel a few days ago and was happy now the tanks were full.

1730 hours, they were well on their way to Rifle Island when the seventeen-year-old handed Len a sandwich to go with his brew, looking at the sea state Len commented.

"Sea is kind to us this afternoon Luv."

"That I like, what time do you think we will be there Len?" The thirty-nine-year-old looked at his watch.

"I reckon about 2000 hours Luv, then we'll sneak into the Gulch as quietly as possible, hope the others get there around the same time."

1900 hours, "I hear a jeep, Vince." The forty-seven-year-old pulled the curtain enough to peek outside.

"No worries, it's Mal, Wendy and Bill, I'll put the kettle on for a drink." Vince met them at the back door still pulling on his boots.

"Time for a drink before we head off?"

Going over the plan, Vince reiterated what Len had said, only two homes this side of the turnoff to the little bay that housed the owner of the *Waubs Bay.* that had around eight shacks in it. The plan was to clear one each on the way, then as quick as possible clear the eight homes in the bay then eyeball the pre 2000 Gardner engine. Next stop would be the esplanade and the four homes there, hopefully arriving at the Gulch at the same time as Len.

1930 hours and Vince turned off to the little bay, watching in the rear-view mirror, Mal and crew were coming out of their last home. The first shack was only small in comparison to the others in the bay.

"Probably one of the original shacks in the area." stated Vince as he stopped in front, smoke was evident from the chimney, Josh covered the back door, while Vince led in the front.

"Dooff...Dooff...and Dooff." Three occupants were all sitting at the kitchen table, Laurel checked the other rooms, called all clear, then out of the corner of her eye she thought she saw some movement, just on the edge of her peripheral vision, as Vince approached the forty-eight-year-old put a finger to her lips and pointed to the bedroom. Vince nodded, then moved her to one side and entered the room, 'well there's not many places to hide in this room' he thought.

"Dooff...Dooff." The ex-navy technician shoots two rounds through the bed, then reaches down to lift the bed up revealing a National bleeding from the leg and the shoulder.

"Dooff," he finished the job. Josh came in the back door and commented.

"Shit mate that was close, we could have missed him." Vince replied.

"Yep, you're right, trouble is how many have we missed before?" Back in the jeep all three TRF members were pondering over the same question.

2045 hours, "Well this is it guys, the home of the old L6 Gardner engine." They were parked outside a magnificent brick home, huge red colour bond shed out the back. Josh backed up Vince while Laurel checked out the back door, finding it open, Vince checked each room in turn, turning to Josh he said.

"Empty mate, not a soul." Laurel met them in the middle and said.

"Looks like Mal's having the same result, no one home, pretty queer if you ask me." Vince opens the door to the shed, enters to find a number of pallets covered with tarps.

"This looks like it," he uncovers the largest item and there it was, the pre 2000 L6 Gardner.

2015 hours and the forty foot RHIB, having turned to port entered the Gulch, on the way up the coast, filling in time, Len had described the place to Jill,

"In-between the craggy rock scape of little Governor Island and the Benoa shoreline, there is this deep ocean ravine, where the town's fishing fleet shelters from the Taswegia Sea swells." Spinning the forty-footer around to come alongside port side, Jill gets a spring line onto the bollard and the thirty-nine-year-old skipper nudges the RHIB closer, while the seventeen-year-old secures the bow and stern lines.

"All good Len," she says smiling, proud of the fact she can now do this with confidence.

2130 hours, "Jeeps coming Len, looks like two sets of lights." Len and Jill watched as the two jeeps pulled up, Len asked.

"How was it guys, any trouble?" Still coming to terms with the loss of Paul,

Vince answered

"Only found one home with anyone there." Mal reported the same.

"Grab your weapon and we will see if the rest of the town is empty" Len was puzzled, so along with Jill they jumped onto Vince's jeep. Mal and his crew went straight past the school to check on homes there, while Vince drove up the main road.

"Looks pretty empty to me, Guys" states Laurel. Driving all the way out of town to the Wildlife Park, the ex- navy technician pulls up in front of the last home, quickly runs in one door and out the back.

"Bloody empty."

2300 hours and both jeeps meet in the middle of town, having searched every back street for signs of the Indonesians, Laurel asked.

"How far to the next property, does anyone know?" Len answered.

"About ten kilometres Laurel, on the right, alongside of the Motel and Winery, Black Hills, then a few shacks at Five-Mile Creek.

"I reckon we might as well check them out to be sure, won't take long." And with everyone in agreeance they headed up the highway.

Monday 9ᵗʰ March 2015 Black Hills Winery

0030 hours, making their way towards the main building Mal stopped in the covered entrance, this award-winning establishment looked stunning in the moonlight. Checking the interior Wendy reported.

"Nobody home here either, and with still plenty of wine on the racks." Bill made a quick dash to the outlying rooms, but it was obvious to everyone there, the place was quite empty. Vince's jeep could be seen coming along the highway from the Five-Mile Creek area, pulling up behind Mal's jeep they decided to make their way back to Benoa.

0900 hours and the group had elected to sleep in the old Benoa Motel down by the beach. Jill and Wendy had risen early to scrounge some tucker. Finding a few tins of baked beans and spaghetti; this would do heated on a small open fire outside the entrance to the motel. Len and Jill made their way back to the *Mary* to call Dick with the news.

"Brrr ... Brrr ... Brrr ... yep, hi Dick, it's Len here mate, yeah all went well, or should I say too well, what do I mean, well there's no one here, yep that's what I said, we only came across one home with Indonesians at home, the rest all the way to Five Mile Creek were empty. Well today we might see if we can move the *Waubs Bay* into the Gulch, then see if we can swap her original donk over, yep found that last night, If we get into trouble we'll call you, right, you too mate."

1100 hours, with everyone on board Len brought the forty-foot RHIB alongside the *Waubs Bay*. The seventy-foot steel fishing boat was riding well at anchor, lashing the RHIB alongside they explored the old vessel. Wendy emerged from the wheelhouse surprised.

"It's like stepping back in time, you know, it's like they just left, little fridge is still going, how marvellous is that, pantry, plates just washed and left on the rack to dry, how would the fridge be still going?" Len answered.

"It would be a three-way fridge Wendy, gas, electric and battery, my guess is it's running on Gas, I saw some huge cylinders out on the stern, two bottles, and the fridge wouldn't use much, we might change them though, I saw plenty at the servo."

Between them all they had a good look around, fuel tanks were three quarters full, water tank the same, Josh and Mal detached the mooring line while Vince and Laurel found the fenders and set them up on the port side, the *Mary* was strapped onto the starboard side and now free to manoeuvre both boats into the Gulch.

A couple of hours later, with the *Waubs Bay* alongside, *Mary* still outside of her, the next job was to prep the boat for taking out the buggered E1 affected motor, while another team retrieved the pre 2000 Motor. Len called for volunteers, Mal admitted to having some mechanical knowledge so elected to stay and help remove the donk, while Josh, Wendy, Bill and Vince worked out how to pick up the pre 2000 engine. Watching the jeep drive away, Len's next move was to get the davit boom on the wharf around and lift the engine room hatch.

1420 hours and arriving at the shed in Little Bay, it didn't take Vince long to spy an overhead endless chain, moving the device over the old engine was relatively easy, next challenge was not.

"We need something to put in on, like a trailer; it's too bloody big to fit in the back of the jeep."

1500 hours, Wendy and Bill drove off looking for the allusive trailer, armed with the measurements, this meant they were looking for a large box trailer or even a boat trailer, leaving Josh and Vince to prepare the engine for lifting.

"Can't we just put some chains underneath Vince and lift it that way?"

"No mate the chains would damage some of the external components, what I'm looking for is a short chain and two lugs to bolt into these lift points." The seventeen-year-old thought that was a good idea.

"Jackpot Josh, just what the doctor ordered." The forty-seven-year-old was holding up two lugs and bolts, Josh lifted up two short chains linked to a large oval ring.

"This do Vince?" The ex-navy technician smiled.

"Spot on mate." By the time Wendy and Bill pulled up with an eight by five tandem trailer, Josh and Vince had bolted the lugs to the engine and prepared to lift in with the endless chain. Josh pointed to Bill trying to back the trailer up the driveway.

"Vince, I think you might need to help Bill." Vince smiled to himself at the efforts the ex-Benoa plumber was doing with the backing, he stopped and yelled out to Vince.

"Mate, backing was never my strong point, can you take over?" The pair swapped jobs: Vince levelled the old jeep and trailer up while Bill assisted winching up the motor.

"Stop Vince that's perfect." They lowered the engine onto the same packed up pallet it was sitting on. Looking around the shed, Vince pointed to the drums of diesel engine oil, filters, etc. that looked like they could use, loaded them, then strapped the huge L6 Gardner to the trailer.

1500 hours, at the Gulch, Len, Laurel, Mal and Jill had removed the cover and nearly disconnected the blown engine; all the fuel lines and electrics were tagged and moved out of the way, the lift lugs were still present, but they couldn't find a chain strop anywhere.

"Jeep's back!" Yells Jill, as she poured the crew a round of drinks, she added.

"I suppose I'll have to make one for everyone now." Wendy said

"No problems Jill I'll help." Vince and Josh climbed down to the engine room and helped with some of the mounting bolts, Vince reporting they had a set of lift chains.

1710 hours, not wanting to take the chance with the old boom block and tackle, they swapped out the endless chain Vince had used to lift it on. So lifting it up enough to clear the wharf they then had to manually pull the boom around so they could lower it onto the wharf well out of the way of the replacement. With the blown motor out and the replacement hooked up Jill yelled.

"Can you hear that?" The seventeen-year-old pointed in the direction of the main road, they could all hear it now as the vehicle got closer. Len yelled.

"Vince, you, Laurel and Josh can you check it out, it's got to be Alliance, if it is run them down and kill them."

1810 hours, Vince and crew dissected the main road, the jeep was now travelling down to Barracouta, having gone through the town centre, Vince floored the old KM450 Light Cargo Truck, the 139HP diesel engine was working overtime, normally with a top speed 104k, the ex-navy technician had it up to the max speed, the speedo's in these vehicles only went to 120, and he had it bouncing on the stops, past the road to Little Bay, and down past Len's auntie's home.

"I see them in front, Luv!" Laurel was pointing half a kilometre in front,

"How many Honey?."

"Can't see Luv." The Alliance jeep was travelling at the comfortable speed of ninety, they obviously hadn't seen the jeep behind them.

Vince yelled over the noise.

"Get them Type 68's ready, round the next bend we'll only be 200 metres behind him and boy is he going to get a shock." Making the left hander at 100 kilometres per hour was not what was recommended, but he still had all four wheels on the ground, then straightening up they saw the jeep in front.

"Boom…Boom…Boom…Boom." Both Josh and Laurel opened up, the 7.62 mm rounds finding the back of the jeep; some went through the canvas, some into the tailgate. This did wake up the driver; he swerved, probably while he was trying to look behind him, he speeded up, and then a head could be seen above the cab.

"Looks like he has a passenger." The return fire came.

"Boom…Boom…Boom." Wild shots, but enough to make Vince angry, downhill on a windy road and Vince was in his element, used to the fast speeds he had achieved on his motor bike, he pushed the jeep right to the limit of the little 139 HP motor must have been thinking 'this is the end' round the last bend they were now nearly in the jeep's back pocket,

"Boom…Boom…Boom…Boom." Laurel and Josh fired two rounds each; the jeep swerved violently to the right, through a farm fence and rolled several times. Stopping above the rolled vehicle, Vince nodded to Laurel, handing her the Type 54 suppressed pistol, she hopped the farm wire fence and inspected the upside-down vehicle, Josh and Vince heard the.

"Dooff…Dooff." A bit puffed out the ex-navy communicator reported,

"All dead but I did get a souvenir, another name tag, this time a Lieutenant Colonel Huje Samira." Vince pondered.

"I wonder where the good colonel was going." Laurel smiled then suggested. "Home maybe, his home was one of those that we cleared the other day."

1930 hours, the pre 2000 L6 Gardner was on the mounting blocks, everyone was buggered, Len called a halt to the proceedings, and they thought they would surprise Vince and his crew with a nice dinner. Wendy yelled out.

"Found some meat in the freezer," she sticks her head out of the *Waubs Bay* wheelhouse,

"Should be alright if it's been frozen all the time, looks like a good piece of corned beef and I have found a pressure cooker." Jill contributes a range of vegetables, and salad components, and she soon had the new potatoes boiling away.

2200 hours and in the dark, the streets of Benoa felt eerie, a slow sea mist had closed in and with the jeep's headlights cutting a mystical path through the soft folds and no home lights, no fireplaces active, it resembled a ghost town. Turning into the street that serviced the Gulch was just as fascinating, all they could see was the two lights coming from both vessels.

2330 hours, climbing into bed at the Benoa Motel, Jill shivered as she waited for Len to have a bird bath, she sure missed the hot shower on board the *Nancy Kay,*

Len had warmed the water, but all they could do was a bird bath, the skipper slid in-between the sheets and was soon covered by Jill's body trying to keep warm. He promised her a hot shower once they got the *Waubs Bay* running, the hot water was gas, and the pressure came from the main engine.

Jill kissed the skipper and allowed his hands to explore, reaching between her legs. Collapsing onto the skipper's chest, still shivering he asked.

"Cold Luv?" She smiled, looking up at his stubbled growth, engulfing herself in his odour, lying there for a few moments she realised that he was still inside of her, a little limp but well and truly inside.

Tuesday 10th March 2015 Waubs Bay and Mary at the Gulch Benoa

0800 hours, Len removed the engine room hatch and swung the derrick boom back to cover the pre 2000 motor sitting in the 8 x 5 box trailer. With Len, Mal, Vince and Bill heaving all their weight on the end of the chain block the mighty engine lifted clear of the trailer sides. Jill, Wendy and Laurel were on the end of the endless chain swinging the great motor over the top of the engine mounts, reversing the endless chain, they slowly lowered the beast onto the mounting blocks.

"Just a little bit more guys." Len was watching the gap to the blocks.

"Push a little bit to me, yeah about 5 mm to go, right hold it, lower away at that." Satisfied once the mounting bolts were screwed on finger tight, they took a rest.

1015 hours and with the mounting bolts done up tight and tweaked with the tension wrench they moved on to all of the peripheral equipment, exhaust, fuel lines, air intakes, electronics, gauges etc. Vince yelled.

"What do you want us to do with the buggered motor Len?"

"Maybe if you pick it up and swing it as far as you can off the wharf, we'll cover it with a tarp just in case we need any parts off it later."

1400 hours, "Right Vince hit the starter mate." The ex- navy technician turned on the ignition then hit the starter button.

"Wurrrr...Wurrrr...Wurrrr...Chug...Chug." A plume of black smoke emerged from the exhaust stack, everyone was grinning like Cheshire cats, tightening the fuel lines again and all the other clamps they lowered the hatch and made it secure. Vince asked.

"What's the plan Len, or do we consult Dick?" The thirty-nine-year-old skipper scratched his stubble.

"Well, we need to put a barricade up to protect us from the north, probably at the bridge north of the Five Mile Creek, then work out what happens to this vessel, where Dick and Doc can use her the most and then we have to work out who's going to crew her."

1724 hours, Vince and Laurel had a round table with Len and Jill, working out who could skipper the *Waubs Bay.*

"It really boils down to either you Len or me," stated Vince.

"I agree Vince, before we ask Dick, do you want to skipper her, or do you want to work between here and Sand Alley in the *Mary* or even the smaller RHIB?" Getting the nod from Laurel, the ex-navy electronic technician replied.

"I think we would rather be in the south of the state, we could back up the Oxford Barricade or the Five Mile Creek one, but that means you have to skipper her are you happy with that?" Len was nodding in the affirmative.

"I reckon Jill, Josh and I could take the boat north if that's what is required, anything to win this war, might as well ring Dick."

"Brrr ... Brrr ... Brrr ... me again Dick, yep, we got the donk changed and she goes like a dream, question is mate what do you want her to do? Ah well we have been discussing this between Vince and Laurel and Jill and I. Well, Vince is happy to stay and back up everything down here, so it looks like I'm skipper and yep, Jill and Josh, right, we will pack some food and set off in a couple of days."

Chapter 18
High Head has a Win

Monday 9ᵗʰ March 2015 Bull Bay Ramat River

0830 hours, Ernie, Belle, Nic, Smokey, Boz and Gaz watched as the FCPB turned to starboard and headed out of the Ramat River. Waiting till the *Nancy Kay* and *Dementia* were secured alongside; Ernie suggested a round table with the two skippers to try and work out the next phase of the operation.

Stepping on board the sixty-five-foot *Conquest*, they joined Santa and crew in the wheelhouse. Joined by Buck and crew off the *Dementia* they excitedly waited for Ernie to start.

The sixty-five-year-old suggested all the TRF troops gather on the quarterdeck of the *Nancy Kay*, he would hold the meeting there.

0900 hours, "Thanks for all your effort, over the last week or so, we certainly kicked some arse, but we have one serious problem, first of all we have potentially too many fronts, and we don't have the manpower to put blockades on all of them. Yes, we have decimated the Alliance in Lawn, and we think from our reccy patrols they have withdrawn to Earth and set up shop there. We did kill their leader, but it won't take them long to replace him. My suggestion at the moment is this-

- Those of you from Bass Island/ *Spirit of Taswegia II* can go back with Santa and the *Nancy Kay* for a rest, Santa's job will be to gather and train a force to help invade St Anne.
- We keep the *Dementia* here to patrol the river and assist with whatever we have to do on the river, that's if Buck is ok with that outcome.
- We also need roving patrols at the extremities like Lawn Central, South Lawn, Ugly Point, Lion Point, Ex, Armada, the back roads between here and Brid, Scott, back roads between Ugly Point and West.

If we can keep the Alliance south of Earth, when the Northwest boys clear across the West, we should have them on their back feet. Before I finish, are there any questions? Yes Tegan?"

"I'm the Medical officer of the *Taswegia II*, what if I don't want to go back to the ship? After all there is nothing for me there, probably the same for some of the others."

"Where would you see yourself living Tegan?"

"Well not in any hot spots, I thought if we could get a few of us together, take up residence close to here, I know a few of us would like to be included in the rest of the war, for instance, I had an uncle who lived at Gary Town, maybe I could use his old place, after all he's not coming back to live there." Ernie could see the logic in all of what the young medical officer had said.

"Alright, let's make it simple, hands up all those that want to go back to Boss Island?" There was quite a lot of murmuring coming from the eighty odd TRF members present, slow to respond

Ernie could only detect half a dozen hands, and these were all Boss Island residents. Smokey took over.

"Are you all happy to continue with the fight, man patrols in and around those areas we mentioned and eventually mount a push East towards St Anne when the time comes?"

There was a general nodding of approval from the crowd, he added.

"Alright, we will leave it up to you to find accommodation, might I suggest the G-Town Hotel, close to the area, easy to guard and not a bad view either, but if anyone has particular dwellings belonging to family, your welcome to inhabit them. We have plenty of vehicles to go around, maybe not quite one each but between half a dozen of you, it should be alright."

1100 hours, the first job was to take twelve members over to the Ugly Point Wharf and collect all the vehicles, Sarge and Henry's teams had acquired. With the vehicles successfully split amongst the members, Ernie and Smokey called for volunteers to run the first roving patrols, while Santa and crew topped up fuel and water, loaded some of the Alliance captured weapons and ammo. Some 400 Type 68 assault rifles, 250 Type 54 pistols, the ammo was becoming light on with only 10,000 rounds of 7.62 (25 average per trooper) and 2000 rounds of 9mm (average one 8 round magazine each).

1300 hours, only eight TRF members were on board the *Nancy Kay* for the return journey to Boss Island, with goodbyes out of the way the sixty-one-year-old ex-navy CD yelled.

"Drop all lines." Santa's crew had slipped the *Dementia* first, then went out away from the wharf astern, allowing Buck to manoeuvre the fifty-five-footer back alongside. Spinning the sixty-five-foot *Conquest* on the spot he then pushed both throttles ahead bringing the boat up to fifteen knots, with everyone waving on the quarterdeck, Santa cleared the entrance to the Ramat River, turned slightly to starboard then bought the boat up to cruising speed, just over planning speed, eighteen to twenty knots. Setting the auto pilot he wrapped his arm around Pat.

"Wonder how Dick and the boys are going?"

His wife of forty-one years smiled, realising that this was the most she had seen Santa since the navy days, she appreciated, that like all sailors, you can take the sailor out of the navy, but you can't take the navy out of the sailor, she thought that 'this was the most alive she had seen him.'

1900 hours and the crew of the *Nancy Kay* could make out the makings of Blackmark in the distance, and with the tide right, they were electing not to eat until they were alongside. This made it easier on them all in the wicked Nor Westerly Sea hammering the boat.

Most of the people on board were in their bunks with the exception of Santa and Vert. Both men were sitting in the chairs, basically holding on when each wave hit them on the port beam, using the seatbelts was the best way to fight the sea state.

"Can't do much about it, Vert, I've backed off to ten knots, any slower and we would be going astern." They just waited until they got closer to land, then as soon as it presented itself, it abated.

"Crikey Skipper, it's almost like someone turned off the tap."

Bringing the sixty-five-footer into Blackmark Harbour was now certainly easier the swell had knocked off, spinning around and coming alongside starboard side to. Vert soon had the springs, bow and stern lines on, running the engine down, Santa eventually shut it off. No one was about, it was like a ghost town, they had seen a bit of movement on the *Spirit* as they passed her, they could make out the dinghy tied up to her cargo doorway.

2200 hours and Vert picked up the scotch bottle, pointing to the skipper as if to ask his approval,

"Why not Vert, been a busy few days, the troops have left us to go home to their beds, good feed girls, what about you Barry, a wee drop?" The thirty-year-old builder nodded in the affirmative. Pat remarked.

"What about us girls' luv?" Giving Rose a wink as if to stir the boys up,

"I didn't think you liked scotch luv." Rose appeared from her cabin with a bottle of Tia Maria and smiled at Pat.

"Now you're talking Rose." With glasses charged they toasted the TRF and the next part of the war.

1400 hours, Gary Town, most of the vehicles had deposited the TRF members from Taswegia II at the G-Town Motel. This luxury motel was built when G-Town was to become another port for the second Strait crossing, unfortunately being a fast Catamaran, it was unsuccessful; due to sea sickness. The sixty-four-room motel was now perfect to house most of the members.

Tegan grabbed a lift into town with Henry and his crew; she would make a home at her uncle's place down by the water on the opposite side of the bay to the motel.

"Thanks for the lift, guys; I suppose I'll see you when you need me, at least I think that's what Ernie meant." The forty-one-year-old knew where the key was and let herself in. She could see evidence of blood in a few rooms, not really knowing whether it was from her uncle and aunty or the Alliance Nationals that moved in after. She figured she would just clean it up anyway.

1700 hours and she was pondering as to what meal she could concoct out of the pantry, not more than a dozen tins of food, it was going to be slim pickings, soon beginning to realise that a modern home was completely the wrong house in this climate, with electric, heating, cooking, hot water there wasn't much she could do.

"Bang, Bang, anyone home?" Tegan heard the banging on the front door, 'who could that be' she thought, then she did a double take thinking this was the way they got into Alliance homes! Grabbing her Type 54 pistol, she gingerly opened the front door, ready to fire off a few rounds if need be.

"Shit Henry you scared the living crap out of me!" Lowering the pistol she asked him in,

"Come in mate, I'm having trouble, can't even offer you a coffee." The ex-copper smiled.

"That's what I thought, so I brought along some help." He returned to the jeep and carried in a gas BBQ complete with wok burner, gas kettle and a huge basket of food, putting her in charge of making the coffees they soon had the makings of a meal on the hot plate, sausages, bacon, onions and tomato, some crusty bread in foil to heat up.

"Well, you have outdone yourself Henry! I'm impressed!" Sipping his drink as he turned the sausages he admitted.

"You know, I was driving back to the Tunnel Complex, and I realised, the contract I had with Charlotte was over and then I thought of you all alone, probably no food so I wanted to officially ask if I could see you, then I thought nah! Don't be a goose, cook her a meal." Tegan was slightly embarrassed.

"Well Henry, I am flattered and well I love the meal idea, it would have been awesome if you had asked me." The ex-senior constable grinned, dropped to one knee and asked her out on a date.

"And to sweeten the deal, I have this, he uncovered a bottle of Shiraz."

"The answer is a big fat yes. I am so chuffed." She kissed him. He returned the kiss, maybe a little more passionate. The medical officer found some candles, setting them up in the lounge room as Henry brought in the cooked delights, finding a couple of glasses he poured the red wine.

2200 hours, "well that was a wonderful meal Tegan, but I think I must be getting back, may I see you again?" The forty-one-year-old couldn't believe it, a true gentleman.

"Tomorrow, show me your town."

Tuesday 10th March 2015 Nancy Kay Blackmark

0800 hours, Vert and Rose, the last to emerge from their love den, Vert dressed in his very predictable blue shorts, Reebok sneakers and army green tee-shirt. Rose on the other hand, usually wafting around in a long cotton Kaftan style dress, today was dressed in a pair of Vert's pale blue shorts, singlet style top and the usual thongs. By the way her breasts were moving, trapped under the singlet it was obvious there was no bra in sight.

"Morning Skipper, Pat, so what's on the agenda for today?" The ex-CD smiled above his steaming hot brew.

"Might do a reccy around the town, try and find some of the locals, I reckon it won't be long before someone on the *Spirit* sees us here and paddles ashore, we will try and get some volunteers from her as well." Pat pointed at the passenger ship,

"Dinghy coming ashore now luv, looks like four people on board."

0840 hours and Captain Bradley Scott climbed aboard the sixty-five-footer first, followed by his first officer, John Williams, Jock Page and making up the four was Wallace Bellows the ship's engineer. Santa introduced his crew and addressed the captain.

"Nice to catch up Captain, how has it been going here while we were away?" The fifty-nine-year-old captain reported.

"Most of the passengers have dispersed amongst the islanders, it's mainly the senior crew that prefer to camp on board, the International Hotel is full of passengers and some crew, so should be a good source of recruits, I presume that's why you're back?" Santa detected some sarcasm in the captain's remark.

"Two reasons, Captain, we delivered some TRF members back to their families and yes we are here to train more troops for a major objective." John asked.

"What has happened to the other officers from the ship, Tegan, Brian, Gary and Jillian has anything happened to them?"

"Not at all John, they chose to stay at Gary Town, I think Tegan is in her uncle's home and the rest are at the Gary Town Hotel with the other TRF members."

The captain and his senior officers enquired as to how the fight was going, Santa and Vert filling the group in with the updated results of the raid on Lawn and surrounding areas, the ex-CD continued.

"At the moment we have active war zones in the following areas, Northwest, the *Fremantle* is at Brownsville and has troops heading to Alfred River and towards Devon, successfully rescued the Bird Island people. Our West Coast members are on the outskirts of Kings Bridge. The Dove group are at Apples, supported by the vessels, *Cougar Anne* and the *Retaliator*, the *Black Ink* is raiding the coastal towns towards Kettle. I believe we have another vessel there, can't remember her name, the Peninsular mob are in control of Soothe and we have just moved into Benoa after the Indonesians moved north to St Anne." Vert added.

"*Tangara* Skipper" the *Spirit of Taswegia II* Captain takes the brew handed to him by Rose.

"I'm impressed, it looks like you or should I say we have a firm hold on our state." Santa did a double take, letting the captains' words sink in.

"I take it from those remarks are we expecting you to join the TRF captain?"

Before the fifty-nine-year-old could reply the second officer butted in.

"I think I can speak for us four, and the answer is yes, we all would like to join the fight." The mood was ecstatic, everyone was shaking hands; the women were given hugs and pecks on the cheek.

1000 hours, Boss Island International Hotel foyer, John had rounded up crew and some passengers he thought would now be keen to join the cause, the group followed John, Bradley, Jock and Wallace to the secluded beach.

Santa and Vert using the same trolley as before, had brought some weapons and made their way to the area used last time for training. As the pair sat, they watched the large group coming up the sandy road.

"Shit Santa, looks like John and the Captain have quite a following, how many do you reckon?" The ex-CD taking his time.

"Got to be a good fifty or sixty mate, and a few women."

1430 hours, with the main part of the training out of the way, the last few were having their turn on the Type 54 pistols, the ex-RAEME soldier commented.

"I reckon that there are about ten that I wouldn't take, too old and too frail Skipper."

"I agree mate, but at least they are keen, might leave it and see if we can use their services in another way. I wouldn't want to turn them down when they are so enthusiastic."

Telling the group, they were required the next day for more training, Santa and Vert made their way back to the *Nancy Kay*, reporting the day's results to the women keen to find out all the gossip.

1700 hours. "How many did we get Luv?" asked Pat. Her and Rose had been scrounging ashore, successfully filling the pantry and had invited the *Spirit* sailors to dinner. Vert had the specs from the shoot.

"Apart from the four officers, we had six other crew members and forty-eight passengers, now out of the crew there were four females and out of the passengers there were twenty females. Fifteen of them were there with their partners, ages ranged from a seventeen-year-old girl passenger (although I suspect she was probably nearer to fifteen and right up to eighty-seven, the Bristol couple, actually he was a good shot, she I wouldn't let near a weapon again."

1810 hours, the crew of the *Nancy Kay* greeted the *Spirit* officers, Rose and Pat had dressed the trestle table out on the quarterdeck, scrounged enough chairs ashore to seat everyone. Pat manned the BBQ, cooking porterhouse steaks while Rose dealt with the new potatoes and salad, wine and spirits flowed abundantly.

The *Spirit* captain leant back in his chair, quite satisfied with the best meal he had eaten in a long time asked.

"What did you think of the troops today, Santa, will they cut the mustard and for my curiosity where will the action be?" Going over the concerns that Vert had brought up earlier, they all agreed it would be a shame if the worst of them could not be used in another way. Not knowing when the offensive would be was a small problem, but they did know it would be at St

Anne, like before an assault by two vessels right into the heart of the town.

Tuesday 17th March 2015 High Head Tunnel System

1000 hours, for the last week, the northern contingent of the TRF had kept the Alliance at bay south of Lawn on the outskirts of Earth. They had a major fire fight on the twelfth near Ex when their truck was ambushed. Eventually they managed to outflank the troops but took heavy casualties, skirmishes on the river were taken care of by the *Dementia* crew. Henry had become a little smitten by the attractive *Spirit of Taswegia II* medical officer, accompanying her on most of the raids and patrols; it was Belle who first commented.

"When are you going to bring her here to meet us?" The sixty-year-old was beginning to sound like Henry's mother.

Going on another raid that night, two jeeps were checking the back roads near West, there had been some clearing three days ago and they wanted to check whether the Alliance had cleared the bodies or not. Henry just smiled.

"Point taken Mum, now who's coming with me? Boz, Claudia and Bill you still ok with the raid? Second jeep going out today will drop members at the wharf and travel upriver on the *Dementia*, they are Smokey, Nic, Boz, and Kylie if your leg is up to it Kylie?"

Tuesday 17th March 2015 55-foot Conquest Dementia Bull Bay Wharf

1130 hours and Buck, Sue, Laurie, May, Nick, Trent and Chris all waiting for the jeep to arrive. They had done a patrol every day with Smokey as pilot. This was another one of these, they had taken to stopping at different jetties along the way, checking if there was any Alliance Nationals or troops hiding out.

"Single up all lines, I can see the jeep." With Smokey, Nic, Baz and Kylie settled in, Buck started the engine.

"Drop all lines." Spinning the wheel to starboard, then going ahead just a touch, he fended off the starboard bow enough to swing her stern out, then going astern straightening the wheel amidships he waited for the boat to nearly stop then turning to port he went ahead, out in the river, he handed the helm over to the river pilot.

1230 hours and the *Dementia* was approaching the Batt Bridge, steaming at eight knots there were four sets of eyes peering through binoculars, constantly panning the sides of the river. Just through the bridge Smokey turned to port hugging the eastern side of the river up into Sprung Bay.

"Might as well do the reverse of last time Buck; never know we might find some runaways."

"You're the pilot Smokey, right crew, check your weapons, magazines loaded, safety's on."

Buck had mounted a Bren gun on a homemade stand that could be used on either side of the boat near the pot hauler. Nic yelled out.

"Movement on the port side, near that boat ramp." The ex-navy river pilot pushed the throttles forward to bring the boat to twenty knots, pushing quite a bow wave in the calm reaches of Sprung Bay.

"Keep your eye on the movement, and someone watch my depth." Buck was peering at the shore; Pat looking at the depth sounder.

"I've got them now!" yelled Buck. Pat added.

"Four metres Smokey." They were within 200 metres of the shore and Laurie could make out three heads, one female, Buck cocked the Bren.

"Engaging now guys, Boom...Boom...Boom...Boom...Boom." The extremely loud pre-1960's gun spat out the .303 rounds out of its thirty-round curved magazine, if anything, this weapon was too accurate and at 200 metres it found its mark.

"Two down, one on the run, silly bitch, she should have stayed where she was, boom...boom, she's down now but not finished." The river pilot headed to the boat ramps small jetty.

"Three metres, Skipper." going astern, the vessel created a muddy concoction as she stirred up the bottom.

Nudging the jetty, Buck and Boz stepped ashore, Boz checking the two heads for vitals while Buck ran the 300 metres to where the girl was dropped. Reaching the woman, the ex-CD petty officer could see that the .303 round had hit her in the pelvis. Determined to not give up she had dragged herself almost 100 metres, un-holstering his supressed Type 54 pistol he held it on the NK Nationals forehead, "Boof."

Tuesday 17ᵗʰ March 2015 Tegan Collin's Residence Gary Town

1130 hours, Henry stopped the old jeep outside of Tegan's house, Boz, Claudia and Bill were in the back, the medical officer smiling as she acknowledged them all. She was dressed in black cargo style pants, a white Spirit shirt and her red woollen jumper, sliding into the front seat alongside Henry the ex-senior police officer leaned over and kissed her. The first display of affection in public startled the medical officer then she smiled, deep down she was touched.

1200 hours, driving across the Ramat River Bridge Boz asked.

"What back road are we checking again Henry?"

"Back way into West, it's the only one we haven't been down for a week, just wanting to know whether the Alliance has been there since we cleared it." Tegan asked.

"Were all the properties occupied Henry when you cleared it?"

"About half and no troopers."

Driving to the West Ramat Highway they turned left, making sure everyone had loaded their weapons with safety's on Henry suggested they sit with their Type 68's upright between their legs, that way if you needed it in a hurry, it was quicker to bring the weapon to bear. Just a few kilometres down the highway they entered Ex, turning right on the back Ex to Devon Road they had to travel about thirty kilometres to the back West Road. Always cautious, the group scanned the sides of the road for trouble. Ernie and team had cleared bodies up to the back West Road, burnt them in a roadside quarry, so the bodies along this road should still be there.

1300 hours, turning left they stopped at the first property on the corner, Boz and Kylie did the reccy and reported no bodies, no Alliance.

"Thanks Boz and Kylie, I'm not sure whether Ernie's mob cleared this one or not, the next house will tell us, it's about 5 kilometres on the left." Stopping in front Henry said.

"Tegan and I will check this one, but still keep your eyes peeled." The pair entered via the back door; the smell of blood was still evident. Tegan had to cover her mouth with a handkerchief, Henry stopped her.

"I'll finish it luv." The ex-senior Constable checked all rooms, meeting Tegan out the back she asked.

"How many bodies Henry?" Wrapping his right arm around her slim waist, he kissed her with all the passion he could muster.

"Twelve my lovely, they need clearing before they decompose anymore."

1500 hours and they found themselves at the outskirts of West, stopping the General M151Diesel Variant jeep on a slight rise overlooking the town the group could see smoke coming from a few chimneys on the main road.

"Maybe another day we should look at clearing this town, might bring it up with Ernie and see how it fits in with the master plan." Turning the vehicle around they headed back to High Head.

Tuesday 17ᵗʰ March 2015 55-foot Conquest Dementia Lawn Marina

1400 hours, Ramat River, *Dementia* easing back on the throttle, Smokey turned to port and the Lawn Marina unfolded in front of them. Trent lowered the binoculars and pointed.

"Movement on the ramp to the Ramat Hotel on the right." Nick and Kylie both picked up the body, and then Buck saw it, Nick volunteered.

"I'll take the shot with my Type 68." Not being able to get the Bren to bear on the target, they gave the twenty-one-year-old apprentice builder the shot.

"Boom...Boom...Boom." A short burst out of the Type 68 assault rifle, at least one round found its mark, now a little closer, Buck reported.

"Looks like a trooper, could be return fire if he's not alone. Smokey, taking no chances went astern and put the fifty-five-footer alongside one of the fingers some 100 metres from the ramp. The downed trooper had crawled behind the power supply box.

"Incoming fire." The Boom, Boom, Boom sending rounds into the side of *Dementia*. With only fibreglass to stop them it wasn't working, with the Bren now able to bear on the man, Buck opened up sending half a magazine into the shore power box he was hiding behind. Silence, did they get him or not, Nick and Trent climbed ashore and tried to flank the trooper, making it to the top level outside one of the restaurants, they opened up on his position. With no return fire they continued towards the shore power box, seeing the man was lying behind it they approached, leaning over the body Trent reported,

"Dead mate." Then from the second floor of the hotel.

"Boom...Boom...Boom, and Boom." An accurate volley of fire rained down on the pair, with no cover from the hotel they were cut down where they stood. Hearing the fire from *Dementia*, Buck and Nic sighted the first-floor balcony, they could see the sniper and Buck opened up with the Light Machine Gun. The sniper was obviously not expecting such fire power, and he stayed outside his cover longer than he needed to.

"Fuck, Fuck the boys are down, cover me!" Buck grabbed Laurie and they ran towards the hotel, Buck went to the fire escape and up to the first floor, on the boat they could hear the loud booms of his Type 68, then finally on the balcony he waved for Laurie to check the boys.

"Sorry Buck, both dead!"

Monday 16th March 2015 Nancy Kay Blackmark

0900 hours, weapons training had been constant every day for the week; and the rest of the crew had been busy doing maintenance. Rose and Pat working on re-supplying the boats pantry with dry and tinned food. Vert had struck a deal with one of the local farmers to swap a Type 68 rifle for a full beast.

Len, Jill and Josh had successfully delivered the *Waubs Bay*, arriving Saturday afternoon; they all took part in the weapons training on Sunday, giving the crew some practice.

1000 hours, full crew meeting including the four officers off the *Spirit of Taswegia II* and the crew of the *Waubs Bay*.

"Thanks for attending, I guess main issue today is to finalise the numbers of the raiding party to be used in the advance on St Anne. The original plan was to train 100 TRF members for the raid with thirty on the *Waubs Bay*, thirty on the *Nancy* and forty on the *Fremantle*. Vert after nearly a week of training, are we any better off?" Consulting his little engineer's notebook

"Stats go like this, all the crew are doing fine, and I might add some of the women are better shots than the men. Passengers, the fifteen couples are getting better and actually quite a competition was developing between them all. The old couple haven't been participating after Mr Bristol, nearly cleaned up a group, swung around whilst pulling the trigger; if it wasn't for John here, we would have six dead members. Mrs Bristol just couldn't work out which way was which, pointing the business end at other members, safety off, I think it would be advisable to give the pair another job. I did find out that before they retired, they ran a restaurant!"

"What about the seventeen-year-old mate?"

"Ah yes, the seventeen, more like fourteen-year-old, the small girl had no problems with the Type 54, took a while for her to get used to holding the stock of the Type 68 tighter, to stop the recoil bruising her shoulder. Poor girl, by last Thursday she had a huge bruise, so I took her off the rifle and just concentrated on the pistol, but if you're asking will she be ok, I'd have to say yes and out of the fifty-eight participants total, we really only lost one. He was just not cut out for this sort of work; he didn't turn up Wednesday and we haven't chased him, so final numbers are fifty-five competent TRF members and two caterers." Captain Scott asked

"Is this going to be enough Santa, If Dick wanted 100 and we can only come up with fifty-five?" The ex-CD replied

"Captain, Dick knows full well you can't force people to take part and to answer the next question before it comes, I am ringing him now." Reaching for the brick phone he dialled the *Fremantle.*

"Brrr ... Brrr ... Brrr ... yeah mate its Santa here, right I'll wait ... g'day Dick, well we have just finished six days of weapons training, yep Len and crew arrived Saturday, no, the bad news is we only have fifty-five total, yep you heard right, oh and two caterers, good news the fifty-three are better than average. St Anne push, right we will continue with the training and try to find a few more members, but I do agree fifty-three good ones is better than eighty bad ones." Hanging up the receiver he continued.

"Well Dick can live with the numbers, the raid on St Anne will probably be in about ten days, we will use the time to get the *Waubs Bay* cleaned up, maybe an engine oil change, and maybe some of the TRF members trained up as deckhands." John added.

"The crew from the *Spirit* should yield the deckhands."

"Fantastic John, we also can send a few of our better shots out for some game, we have to keep the freezers full, so I'll leave that up to Vert to organise."

Tuesday 17th March 2015 Bull Bay Wharf

1800 hours, Henry, Tegan, Boz, Claudia and Bill watched as the *Dementia* eased alongside the wharf, taking the mooring lines from Nic, Henry could tell the mood was sombre. Engine shut down they assembled on the aft deck, and it took a while for Henry's lot to notice the absence of Trent and Nick. Henry asked.

"Shit raid Buck?" The sixty-one-year-old went on to describe the ambush at the marina and the loss of the two boys, they had recovered the bodies and were going to bury them in the G-Town Cemetery alongside the other TRF members that had fallen.

Wednesday 18th March 2015 Tegan's Residence Gary Town

1700 hours, returning from the burial services for Trent and Nick, Henry pulled the General M151Diesel Variant jeep up in the driveway to Tegan's uncle's home, the medical officer remarked.

"Dinner is on me tonight." As she walked the few paces to the front door, Henry admired the way she looked. Choosing to wear a uniform skirt to the funeral, it was the first time the medical officer had been out of slacks, whether this was because of the attention Henry was giving her or not, she felt more like a woman that day, the blue skirt was above the knee showing quite a bit of her shapely legs, the top was simple, a white bodice with pretty lace around the top dipping at the cleavage just enough to show off her curves.

"What are we dining on tonight my dear?" She loved the way Henry spoke to her; she loved the fact he was doing it right.

"Never you mind," she playfully replied. Henry wrapped his arms around her waist, holding her tight against his body, he kissed her passionately.

"Bribery will get you nowhere, just fire up the gas stove for me." Smiling Tegan had thought about the last week or so, Henry had been the perfect gentleman, nothing improper at all about his manner.

1900 hours, pulling the cork on a bottle of Bubbly extracted from the 12-volt car fridge, the ex-senior constable poured the two glasses and watched as Tegan served the meal, she had managed to salvage fresh vegetables from her uncle's garden, adding them to a couple of tins of spaghetti sauce with meatballs served over packet fettuccini pasta and grated parmesan cheese, she could already tell he was impressed.

"Fantastic luv!" she leaned over and kissed him.

2010 hours, dishes done, the last of the wine topping up their glasses, they were lounging on the huge couch, reminiscing about watching television, having power, the things they used to take for granted. Henry was sitting with the couch reclined while Tegan lay along the couch over Henry's lap. Looking up at the forty-four-year-old's face she admired his many features, short, cropped hair, clean shaven with the hint of aftershave, she rubbed his chest and neck while he caressed her breasts.

Friday 20th March 2015 TRF Patrol Lawn

1700 hours and Ernie, Belle, Boz and Kylie had left the funeral and headed into Lawn for their bi-weekly reccy, keeping an eye on Alliance occupation. Passing Duck Point they prepped their weapons, as usual they all had pistols and webbing along with the Type 68-assault rifle, all loaded with spare magazines. The aging jeep was having trouble getting up some of the hills along the way, the Willys MC 60 hp engine struggled with the four passengers, weapons and ammo.

On the outskirts of Lawn, they stopped overlooking the approach to the city and the suburb of Invers. Using the binoculars, Ernie and Boz were scouring the horizon for signs of movement, a person or a vehicle, because where there was movement there was trouble.

"Can't see any movement uncle Ern."

"Nor I Boz, we'll take a swing through the middle of town and check." Driving along the Invers centre they soon found themselves driving past the town hall, the old alliance HQ. The town was beginning to resemble something out of a horror movie. Shops had their windows smashed, contents out on the street, evidence of wild dogs violating the Alliance corpses. Kylie admitted to the group.

"I hate this town now, it's too spooky with no one around, gives me the creeps." She snuggled into Boz's arm and tried not to think about it. Ernie pulled up outside a well-known supermarket as Belle wanted to check out the shelves, whether they were empty or maybe something left to add to their pantry.

"We'll come with you, aunty Flood." With the three of them disappearing into the Woolworths store, Ernie was starting to get the jitters, he found his eyes were everywhere.

1800 hours, Inside the huge supermarket Belle was quite surprised to find a lot of items were still on the shelves. Mainly tinned stuff that was a bit way out and maybe not to everyone's liking. Kylie found a selection of beans that had fallen down behind a display board.

"Look at this Belle, Kylie holding up chilli beans, beans in black bean sauce, beans and mince." Boz found a selection of mixed lollies, some of the bags were split but he did manage to select some that weren't. Belle was in front of the Asian section and found tinned Shitake mushrooms, bean sprouts and tinned lemongrass.

Making their way back to the escalator their attention was drawn to movement over the road. Stopping at the huge window overlooking the road it looked like a patrol of Alliance troopers, six or seven of them on foot. They obviously hadn't seen Ernie, and the jeep parked around the corner between the road and the undercover car park. With nothing except their pistols, they felt a little under armed. The trio emerged at the bottom of the escalator and now at the same level as the troopers. They had a problem, to get to the jeep they would have to expose themselves when exiting the shop to turn down the lane to the car park. The troopers didn't seem in a hurry to move on and at one stage it looked like they were coming across the street, Boz has an idea.

"We make a noise, they come to investigate, and we ambush them." Kylie wasn't sure she liked the idea; Belle was sitting on the fence.

"After we make a noise Uncle Ern will come to help us." Boz sent the girls back up the escalator while he hid underneath it, he had arranged for Belle to send a shopping trolley over the edge making a noise.

"Rattle, Rattle and Bang." The trolley certainly made a noise, Boz couldn't see from where he was hiding but Kylie could and telling him as they approached the doors.

"Two, no four are coming across the road towards you now and two more after that, four metres behind the first group."

The young assistant river pilot could hear the door open, whispering voices then footsteps on the escalator. He waited a few seconds hoping the door would open again, it did, a few seconds more whispering voices then footsteps on the escalator again. Boz crawled out from under the steps at the same time Belle showed herself at the top, with the six troopers trapped between Boz and Belle, and not having their weapons drawn, they were stuffed, Boz held the pistol with both hands to steady his aim.

"Boof...Boof...Boof." The supressed rounds finding their mark on the last three.

"Bang...Bang...Bang...Bang." Belle's un-supressed weapon, a lot louder cutting the first four down, the whole six falling backwards down the steep stairs. Boz was also watching the two troopers still on the other side of the road,

"Boom, Boom, Boom, Boom," their type 68's bellowed out their 7.62 mm rounds, smashing the glass in the door and adjacent window, making Boz seek cover, the pair were peppering the top floor, now aware that is where they thought the threat was coming from. From his cover the twenty seven-year-old could see the troopers casually walking across the road all the time peppering the top floor then.

"Boom...Boom." The sound came from the alley way cutting the troopers down. Boz yelled out.

"Are you two alright up there?" Kylie stuck her head over the balcony.

"Yep, we're fine, was that Ernie?" The sixty-five-year-old checking the vitals of the two in the street,

"Dooff." Looks like he had to finish one off. The girls hauled their booty down the escalator stepping over the dead bodies, Ernie complained.

"Last fucking time I bring you all to go shopping."

Chapter 19
Alliance Re-Groups

Wednesday 18th March 2015 New Lawn HQ

0800 hours and the newly promoted Major Pin Lim Ho had withdrawn his troops to Earth. The action at Duck Point had failed, with the rebels successfully over running his men, one of the major problems was lack of ammunition. He had sent out snipers to try and ambush the rebels, one set at the Lawn Hotel overlooking the marina, he was fully aware that the rebels had sea power, so he also sent out roving patrols, no vehicles to be more stealth like.

"Give this to the courier going through to Kings Town Corporal." The forty-two-year-old major had outlined his concerns to the general, mainly lack of ammunition and he was also running out of men. From the original 75,000 troops he landed with they now only had 8,000 and half of these were in homes as guards, but the ammunition was really bad, each man would only have around 1 magazine's worth, his back-up supplies were sitting at around 2000 7.62 mm and 500 9 mm.

Wednesday 18th March 2015 Kings Town HQ

0800 hours, the general was sitting at his desk pondering over the last week's events, the humiliating defeat of the raid on Soothe, the untimely death of his Senior Lieutenant Lum Si Gow. The forty-year-old veteran's loss truly saddened the general; he had the pleasure of seeing the combat veteran come up through the ranks and had served with him against South Korea when he was a sergeant.

Two days ago, at his weekly meeting the outcome was not much better, he had not received a report from Devon or Brownsville, although the one from Lawn looked promising with two major offensives against the rebel force. He was looking forward to today, this was the day when the huge Incat would be launched, and his engineers had reported they were ready for sea trials.

"Come Captain, let's go and inspect our navy!"

Pulling up outside the old Incat boat shed, the general was optimistic about the huge catamaran.

1000 hours, "Captain, what's the old engineer's name again?"

"Guhn Kuhn General."

"Ah yes, thank you Captain." The pair entered the huge building that housed the eighty-five metre Cat.

"Good morning Guhn Kuhn, I see you are ready to launch the boat" The seventy-eight-year-old looked at the general, not really liking the way he had been coerced into the job in the first place.

"Yes General, all is ready if you want to launch today?"

Jun Lee was urgently needing some sea power, he had a squad standing by and three of the *Warrnambool's* crew, that were ashore drunk when their patrol boat sunk alongside the refuelling wharf, the marine experience was what they were sadly lacking.

"Well, Guhn, let's see it in the water," the old motor mechanic releasing the brake on the huge winch slowly, fully aware that with no power to drive the winch, this would be a one-way journey down. The cable inched off the drum, the metal train wheels screeched as they rotated along the track, having had no use in quite some time. Guhn watched as the winch drum heated up. Hoping it would not fail; two of his helpers were on board the huge Cat, along with the general's mixed up crew. Pouring water over the brake drum kept it cool enough to continue.

1200 hours, with the Catamaran in the water still attached by the cable, Guhn instructed the ex-*Warrnambool* sailor to start the main engine. The retired motor mechanic had managed to find an old hydraulic pump and alternator to bolt on to the front of the huge 100hp Lister engine.

The vessel's steering was hydraulic, and the alternator supplied power to tll stophe high voltage system, running instruments. The large capacity batteries he scrounged would be dual purpose, starting all low voltage systems on board. A rumble came from the bowels of the huge Cat, the Lister was running, the Morse cable system for operating the gearbox was tested, and the Wartsila Water Jet pump was working. The general was excited and wanted to get on board for the test run. Once on board, the pair sat up on the bridge while the makeshift crew ran around.

"Slipping the cable now!" Yelled Guhn, as he watched the vessel move backwards, the senior sailor from the *Warrnambool* was elevated to captain of the vessel, his original role was watch keeper.

Moving the starboard Morse control to astern, the giant vessel responded slowly and moved astern out into the bay. Spinning the ship's wheel to port, the helmsman moved the starboard Morse control ahead, the giant catamaran was slow to respond to the wheel and at one stage the vessel came close to hitting the wharf on the starboard quarter. Now mid-stream in the river, they moved towards the Kings Town bridge, past the old Zinc Factory, the general was impressed,

"What do you think Captain, is this good enough to go up against the rebels?" The forty-year-old thought about all what he knew about ships.

"I guess it depends what armament we will be putting on board sir, and how much faster it goes." The general beckoned to the helmsman.

"Push her up to full speed sailor, and let's see what she can do." The ex-*Warrnambool* sailor turned to the general.

"This is as fast as she goes sir, six knots."

"Start the other motor man!" The general was showing his annoyance. Looking at the now irate general, he had trouble spitting out the words.

"There is no other motor sir."

"What, do you mean, no other motor, this is a Catamaran, I might not know too much about boats, but I do know there is supposed to be two motors on a Catamaran." Guhn was listening and tried to walk away from the bridge when, the general yelled for him to present himself and he did so sheepishly.

"I could only find the one suitable engine General, and it has taken all this time to prepare it to replace the original, we had to find hydraulic pump and alternator." The captain and the general could see the man was truly upset.

Piloting the huge vessel into the main wharf area of Kings Town was not as easy as it appeared; the steerage was unresponsive to starboard and not much better to port but they did manage to get her alongside. Jun Lee was aware that even if they did find another motor, it would be impossible to winch the vessel back up the slip where she was built.

"Captain, work out what type of weaponry we can install and how many crew do we need, I have a plan to test her out, we can run a patrol down the channel, and destroy the rebel's vessels, oh and Captain, I don't like the Japanese name 'AKANE' we must rename the boat!"

Thursday 19th March 2015 on board NK Catamaran 'Gin Gum Kim' Kings Town Wharf

0900 hours and work had started in earnest, the general was throwing everything at the conversion, he had the captain working on the crew, weapons and painting over the Japanese name in favour of the name the captain had suggested, the *'Gin Gum Kim'* after their President.

With no real heavy, or even their light machine guns to use, Li Chun looked towards the Ultimax 100, an Indonesian weapon, he had managed to acquire two of a month ago in a back handed deal with the Indonesian supply and logistics Captain Raja Atmadja, along with 2000 5.56mm rounds. He wanted to keep them up his sleeve for a rainy day.

These would be mounted on the bridge wings, the only other major fire power he could muster was the Type 69 RPG's – these rocket propelled grenades he had good supplies of, but they were spread out to the outer posts, all he could muster in Kings Town were six, these would be shoulder mounted and used wherever necessary.

1200 hours, and Li Chun was overseeing the last of the work on the eighty-five metre Catamaran. He had sourced what crew he could, apart from the ex-*Warrnambool* sailors already acquired and the old engineer, he found six troopers with some sea experience.

The next headache was to organise fuel, Guhn had wrongly assumed the tanks on the huge Cat were full, but he was grossly mistaken, with only enough fuel on board to test the original engines, it was a miracle they didn't run out on their way to the wharf.

1500 hours, General Jun Lee arrived on board amongst the scurrying of men, loading ammunition and weapons. He asked the obvious question,

"How goes the work captain, are we still on track to sail tomorrow?" Li Chun was embarrassed and showed it, stuttering badly.

"Still waiting on fuel sir." Jun Lee was not amused.

"What seems to be the hold-up?" The captain explained that all the fuel recovery trucks bar one was north of Kings Town and couldn't be contacted, the only one left had just transferred all its fuel to the hospital.

"How long to re-fill it, Captain?"

"We are hoping by 2100 hours sir." Walking off, the general turned and said,

"Make it happen Li; I want this vessel to launch an attack tomorrow at dawn."

Chapter 20
Frog Island

Monday 16ᵗʰ March 2015 sixty-five-foot Conquest Retaliator Apples

0800 hours. Finished with breakfast, washing up out of the way, Riley and Liz were waiting for Mick, Rona and Christine to join them. With the bad weather abating, they had decided their support was better utilised back on the peninsula. The two vessels had been in the area for over a week, concentrating on clearing every back road from Clem's Saddle, north of Apples on the main highway and Veronica Sands on the coast road, which meant that they held all the ground south.

The *Black Ink* was clearing from Veronica Sands to just south of Kettle. It had been a long slog for the TRF after the injury of Brian, but now it was time for the *Retaliator* to return to Crayfish, there wasn't anything more she could do here. Riley yelled.

"Single up all lines." The twenty-year-old skipper hit the starter on the 1000 HP V12 Caterpillar Turbo engine. Riley and Liz watched as a jeep approached them, it was Nobby and Brenda along with the *Retaliators* crewmen, Mick, Christine and Ron

Barr, newly recruited from the *Black Ink*. After running around to Veronica Sands, the group had been way out back, checking the outlying properties west of Apples.

Nobby stood on the jetty as the three hopped aboard.

"Safe trip home mate, I must say it has been great having you guys help with the clearing, maybe we'll catch up in the end at the piss-up? Oh and say hello to Sarge and Annie when you see them." The skipper acknowledged.

"Thanks Nobby and Brenda, sure will, good luck with it all, not sure when I will see Sarge and Annie, but I'll pass on your regards, maybe we'll all catch up in Kings Town?" Ron and Mick helped Liz drop all lines, the twenty-year-old screwed off the starboard bow fender then went astern, out in the middle of the Apples river he straightened the sixty-five-footer then span on the spot. Before moving off, everyone waved at Baz and his crew on the *Cougar Anne,* also midstream waiting to take the sixty-five footer's place alongside. Riley addressed the trio.

"You guys, must be buggered, might as well get your head down, Liz

and I will be ok." Mick spoke for the group.

"Thanks Riley much appreciated, we've been on the go all night clearing way out west, after getting Ron, Christine and all their gear, quite a surprise how many properties were occupied, reckon we cleared about fifty homes, I think it was Shane and Rachael who might have come across a pocket of locals hiding out in the hills, trouble is, with us lot driving the Alliance jeeps they are still afraid of us."

Monday 16th March 2015 ninety-foot Black Ink

1800 hours, south of Woodsville, Harold had worked the shore for over a week, sometimes withdrawing to Legs to re-coupe if the weather permitted.

Everyone was still coming to terms with Steve's death, they now found it better to land, clear for five or six hours then withdraw, they had done this from Veronica where they sometimes came across TRF members from Nobby's group to Woodsville.

Tying up at the Middletown jetty for the third time in a week, the thirty-year-old skipper could see the two Alliance jeeps where they left them.

"Right, I reckon if we concentrate on the couple of roads we missed last time. Shayne, Ivan and Deb will check that out, while the Sweets, Pat and Cindy run the coast road again, that's if you're up to it Pat?" The fifty-nine-year-old light housekeeper nodded in the affirmative. Shayne yelled as he leapt ashore dragging Debra with him.

"See you guys around 2200 hours then."

"Sounds good to me Shayne, we might even stay alongside here instead of withdrawing to Legs." Ivan beat the orchard worker to the driver's side.

"I'll drive mate." Shayne and Deb cuddled up in the back seat. Warming the old jeep up they watched as the other team prepared themselves, Shayne yelled

"Got room for one more here, oh and weapons check please,"

"I'll come with you!" yelled Pat as she hopped in the front alongside Ivan; Type 68's between their knees, loaded and on safe, Ivan sat his Type 54 pistol in the door holster. Driving around ten kilometres, they turned left up a dirt road they had cleared before, five more kilometres they came across a turnoff to the left.

1930 hours, "we haven't been down this road, so eyes peeled from now." The sun was hidden by the massive trees lining the dirt road, slowing down to twenty kilometres per hour they scanned either side of the track for driveways, Deb commented.

"Who the bloody hell would live out here, I can't even see power lines." Shayne added.

"They might come in from the other end luv, or they might just be off the grid." Ivan slowed down even more and stopped adjacent to a driveway.

"Can't see any light, what do you reckon?" Shayne answered.

"Just drive up, bold as brass mate." The ex-accountant slowly punched the jeep along the track that vaguely resembled a driveway, stopping at the front door to a nice-looking cottage, the post 2000 vehicle was still in the carport. Shayne hopped out and belted on the door, Deb and Pat backed him up, after what seemed like an awfully long time they heard a scuffle behind the door, a female called out

"neoneun mueos-eul wonhani" or 'what do you want' Deb yelled back the only phrase she could remember

"mwoga munje ya!" or 'what's wrong', there was silence, muttering then the door opened, safety chain off. Shayne heaved against the timber and glass door knocking the old lady over, stepping over the woman

"Dooff!" Shooting her in the head, motioning to Deb and Pat to take a room each while he worked the rear of the home. With slightly louder Dooff's behind him the twenty-three-year-old orchard worker pushed open the middle door into a kitchen come dining room, the old man was sitting at the table, through the NVG's Shayne could make out a weapon leaning against the bench.

The old man was pretty fast for his age, Shayne thought this was possibly a retired trooper, he got to his assault rifle but failed to bring it to bare.

"Dooff...Dooff." The 9 mm rounds hitting the man in the upper body making him head butt the bench. Shayne yelled.

"All clear!" The two women both added.

"All clear here."

Meeting them in the passageway they reported four more bodies across the two bedrooms, collecting the rifle and what ammunition he could find they loaded up the jeep, Deb secured the sanitary items and Ivan was excited to learn all about it, he counted the ammo.

"Shit Shayne, not much ammo, only twenty-four rounds and If I remember rightly, we haven't seen a trooper for quite a while." The twenty-three-year-old agreed.

2000 hours, Julie, Julia and Rod Sweet were in the jeep driven by Cindy, had made it as far north as they had been before, all the homes that had been cleared were still bearing the bodies of the Nationals, no one had cleaned them up, meaning the TRF members concluded the Alliance was grossly under manned.

Tuesday 17th March 2015 sixty-five-foot Conquest Retaliator in the Channel

0900 hours and having tried to round the southern tip of Frog Island the day before, they were beaten back by the weather, with a huge swell coming in from the southeast it was just too much for the sixty-five-footer, so Riley had decided to turn around and come up the channel trying to avoid the big swell, and electing to anchor at Legs.

Giving the crew a well-earned rest, Liz had pulled a whole frozen chicken out of the freezer for dinner the night before but due to the sea state she waited until they were at anchor, so a late dinner of roast chook, baked spuds, gravy and dehydrated peas was washed down with a cold beer.

Ron was first up; by the time Riley emerged from the skipper's cabin the twenty-nine-year-old winemaker had the hot drinks well underway.

"Drinks poured Skipper, and the toast won't be far away." The smell of fresh coffee and toast had its effect, and the rest of the crew emerged like rats from a sinking ship, Liz still brushing her hair.

"Thanks Ron, might just keep you on, everyone happy with toast, I can try and find some tinned wonders?" With everyone saying the toast would be fine, Mick asked.

"What's on the agenda today, Skipper, hope we aren't going south again?" The thirty-eight-year-old farmer was still trying to orientate his body without the swell they were in yesterday. Ron concurred, and Liz sat on the skipper's knees looking up at the twenty-year-old.

"I don't think Riley would do that to us, would you Riles?" The skipper smiled "Well I did consider it but was persuaded not to do it, I thought we would touch

base with Harold this morning and offer our support as a gun ship if he wants us."

1100 hours, "Weigh anchor!" With the last of the chain off the bottom, Riley went astern into deep water, the anchor secured he spun the sixty-five-footer around and headed off up the channel. Reaching for the UHF he thought he would try the *Black Ink,*

"*Black Ink, Black Ink,* this is *Retaliator* do you read me, over?" he waited for a few seconds.

"*Retaliator,* this is *Black Ink,* go to 72 over" the twenty-year-old flicked the radio to channel 72.

"*Retaliator* this is *Black Ink,* thought you might be halfway home by now?"

"Too bloody rough Harold, swell was around six metres on the nose, thought we might come and give you a hand while we travel up the inside, that's if you want help?"

"We have pretty well wrapped it up as far as Kettle, the *Tangara* has been running raids from Denis Point to Kettle for a week, but they could probably use your 50 Cal for some passing raids at the marina." Switching to channel 16 again Riley tried to raise the *Tangara*.

"*Tangara, Tangara* this is *Retaliator* do you read me over?" The skipper knocked the throttle forward to give the sixty-five-footer some more speed effectively closing the gap for the radio.

1300 hours and they were off Woodsville; Liz tried again on the UHF

"*Tangara, Tangara* this is *Retaliator* do you read me over?" She enjoyed sitting in the navigator's chair.

"*Retaliator*, this is *Tangara* loud and clear, go to 78 over." the nineteen-year-old clicked the set onto channel 78.

"*Retaliator* receiving on 78, how are you going Alf?" The eighteen-year-old reported on the raids they had done over the last week, they had sat still for three days because last time they approached the marina the Alliance tried to spring an ambush, quick look by Merv and cover fire from Sam he did a quick retreat.

Alf suggested the sixty-five-footer raft up alongside the *Tangara*, then when the weather was right, assist when the *Tangara* made its next assault on Kettle, the weather was still blowing in from the southeast so they might have to lay over for a day and with no real pressing engagements waiting for them at Crayfish, Riley decided they would wait.

1600 hours, they entered the Denis Point Bay and came alongside the fifty-six-foot ex-cray boat. Neatly rafted up, it was great to catch up with Alf, Shakira, Mervin and Samuel again. Invited on-board the Conquest for dinner, they combined pantries, Mervin, Shakira and Liz all showing their culinary skills, Mervin supplied three lovely salmon to which Alf made smart work filleting and de-boning, some homemade wedgies and a salad compliments of someone's garden ashore at Denis Point.

Now Mervin wouldn't say, but they all suspected Gladys Ponder was the donator except she didn't know it. Alf proposed a toast

"Great to drink real cold beer from a fridge again and well here's to our raid, this time if they are waiting for us, we have the greater fire power from the 50 Cal."

Wednesday 18th March 2015 ninety-foot Retaliator and Tangara Denis Point

1800 hours, "what do you reckon Riley?" The eighteen-year-old Alf was asking for a weather report.

"Looks like the wind has dropped right off Alf, I reckon we go tonight, what's your plan of attack?"

"Leave here around 2100 hours, that puts us in the marina about dusk, I'll aim for the main finger again but won't tie up, if they are expecting us they'll open up, so if you could come up behind them on the other side of the main finger they will be stuffed, once we shut them up, I'll tie up and continue with the clearing, if you guys can stand cover, in case they attack the boat, that would be great."

"You don't want us to help in the clearing then?"

"Nah, I reckon if you shoot them up for us that will do, there looked like a small party of around a dozen troopers."

2215 hours and *Tangara* was on final approach to the main marina finger, the night was still, a welcome change from the last few days where it blew a gale. Inside the cove there was no wind whatsoever. Alf put the fifty-six-footer astern, and the L6

Gardner effortlessly stopped her. Like last time, no one showed themselves, then came the rifle fire.

"Boom...Boom...Boom...Boom." The weapons were showing their muzzle flashes, coming from behind a small shed, probably a utilities space. Alf went astern out of range to the splintering rounds making a mess of the *Tangara's* wheelhouse.

2230 hours and out of the corner of their eyes, Mervin and Shakira caught sight of the *Retaliator* steaming past on the other side of the finger. The 50 Calibre Machine Gun mounted amidships opened up on the Alliance position.

"Boom...Boom...Boom...Boom...Boom...Boom...Boom." The half inch projectiles spitting out of the barrel of this heavy machine gun at the rate of 600 rounds a minute, chopped the little galvanised shed to pieces, literally shredding the shed, the contents and the men crouched down behind it. Riley stopped the sixty-five-footer just twenty metres from the Alliance ambush position, a quick look through the NVG's and the twenty-year-old nods to Liz where she was hanging off the UHF.

"All clear Alf".

Thursday 19ᵗʰ March 2015 fifty-six-foot Tangara Kettle Marina

0200 hours, with the ex-cray boat secured and *Retaliator* keeping watch, all the *Tangara's* crew went ashore. Mervin was happy to be back in the thick of it and paired up with Samuel, they headed for the main road behind the homes above the ferry terminal, while Alf and Shakira went to the homes beyond the hotel and to the right, along the main road. Alf pointedp to the hotel.

"I think we might just do a walk through; in case they have replenished it with more troops." Shakira knew the way and made her way in the side door and up the stairs on the right of the building. Emerging in the large dining room, she could see evidence someone had been there, the first thing that struck her was all the bodies they left inside the double front doors were gone.

"I'll check the rooms luv if you do the kitchen?" Shakira released the safety on her pistol and approached the double flip doors to the kitchen. Peering through the round glass windows the twenty-year-old could see a trooper sitting at a bench with his back to the door, afraid that the doors would squeak, she knelt down as she pushed the right hand side door inwards, the trooper turned around to see who moved the door, not seeing Shakira he returned to what he was doing, the twenty year old aimed and fired from where she was.

"Bang!" The 9 mm unsuppressed round, hitting the man squarely in the back. Checking the rest of the room, Shakira exited the kitchen to find Alf returning back from the accommodation rooms.

"How many luv, heard the shot just the one?" The twenty-year-old smiled. "Just the one what about you?"

"Twelve rooms, all look like they are occupied but empty; I reckon they were our welcoming committee out in the marina."

0400 hours, Mervin and Samuel peered into the window, there was a candle flickering in the room, a trifle odd for 4am. Merv decided to try the back door, they had been having a good run, sixteen homes, eighty-four Nationals and only one trooper, this was the furthest they had travelled away from the marina. Pushing the back door inwards, Merv entered first, his NVG's scanning the back room for movement. Most of the houses they cleared probably would have had to hear the barking 50 Cal earlier, possibly why a lot of them were awake, the sixty-eight-year- old whispered.

"You take the right, and I'll do the left." With a nod from Sam, they started down the hallway, Merv put his ear to the lounge room door, then squatted down before he pushed it open.

"Boom...Boom." The assault rifles 7.62mm rounds would have made short work of him if he wasn't squatting, through the NVG's he detected the trooper sitting against the outside wall, which was why they couldn't see him from the window.

"Dooff...Dooff...Dooff." Merv's supressed pistols three 9 mm rounds were very accurate, two in the chest and one in the forehead. He could hear Sam's slightly louder shots through a pillow and the final body count was seven.

Sam emerged from the bathroom with a garbage bag full of booty, meeting Merv with the trooper's weapon and webbing slung over his shoulder, along with a surprise, a type 54 pistol and ammo to suit both weapons. Smiling at Sam,

"Reckon we have done enough tonight mate, let's head back." The twenty-three-year-old collected the other four rifles out the front, and added the garbage bag to the others, between them they had quite a haul, five Type 68's and one Type 54, a shit load of ammo and two big bags of sanitary items.

0510 hours, Alf was creeping up behind Shakira at the pairs last home; he was letting the twenty-year-old get some experience going first. In the moonlight Alf could easily make out the very nicely rounded backside now only inches in front of him, the eighteen-year-old couldn't help himself, lightly pinching her between the legs on her inner thigh, she playfully slapped his hand away, he did it again, she groaned, he whispered.

"Shush luv." The twenty-year-old turned, grabbed Alf by the shirt front, shoved her tongue down his throat then whispered.

"You'll keep you bastard!"

Opening the door the pair made their way through the huge lounge room to the two bedrooms running off it, first room had a couple sleeping.

"Dooff...Dooff." The supressed pistol working a treat, both 9 mm rounds shattering their temples as it entered. Second room yielded two sets of bunks, four kids, beckoning Alf to help, Shakira didn't want to use the louder unsuppressed weapon.

"Dooff...Dooff...Dooff...Dooff." Shakira checked the last room, finally whispering.

"All clear."

0600 hours, in the dawn light, the pair made their way back through the hotel, downstairs and out onto the main marina finger. This pontoon would have to be 600 metres long with fifteen fingers off each side, each one of those could hold at least thirty vessels on each side, Alf was mentally adding up the number of vessels all up, catching up to the twenty-year-old he slipped his arm around her waist saying.

"Fuck Shakira, this marina has the potential to hold 1800 vessels. Phew that's a lot of money." They could already see Merv and Sam aboard, slipping the lines as they hopped over the guard rail, Alf grabbed the VHF.

"Thanks for the babysit Riles, we might head back now, are you joining us?"

"Nah, thanks all the same, we might head back to Crayfish, what's your next move?"

"Same, small raids until the Dove group make their way up the channel, same with *Black Ink* and *Cougar Anne*, we will get as close to Kings Town as we can and then wait for reinforcements from Dick, catch you later, *Tangara* out."

Thursday 19th March 2015 Cougar Anne Apples

0730 hours and Baz fired up the fifty-foot-steel ex-cray boat, the 600 HP GM fired first revolution. Planning to head up into the channel proper, first topping up fuel tanks at the old salmon farm complex at Port Apples, Nobby and Brenda had just pulled up to see them off, Shane and Rachael also pulling up with Matilda, Pete and Delilah, Shot as well. Baz spoke first.

"We'll head off Nobby, not much more we can do from here, but I reckon they will need our help on the water closer to Kettle." The forty-six-year-old ex-trail boss replied.

"Yes, I am pretty happy with our progress, we still have a fair bit to do out in the back blocks, and I guess our goal is to get everything cleared from Kettle South, then we can start to look at Kings Town proper, but I'll leave that logistics to Dick, keep your head down, talk later."

0800 hours, "drop all lines." Baz fended off the starboard bow and went astern from the salmon wharf; with all tanks full he was happy. Steaming down the river, the water was dead calm; reaching for the brick phone he dialled Harold.

"Brrr … Brrr … hi Harold, yep, it's Baz, yes, we are on our way, oh I reckon we are off Sausage and Eggs Bay, where are you? Ok why don't we all meet up at Dennis Point Bay, yep understand. Riley has gone back to Crayfish, what only today, I thought he would be there by now, yep understand, weather was shit, oh glad he could be of some assistance to Alf, righto mate see you tonight."

Thursday 19th March 2015 Cougar Anne on approach to Dennis Point Bay

1930 hours Lyne pointed to the *Black Ink*.

"Looks like the *Tangara* has rafted up to her, will we be able to do the same or will that be too much?" Bringing the *Cougar*

Anne alongside the ex-squid boat they soon made short work of securing the old girl. There were plenty of handshakes, hugs and a genuine welcome to all.

Squeezing into the *Black Ink's* saloon was a feat in itself but squeeze they did, another feed of salmon and fresh vegies went down particularly well with Baz, Lyn, Sid and Craig. A night of stories unfolded over a few drinks, the mood was high, although there was plenty of toasting their dead comrades well into the night. Cindy stood the middle watch, being the only non-drinker; she was to wake Harold at 0400 hours for the morning watch.

Friday 20th March 2015 Cougar Anne, Tangara and Black Ink at anchor Dennis Point Bay

0630 hours, morning watch and Harold, finding it hard to maintain consciousness, something to do with the excessive alcohol the night before wandered out onto the stern to relieve himself. With the zip done up he took a moment to glance around at the placid water, his eyes did a sort of a double take as he looked towards Kings Town.

In the distance he could detect another vessel, but not just any vessel, this one seemed a lot larger. He made it back into the wheelhouse to grab the binoculars at the same time Julie was making coffee.

"Wake everyone Julie, we have company and when you're finished here, wake the other two vessels as well, quick smart." Julie, still mumbling with displeasure disappeared below and opted for the 'bang rather loudly on the cabin door' approach. Harold could hear the abuse coming from below as weary heads appeared.

Climbing over the railing to the *Cougar Anne*, she was met by Baz coming up into the wheelhouse. Explaining what Harold had said, it was obvious the ex-navy petty officer clearance diver had seen enough action to realise trouble was bearing down on them, albeit not fast but coming their way.

"What do you make of her Harold?" The *Black Ink* skipper dropped the binoculars, as all three vessels crew appeared from below like a poorly organised fire muster.

"Looks awfully like a huge catamaran, you know like the ones that International Catamaran's builds, I'm puzzled she should be travelling faster or maybe they haven't seen us." Baz raised the binoculars and was soon joined by Alf and Merv, all looking at the huge ship.

"Start main engines everyone; I don't like the look of this."

Baz was studying the huge cat, Sid and Craig quickly got the main started when Baz remarked.

"Looks like she is labouring to port Harold"

"What do you reckon, only one engine operational?"

"That would be my guess, and not very quick at that, maybe that's the only pre 2000 engine they could find, I put her about three miles away."

With the rattle of the *Black Ink's* anchor chain running through the Hauser pipe and the *Tangara* and *Cougar Anne's* mooring lines dropped the three vessels remained close enough for the skippers to come up with a plan.

"Keep off the radio Harold, and Alf, the Alliance will probably be scanning, if you need to talk, use the brick phones. I'm no naval strategist and I don't know what weapons she has on board, but we can't stay here, make your way around the point to the old ferry terminal, I reckon the *Black Ink* and us can sort of hide behind the infrastructure. Alf if you head over to the marina and hide out amongst all the other vessels, it'll make it harder for them to see you."

"What do we do then Baz?"

"When they come into range of our RPG's, let them have it, we also have the 50 calibre machine guns, and they will outshoot anything the Alliance has."

0845 hours, the *Black Ink* and *Cougar Anne* rafted with one amidships mooring line, neatly hiding behind the ferry wharf. The two crews watched as Alf led the *Tangara* back to the Kettle Marina. Craig yelled.

"There she blows." Using the age-old Whaler's cry for sighting a Whale. Questions were fired from most of the women, how are we going to fight such a large ship, etc. etc. Harold had Peter read out the range from the radar screen, watching the huge cat labour its way towards the channel.

"Doesn't look like they have seen us Baz, they're heading right down the middle of the channel."

"Question is mate, are they going to be in range when they are abeam of us, because that's when the game is up, they'll see us for sure." Half an hour later.

"She's trying to turn to starboard, shit I reckon they have seen the *Tangara*." Gunfire could be heard as the Cat opened up fire in the direction of the *Tangara*,

"Light machine gun, time to go to the rescue." Baz ordered the mooring line dropped and pushed the fifty-foot ex- cray boat to full ahead, Sid and Craig were already manning the 50 calibre, making sure a second box of ammunition was close by. From the stern, the huge catamaran looked even bigger and appeared to be light in the water. Machine gun fire still echoing from the bow, Baz steered the *Cougar Anne* straight for its stern, looking astern he could see the slightly faster *Black Ink* about to overtake them.

1030 hours. They were only one hundred metres from the Cat's stern, Harold was a beam of them on their starboard side, no one seemed to looking anywhere except straight ahead at the *Tangara*, who was by now under way trying to dodge the Alliance battleship. Close enough to see the name on the stern.

"*Gin Gum Kim* and looks like we have company on her stern, someone is setting up a machine gun, fire when ready Craig." The half inch projectiles cut the two-man team to ribbons and did a fair amount of damage to the superstructure.

"The alloy is no match for the 50 Cal luv, they punch straight through."

"RPG smoke, coming from the starboard quarter, looks like they are firing on the *Black Ink*." The smoke trail could be seen marginally missing the ex-squid boat as Harold turned towards the Rock Propelled Grenade. Shayne hanging onto the end of the 50 Cal mounted on the bow splintered the bridge of the huge cat, making the RPG operator have second thoughts on sticking his head out to take another shot.

1100 hours and the 50 Cal's were keeping the stern and starboard sides of the Alliance battleship at bay. While still taking sporadic light machine gun and rifle fire, the *Cougar Anne* moved up the port side where Sid was preparing to fire their RPG.

"Where do you want me to aim Baz?"

"Bridge, mate, wait till we are abeam of the wing."

At the precise moment the fifty-footer was in position, they saw the Alliance trooper shoulder his weapon and pull the trigger. The smoke trail could be clearly seen snaking its way towards the *Tangara* still trying to dodge the incoming fire from the bow of the huge cat. Sid let his rocket go and over the shorter distance it contacted the aluminium bridge, accurately entering through the port bridge wing door and exploding in a fireball.

The huge Catamaran seemed to hic-up, still surging ahead on its slow starboard engine while the aluminium burnt fiercely, extending its fiery arm throughout the vessel, then the fuel tanks heated by the flames, erupted. Turning to port to avoid the intense heat, Baz, Lyn and the crew could only look forward.

"Come on Alf, turn! Turn the bloody boat, fuck it's going to hit them." From their port position, looking past the bow of the cat, they could make out the *Tangara* as she exploded in a mass of splintering timber, and diesel burning. Right on the edge of the RPG's range it was a fluke the Alliance trooper hit anything.

Chapter 21
Brownsville

Wednesday 18th March 2015 TRF Elite and Queen Members
Wynn Highway

"Looks like the rest of the group Reg." They could now see the truck with Rusty and his lot, then the jeep carrying Grant and Brittney emerge out of the dark. Having scouted ahead towards Wynn, the group had successfully cleared a number of homes. They were surprised to find a few on the outskirts empty.

"Hey Tom, lights coming up behind us, let's hope it's Sarge and Dick's."

Gathering everyone around, Dick and Sarge caught up with the stats, Reg had lost three more troops and Tom had one wounded.

"Where is Chris?" asked Sarge.

"Should have been behind me." reported Grant.

0400 hours a lone set of lights appeared from the direction of Wynn. Pulling up there were two obvious points to consider, first, Chris was wounded and second, they had an extra two in the jeep.

"Have a look at Chris's arm, Sarge and who do we have here?" Looking at the slightly busted up male being held up by a woman in the back seat.

"Let me introduce John and Ester Webster from Wynn, they have been on the move ever since the Alliance came to town, but I'm sure when he can talk properly, he'll explain it himself. We burst into this home where he thought we were Alliance and opened up on us. Hearing the familiar sound of the Type 68, we thought they were the Alliance, then it all gets a bit hectic, John shoots Chris in the arm, Chris returns fire and in the onslaught of fending off Ester, one of our guys slams the butt of his weapon at John's head. Realising they were Taswegians it all came to a halt after the dust settled." Ester confirmed the account but was too distraught to tell the rest of the story.

"Take Chris, John and Ester back to the Fremantle, the ladies will patch them up. Tell Doc we're on track and will meet the Freo in Wynn tomorrow night."

1000 hours, Dick, Sarge, Thomas and Annie took the coast road while the other TRF members dispersed down the main road checking the little side roads missed on the first rotation.

"Bummer about losing the three men Dick." Annie was visibly upset having just got to know two of them on Queen Island. Dick decided not to comment, just rubbed Annie's neck. The twenty-eight-year-old horsewoman leant into Dick's comforting arm, staring out at the sea. The day was overcast, the sea took on a dirty grey colour, the white caps could be seen far out to sea, the foam left behind when the waves crashed over the rocks resembling the foam on the top of a good cup of coffee or a badly poured beer.

1500 hours, Dick pulled up at the Wynn fisherman's wharf in front of the overhead fuel tank.

"Good thinking Dick." Thomas and Sarge blurt out together.

"Great minds think alike." Thomas leaned over Annie, and whispered in her ear, all the time snapping his fingers to get Dick's attention, being deaf the ex-CD had no hope of hearing Thomas, but Sarge was quick to give him that 'what's up' look. The seventy-two-year-old ex-regimental sergeant major, pointed to the old fish shop on the wharf, he had seen a person dash from the annex to the shop door and disappear inside.

With his 9mm drawn and off safety, he took just a few seconds to cover the ten paces to the annex, motioning Sarge to cover the back entrance to the shop, he entered. Sarge looked back towards Annie taking cover behind the jeep while Dick continued to fill its tank.

"Bang... Bang... Bang... the rear flyscreen door opened, and a young trooper emerged holding his left knee, fumbling he had no time to ready his rifle and was swiftly shot by Sarge. Entering the back room, it was evident the trooper and family had been hiding out for some time, Thomas suggested there was evidence they had been living there for weeks which suggested a deserter.

"All clear!" yelled Sarge, back in the direction to Dick and Annie.

Continuing on around the coast road, they stopped a few times to check out possible hiding places, dead Nationals were everywhere, the evidence of the TRF members coming through the night before was a stark reminder of the horrors of war. Swinging back out on the highway they continued southeast towards Stone,

"How far do you want to go Dick?" asked Sarge.

"Just till we hit Alliance again, I told the others to continue to run parallel to the highway for half a day then all meet back at the Fremantle." Dick and Thomas swapped places; the ex-CD was weary and sat in the back alongside Annie, the mood was silent and eventually the homes were back, overlooking the highway, then the railway lines, small shrubs were in-between the line and the small rocky beaches, although the sand wasn't yellow it was almost the colour of grey, Annie pointed to a worn-out sign.

"Watcome Beach." Wildflowers were everywhere.

"Red Hot Pokers." claimed Annie, happy to pass on her botanic expertise.

1900 hours and opposite a small island, they found the 'Lesbians' Café'. Looking towards the sea, from this unusually named business, Dick commented that the rocks had taken on an almost black colour, the pebble beaches and a smitten of sand, if it can be called that. Electing to call it a day and rest, Sarge worked out the watch keeping, they drew straws. Annie and Sarge up first till 0200 hours then Thomas and Dick to first light.

Dick got the gas burner going and salvaged enough for a feed and a coffee, courtesy of the sachets in Sarge's pocket.

Thursday 19th March 2015 TRF Elite in the hills on the outskirts of Wynn

0900 hours, Rusty Gowen pulled the old KM450 Light Cargo Truck up outside a house, Grant and Brittney were in the next street when they heard it.

"Whoomph!" They could make out the black acrid smoke billowing up towards the clouds and quickly made the short distance to its source.

"Fucking hell Britt, Rusty's truck, it's gone!" The thirty-four-year-old professional shooter was more concerned about the Alliance trooper reloading the RPG.

"Mate, take out the shooter!" Grant had a head on the bloke and took the shot, the RPG swung around and took off at a forty-five-degree angle, hitting the home down the street. After ten minutes of return fire from another Type 68 there was silence.

"They're heading out the back, I reckon the bastards are out of ammo." Brittney was pointing to the two troopers trying to get over the back fence, stupidly still carrying their weapons, Grant shot the first in the back halfway over, while Brittney took out the second, halfway across the common on the other side.

"Nice shot Britt must have been 700 metres."

Thursday 19th March 2015 TRF Elite FCPB Fremantle Wynn Wharf

1726 hours, Sarge drove the jeep down the ramp to the Wynn Wharf, the scene of the shooting at the old fish shop. It was evident the TRF was a vehicle short.

"I wonder where Rusty is?" questioned Dick as he jumped out.

The Fremantle was still running main engines, her timely arrival, with all mooring lines secure, meant the sombre reality unfolded. Grant and Brittney re-told the story, and everyone was consoling Rusty's brother Reg. Doc organised sentries and declared splicing the mainbrace in Rusty's honour. After cleaning up Dick, Sarge, Chris, Tom, Grant and the newly recruited John did a head count.

"I make it twenty-two plus John Hammer's seven, that's twenty-nine plus the crew"

"Not true Dick, it's thirty-one." The fifty-six-year-old infantry sergeant grinned pointing to Ester and himself.

"Sorry John, I was going to get around to you two sooner or later, how are you both feeling?"

"Great now thanks to Nari and the rest of the crew, we've been well fed, showered and dressed courtesy of everyone on board, now it's our turn to help. What can we do?" Doc looked at Dick then said.

"We reckon, with your training, if you want to, it would be more beneficial to run the TRF from here, when the Fremantle leaves Brownsville in a couple of days we want someone of your calibre to take charge of operations here, what do you think?"

"Does this mean we might get to go home?" Ester was looking longingly at John.

"Could be luv, could be."

Friday 20th March 2015 FCPB Fremantle on approach to Brownsville Harbour

0800 hours. They had left Sarge's jeep for the rest of the TRF; John was quick to establish his leadership and spread a couple of troops from Grant's jeep. The brief was simple, kill anyone Alliance between Stone and Brownsville, meeting up with the Fremantle later on today.

With ammunition replenished and spare weapons issued, the three jeeps and a truck dispersed around 0300 hours after only four hours sleep. Doc called for main engines at 0300 hours and the *Fremantle* slipped lines twenty minutes later.

"Starboard 20 Dick, steer *zero nine five*."

"Roger that Skipper, steering *zero nine five*."

The short hop down the coast to Brownsville didn't take long. This commercial shipping port was the home to the *Spirit of Taswegia* 1 and 2 along with most of the major freight ships.

"Starboard 30 Dick, bring her into the channel, Jack, can you take over, 40–60-gun crew close up, we have hostiles on the port beam, incoming gunfire, Sarge can you man the 50 on the port side?"

"Already on it, Skipper." Sarge had brought the weapon to bear and started firing into what looked like a small brick building down on the waterfront.

"Looks like an old pumping station, their well dug in." Dick trained the 40-60 to port while Thomas loaded a clip.

"Boom... Boom... Boom..."

"Looks like that's a hit Doc!" reported Jack, looking at the smouldering remains.

"Just a pile of bricks now Dick." Thomas was patting the ex-CD on the head.

1200 hours, bringing the FCPB alongside the old *Spirit* berth, Doc tucked the stern in front of the rear loading ramp the *Spirit* used to use.

"Finished with main engines Annie." With a smile the horsewoman darted below grabbing her earmuffs as she entered the hatch. Jack wasn't even halfway to the hatch when the first main engine shut down, Doc yelled.

"Shit Chief you might be out of a job, the girl's on fire."

Dick, Sarge and Thomas went for a wander, making sure they were well armed, rifles and pistols. Working their way through the freight terminal they checked all floors and buildings. Through the main access gate, they approached the first home.

"All clear, bodies everywhere, looks like our guys have beaten us to it." Sarge was already three homes in front. Dick and Thomas checked out the shop adjacent to the terminal entrance and discovered trooper's weapons in one of the rooms.

"Looks like someone forgot to collect these, Dick."

"Or they are still here?" whispered the ex-CD. Opening the back bedroom door, they found the trooper sound asleep.

"Dooff." Thomas yelled.

"Found some transport Dick." The ex-CD emerged holding up a name tag Senior Lieutenant Bin Pin'.

"This would be why he had a jeep; question is what was he doing here on his own?" The ex-RSM smiled as he mounted the General M151Diesel Variant jeep and turned the key to pre-heat.

"Deserter or coward?" Dick looked at the RSM, the building, its aspect on the town,

"You could be right mate, but it doesn't matter now, does it?"

1400 hours and they could hear gunfire coming from over the river, it wasn't long before a jeep pulled up on the wharf. John and Ester jumped out; the other two boys lit up a smoke while the pair made their way to the bridge.

"Area Command reporting in sir." John stood to attention and saluted Doc smiling like a Cheshire cat.

"At ease Sergeant." Everyone on the bridge just burst into laughter.

"Just give us the update Sergeant!"

"Well town centres, both Devon and East Devon are clear; the team is clearing the outskirts. We found their headquarters or what we thought was, funny thing though nobody there over the rank of corporal, no officers at all." Thomas yelled from the flying bridge.

"We know where one of them was!"

Dick filled John in with the discovery of Senior Lieutenant Bin Pin and the RSM's thoughts on the matter.

"He was just a kid, early twenties I reckon."

1530 hours, Patch, Lauren, Nari and April emerged from below, armed with shopping bags.

"We're going on a reconnaissance, hunting groceries; do you want to tag along Ester?" The South African looked at her husband.

"Are we going anywhere John?"

"No dear, all good, we might stay, but I will set the rest of the crew up at one of the hotels along the esplanade, you go along."

"We'll drop some groceries off on the way back then." Jack came up from below, reported on the status, suggested refuelling the next day, then smiled at the women as they left.

"Wait for me, I might tag along." Reaching for his weapons, he gave the rest the thumbs up.

1705 hours and after searching nearly all the homes in the greater East Devon area, the old M151 was loaded to the hilt, tinned food, rice, pasta, fresh vegetables, spices, fresh beef, cured hams, bacon etc. Dropping a selection off for the TRF Elite Squad at the East Devon Motel they headed back to the *Fremantle*.

"Might take a slight detour ladies, there is a live crayfish wholesaler up this street."

"Won't they be off Jack?" asked Nari, wondering if the delicate crustations could survive in a tank with no feed since the E1.

"I'm more worried whether anyone else has thought to take a look." Patch stopped the jeep outside a bland building front; from the outside it looked derelict, the windows had been painted white from the inside. Jack tried the front door; it felt like it was screwed in place.

"Wait here ladies while I go in the back way." They watched the ex-sniper disappear.

Jack found the back door ajar; the place was a mess outside with rubbish everywhere, entering the back room he thought he heard female voices, stopping he strained his ears then satisfied it must have been the girls sitting in the jeep, continued into the passageway. The air was stale and with not much light he found it hard to see, that musky smell of old seafood and damp. The first room he remembered had one tank in it and yep, still did, he grabbed the catch net and swirled it around the greenish water coming up empty.

"Whack!" Something came down on the back of his head, funny thing was it had no power to it, certainly shocked him but didn't do any real damage. Turning around and grabbing the perpetrator he found himself staring at a girl not much more than twelve, brandishing the weapon she hit him with.

The two foot piece of PVC plumbing pipe was about to take another swipe when the ex-navy CD poked his Type 54 pistol into her chest and pulled the trigger.

"Boof." Letting her slide to the floor, he could hear footsteps running back down the passage, leaning out the door he could just make out another figure escaping.

"Boof...Boof." His first shot ricocheted off a drum, second found its mark. Checking his catch, he found another girl of a similar age, looking at her face, he thought 'pretty little thing' sensing someone was behind him he drew the pistol and span around.

"Fucking hell, Patch scared the shit out of me."

"We were worried about you Jack; we heard the shots." April entered, then Lauren, Nari and Ester, smiling the ex-CD joked.

"Were you all in for a piece of the action, what if someone stole the jeep with all the food in it?"

"Sorry Jack didn't think of that!"

Back onboard, Doc was going over the next part of the plan; he had the charts out and was plotting the course back to Bull Bay, then through Banks Strait and down to Ansons Bay. Dick and Sarge were milling over the book with all the brick phone numbers, while Annie was perched in the skipper's chair.

"Might do a ring around, Skipper and get a sit-rep on how we sit within the State"

"Great idea Dick, so Sarge will mark the positions on the Taswegia map?"

"Yep, that way we might be able to identify the bits we missed."

1900 hours, "Brrr … Brrr … Brrr …Oh g'day Blue how's it all going or more to the point have you advanced and what are the casualties?"

"Well Dick, we have cleared all the way out to the Wall in the Wilderness and set up a barricade, numbers - eighty-six Alliance dead, we have lost four and six wounded. The weather has cleared, and the snow has disappeared."

"Sounds fantastic mate, I'll do the ring around and get back to everyone with an overall appraisal."

"Brrr … Brrr … Brenda, it's Dick how's everyone and can you give me an update?"

"All good Dick, Nobby's out on patrol, I've got the phone at Apples. We have cleared all the way to Clem's Saddle, still clearing the back roads, Shane and Rachael were doing the tally's last night, looks like around 2367 Alliance so far."

2000 hours and Dick called a full meeting in the *Fremantle's* junior sailors mess, and then promptly handed the proceedings over to Sarge. The ex-Sapper had the map of Taswegia on the bulkhead, shaded out in different colours.

"Welcome to the TRF update, thanks to all those billeted ashore for coming. As you can see by the different colours, I crudely drew on the map, we have control of the following marked in light blue-

- Johnny and the peninsular TRF have the whole peninsular up as far as Oxford in the north, Mid-Point to the west.
- Mona Commander has control from Wattle in the west to Devon outskirts in the east and just outside Brownsville in the north.
- John, our newly appointed northwest commander has secured all the northwest tip to Devon.

- Blue Bone has control all the way east from Queen to the Wall in the Wilderness.
- Harold and his pirates on the *Black Ink* have control from Wood in the south to Kettle in the north, including Frog Island.
- Len from Oxford in the south to White Distillery in the north.
- Santa is training the locals and Taswegia II passengers on Bass Island.
- Buck controls the Ramat River and the northern coastline from High Head to Reed Lagoon.
- Ernie's tunnel rats- High Head in the north to Earth in the south and all the way to Scot in the east and Reed Lagoon.

The red section through the middle represents the NK Alliance while the light green represents the Indonesian Alliance." Sarge went on to report on the frontline TRF clearing teams, it seems the Alliance's ammunition supplies or lack of them will be their undoing well before we beat them outright. It has been reported that some troopers have as little as five rounds in their possession when killed.

On the other hand, this does not seem to be the case with their Indonesian counterparts. They appeared to be fully kitted out with up to 100 rounds each. After the strategic withdrawal from Benoa north, the Indo Alliance has dug in with temporary camps set up at Bin Bay all the way north to Eddystone Light, including Ansons Bay. A small Garrison at St Mona is spread thin guarding Nationals in over 500 homes between Elephant Pass and Conara.

The main Garrison at St Anne covers from Scott to past Reed Lagoon and down the coast to Two-mile Creek, Dick replied.

"Thanks for that Sarge; it gives us a real time look at what's happening now and how our hard work has paid off, Yes John?" The ex-army sergeant stood.

"You boys, oh and girls have done a fantastic job, seeing this map has made me realise one thing."

"And what would that be John?"

"Well Dick, the fact that we are winning this war, when I first came onboard and listened to all the stories it was a bit hard to take it all in, I thought you had maybe had a few skirmishes, but this is fucking awesome!" Doc addressed the team.

"From my point of view and maybe Nari's, who have lived the horror of the Alliance day in, day out, I can truly say you lot are bloody geniuses. And of course, this whole thing was started by Dick, Patch, Jack, April, Sarge and Annie."

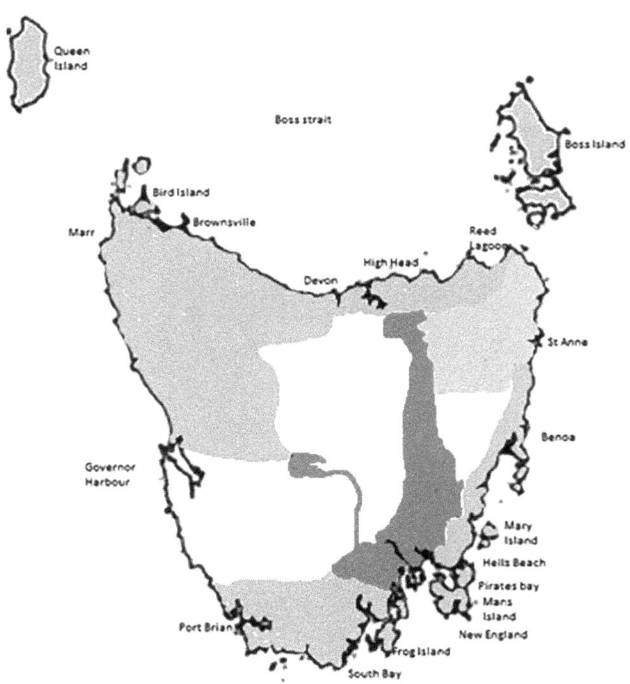

Chapter 22
Peninsular Verdict

Monday 16th March 2015 Strong Fort Bay Cemetery

1200 hours, "We commit the body of Helen Crawfield to the earth, may God rest upon her soul." Johnny was becoming accustomed to conducting a burial service, the perfect place was a small patch of grass at the original settlement where they chose to bury the members killed by the Alliance.

The mood was sombre to say the least; it had taken Wendy Black, a week to conduct some sort of autopsy. Robert Crawfield wanted to assist but because of the relationship to Helen, Johnny refused to let the sixty-year-old dentist see the body. Wendy called upon her friend Joan, the retired nurse now running the triage at Crayfish to assist with the grisly task of gathering evidence from the rape and heavy beating the girl received.

With no real forensics available, Wendy used old fashioned methods, taking snapshots of blood, semen and hair samples, they retrieved from Helen's body with the powerful microscope.

1600 hours, in Johnny's residence, the old ranger's house, they met, Johnny headed up the investigating team. Wendy, Joan, Graham and Roberto sat around the kitchen table each holding a small clean glass of neat scotch.

"Well girls give us what you have?" The forty-four-year-old Benoa nursing sister cleared her throat,

"I must say Johnny, this has not proved easy, and I didn't really want the job, oh getting the samples from poor Helen's body was easy enough, I have performed plenty of cervix swabs in my life, getting minute skin and blood samples from her bruises caused a bit more of a challenge but one Joan and I finally achieved. However, I'm not sure I liked the method of retrieving the samples from young Max." Graham answered in defence.

"Well Wendy, if he had cooperated it would have been simple, but as it was, he fought us tooth and nail, so we took the samples by force and in the end had to sedate him with one of those bloody horse tranquilisers of Dick's." Wendy pulled a face,

"Still Graham and Roberto it was a horrific affair, but you did get them. The internal swab of Max's penis resulted in a positive match to some of the semen found in Helen."

"Some, what the fuck do you mean SOME?"

"Just what it means Roberto, there was evidence of other semen present, also Max's blood and skin tissues did not match the bruising found on her, although this was really hard to determine.

Monday 16th March 2015 Old Coach Depot outside Soothe

0930 hours, Leaving William Dart and David on watch at the mid causeway, Will and Eleanor entered the old coachl depot finding a sleepy Mick J putting the kettle on.

"How's it been Mick?" asked Eleanor, still shaken after the full-on assault from the Alliance only four days ago.

"Pretty quiet Luv, what about the causeway?"

"Same." Will butted in, handing El a cup. Hearing the morning watch, aka George and Clinton snoring, the three of them sat outside overlooking the carnage that had ensued, the burnt out remains of the five trucks and just a couple of hundred metres down the road the shell of the last truck.

"Bloody hell Mick, that was some shot, on the run and at that range, tell me what the final count of dead Alliance was?"

"237 mate; we could recognise some NCOs, and we think the 'piece-de-resistance' was an officer in the last truck." Will reported after he finished sniping that day, he collected what weapons he could that weren't damaged, funny thing was ammunition was scarce, quite a few of the Type 68's were empty.

El brought up the subject that they were all dreading; the funeral of young Helen Crawfield that day.

"I wonder how they are going sorting out the autopsy."

"Bugger of a situation El, I like young Max but from what we have heard, it wasn't looking good for the lad." Mick turned to face the pair.

"I just don't see Max killing the girl, slipping a bit into her, yes, but not anything else, he thought the world of her, I remember when he used to come and deliver the salmon to us, you could see the change in his demeanour."

Sitting there in silence the trio pondered the events of the last three months, Will reported on the activity at Mid; he had done a stealth raid one night creeping alongside the causeway to the Isthmus of land that jutted out into the Pittwater.

The Alliance holding point was based in a house that sat above the road on the left-hand side of the highway, a truck strategically placed across the highway with two sentries. He reckoned that a couple of them could conduct a raid on the outpost but because he was not sure how many were bunking at the Mid Hotel it would be too risky, although he admitted it would bloody their nose.

1130 hours the pair ran into Graham bringing a fresh supply of food,

"G'day Will, El, sure glad you needed supplies today, I hate bloody funerals!"

"Any news on the push towards Kings Town mate?"

"Nah I think this thing with Max has rattled Johnny, and he just wants to get to the bottom of it, although I did hear things are going well up the coast and we have control of Benoa. Vince and Len even got an old fishing boat converted; they would be on their way to Bass Island by now. I think Johnny said the TRF holds all the way to two-mile creek, oh and we have been kicking arse down the channel."

Friday 20th March 2015 Crawfield property Falcons Neck

1000 hours, Roberto and Graham had procured the services of Sid to take another look at the crime scene, Graham had combed the area Helen's body was found, so Roberto took over, leaving Sid and Graham scouring the surrounding bush, sitting on a stump Graham surmised.

"If I was going to do such a thing to a pretty young girl, oh and I was not Max but some other bastard. I think I would have been watching the property for some time, working out her comings and goings, so how long had Max been taking Helen on his deliveries?" Sid sucked in a breath still finding it hard to come to terms that his 'little girl' was dead.

"Max had asked us a few Sundays ago, we hated the idea at first, nothing to do with Max, Ellen and I just thought Helen was just too young. It was only Saturday night that Ellen reminded me what age she was when we first went out, so we gave in and allowed Max to officially take her out." The last words came out amongst tears when Graham gave the grieving father a squeeze on the arm,

"Mate it's alright lets, change the subject, ok who else could have done it? It certainly wasn't the young lad of the Jones's, what's his name? Roger."

"He's only twelve, mate." managed Sid.

"That leaves Mick Jones and old Cedric Bilton."

"Cedric's too old and Mick has been on duty at Soothe ever since the push."

"What if it wasn't one of us?"

"Sid, you mean someone from another area. Doesn't seem possible, anyway I think Roberto and Johnny have ruled that out."

"What if it was some Alliance deserter, you know some scum to scared to fight and has been hiding out ever since we cleared the peninsular."

1300 hours, over a cold lunch, courtesy of the Biltons, the pair ran their idea past Roberto.

"Interesting theory guys, let's break it down, we cleared this area on the 27th ^{of} January, clean up started 29th but not in this area for say another week or two and I think you moved in when Sid?"

"15th February Roberto"

"So, this deserter or shall we call him the 'Perp' has been living rough for over a month, there's plenty of dense bush down this road and a few shacks that haven't been occupied, are you thinking what I'm thinking?"

"Yep!"

0600 Saturday 21ˢᵗ March 2015 Norfolk Bay Road one kilometre past the Crawfield property

The retired concreter stepped out of the security jeep and stood alongside Graham, Jack and Johnny. The ex-farmer from Julia Bay had a long conversation with Dick and Sarge the night before and ran Graham and Sid's idea past them.

"Dick and Sarge were in agreeance with Graham and Sid, it's possible we have a rogue trooper, or even a NK National." Johnny was strapping on the webbing holster that housed his Type 54 pistol, still not one hundred per cent happy about the whole hunting killing thing. Reaching for the Type 68 assault rifle and spare ammunition clips the ex-farmer was watching the other two, obviously comfortable dealing with weapons, the pair had come a long way from the railway and courier driving.

"Right, you two ready?" Sid looked at Graham.

"Mate we were born ready, let's do this shit, how do you want to tackle it?"

"Taking advice from Dick last night, he suggested on foot, so we don't let the bastard hear us barrelling down the road in a jeep. From memory the road runs for about fifteen kilometres from the start, so we've got about nine to go and around twelve shacks. Graham, if you take point, I'll follow you and Sid if you can run parallel to me but about 100 metres in from the road, we should have it covered."

0630 hours and the trio continued to the first home, a vertically clad timber shack, looked like one - or two-bedroom, Graham drew the pistol and entered the back door, Johnny backed up while Sid covered the front.

"All clear" The next dwelling was just in sight, a slightly newer building of brick and colour bond roof job. Sid went in first followed by Graham with Johnny watching the front.

"All clear guys but come and look at this." Graham and Johnny found the ex-railway worker standing over a combustion stove in the kitchen, not really seeing what he was worried about, he could see their looks of query over their faces as he points to the stove. Not wanting to appear stupid Graham asks.

"What?"

"Mate it's still warm."

"Well, that's thrown a curve ball, I guess it proves we were right, some little slope is living up and down this road preying on our girls." Sid was obviously emotional, and Johnny took him outside to calm down, Graham looked out the window.

"Fucking hell, a vehicle, quick run and stop it going any further before they give the game away, who the fuck would be driving down here this time of the morning anyway." Being the youngest of the three, the ex-courier driver made it to the road just as the jeep drew level.

"Bloody hell Wendy, what are you doing, you could have ruined the whole operation!" The ex-nursing sister blushed at the outburst but as Johnny and Sid joined them, she let fly.

"Well, you bloody upstart, I've been up all night going over the semen specimens, realised you were possibly running into trouble so drove here with no sleep to warn you, and all you can do is yell at me, well fuck you." Johnny put his arm around her and gave Graham one of 'those' looks,

"Sorry Wendy, I'm just worried the jeep would have given us away, anyway what's so important to drive here, we already know we're looking for a slope and what do you mean running into trouble?" Taking a deep breath.

"Remember when I said the whole autopsy was to determine with the equipment we had, well after working right up to 4.30 this morning I discovered why, there is more than two samples of semen?"

"Shit, does this mean she was raped by two slopes?"

"No Sid, I'm sorry but I have isolated six so far!"

"Fuck, thanks for the warning, Wendy, this means we are walking into a half a dozen or more NK Nationals."

"Or troopers Graham, now that changes things, armed troopers will be difficult to kill."

"We had no trouble killing them a month ago Johnny, what's the difference now?"

"They will be expecting someone to come looking mate, that's a bit different."

1900 Saturday 21ˢᵗ March 2015 610 Norfolk Bay Road

Johnny had called in reinforcements, the recently returned *Retaliator* crew of Riley, Liz, Ron, Mick S and Christine. Riley's jeep pulled up behind Johnny's and with introductions out of the way Johnny outlined the problem and the possible numbers they were dealing with.

"I think we should split into two teams." suggested Graham.

Knowing the peninsular leader was not fond of patrols like this, it was suggested Johnny sit this one out and ride back-up in his jeep, and after much discussion Christine volunteered to drive Riley's jeep, keeping their distance. Graham would lead the first team of Sid and Ron while the twenty-year-old skipper would lead Liz and Mick S.

"I'll take Sid and Ron away from the road, we will cover the second half a kilometre, so Riley if your team can cover the first half a kilometre. Spread out so you are still in sight of each other, if the bush gets denser, move closer but at no time are you to be out of sight from the next team member. No talking, Type 68's at the ready with safeties off. Remember these could be battle hardened troops or cowards, either way, watch each other's backs. Now some of the houses are a long way from the road, so we will cover them, the rest closer to the road Riley's crew will cover, any questions?" Ron raised his hand.

"Won't it be difficult to see in a couple of hours?" Riley smiled.

"Got you covered Ron" as the young skipper handed the NVG's around.

"Team leaders will tell you when to put them on to adjust to the dark."

2010 hours, spaced around one hundred and fifty metres apart they moved forward in a traditional military Emu parade, lined up abreast. Each team member with their assault rifles in the ready position or 'low port arms' as it used to be called, were constantly scanning the horizon, with a full clip plus one up the spout, the Type 54 also fully loaded in its webbing holster.

Riley gave the signal for them to put on their NVG's; they had been told how to get used to them, practice touching their rifle as if they were going to reload. Somewhere, half a kilometre to his right Graham was signalling for his team to do the same. First house was in Riley's line of fire, Mick moved in to assist the skipper clear the building while Liz covered the front of the house to the road. The all-clear signal of thumbs up was given, and the pair resumed their position heading due west.

2120 hours and Graham stopped dead, lowered his hand to Sid meaning they would crouch down, Ron saw what was happening and did the same but not knowing what Graham wanted, he worked his way over to the leader's position whispering.

"What gives mate?" The ex-courier driver drew them together.

"If you look closely, you will see a dim light through the opaque toilet window. I think we have the jackpot gents."

"Do you want me to get Mick's attention?"

"Can you do that without giving us away?"

"Sure, I'll give a bird call, Mick and I have already discussed it."

2145 hours, all six TRF members were squatting on the now lightly frosted with dew grass, some ten metres from the side of the house. It was decided that Graham, Sid and Ron would enter the back door in fifteen minutes while Riley's team covered the front door and the only other exit, a sliding glass door on the other side. Riley had issued all members with Type 54 suppressors and supervised them being fitted, their Type 68's to be left outside.

The air was as still as could be, absolutely no wind, quite common for autumn and the temperature was now close to zero. A frost was gathering, and all members were glad of the warm clothing they elected to wear.

2200 hours, Graham slipped the back door in, remembering what Sarge and Dick had taught them he entered the room below the door handle height and quickly scanned the room, beckoning his team in behind him. Motioning to take the pistols off safe he stood; his nostrils confirmed the room was the kitchen dining combined, with two doors leading away from it. Sid moved to the one on the right while he and Ron took the left. Opening into what looked like a small bedroom his nostrils worked their magic again; a strong garlic smell with a hint of male body odour told the ex-courier driver he had company.

Detecting the rise and fall of the man's chest was clearly visible through the NVG's and he quickly aimed and fired.

"Dooff...Dooff." the 9mm hollow point rounds made short work of the man's torso. Back in the kitchen they heard the slight sound of a creaky floor to their right. A quick look revealed Sid still trying to make his way across the lounge room; it looked like two doorways off this room to the right, obviously more bedrooms.

Sid pointed to the room in front of him, while Graham pointed to the one to the left. It was Graham who opened his first, 'all clear' he thought, smiling and just about to remove his NVG's Sid opened his door.

"Boom!" The forty-year-old ex-railway worker's body was propelled back out the doorway with all the thrust that a good twelve-gauge shotgun can deliver. Ron was closest and dropped to the floor as the irate NK Trooper fired again.

"Boom!" The gun sprayed its deadly load across the room and into the glass wall cabinet, shattering its glass front.

"Dooff...Dooff...Dooff." Ron fired three shots, the first hitting the trooper in the torso, second missed but the third hit him in the neck spraying arterial blood everywhere.

"Dooff...Dooff." Graham shot the man at close range in the head. Holding out his hand to help the winemaker to his feet,

"Shit, mate, are you alright?" Graham looked at the still smoking body of his mate, or what was left of it. The twelve-gauge shot, probably number two shot load literally punched a twelve-inch hole through his chest and out of his back.

"At least it was quick mate." The twenty-nine-year-old didn't know what else to say.

0135 Sunday 22ⁿᵈ March 2015 848 Norfolk Bay Road

Moving quickly away from where Sid met his demise, they regrouped on the road and waited for the back-up jeeps. On arrival, Johnny could see the group were visibly upset and twigged when Sid was absent, that they had either an injury or death. Christine slowly rolled to a stop alongside Johnny's jeep.

"Tell me what happened?" The peninsular leader was addressing Graham,

"Three of them holed up mate, all troopers, and armed to the teeth, the good thing is we got two of them using the

NVG's, but Sid's bastard was obviously expecting trouble. He let Sid have the full force of the twelve-gauge shotgun, young Ron here hit him three times and I finished him off. A full search of the rest of the house came up empty." Liz was comforting Christine, the nineteen-year-old was becoming accustomed to the killing, something that Christine still found extremely hard.

"If you guys can continue on, Christine and I will retrieve the body, not sure when I will tell Ellen. I just hope you can kill the others, so we can at least have some closure for the murder of Helen, this is going to completely devastate her, first her eldest daughter, now her husband."

0245 hours and two kilometres further on, the group continued the Emu picket line, just the five of them, sticking to around one hundred metres apart, Liz on the road end and Ron on the bush end. The next home loomed up out of the fog that was now drifting in from the bay. something that was a familiar occurrence; after consulting each other they decided to close the gap to twenty metres.

This house was very close to the road with only a driveway the size of someone in town. Riley, with backup from Liz, took the front door, while Mick S covered their backs, the twenty-year-old skipper tried the handle, locked, and the sliding glass window alongside was cracked to allow air flow. A simple push to the side and cutting the flywire revealed a hole big enough for Riley and Liz to enter.

Finding themselves in a sitting room decked out with comfy chairs and the television, the pair negotiated the furniture and into the hallway, looking right Riley could see Graham and Ron in the kitchen. Thumbs up from Graham and they converged on the four doors between them, being aware it could be a trap, the skipper laid flat on his stomach, looking at Liz off to one side, he motioned for her to push the door open.

"Boom...Boom...Boom." The unmistakable sound of an angry Type 68 assault rifle was prevalent. From the intensity of the blasts, whoever was on the other end was close, very close.

Riley rolled into the doorway, praying the NVG's would not let him down at such a crucial time.

"Dooff ... Dooff." The Type 54 semi auto pistol delivered its 7.62 mm hollow point rounds right on track striking the Alliance trooper square in the chest. At the same time the door on the other side of the small hall opened, almost knocking Graham over as the trooper rushed out with his Type 68 on the hip. Acting quickly, he slammed the butt of the weapon into the back of Graham's head sending the thirty-eight-year-old ex-courier driver to the floor.

The Alliance trooper pulled the trigger prematurely.

"Boom!" As Graham was hitting the floor, the round completely missed him imbedding itself into the flooring; Ron brought his Type 54 around to bear on the assailant and squeezed the trigger.

"Dooff." At the same time another shot.

"Dooff." Liz was already squaring off at the trooper but missed his torso because of his action against Graham, hitting him in the side of the head.

0420 hours, Riley was laying on the floor in the doorway, Liz sitting alongside the skipper leaning against the wall. Ron was kneeling alongside Graham who was wiping the blood off the egg-shaped bump on the back of his head, Ron started to speak.

"Fuuff ..." He was muffled mid-sentence as Graham placed his hand over the winemaker's mouth. Signalling to Riley and Liz there was still one room to go, the twenty-year-old skipper had momentarily forgotten all about the door directly opposite. He tapped Liz on the shoulder and pointed for her to get away from the door while he positioned himself in the prone position then started to moan.

"Ahhhhhh, moooaann, groaaaan, help me, I'm hit, shit is anyone there? Graham, Ron where are you? Fuck they're all dead, ahhhh ..." Ron went to help the skipper thinking he was really hit, Graham blocked his motion with his arm, Liz was grinning at her boyfriend's performance. It worked; a noise came from within the room, possibly the trooper getting out from under the bed then.

"Dong·mu, Lok." This confirmed there was someone in the room, but how many? None of the TRF understood the words; Riley repeated his moaning performance, a little quieter this time.

The timber internal door handle turned ever so slowly, and the door opened, what the trooper would have seen was pretty much nothing, unless he had an NCG. The skipper had full vision, although with a green tinge, the trooper was actually an officer and when in the middle of the doorway he looked left and right, Riley could almost hear his brain straining to see.

"Dooff ... Dooff." The 9 mm rounds easily finding their mark from six feet in range. Liz stood up, so did Riley, they were joined by Ron and Graham. Liz found a chair and sat the ex-courier driver down to administer first aid,

"Dong·mu, Gim" Everyone froze 'shit not another one' thought Riley.

"Dong·mu, Gim" A little more urgent this time, still no movement from inside.

Riley motioned to Ron to back him up, and the twenty rear old peered around the door into, what looked like a kid's bedroom, single bed, walls decked out with boy stuff, model planes, what looked like a remote-control tank on one of the shelves. Ron checked under the bed giving Riley the thumbs up, 'where the fuck is he?'

"Dong·mu, Gim!" 'Now I've got you, you little rapist' pointing to the double wardrobe the pair levelled their 54's,

"Dooff ... Dooff ... Dooff ... Dooff." Placing four shots at random spacing's they witnessed the door opening and the trooper tumbling out.

0510 hours, "Dooff ... Dooff." Two more rounds to finish him off. Ron and Riley dragged the body out the front door and into the morning light, Graham sporting a head bandage dragged the officer out,

"Looks like two officers, the first has got two pips on his shoulders, my guess is a lieutenant, the last one and the coward hiding in the wardrobe is something special, he's also got two stars but they're larger, I think this prick is a lieutenant colonel."

Chapter 23
Numbers

Saturday 21ˢᵗ March 2015 Kings Town Wharf

0600 hours. Jun Lee stood where the huge catamaran was moored the day before, half expecting to see it back from its first sortie down the channel; he took in the smells of salt air and the stale smell of fish. Movement was virtually non-existent, and the sixty-year-old general surveyed the buildings surrounding the ancient harbour, still in awe of its history, his thoughts drifted back to Pyongyang, North Korea's capital, an ancient city located on the Taedong River about 109 kilometres (68 miles) upstream from its mouth on the Yellow Sea. He remembered only too well where the super tankers were built, the Naval Nampho shipyards, his many visits to oversee the production. While both naval and army defence headquarters were in Pyongyang, the Yellow Sea Fleet Command was situated at Toejo Dong; the KPN (Korean Peoples Navy) has twenty bases split between the two coasts (Sea of Japan and Yellow Sea).

0710 hours, back in his office, he peered longingly down the river looking for the *Gin Gum Kim,* 'where is Li Chun' he thought, usually already at work when the general arrived, he was beginning to have a terrible thought. Yelling at the first clerk to arrive,

"Where is Captain Li Chun?" The corporal wishing he hadn't come to work early replies.

"Last time I saw him sir, was on the mighty catamaran organising ammunition and the fuel truck around 2000 hours Thursday evening."

The general was in meetings all day yesterday and was confident Li was organising his horse troops for another raid. Maybe he is still with them.

"Send a messenger to the horse stables at East Kings Town; find out if Captain Chun is there or if he was present there yesterday."

0900 Saturday 21ˢᵗ March 2015 Kings Town Headquarters

"Come in Corporal"

"A messenger to see you sir"

"Ah good, at last some news from East Kingstown?"

"Sorry sir he's from Kettle." The messenger handed over the written report from the Kettle commander. Jun Lee read the words and sank into his chair waving the young soldier away.

General

At approximately 1100 hours yesterday a fierce naval battle was observed in the channel some five miles from the Kettle Marina, our lookouts reported a huge catamaran midstream chasing one vessel, this may in fact be the one that was moved from the marina some weeks ago. This catamaran was being chased by two other vessels, these have been seen at other locations up and down the channel and are confirmed to be the rebel forces.

Rocket Propelled Grenades and machine gun fire was reported constantly between the three vessels, lasting for approximately two hours. It appears the timber vessel being chased was hit by RPG fired from the catamaran destroying it completely but unfortunately another RPG hit the catamarans bridge superstructure, this erupted in a fireball stopping the vessel dead in its tracks. After thirty minutes the great aluminium beast slid under the waves, there were no survivors.

Min Dong Senior Lieutenant
Commander Alliance Forces
Kettle

Monday 23rd March 2015 Kings Town Headquarters

0900 hours and time for the weekly update on casualty numbers and operations status. Jun Lee's clerk was chasing up the final messengers from the various areas for this very important situation report. Since the death of Senior Lieutenant Lum Si Gow in the debacle at Soothe, the general had not enjoyed the meetings.

Standing in front of his whiteboard, Jun Lee wrote down the headings while his senior sergeant read the reports from the various messengers-

"Sir, the following reports are in-

- Oxford
  - No report from this area, reported to be in rebel hands although Alliance horse troops were operating in the hills west of there, in actual fact that is why he had not heard back from them.

- Mid-Point
  - 400 strong Alliance blockade was holding firm although some night-time raids had taken place by the rebels with only three killed.
  - Ammunition was down to seventy per trooper on average, none in reserve.
- Mona
  - Last report from this area had the Alliance troops on the run back to Devon to re-group, no word since last week.
- Wattle
  - This had fallen into rebel hands.
- Devon
  - This had fallen into rebel hands.
- Brownsville
  - This had fallen into rebel hands.
- Kings Bridge
  - Alliance troops had withdrawn to the wall in the wilderness, the 200 strong company was well supplied, the fighting at Kings Bridge saw the loss of 245 troopers and seven wounded.
- Wood
  - A detachment from Kettle had engaged the rebels and set up a barricade near the back road to Swan, they sustained heavy casualties losing 105 and thirty wounded. Ammunition levels were low with an average of twenty-five rounds per man.
- Kettle
  - The Garrison north of Kettle still stands even though the rebels had systematically killed all the Nationals in the area, what they missed were relocated to Queens. Garrison strength was 410 with an average of eighty rounds per man.

- Indonesian Alliance
  - A messenger had made their way from St Mona reporting a strategic withdrawal from Benoa to St Anne, Indonesian troop numbers were good with reports of around 40,000 left of their original 75,000, no mention was made of the 10,000 on loan to the NK Alliance.
- Lawn
  - Heavy casualties and with the Lawn Commander Lieutenant Colonel Lee Bowe dead, the area was in chaos, what troops were left had withdrawn to Earth. It was reported ammunition was non-existent.
- Reed Lagoon
  - Small garrison of Indonesian troops had control of this small Northeast outpost.
- Earth
  - 15,000 troops under the command of Major Pin Lim Ho, recently promoted.
- Scot
  - Garrison of 5,000 troops covering a vast area, NK Nationals were systematically being exterminated by rebel forces, ammunition supplies still good and some in reserve.
- Lakeside
  - Captain Tun Kim and his 1000 strong garrison was stretched from Wall in the Wilderness in the west to Oxford in the east, ammunition levels high, currently rooting out rebels in the Red Mountain area assisted by the horse troops.
- St Mona
  - Indonesian Garrison of around 5,000, good ammunition supplies."

General Jun Lee Sung stared out over the Kings Town Harbour; he seemed in a daze; the sergeant wondered whether the general actually heard anything he had reported.

"Thank you, Sergeant, and to all of the messengers making their way here today you are dismissed. Oh Sergeant, call a full staff meeting at 1300 hours!"

1300 hours, the main hall of the Taswegian parliament was an awesome room, full of exotic Taswegian timbers and the furniture was covered with lush red and gold leather upholstery. Jun Lee always loved the smell of the leather, and he could swear the timber gave off a wonderful aroma.

A full staff meeting was not what the name suggested, because of the time it took to get messengers to the outlying areas it really meant the meeting consisted of the garrison senior staff and the general's headquarters staff. Looking out over the room at the rag tag bunch of officers and senior NCO's he started,

"Welcome, I have brought you all here today to bring you up to speed on the situation around the state. The outlying messengers have returned to their areas with my orders for the next phase, before you are the outcomes of that meeting"

Jun Lee unveiled the whiteboard and gave the room time to digest the information written on it. A hand shot up from the left of the room.

"Yes Lieutenant?" the rather young, faced trooper wearing sergeant stripes was taken aback by the comment, not sure if the general was addressing him.

"Er sorry sir, Sergeant Sonny Li Kim here, I'm in charge of a troop stationed between East Kingstown and Bridge, I was wondering whether we could be of some assistance to the horse troops in the twaddle area?" The general smiled.

"That's why you are now Lieutenant Kim, great suggestion, we should have more forward-thinking troopers and maybe we would not be in this situation." Another hand.

"How are we going overall General, are we going to lose the battle and what news of our much-needed ammunition re-supply."

"We can only hope that the next convoy arrives soon Major Go, although it is grossly overdue, I fear it was caught up in the nuclear blasts and we have to deal with the ammunition shortages ourselves." The thirty something Major stood.

"I have a suggestion re the ammunition sir, we send out orders to restrict shots fired to confirmed kill only, issue a fixed bayonets order to all troops and stockpile what other weapons we have. Do we have numbers on our 9mm ammunition sir? I see all your reports only mention the 7.62mm." Jun Lee had not thought of this and summoned his clerk to take a memo to all outlying areas.

"Good question Major now Sergeant, take the following memo to be delivered to all areas,

- Report 9mm ammunition supplies ASAP
- General Order to fix bayonets
- Restrict shots to confirmed kill shots as of now
- Report on all other weapon stocks, RPG's, Grenades etc.
- Conscript all male Nationals above the age of 16 and train them to fight

"This will not go down well with the Nationals sir, it was part of a mandate when they were picked to come to Taswegia that they would not be required to fight, they were to have nothing to do with the annihilation of the Taswegians."

"They might not have any choice if it gets any worse, oh and Sergeant, break open the emergency ammunition supplies!"

Chapter 24
Battle at Ansons Bay

Saturday 21ˢᵗ March 2015 FCPB Fremantle Brownsville Harbour

0800 hours, Dick, Sarge and Doc seated on the bridge, Sarge still armed with the whiteboard, the forty-five-year-old ex-sapper listed the vessels that were currently or would be operating in the Northeast.

- *Nancy Kay* crew plus one *Spirit* officer, one crew and eighteen passengers
- *Waubs Bay* crew plus one *Spirit* officer, one crew and fourteen passengers
- *Fremantle* crew plus two *Spirit* officers, four crew and sixteen passengers

"We need to put an invasion plan together for the main push against the Indonesians, we have not really banged heads with these troops yet, but this will change."

Dick looked around the bridge, accepted the brew from Jack as he emerged from below, the constant drone of voices emulating from below, he knew these were Patch, April, Nari, Lauren and

Nettie. Thomas presented after a reccy of the local shops with whatever the seventy-two-year-old ex-RSM could scrounge.

"How did you go Thomas?"

"A few dozen bottles of wine to add to our supply, courtesy of the East Brownsville bottle shop Doc."

"Nice, we're just compiling the plan of attack for the Indonesians mate; so far, we thought the three vessels would be as per Sarge's whiteboard. *Nancy Kaye* and *Waubs Bay* would bring the trained troops from Bass Island, rendezvous with us to take our contingent, numbers given to us by Santa were six ex-*Spirit* crew, four officers and forty-eight passengers, a couple of which should probably not go ashore and be used for the raids. Split up as displayed on the board, oh and the older couple, the Bristols will help on board the *Fremantle*, I'm quite sure Nari, April and Lauren can occupy them appropriately."

"Don't forget Patch and Nettie Dick."

"Haven't forgot them mate, they will be operating the RHIB, have to have someone to coxswain her into the drop off points."

1200 hours and with the boat's numbers worked out, Doc took over with the logistics.

"Around 2200 hours on the 26th of March, the *Fremantle* will anchor off the entrance to Ansons Bay, East Coast Taswegia, where Patch and Nettie will relay RHIB team one just inside the channel at Policeman's Point. This will consist of Sarge, Thomas, one *Spirit* officer, two *Spirit* crew and seven passengers." Sarge continued

"Thanks Doc, yep, we will land and clear the area, only about half a dozen shacks there, but as it's a popular camping ground and the Indo's may have used it as a tent city. Because of its distance from the main area of Ansons Bay I'm hoping there will be a jeep or truck for us to scrounge for transport.

Our mission will be to clear all the farms between Policeman's Point and Ansons Bay, hopefully rendezvousing with Dick and team two sometime during the night."

"Right after Patch and Nettie deposit team one, they will return to the *Fremantle* and collect team two, this will take them through the channel and across the bay to the northern shore where the road finishes, and this should be around midnight. Team two will consist of Dick, Jack, one Spirit Officer, two Spirit crew and seven passengers. Their mission will be to start clearing the shacks; well, you can't really call them shacks now, because most of them were permanent residents and fairly substantial homes. Taking numbers off the Taswegian street atlas it looks like around two hundred homes in the area, if we call the boat ramp ground zero and where the two teams meet up this should be around 0400 hours, then combining they can continue to clear the southern section of the small settlement, hopefully completing the task by sun up, any questions?"

"What happens to the *Waubs Bay* and *Nancy Kay* Doc?"

"Yes Thomas, good point, they will steam in company with us till we anchor then continue on to Humbug Point and the entrance to Georges Bay. Now the *Nancy Kay* has crossed the bar before when she and the *Dementia* carried out a stealth raid on St Anne, the tide should be right for the *Waubs Bay's* slightly deeper draft. *Nancy Kay* will deposit a team ashore at the boat ramp and jetty where they saved Rose, Barry, Nick and Trent, they will find transport and start clearing the point working towards St Anne.

Both vessels will then enter the bar around the same time as Dick and team two go ashore and steam straight to the main wharf area arriving around 0100 hours. The mission will be similar to last time; Santa will lead a team and continue to clear the town from the main wharf while Len and Josh lead another team from the slip area. If they give the town till say 0530 hours, then withdraw to the middle of the bay and anchor." Dick took over.

"*Fremantle* RHIB will extract teams one and two at 0700 hours from the boat ramp, and then back to us. Whatever is not cleared will have to wait, our brief will be to hit them fast and hard. We will steam down the coast to stand off The Gardens, the 40-60 crew will close up and commence bombardment of the twenty homes there, now they are right on the waterfront so shouldn't present a problem, I admit it is a shame we have to destroy these homes, but it was felt it quicker to do this on the way to Bin Bay where the RHIB will deposit two teams again, one to clear Bin Bay proper and the other to reccy Humbug Point where it is expected there will be a huge tent city. This area is usually a camper's paradise, and we may elect to bombard this area as well."

TRF Vessel Waubs Bay photo taken by Author

Sunday 22ⁿᵈ March 2015 TRF Vessel Nancy Kay Blackmark Harbour

0945 hours, as Santa watched the small tender make its way from the *Spirit of Taswegia II,* his thought process was interrupted by Pat trying to hand him a coffee, and a squawk on the VHF.

"*Nancy Kay, Nancy Kay this is Waubs Bay, Waubs Bay* over." The ex-Navy CD reached above his skipper's chair and squeezed the transmit button.

"*Waubs Bay* this is *Nancy Kay* receiving loud and clear, is that you Len, what's your position?"

"Just entering Parry's Bay mate, sorry we're late, had a few engine problems, will tell you when we get there, eta- 1200 hours."

"Come in Bradley; help yourself to a brew, kettle's hot." The *Spirit of Taswegia II* Captain eased into the bench seat around the small table in the wheelhouse of the *Nancy Kay.*

"Thanks Santa, any news from The *Fremantle*?"

"Yep, I gave Dick the stats we went through yesterday and he has come up with the split between *Waubs Bay,* us and them.

We sail Tuesday morning and rendezvous with the *Fremantle* at Swan Island where they will take their TRF contingent, two *Spirit* officers, four crew and eighteen passengers. I'm suggesting we carry them along with our contingent of one officer, one crew and fourteen passengers, the *Waubs Bay* will carry the same." Looking at Bradley and the Captain, he guessed Santa's question.

"I'll go with the *Fremantle* along with Jock, my second engineer that leaves John and Wallace to fill the other two berths, one with you and one with Len."

"Speaking of Len, he'll be here soon, I'm suggesting we stick to the rest day today and do one more round of range practice tomorrow. Introduce the *Waubs Bay* crew to their TRF contingent while Pat, Rose, Jill and maybe Barry revictual both vessels, when the practice is over, we will stow all the weapons and ammo on board. I know Dick and Sarge will want to swap over to Indonesian weaponry, oh that reminds me Vert pull out the SS1-R5 Raider Assault Rifles we have in stock along with say 500 rounds, just so everyone can get accustomed to it."

Monday 23rd March 2015 TRF Vessel Waubs Bay outside the Nancy Kay Blackmark Harbour

1700 hours and with introductions out of the way, Jill had joined forces with Pat, Rose and Barry successfully relieving a local farmer of a whole beast, cut up after being hung for a week. Added to this were spuds, fresh veggies and a selection of seafood, enough to feed one hundred personnel.

Range practice went well with all members trying the Indonesian Raider Assault Rifle, the weapon performed similarly to the Type 68 of the NK Alliance, but the projectile was smaller. Vert showed them the Pindad P2 Semi-automatic Pistol and a few rounds were fired, but because this was just another 9mm pistol he decided to save the ammunition.

Bradley and the other *Spirit* crew members supervised feeding the rest of the TRF at the International Hotel, letting them have a drink on their last night. The crews of the *Nancy Kay* and *Waubs Bay* were joined by the officers for a last supper together.

"What times kick off tomorrow, Santa?" John, the lanky first mate was just a tad nervous not really knowing how he would perform in battle; he looked at the other TRF members present,

"I'll be honest, I'm scared, I know Santa is probably the most experienced here tonight, but I look at Len, six months ago mate you were a fisherman and Jill, shit you're only seventeen, how the fuck do you do it?" Jill smiled and held up her hand.

"Let me answer this, Santa." Squeezing Len's hand and placing her other arm around the ex-CD's neck.

"You know what John, I'm scared too, I bet if you asked them, hell everyone would be scared, even Dick, Jack and Sarge, the most combat ready out of all of us. Dick once told me when we cleared a chook farm it was healthy to be scared, it sort of honed his wits and made him that much more responsive, ready for action, he said it used to make his brain run faster. Trust your training John, Captain, hell you couldn't have got better trainers than these guys here. Shit here I am sounding like an old pro! Don't say a word Len, I, like everyone else on Taswegia will be happy when the fat lady sings, or in this case the general." Santa answered John's question.

"We sail at 0900 hours, rendezvous with the *Fremantle* at 1300 hours." Rose pulled out a couple of bottles of port, something she had come across while scrounging for victuals earlier in the day, these came with a dozen shot glasses and were soon issued out.

"A toast to, well I don't know, us I suppose, you know the good guys, oh I reckon it should be to Dick and Patch without them we wouldn't be here!" Standing, the group fell silent for a minute, each one mulling over their thoughts, what had happened in the last three months but more to the point what was going to happen in the next three.

2100 hours, meal out of the way, Vert and Rose retired to their cabin, the *Spirit* crew and Barry returned to the International Hotel. Well Barry had a girl he was interested in, Josh and port didn't get on, so the nineteen-year-old fell into his bunk on the *Waubs Bay*, leaving Santa, Pat, Jill and Len lounging outside on the aft deck.

"Tell me how you first met Dick, Santa?" The sixty-one-year-old ex-clearance diver smiled.

"Ninth of October 1969, Kingstown Marine Building 0900 hours, there were eleven of us, all fifteen years old, none of us knew anyone else. I must admit, I would have looked like a real posh bugger carrying my tennis racquet.

At 1000 we were ushered into some bloke's office where we swore allegiance to Queen and country, we then had twenty minutes to chat amongst ourselves before the bus came to whisk us away to the airport, then we flew to Milbourne then finally Perth in Western Australia. I think we finally made it through the gates of HMAS Leeuwin and to our accommodation block after SCRAN that night, they split us up between the two divisions."

"Were you in the same division as Dick?"

"No, I ended up in the other division, nothing flash about the choice; I think the navy just worked alphabetically, Dick's surname 'Mann' fell in the middle, so he went to Rhoades while mine 'Saunders' went to Howden." Pat commented.

"You know, you've never told me that story!"

"Pat my love, there is plenty about my navy career I haven't told you" Standing, Pat grabbed Santa's ear and pulled him towards their cabin, smiling and with a wink at Jill.

"You bastard, you'll keep."

Tuesday 24th March 2015 TRF Vessel Nancy Kay Blackmark Harbour

0850 hours and the *Waubs Bay* had already loaded their TRF troops while Jill had slipped the lines, she was now standing off the wharf waiting for the *Nancy Kay* to do the same. Vert emerged from the engine room like some apparition, stuffed his rag into his shorts back pocket and gave Santa the thumbs up signal.

The V12 Caterpillar 1000 HP Turbo Diesel Engine turned over, firing on its first rotation, a puff of black smoke escaped from the exhaust and the rumble of the powerful beast shook every part of the vessel. Barry was dropping the mooring lines and as soon as the last one was on deck, Santa went ahead spinning the wheel to starboard edging the bow of the sixty-five-foot Conquest into the huge truck tyres being used as fenders.

Going astern Pat hit the ships horn three times and soon was heading out to open water. *Waubs Bay* falling in astern of her they passed the huge bow of the *Spirit of Taswegia II*, both were absolutely dwarfed by the towering ship. Turning to port, Santa came around to *one seven nine* degrees and set the auto pilot, Pat asked for the heading and reached for the VHF handset.

"*Waubs Bay* this is *Nancy Kay*, suggest course to steer, *one seven nine* degrees."

Monday 23rd March 2015 FCPB Fremantle Bull Bay Wharf

2100 hours, Patch and Dick stood holding hands at the top of the gangway as they watched their friends drive away. The night air was still and with the river hardly moving, *Fremantle* was very stationary, she had arrived just after lunch, giving the crew the afternoon off while catching up with Ernie, Belle and the High Head contingent. Catching up with all the details was well worth it; this also gave Dick and Sarge time to lay out plans to the group and what they saw as their involvement when they attacked the Indonesians.

Ernie, Belle, Henry and Tegan had enjoyed an evening meal aboard, all understanding their part to play. They were to back up with attacking at Reeds Lagoon and Scott, they had conducted some clearing raids in the past and noted Scott still had 4-5000 troops. This raid was planned for the same night as the *Fremantle* swooped on Ansons Bay. Henry and a team of twenty would attack Scott while Ernie and another twenty would attack Reeds Lagoon.

"Great evening Chook." Hugging his wife, Dick relaxed.

"Looks like another romance blossoming between Henry and Tegan?"

"And why not, he's still young and she's certainly a good-looking sort!"

Joining everyone in the Junior Sailor's Mess Doc raised his glass of cabernet sauvignon.

"Well, here's to tomorrow night, it's been a long time coming and thanks to Sarge, Jack and Dick well planned." Jack commented.

"Let's hope Santa and Vert has trained them well enough to do the job with minimal casualties."

"What time do we rendezvous with them Doc?"

"1300 hours Nari, oh and we have an elderly couple to make use of, they won't be going on the raids."

"We use them in galley and sick bay my man no problems."

"How did you go Nettie and Patch checking the RHIB this afternoon? I see Dick launched it for you to have some practice,"

"After a few runs we kicked arse Doc, and then Patch had a go."

Everyone laughed, they could see the funny side, and even Patch knew she was not all that coordinated with things mechanical, especially when it involved balance as well.

"I think Nettie will be the main coxswain and I will be the deckhand, as long as Nettie can keep the darn thing still."

Tuesday 24th March 2015 FCPB Fremantle entering Boss Strait

0900 hours, Annie and Jack were finishing rounds in the engine room, Patch and Nari lookout, Dick was on the wheel, Doc in his chair and everyone else was on the flying bridge enjoying the sunshine.

"Starboard 20 Dick, steer *zero six nine*, revs for twenty knots"

"Roger that Skipper *zero six nine*, twenty knots." The FCPB responded quickly to the helm in the slight sea conditions, the bow soon porpoised up and down in the following swell pushing a bow spray out either side on the downward plunge. Temperature was a hazy twenty degrees; wind five knots from the Northwest.

1200 hours, Patch and Lauren put together a ploughman's lunch, they had got used to sitting the huge trays on top of a damp towel on the Perspex topped chart table, crew could just help themselves.

"Swan Island and two other contacts well and truly on radar Doc, distance to run four miles."

"*Nancy Kay, Nancy Kay,* this is *Fremantle* over."

"Receiving *Fremantle,* where do you want to transfer, over?"

"I reckon we'll make for the lee side of the island, less swell Santa."

1315 hours and *Fremantle* stopped in the lee of Swan Island and dropped anchor, with Santa on final approach to the starboard side in the *Nancy Kay,* the *Waubs Bay* standing off. Barry handed Thomas and Jack the amidships mooring line, this was all that was needed to hold the two vessels together while they rafted up and transferred troops. Len brought the *Waubs Bay* alongside the port side and did the same.

Dick hopped aboard to say hello, giving Pat a hug the ex-CD made it to the wheelhouse to catch up with Santa and Vert. With the TRF team already topside they were merrily hopping over to the *Fremantle,* last one off was Bradley. The *Spirit* Captain waited till Dick was finished then joined him aboard Fremantle. It was decided because there was only twenty-four nautical miles to run for Ansons Bay they would wait there until 2000 hours.

2000 hours, with all crews back aboard their respective vessels, Doc ordered weigh anchor, Jack and Patch manned the windlass while Annie looked after things below.

"Slow ahead Dick, steer *one two seven* revolutions for ten knots."

"Roger that Skipper." Finished with the windlass, Jack and Patch watched as the other two vessels fell in astern. Jack declared.

"My shout for the brews Patch." The ex-CD sniper disappeared below collecting other orders as he went.

2130 hours, the *Waubs Bay* and *Nancy Kay* had overtaken the FCPB making their way to Humbug Point before *Fremantle* turned in to drop the first team off.

"Starboard ten, steer *two one zero* revolutions for five knots." Dick eased the patrol boat around under the point that housed Eddystone Lighthouse, the usual lookouts, Patch and Nari with Thomas reading the depth out as they got close to shore. Running down parallel to the coast they were headed towards Policeman's Point, hoping to get some reprieve from the swell before they anchored.

"Ten metres, Skipper." called Thomas.

"Slow astern, all stop, drop anchor."

Tuesday 24th March 2015 FCPB Fremantle off Ansons Bay East Coast Taswegia

2210 hours, with her anchor on the bottom and a suitable scope of chain deployed, Doc ordered the RHIB deployed while Sarge was issuing weapons and ammunition to the teams.

"Team one stand by." Patch and Nettie were already in the RHIB; Nettie had the twin 150HP Mercury Verados idling while Patch held on to the short painter holding them alongside. Sarge, Thomas, John, the two crew and the seven passengers that made up the team quickly seated themselves aboard the RHIB. Patch let go and the young eighteen-year-old Nettie Crumb thrust the throttles ahead not quite to the plane, taking heed what Dick said about making too much noise, the trip into the Policeman's Point boat ramp took only five minutes. Nettie nudged the bow of the twenty-two-foot boat against the crumbling concrete ramp, Sarge jumped ashore and held the boat straight while everyone made it ashore. The eighteen-year-old went astern and spun around for the return journey.

Tuesday 24th March 2015 Team one Policeman's Point

2250 hours, Sarge had gathered the team for the last-minute prep talk; he had already sent three members to the closest house to try and acquire some transport.

"John, you stick with me and you two ladies over there, Thomas can you take Jock and the rest down to the camping ground, see what's about, remember NVG's for those that have them and suppressors only, you've only got the rifles for emergencies." The forty-five-year-old ex-sapper watched them disperse, the first home was occupied, on approach he was met with an excited female member telling him they found a jeep, the girl was that excited Sarge had to clamp his hand over the woman's mouth to stop her waking the neighbourhood.

This was the right time to give them a lesson on how it was done; gaining entry through an unlocked sliding glass door Sarge led three of them to the first bedroom.

"Dooff ... Dooff." The first two Indonesian Nationals were disposed of, next room same outcome, next room three kids, this brought the three team members to a halt, but the ex-sapper didn't miss a beat, knowing they would find it difficult to kill children in cold blood, especially the females. Gathering at the jeep John whispered.

"Sarge, I'm impressed, how do you do that?"

"You'll get used to it mate." They could detect the supple sounds of the suppressed 9mm Browning pistols doing their job in the campsite area.

Just after midnight, having completed all the tents and homes in this area, they loaded into the jeep and made their way west.

"First farm is about two kilometres team, John, you, plus one take the front, Jock you and Thomas take the back, the rest of you with me, we'll check the sheds, pay attention if you find any meat hanging, we'll take it with us." A hesitant first officer led the way in through the front door, it wasn't long, and Sarge gave the thumbs up after hearing the familiar 'Dooff … Dooff'. Thomas met John in the middle of the farmhouse then reported to Sarge out back, one of the crew whispered loudly.

"Found a pig hanging in the kill house!"

"Great work team, now I know none of you have been on a clearing raid before, but I have one thing to report" John was quick to comment.

"What, that we're doing a great job Sarge"

"Well that too, no there has been no troopers, normally with the NK Nationals there would have been house security, now that means it's easier for us to kill them with nobody shooting back, but it also means, if they are not here, where are they?"

"Waiting to ambush us down the road Sarge?"

"Fucking hope not Jock, but we will have our wits about us."

Tuesday 24ᵗʰ March 2015 Team Two Ansons Bay

2320 hours and Nettie brought the RHIB back from the plane and following Dick's direction turned to port, the ex-CD specialist was heading towards the last home on the bay.

"Bring her in here girl." The bank was three foot above the waterline and after Patch found a secure tree root to tie the bow to, Dick clambered up the bank and onto the back lawn of a home, followed by Bradley, Wallace, the crew and with their tail man Jack they assembled. Patch waved as the RHIB spun and disappeared into the inkiness of the night.

"Ok, we'll split into six teams of two. Bradley with one passenger, Wallace with another, Jack with one, other crew member, sorry luv forgotten your name, with one, two together and one with me, you all know the drill, some of you have NVG's and suppressors only, take no risks, where possible go in the front door, remember bad guys always go in the back door so they are less likely to expect us to go in the front. Anyway, that's my reasoning; we'll meet up at the end of this street to re-group."

0130 hours. All teams were progressing well; most homes yielded at least eight Indonesian Nationals, Jack had to go back three homes when he found out the team of two passengers, the one couple couldn't bring themselves to kill the children.

Thomas wondered whether to bring this up with Dick when they met at the end of the street.

0240 hours, the team gathered out the front of an old shop, it looked like it had been closed for years so no one cleared the place. They sat on a short brick retaining wall and caught their breath. Dick squatted facing the group, while Jack stood behind the ex-CD; Wallace and Bradley were given the task of collecting the stats of the night, Dick whispered to Jack.

"Mate I don't like this, this is weird, no troopers. Has anyone come across troops?" There were murmurings from the group, some of the new crew didn't understand and were horrified when the learned that usually there was armed troopers guarding the Nationals.

Jack placed his hand on Dick's shoulder, and in the moonlight the ex-CD could make out a shadow coming from within the old shop, Jack moved around the back of the shop, Dick waved to Bradley making a signal for everyone to hit the deck.

"Dooff … Dooff …Dooff … Dooff … Dooff, bang, bang." The distinct sound of the supressed 9mm Browning followed by the Pindad P2 Semi-automatic Pistol's unsuppressed muzzle blast. Dick was quick to make it to the front door, shouldering the near rotten covering, he spewed into the main room where Jack was taking cover behind an old fridge, receiving the P2's rounds from behind the counter.

From Dick's vantage point thru the NVG's he could see the perpetrator and when they realised someone had crash tackled the door they were confused for a second, not knowing which way to fire, which was all the sixty-one-year-old needed.

"Dooff … Dooff." The two 9mm hollow point rounds both found their mark hitting the young Indonesian soldier in the head and chest. Dick asked.

"You alright Jack?"

"Yeah mate, took some bark off my knee, I got four but missed the fifth, so it's still hot, get my drift?"

"Roger that, in this room or out the back?"

"Can't be out the back, he headed this way, and I don't think the one you shot are one and the same." Taking a moment to let the dust settle, Dick could hear Bradley calling from outside.

"Wait one." Dick crawled to the body on the floor, checked for a pulse, extracted the P2 from his hand then sat with his back to the counter facing the old cool room.

"You right Jack if I make a noise?" The ex-sniper knew exactly what his mate meant.

"Fire in the hole"

The F1 fragmentation hand grenade (F1 grenade) didn't have far to go, Dick had no trouble aiming through the open doorway to the cool room, designed to produce a lethal radius of 6 m (19.6 ft) and a casualty radius of 15 m (49 ft) this was well within the specs. The 4,000 2.4mm steel ball fragments arranged to "achieve uniform distribution of lethal fragments through 360° upon functioning." The 5 second timed fuse ran out, and a blast with an equivalent explosive composition mass of 62g of RDX annihilated the room.

"Did you hear the yelp, Jack?"

"Yep, certainly sounded like someone was not happy mate."

0300 hours, Dick and Jack were met by a couple of the women and Bradley.

"What the hell happened here Jack, one moment you were here and the next you've shot the bad guys?"

"Not all of them Captain, if it wasn't for Dick nailing the one behind the counter and sorting the last one with the grenade, I'd be toast!

"Problem is now all the neighbours heard the noise, but we know why we haven't come across any troopers, they were stationed here as security, question is are there any more little outposts?"

Wednesday 25ᵗʰ March 2015 Team One Ansons Bay Main Road

0300 hours, having wrapped the prime piece of pork in a water-soaked hessian bag, team one continued to clear the next nine farms, this took them around the southern part of the bay and over a small bridge which housed the creek feeding the bay. In the moonlight Sarge could easily make out the tannin in the water, a brown froth gathered where the free-flowing creek met the bay. Hearing the explosion twenty minutes earlier brought them back to reality.

The M35A3 variant jeep carried the team towards the next home; they were certainly closer together here, not like the farms, Thomas had pointed up the road to where it turned abruptly to the right.

"I guess this is the entrance to the little township itself mate."

Letting the teams of two off at each home meant the jeep was well towards the corner, Sarge looked back and could already see the members emerging from the homes, the slight 'Dooff … Dooff' sounds becoming more familiar.

0400 hours and fifteen homes down, they could see the boat ramp in front of them; this was where they were supposed to meet team two.

"There they are Sarge?" John was pointing to the M35 2-ton cargo truck used to move team two around.

"Howdy partner, fancy seeing you here." Jack was displaying his usual dry humour.

"Any trouble Sarge?"

"No mate, but by the sounds of the bang a while ago you have?"

"Yeah, we found a rat's nest bunkered down at the old shop."

"Rat Sac?"

"Nah F1."

0430 hours team one took the low road along the waterfront while Dick's team two went inland, a road that ran one block back from the coast road. It was decided the Indonesians to save troop numbers elected to put a small garrison there instead of home security, this might have saved them troop numbers but may have been their undoing.

Wednesday 25th March 2015 Team One Ansons Bay Waterfront Homes

0450 hours and with the boat ramp behind them; Sarge split them up into their smaller two person teams. This time he paired up with the forty-eight-year-old chef, Terri, a solidly built girl with short auburn hair, obviously not afraid of hard work she had revelled in the killing.

"Thanks, Sarge, for asking me to pair up, really appreciate it."

"No problems Terri, just do what I do, and we'll be ok."

Looking ahead at the line of homes, he smiled to himself thinking 'fuck it will be daylight soon'. Halfway along the team encountered just that, the first Indonesian National upright and definably awake. Luck be with them, it was Thomas and a woman passenger that entered the front door only to be confronted by an old man preparing for his morning wash, stripped to the waist it was obvious the bathroom was his destination.

"Dooff ... Dooff." The ex-regimental sergeant major peering through the NVG's didn't hesitate to shoot the man, quickly followed by his wife following him. Thomas nodded to his partner to clear the next room, she hesitated at the door, this he guessed was a children's bedroom.

"Dooff ... Dooff ... Dooff." He was right, smiling at the thirty something partner he just gave her a slight hug as if to say, 'it will be alright'.

Wednesday 25th March 2015 Team Two Back Street Ansons Bay

0500 hours, better watch our step Liz, the bastards could be awake, Dick was whispering to his current teammate, Liz McDonald, a thirty-six-year-old *Spirit* kitchen hand. Liz had trouble earlier in the night; she froze and left three kids after not being able to shoot them. Jack had to go back and deal with it, finally mentioning it to Dick after the rat's nest was dealt with.

"You lead Liz, I'll back you up" Dick was feeling pretty good about the clearing, mainly because with no troops attached to each home it meant the clearing could be accomplished faster with no fear of being shot at. Armed with the NVG's, the kitchen hand pushed the first bedroom door open to find the woman sitting up on the side of the bed putting on a blouse, while the male snoozed on the far side of the bed.

"Dooff." The hollow point round hit the woman in the chest just right of centre, killing her instantly, Liz moved closer to the bed and took aim again.

"Dooff." Just as she fired the male moved, the round must have grazed his shoulder. Waking to a bullet wound must be bad, but to open your eyes and see a white woman taking aim for another shot would be worse.

"Dooff." Second shot hit him in the back but didn't kill him, being diligent must be a trait of her job, the girl just walking around to the male now moaning and placed her barrel to the man's temple and pulled the trigger. Not anticipating the power of the blast Liz was not prepared for the brain splatter that eventuated, hitting the bedhead and back over her front.

"Shit, fucking hell, Dooff." Dick moved forward to stop her from firing another shot, she was obviously upset.

"Settle girl, it's ok."

"No, it's not, I've got blood and shit all over my shirt, what is that stuff, no don't tell me its brain stuff." Before Dick could do anything, else Liz had literally ripped her shirt off throwing the splattered blouse onto the bed, knocking her NVG's off in the process.

"Voices were heard from out in the passageway, Dick assumed the distraught mumblings from Liz had woke the rest of the family 'Shit' he grabbed the half-naked Liz, clamped his hand over her mouth and dragged her behind the door. Words were being spoken as an older woman entered the room.

"Dooff." Dick grabbed the old lady's body and eased it to the floor, putting his finger to his lips, giving Liz the shush signal he exited.

"Dooff ... Dooff ... Dooff ... Dooff." Liz could hear the bodies hitting the floor but still couldn't bring herself to move.

0530 hours and with the house cleared, Dick found Liz still standing over the dead National in an almost defiant stance. The ex-CD put his arm around her bare shoulder and moved her outside. Void of the partial darkness, the CD had failed to see she had no bra, or maybe she ripped that off as well. A well-proportioned girl with firm breasts, nipples standing up in the early morning chilly temperature, all he could do was strip off his shirt and place it around her. Feeling the cool morning air on his tank top clad body he now was confronted by the dawn, now peeping its warming head up over the low shrubby headland between him and the horizon. His thoughts went to Patch and the rest of the *Fremantle* crew just on the other side; they would all be worried for their safety.

"Sorry Dick, I don't know what came over me." The thirty-six-year-old looked terrible, seeing the spray of blood had not only confined itself to the blouse. Moving over to an outside water tank, the ex-CD encouraged Liz to wash her face, he did the same suggesting she would feel better, he didn't want to alarm her to her looks. Finding a towel from inside, they dried their faces.

"Feel better Liz?"

"Much, thank you and thank you for your shirt, are you sure it is alright?" Dick smiled.

"Oh, I think it's much better this way, you know control the red-blooded members not getting too excited." Liz blushed, finally realising that she had been naked, not something that came naturally to her.

"Looks like we've got company." Pointing to the number of Indonesian Nationals wandering out onto the road. Bradley exited the next house up with Lesley, a fifty-year-old housekeeping superintendent close in tow. Giving Dick one of those 'what do I do now' looks they all just walked towards the M35 2--ton cargo truck. Jack, already there with another

Spirit passenger was surprised when an Indonesian National approached the jeep, obviously not aware of the danger, the fifty-one-year-old ex-CD specialist sniper just nodded at the woman, grabbed her shoulders and marched her back to the front door she emerged from.

"Dooff." Beckoning for his partner to join him they proceeded to clear that home. Dick was aware that this was out of sequence, something they would either have to deal with or withdraw to the extraction point.

Wednesday 25th March 2015 Team 1 Ansons Bay Creek

0600 hours, Sarge and his team had just finished the line of homes before the tannin spewing creek, the last half a dozen, the occupants were up and definitely in the way, shooting people during daylight came as something new to the ex-sapper, usually done in the dark of night looking through the green haze of the NVG's.

"One hour to extraction Thomas, pass the word, we'll hop through this yard and help Dick and team two out."

The six team one pairs soon had the top end of the street covered, with no need to stealth it was fast, very fast, that fast in fact Terri just watched in awe of the forty-five-year-old ex-sapper virtually run through each house, shooting, reloading, shooting, before long the chef was leaning against the front gate post puffed out, she couldn't keep up with him.

"Fucking hell Sarge, you're a machine, what a marvellous example of testosterone, if you weren't hooked up with that lovely little girl, what was her name, Annie, I'd strap you on myself!"

"Don't take on older women." he grinned.

"Boy with me, you'd have no choice." Looking back at the three homes, Sarge thought 'fucking hell, she means it'.

"Right oh, team on me, in the jeep."

0700 hours and Jack was finishing the last home, when Dick and Sarge could hear the distinct sound of the twin 150HP Verados humming across the bay.

"That will be our taxi?" He was waving both vehicles to follow him to the boat ramp. Back on board the *Fremantle*,

"Brrr ... Brrr ... Brrr, hi Santa, how's it hanging, shit no good mate, yep that timing will work, see you then."

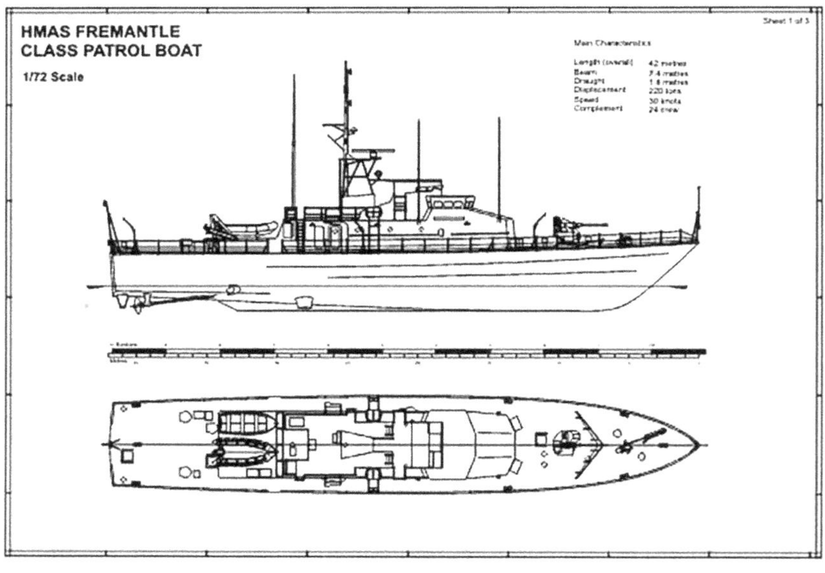

Chapter 25
West Coast takes a hit

Thursday 12th March 2015 on approach to Gorm West Coast Taswegia

0900 hours and Lou had convinced the good doctor Alex, to accompany her for the changeover come re-supply run again. Doing one of these a fortnight, this was not hard to do, as the Strine Hospital was pretty quiet and after talking Bob Silver into helping out, it was easy to leave them, after all he had the help from his newfound family Gill, Margo and Hugo, the four of them had lived on Bob's yacht at Port Brian.

The old KM450 Light Cargo Truck laboured as it always did, climbing up out of the mining town of Queen, the windy steep road nearly killed the fifty-year-old truck.

"Glad you could come with me luv." The fifty-one-year-old blonde ex-trail guide slid her hand into the doctor's lap.

Alex, in the beginning, was just attracted to her voluptuous body but had become smitten with the woman, this highly sexed woman was starved for male attention when he came along. This, as someone not from the coast therefore not part of the gossip which had followed her, pretty much ever since she split from her husband a long time ago, she swore that she would never give the locals the satisfaction of knowing anything about her sex life, that's why she had none, by choice.

1000 hours, the hill didn't win, the old truck made it to the top, then started down towards the old mining town of Gorm. Past the famous gravel football oval, the TRF member sitting up front was smiling to himself 'crikey if I wasn't sitting here, they would be at it like rabbits' the replacement had known Lou most of his life and was well aware of the rumours floating around about her.

"Boom ... Boom ... Boom ... Boom." The sound of automatic fire came that surprisingly it nearly sent Lou off the road in fright.

Alex heard the passenger side window shatter, the rounds passing across on front of them and crashing out of the driver's side window, some imbedding themselves into the driver's door pillar.

"Shit, where the fuck did that come from, boy we were lucky there, anyone hit in the back?" Yelling came from the frightened troops sitting behind her, the rattle of the automatic gunfire still chasing after the truck. Alex turned to get a clearer look in the back saw that the TRF member beside him had been hit in the throat and was quietly bleeding to death.

"He's hit Lou." Lou slowed down, reaching up he checked the man's pulse,

"Dead, don't stop!"

"All ok back here" called someone.

The fifty-one-year-old stopped alongside the Gorm Hotel, a derelict concrete shell of a building. Alex dismounted and with help from another dragged the dead man out and onto the grass, the most experienced man in the back took a look to see if he could see where the gunfire might have come from.

"Looks like the only real place with good cover was the pump shed on the other side of the dam, halfway up the bank, this gave good cover and high ground for vision.

"I'll take two men Lou, and rouse them out; the rest will cover the road behind you"

Alex and Lou watched as the three men disappeared to the right of the dam, they had 300 metres of bushy cover then only thirty metres to the shed. The rest of them spread out up the road, the last of them drawing fire again.

"That was helpful." stated Alex watching the smoke coming from the pump shed.

"Dickheads should have stayed still and just moved on but it's too late now, our guys will nail them."

"You sound like you're on their side Alex?" As she tries to strangle the doctor shoving her tongue deep into the fifty-nine-year-old's mouth.

"Not at all Luv, just pointing out their downfall." He broke free and shoved his hand down Lou's shorts finding the sweet spot.

"Oooooooh, you're a bastard doc!"

1200 hours and it had gone quiet for the last half an hour, not that Alex and Lou would have known, they were pre-occupied exploring each other's bodies.

"Bang ... Bang, got them." yelled someone; Alex tore away from Lou's clutches in time to see the men re-appear from behind the pump shed.

"Looked like just kids Lou, been living it rough for a while I reckon."

Mount up or Blue will wonder what kept us, they had three hours to go to the last known position of their troops, or by now the ex-SAS sergeant was hoping to be as far as Kings Bridge or even on towards the Wall in the Wilderness. The truck hadn't even moved a couple of feet when Lou swore.

"Fuck, those bastards shot one of our tyres."

"Could have been worse Luv, might have shot two, we only have one spare, now that would have been a problem." Lou grinned.

"Not really, I know where there is an old caravan up behind the hotel ruins, used to be a pop-up restaurant there, we could have holed up there for ages, and after all we have plenty of tucker." She was pointing to the crates of supplies sharing the rear with the men.

1630 hours, with the Kings Bridge Hotel coming up on the right-hand side, evidence of heavy fighting was everywhere. A pile of Alliance bodies off to the left over the road, was being doused with a petrol- diesel mix then ignited. The café on the left was now the makeshift camp kitchen, men could be seen tending the outside cooking fires, pulling up, Alex yelled through the broken glass.

"Hi Anita, how's it going?" The fifty-year-old came over and greeted them.

"Great to see you guys, Blue thought something had happened to you, he's down the road just outside the Wall, got most of them held up there, can't be many of them left, it won't be long, and they will retreat."

Backing the truck up to the café, the men quickly unloaded the contents, the camp was looking a little more professional now. They could hear the hum of the generator from over behind them in the bush, keeping the fridges going and giving light for the café and cabin park office next door, this was Blue's HQ.

"Come in Lou, Alex, I'll make you a coffee."

1800 hours and Alex could see a jeep coming up the road towards them, pulling in, Blue climbed out along with half a dozen men, ready for first meal serving.

"G'day Lou, Alex, had a bit of trouble, eh?"

The pair filled him in with all the details; he was most excited to find out about the kids and the automatic weapons.

"We lost a couple a week ago, they scarpered into the bush by the old Hydro Dam a couple of clicks back up the road, and they had been sniping us for a few days when we got wind of where they were hiding out. I'd lay money it was the same pair, the timing works, it would take them that long in this terrain to make it that far, just glad you're both alright."

"It was a close encounter Blue; bloke beside me caught one in the throat, lucky it didn't hit anyone else"

2100 hours and with the meal over, Blue had driven the second meal relief back to the front. Anita pulled Lou aside telling her the second cabin was vacant; she assumed that Alex and she would not be travelling back in the dark. The twelve TRF members going back with the pair the next day were enjoying a drink at the Kings Bridge Hotel, their accommodation while rostered on there. Blue and Anita insisted Alex and Lou join them for a drink with the troops; there had been some particularly difficult firefights the previous week.uc

The NK Alliance had bolstered troops and mounted an offensive, nearly catching the TRF members off guard, if it wasn't for a couple of the relief guys taking a call of nature, one squatting and one keeping guard they wouldn't have seen the squad of men crawling up a bank trying to outflank them. The hero, Grady tells the story, leaning against the huge six-foot open fireplace at the hotel.

"Well. I'm taking a shit, you know concentrating hard on the matter at hand when I think I hear voices whispering, cept I can't understand them so I start whispering out to them, now I think they are my mates pulling the piss, any way they obviously can't understand me, so I whisper louder, louder and so on, before long we're nearly shouting at each other, my mate pushes through the bush asking what the fuck I'm doing when one of the gooks stands up to see where the whispering is coming from. He sees me, with me strides down and a jumper on, I suppose I looked like one of them, next thing about four of them come forward all friendly like, I wiped my arse and pulled the dacks up, but my mate here recognises them and yell's 'shoot the fuckers' next thing I know we're still standing there and there's a dozen of them dead." Alex and Lou were gobsmacked.

"Wow, what a story, you'll live off that for years mate." Grady just laughed.

"Nah, I was taking a shit like I said, the gooks came through the bush and were just about to cancel my ticket when old Red here blew them all to hell." Blue smiled.

"Like you said Lou, either way they are both good stories."

Friday 13th March 2015 TRF Outpost Kings Bridge

0430 hours, Alex couldn't sleep, he kept thinking of the man's story from the night before, what a hoot, he turned to face Lou and decided it was his turn to instigate the frolicking. The early morning desire to go for a leak always enhanced the size and intensity, and armed with this, he found it easy to enter the fifty-one-year-old, still well lubricated from the night before, he soon had Lou reaching for his head and kissing the good doctor.

"Mm, you're awake early, not that I'm complaining."

0900 hours and Lou pulled the KM 450 Light Cargo Truck up outside the Kings Bridge Hotel; they had said their goodbyes to Anita and Blue and prepared for the return journey. Blue had one of his men repair the spare wheel at the old garage, you know just in case.

Monday 16th March 2015 Mona Outpost West Coast Taswegia

1200 hours and Griz, the misfit from Wattle was getting used to his position of power, having moved with the TRF from Mona down the road towards Sheaf, he had held the position since the *Fremantle* boys had moved back to Strine. This morning was like all the others in the last week, but he had an inkling things would change, it had been too quiet for his liking. Having just changed watches, the boys were perched either side of the cutting above the road, this was the easiest position to guard, today he decided to place four members on each side and made them take extra ammunition.

Two weeks ago, they had come up with the idea of dragging a derelict ten-ton truck from up outside Mona to the cutting and block the road with the huge beast. Some of the crew thought he was nuts 'what if we need to get past, it will be in the way' these were some of the main concerns, but Griz was adamant this would be needed before long.

1430 hours and a report had come in from the cutting; they could hear engine noises coming from down the road towards Sheaf. Sending a two-man reccy team to see what was happening, Griz bolstered numbers just in case. Full complement for the outpost was twenty four men; weapons were the Type 68 Assault Rifles, a few 9mm Type 54 pistols, one RPG and one Ultimax Light Machine Gun, compliments of the Indonesian Alliance, or should

I say the *Fremantle* and *Warrnambool*, the big problem was the ammunition for this, being 5.56mm they had ran out a week ago, during a fire fight they expelled all available ammunition for this weapon.

"Hey Griz, reccy team is back, looks like they are getting ready for an offensive, a couple of trucks and about forty men."

Monday 16ᵗʰ March 2015 TRF Vessel Christa Leanne Grass Harbour

0900 hours, Harry, Jill and Gary had slotted into their roll of transporting TRF members between Grass and Stone and today was similar, except for a report of TRF members missing on Kangaroo Island. Word had come back that John Hammer's stockman, Billy Short and his girlfriend Tracey Webster borrowed one of John's dinghies to row across to Kangaroo Island to go Mutton Birding, this was a week ago and they haven't been seen since.

"Engine checks been done Harry, all good below." The twenty-four-year-old skipper pushed the starters bringing the twin VOLVO TMD 100A, 250 HP engines to life; Jill was already assisting Gary in slipping the lines with some help from people ashore.

Joining them for the trip were four Elite members on their way back to Taswegia after a week's spell. Tom, Reg, Grant and Brittany were stowing their weapons and ammunition, quite familiar with Harry and the crew of the *Christa Leanne*.

"How close can you get us to the island Skipper?"

"Should be able to get you within rowing distance mate, I'm not sure what's there, I have only passed the island, and to be honest not paid much attention to it.

Jill, assisted by Brittany poured the drinks as the eighty-five-foot ex-squidl boat negotiated the couple of sunken wrecks in Grass Harbour.

"What does the tourism guide say about this place Jill?" Flicking to the relevant page the eighteen-year-old read.

"Not much it seems, all it says is that Kangaroo Island is part of the Petrel Group, it's a 125-hectare (310-acre) unpopulated island, located in the Boss Strait, close to the Bird Island, in north-west Taswegia, it goes on to say, the island has been used for grazing cattle, Mutton Birding and is surrounded by extensive mudflats."

"Not very informative Tom, I guess it will be suck it and see, the navigational chart says reasonably deep water on the western side, just mudflats on the side facing Bird Island, might do a circumference and check it out, eh?"

"Wouldn't recommend that Skipper, if there's NK Alliance there it will give them the upper hand."

"Surely Tom, this is just a look for Billy and Tracey, the Alliance wouldn't have the means to get there."

"Billy and Tracey got there, what's the difference, after all it's only a mile to row from the mainland?"

"How long before we are there?"

"Forty-two miles to the turn between Four Hammock and Shooters Island then twenty to run to the western side of Kangaroo Island, so about five hours give or take."

0400 Monday 16th March 2015 TRF Outpost Kings Bridge

"Mount up boys, let's surprise the bastards," Blue and twelve of his TRF best were going to give the NK Alliance a bloody nose 'this has been going on too long' thought the fifty-six-year-old ex-SAS sergeant, they were close to the 'Wall' but just couldn't seem to break through. The garrison there was getting reinforcements; it must be, because each time they attacked, there seemed to be more troopers.

0415 hours, pulling the KM450 Light Cargo Truck up 500 metres from the entrance to the 'Wall', men dispersed left and right, the car park had multiple entrances, they had been there many times before.

With the truck hidden from view, they crept forward on three fronts, Blue could just make out the front of the building that housed this sculptor's creation, the stainless-steel bollards in front of the path leading to the front door, reflecting in the moonlight. TRF members on the left, made their way to the kitchen entrance of the old café located inside, while the right-hand side went to a side door used to load the tons of firewood needed to keep the building at an above freezing temperature by the huge six-foot open fire. Now this was only warming directly in front, the rest was purely for optical appeasement.

The fifty-six-year-old and four members crept towards the front door, past the glistening bollards, he shivered, and even though it was March the temperature was a very chilly minus one.

"Wait mate; give the others time to get to their respective doors." Opening the huge front door Blue entered, and went left to the little counter that housed the tourism desk, this was in-between the front outside door and the inner doors, sort of like a vacuum or air lock to keep whatever heat was inside there.

"Stop!" Blue stood and beckoned the others to get up, they opened the inner doors to meet the right-hand team coming through the wood door.

"I'm a bloody dickhead guys, look outside." He was waving his arms around in a circle.

"Did you see any vehicles?"

0515 hours. The left-hand team appeared from the other end of the building as the early morning sun started to show its warming head.

"What, you reckoned they have done a runner Blue?"

"Maybe strategically withdrawn, what's the next place they would be better set up to fend us off?" The ex-SAS member was not familiar with the surroundings; one of the team, a local from Queen raised his hand.

"That would be the fourteen-mile road turnoff the one to Laughing Jack Lagoon, well that's where I would set up a post, and any further towards Bronte would mean we could just go around them on the fourteen mile."

Monday 16th March 2015 TRF Mona Outpost West Coast Taswegia

1700 hours and the gunfire was deafening! Griz could hear it from his makeshift headquarters, some two kilometres from the cutting. Having tried to outflank the cutting guards, before the Alliance were making a two-pronged attack. One prong - the same as before, up the long dirt track behind the position, this Griz had anticipated leaving four members set up either side of the track. The other prong, well this was going to be a great surprise to them, they must have thought if they drive the lead truck really fast into the cutting, they will break through the flimsy barrier, albeit under immense fire from the TRF members above, but at least they would get through and attack the HQ. Well, this was ok except Griz placed the ten ton dump truck in their way.

The KM 450 truck loaded with troopers barrelled around the corner at ninety-five kilometres an hour, fire was raining down on them, and then the driver saw it, with a screech of brakes to try and stop hitting the thirty-ton beast, all the time his superior said.

"Do not stop, we will be cut to pieces." The man was confused, but he did realise one thing, 'this was the day he would die'. The KM450 hit the heavily laden Western Star Truck right in the middle, the nose of their truck burying itself under the body of the dumpster. Type 68 7.62mm rounds were dancing all over the canvas clad KM450, killing most of the troopers instantly. The driver and his NCO still alive, after the crash were protected from above by the overhanging pile of twisted metal. The corporal had his legs pinned.

"Trooper, go, save yourself, I will fight to the end."

Southern Side of the Cutting, Mona Outpost West Coast, Taswegia

1730 hours and with all the noise coming from the cutting, the NK Alliance lieutenant couldn't have known the carnage that awaited them; he had his orders and stuck to them.

"Advance men, follow me!" The twenty-three-year-old moved out into the dirt track and led his squad of a dozen men towards the back of the cutting,

"Boom ... Boom ... Boom." The first three men alongside the lieutenant fell to the ground, they returned fire but with no real targets visible, it was futile, finally sighting movement in the bushes he ordered them to open fire.

TRF member Brian felt the 7.62mm round enter his side from the right as he tried to get a better firing position, something he would regret, he didn't feel it exit and hit the granite boulder, a left-over reminder of excavating the cutting. With all movement stopped from the KM450, Griz and two members surveyed the wreckage all the while being covered from above.

"Mate, check the back of the truck for anything still alive."

"Bang ... Bang." A member finished off a couple still moving in the rear. Griz made his way to the Western Star's Mona side; he noted the great truck hadn't moved at all after the impact with the KM450. Crouching down, he looked at the cab of the Alliance truck.

"Bang!" He didn't see or feel the 9mm round exit the driver's Type 54 pistol and enter his throat, 'shit' his hand went instinctively to cover the wound, now spurting bright red oxygen impregnated blood frothing through his fingers, the NK Alliance driver now clearly in sight.

"Bang ... bang." Both driver and trapped NCO were silenced by the man checking the back of the truck,

"Medic, Griz has been hit, fuck he's done for."

Monday 16ᵗʰ March 2015 TRF Vessel *Christa Leanne* Kangaroo Island

1400 hours, Harry brought the eighty-five-footer back to five knots as he rounded a small headland on the western side of the Island,

"Twelve metres Harry" called Jill. Tom and team were already out on deck getting ready to deploy the sixteen-foot tinny. Taking the *Christa Leanne* in as close as he possibly could, Harry went astern just as the sounder alarm went off.

"Four metres Harry." A startled Jill reported just as Gary slipped the anchor and watched the chain slow down as the plough anchor hit the muddy bottom below.

"Boom ... Boom ... Boom ... Boom." The thunderous sound of an angry Type 68 Assault Rifle was quite deafening inside the secluded bay, rounds were ricocheting off the ex-squid boat's hull and superstructure.

"Boom ... Boom ... Boom ... Boom." Grant and Reg were returning fire,

"Got him, he's over on the right, a stump down on the foreshore."

The professional shooter, come Elite Squad sniper settled down with her new best friend, a SLR special, a gift from Jack, her hero, this 7.62mm Self Loading Rifle came with muzzle brake and powerful telescopic sights. Looking through the sights was like blowing the scene up tenfold, the thirty-four-year-old could easily see the stump and the Alliance trooper trying to hide behind it, smiling she thought 'yeah mate you might have your head and body behind it, but I can still see your backside'

"Dooff … Click …" the 7.62mm projectile entered the man's left hip, shaving a small piece of bark off the stump as it went past, straight through, exiting his right hip making mincemeat of everything in-between.

"Nice shot Britt!" After a quick look through the binoculars, Harry couldn't see anything on the shore, well there wasn't any other cover.

Tom, Reg and Grant had the tinny over the side and helping Brittany they set off towards the shore, a few pulls on the oars and they were there. Harry and Jill covered the four from the quarterdeck.

"Where's Gary Luv?"

"I'll go look, probably securing the anchor."

"FUCK Harry, Gary's been hit; ooh I think he's dead!"

Monday 16th March 2015 Strine Hospital

1200 hours, Lou had dropped Alex off for his afternoon appointments. He had taken to seeing a few locals after lunch, Bob and his sidekick Gill covered the early shift preferring that to the afternoon, the sound of an old truck pulling up alerted the fifty-nine-year-old ex-endoscopy specialist.

"It's Dr Phil Hyland, doc, I think he's had a heart attack!"

Alex and the young relation of Phil's carried the old doctor inside to a trolley, checking his vitals; Alex quickly placed a mask delivering what little oxygen he had left, searching the drugs cupboard for Adrenalin, coming up empty, 'shit' he thought, he remembered that the drug was not really helpful for the brain but in extreme cases would aid the heart attack, also helping to restart it, Adrenaline increases your heart rate, elevates your blood pressure and boosts energy supplies.

1430 hours, Lou dropped in for afternoon tea, well that's what she called it, today saw the good doctor literally up to his elbows in work, apart from the aging doctor Phil, he was treating an early delivery, a laceration of the thigh and what he suspected as the venereal disease, syphilis.

"Well, I leave you for half a day and look what happens?" The blonde was having a dig at Alex, mainly because her afternoon, the way she saw it happening had just been turned upside down.

"Seeing you are bored Doll, better give me a hand."

"Anything for you Hon, what do you want done?"

"Check the woman out, time the contractions for me and let me know how close together they are, while I finish stitching up this thigh." Looking at the ten-inch cut on the man's leg nearly brought the fifty-one-year-old undone.

"Fucking hell, how did you do that mate?"

"No good trying to talk to him Doll, he passed out ten minutes ago, probably a good thing, it saves morphine"

"How's the old doc going?"

"Unfortunately, not good, his heart is just worn out, it's not pumping enough blood out, and flow rate is only about thirty beats a minute, if I was in a proper hospital with all mod cons I would be recommending a pacemaker."

1900 hours, Lou and the good doctor left Bob and Gill to cover the night shift. Just as she was reversing the jeep, Bob flagged them down.

"Dr Phil didn't make it Alex, sorry."

The drive home was in silence, either one not knowing what to say to the other, Lou had known Phil all her life, well he was the one that delivered her, and Alex had befriended him as a medical professional.

"I love you Alex!"

The words resonated in the air, he had known this for some time but had never actually heard Lou say them, she squeezed his hand as they entered the old shack she called home, and he pulled her towards him pressing her breasts into his chest and kissed her passionately.

"I love you too!"

FCPB *Fremantle* at Anchor Skeleton Cove

Chapter 26
Bin Bay

**Wednesday 25th March 2015 FCPB Fremantle
at anchor outside Ansons Bay**

0800 hours and with the two teams aboard, and the RHIB strapped to its harness, Doc operated the Hiab lifting the twenty-two-footer onto its cradle.

"Successful raid guys?" Doc along with everyone left on board was keen to hear the outcome.

"Briefing in twenty minutes Skipper, a feed and a shower first." All team members disappeared to the various parts of ship, females were to use the senior sailor's heads and showers, officers, plus Dick, Sarge and Jack and partners could use the officer's heads while everyone else used the junior sailors.

0900 hours, Nari, Patch, Lauren, April and Nettie had put on a feast of a breakfast, more like a full English breakfast, and with the numbers up to thirty-two there was plenty of it. The Bristols were gainfully employed helping out in the Galley, Mr in charge of the double six-slice toasters and Mrs on whipping up a batch of scrambled eggs, the best they could do with powdered eggs.

"Ok sit-rep on last night raids, I'll do team two, Sarge will fill you in with team one. First of all, let me say everyone did a sterling job, seeing as it was a virgin raid for most. I think everyone got to use the NVG's and everyone bloodied their weapons so to speak." He could detect shivers coming from some of the female *Spirit* passengers still not sure how to handle the whole killing scenario.

"Jack kept the numbers from last night, they read like this - 127 homes to the boat ramp from where we were dropped off, this yielded 1016 Indonesian Nationals and only six troopers, these were not house security but a small garrison in the old shop. The second part heading up Back Street meant we cleared 67 homes yielding 603 Nationals, over to you Sarge."

"Thanks Dick, team one dropped in on Policeman's Point and between there and the boat ramp saw thirty-four farms and various tents out on the point, yielding 728 Nationals, numerous fresh veggies and one pig." April added.

"Yes, thanks for that Sarge, most appreciated and it has been put in the cool room.

"No, thank the team April, they did a great job collecting it all, ok next bit was up the bay side road meaning we cleared eighty-five homes or 688 Nationals before helping Dick and team two finish Back Street. I would like to personally thank my 2IC Thomas and John for their efforts." Doc addressed the crew.

"Bloody fantastic, so just over 3,000 Indonesian Nationals were killed, this is a great victory for the TRF, but I fear we will be looking at a lot more casualties in the next two battles. I'll hand you back to Dick to lay out the next part of the plan."

"Thanks Skipper, well I think we will be getting our heads down first up and well deserved, let's say to 1600 hours, then an early SCRAN, while the *Fremantle* makes her way to The Gardens, where the 40/60 crew will close up and blast the twenty homes or so, this is approximately five nautical miles away, steaming time less than half an hour. Our next stop is Bin Bay, another five nautical miles, we will anchor on the top side of Humbug Point at a place aptly called Skeleton Bay where the RHIB will do two runs. Team one there and team two around the point towards Humbug Point at a place called Dora Point. From here it's across the dirt road to clear the twenty homes overlooking Dora Point."

1000 hours. It didn't take Dick long to get out of his lounging clothes and fall into their bunk alongside Patch, similar scenes were playing out around the ship while a small crew monitored the shore for signs of activity.

1600 hours and the ship was a mass of people waking up, washing, showering, taking advantage of the mild afternoon weather on the upper deck. Dick came to, through Patch's use of an early morning erection, although the time of day was wrong, Dick's body didn't know that.

"Best sleep ever Chook, and boy what a way to wake me up." The ship's broadcast squawked.

"Weigh anchor." The sounds of the 3,200 HP MTU main engines rumbling through their underwater exhaust were already filling the air. Slapping Patch on the rump as he exited for a quick shower he thought 'it's great to be alive'.

"Port ten steer *one eight two* revolutions for ten knots." Annie replied with a cheeky grin.

"Roger that Skipper." It didn't take long for the FCPB to cover the five nautical miles, arriving off 'The Gardens' at 1625 hours or just below it to a little cove called Seaton Cove. This was a pure white sandy beach, surrounded by overhanging foreshore, sporting a dozen luxurious homes, built there for one purpose only, the view.

40/60 Bofors Gun

"50 Calibre and 40/60 Gun crews close up!" Dick chose Jack to stand above him in the loader's position while John and Jock would keep the ammunition up to the mount, out of the ready-use lockers in the front of the bridge superstructure. Sarge was quick to uncover the Starboard 50 Cal mount after bringing up a couple of boxes of rounds and with the assistance of the old RSM, he soon had the beginning of the belt in the breach, locked into place and the cocking lever pulled back.

On the forecastle after a quick lesson on what was expected, and to be aware of the guns firing arc, Dick turned the hydraulic motor on and pulled the stop pin up to allow the gun to rotate. Jack pulled the first clip out of the rack to the right of the gun, pulled the cocking lever back and rammed the first rack into the breach. Dick with both hands on the joystick depressed the dead man controls, rotated and elevated the barrel to bring the first home to bear. Squeezing the trigger while keeping the main part of the target inside the spider's web site was not as easy as it looked. The motion of the vessel moving with the swell meant the barrel sometimes had to be constantly moved up and down to compensate.

"Boom ... Boom ... Boom ... Boom." The first clip expelled, with Jack quickly replacing it with another, the clip bar pushed out of its shute and onto the deck.

The 40mm high explosive, direct action rounds, found various parts of the first home, wreaking havoc on the home's façade. Mixing the rounds up, the loading crew placed WP rounds in amongst the HE, these were nicknamed Woolley Peter or better known as White Phosphorus. White phosphorus is used in smoke, illumination and incendiary munitions, and is commonly the burning element of tracer ammunition. In this case it didn't take long for them to introduce the burning element.

1700 hours and some twenty-five clips later, the 100 mixed rounds had reduced the stately homes to rubble. Sarge was then given the nod to finish off whatever was left, anything that even looked like it was moving was targeted, the half inch hollow point rounds hitting with a punch expanding from half inch to four inches on impact.

"Well done team, we might leave the gun racks loaded for the next bit but stand down." Doc manoeuvred the patrol boat around and headed down the coast towards Bin Bay, passing Sloop Rock, Sloop Lagoon, Taylors Beach and Cosy Corner, some of these had Indonesian Nationals camping along the foreshore in tents 'save these for another day' he thought.

Wednesday 25th March 2015 FCPB Fremantle at Anchor Skeleton Cove

1800 hours, the *Fremantle* nosed into Skeleton Bay. It was still daylight, but they were hoping, because of the rough terrain, no one would be looking towards the sea.

"Deploy the RHIB." Patch and Nettie with plenty of help, lowered the twenty-two-foot boat into the water.

"Team one ten minutes to go." broadcasted Doc on the internal speakers only. Sarge was outside the armoury issuing weapons and ammunition to both teams, handing the keys to Doc as he made his way to the starboard side aft, where the RHIB was waiting, the rest of his team already seated. Patch untied the painter, smiled at the young eighteen-year-old and said,

"Here we go again Nettie!"

Two hundred metres later the RHIB nudged the pure white sand at Skeleton Cove; Sarge rounded his troops up on the rocks, giving his mate's wife a wave as they sped back to the *Fremantle*.

"Right, this is the same as yesterday, it all starts up this bank and across the road to the houses, suppressors only, no NVG's needed at the moment., same teams as before, mix it up with who goes first, be wary these may have security forces." Holding Terri back while the rest scaled the short bank to the road.

"We'll go last Luv and pick up the rear."

1905 hours and team two hit the rocky beach at Dora Point, the ex-CD kissing his wife as he was the last to leap ashore.

"Take it easy Dick." The ex-CD could detect a tear in Patch's eye, he blew her a kiss as he gathered the troops. As he approached the group he could see Marie, the housekeeper in tears, thinking quickly, he waved for the RHIB to return to the beach.

"What's up girl, wow that looks nasty, Wallace can you go back and let Nettie and Patch know they will be transporting Marie back to the ship? Looks like she has badly sprained her ankle."

"No probs Dick." The *Spirit* engineer was soon relaying the message and with the help of Bradley and a couple of *Spirit* passengers, they soon had the girl sitting in the bow of the RHIB.

"Really sorry Dick, I must have slipped on these confounded slippery rocks."

"Don't worry about it, you're not much good to us injured and just a liability, best place for you is with Nari and Doc."

1935 hours, Dick took the odd man to make three in his team; they climbed the steep set of steps and crossed the road towards the first home. Jack and partner climbed the front steps to their home, being still daylight, it foiled them to see children playing outside, killing them in their beds is one thing but trying to shoot a kid whilst running around is something else, sort of like shooting a bunny on the run.

First home was Jack's, the ex-Sniper made it inside to confront an Indonesian trooper sporting a SS1-R5 Raider Assault Rifle, the trooper didn't know which way to look, not sure what to make of Jack under his signature cowboy hat, the suppressed 9mm Browning was quick to bring the matter to a close, hitting him between the eyes, with literally no sound Jack was free to exterminate all those inside, the female passenger could only look on helplessly.

"Pick the rifle and ammo up luv; don't forget to go through his uniform to get all his ammo, and maybe check out his room for more, don't forget the other supplies!"

"Yuk, this is disgusting" as she gingerly fingered the contents of his pockets. Jack just looked at the girl.

"After you just witnessed me blowing his brains out you think going through his pockets yuk, fucking hell luv, grow up." Back out on the road, Jack called the girl over.

"Sorry luv, I was a bit harsh on you inside."

"No Jack I should be the one apologising to you, I was being childish and with everything you and the other TRF members are doing, or by God have done so far it makes what I am doing pale in significance."

Wednesday 25th March 2015 Team Two Skeleton Cove

2100 hours and Dick let the thirty-six-year-old kitchen hand lead the first five homes, four of which yielded house security. As the light was fading, this made it easier to enter homes unseen.

While clearing a large home, Jack detected the sound of an assault rifle letting rip coming from the house next door. Quickly finishing the job they were doing, the pair ran to the home to find the captain lying in a pool of blood and his partner dead on the floor, following the blood trail up the hallway, Jack shot the Indonesian trooper in the head as he tried to crawl away, the good captain shot the man in the groin after he in turn shot the captain's female partner. All the other members of the house had scarpered.

"Fuck, grab that tablecloth luv." Wrapping it around the captain's wound a nasty shoulder one, in and out. Stemming the bleeding, the pair managed to get Bradley outside in time to meet a jeep procured from down the road. Wallace pulled up and between them the managed to get his captain in the back.

Whistling Dick's attention, they soon had the patient to the little boat ramp and jetty alongside the now de-funked tourist business. Dick used his portable VHF to call the ship and ordering an ambulance, directing them to the jetty by torch.

"Shoulder wound Patch, losing blood fast, big hole, get him to sickbay ASAP.

"*Fremantle*, this is Dick, the Captain has a large hole in his shoulder, doesn't look like any bones hit but I could be wrong, losing blood, RHIB on its way back to you now"

"Roger that Dick, will pull out all stops to get him below, do you want me to send the RHIB back to the jetty you know, just in case of another casualty?"

"Probably wouldn't be a bad idea, make sure they are armed, and I might leave Wallace with them."

Wednesday 25th March 2015 Team One between Dora and Humbug Point

2300 hours, Sarge and his team could hear the assault rifles barking over the hill,

"Only hope they are alright " blurted Terri feeling just a little scared with all the shooting.

Team one, had finished the homes and were working their way through the myriad of tents and bush lean-tos on Humbug Point. The place was littered with them, obviously a go-to-camping destination in its day, it was well equipped to carry the Indonesian makeshift city, two large ablution blocks complete with showers, water supplied by huge tanks collecting water off the roof.

One problem soon became apparent to the ex-sapper, remembering where they had been.

Thomas and offsider hit the jackpot, a jeep, but what comes with good news also comes bad. The Indonesian chief warrant officer was an elite *Korps Marinir*; these Indonesian Marine Corps were the Indonesian navy's ground troops. The division was created on 15 November 1945 and is the country's main amphibious warfare force and quick reaction force against enemy invasion.

Entering the last home before the tent city, both members cleared the bulk of the home, only yielding two females and one old man. Thomas was surprised to see the warrant officer sitting on the back porch having a cigarette, the aging Marine turned to see Thomas level the Browning, he was reaching for his own Pindad P2 Semi-automatic pistol but this time, as the seventy-two-year-old ex-RSM already had his weapon ready, it was too late. The 9mm hollow point shot the man through the heart. Curious about the man's uniform, Thomas lifted the tunic off the kitchen chair on the way to the jeep.

0100 hours. The camping ground at Humbug Point was like a rabbit warren, with the area cleared just enough to house the tents in-between the trees, almost every camp area was under the shade of the gum trees, a well thought out idea by the local council, 'bet they had no idea it would be used by invaders after killing all of us' thought Sarge.

"I thought the tents would be a piece of piss, but they're a pain, trying to untie the tabs or worse still the zip tie's means you fumble too much, that's ok if it's just Indonesian Nationals but if there's a trooper inside, we're too vulnerable." The ex-sapper was whispering to most of his team, all of a sudden, the sound of gunfire from the next group of tents,

"Bang … Bang." Sarge with Terri hot on his tail made their way to where the sound resonated from, crouching as he went, he soon realised what had happened. John and team member were trying to gain access to the tent, when the trooper inside started firing right through the material.

"He must have got wind it was us." The half-dressed trooper was standing over John who was obviously wounded, the other half of his team was clearly seen crouching behind the rear of the tent, to throw the man of guard, all Sarge could think of was to mutter the bit of NK Alliance he had learnt.

"Mwoga munje ya!" or 'what's wrong. This was all it took for the trooper, who was preparing to finish John off to hesitate.

"Dooff … Dooff." The 9mm rounds hit the man's upper torso, not an easy shot at some 200 metres.

Picking up the quite distraught team member from behind the tent, Sarge quickly dispatched the rest of the contents with

Terri standing guard. Then trying something different, while Terri whistled Thomas over to see to John. The forty-five-year-old ex-sapper pulled his bayonet and ran a slit down the back of the next tent, leaned in through it and shot all six inside 'much easier he thought'

"How is he Thomas?"

"Two wounds mate, one through the side under the ribs and the other through the thigh, both serious enough, we need to get him back to the *Fremantle*."

"Jock you and your mate carry John back to the vehicle and get him to the extraction point, Patch, Nettie and Wallace should be there, they'll know what to do, they will warn Doc and Nari, the rest of you draw bayonets and do what I do."

Thursday 26th March 2015 Team Two Bin Bay

0200 hours, Dick with two men down and one running security at the jetty, decided to re-group and make three teams of three. This was working well, Jack took one female and one male passenger, Dick with Liz and a male passenger leaving the last three passengers to work together. Two 9mm suppressors per team meant the third person was only to shoot if really needed to, with one team clearing the couple of shops sitting above the road; the ex-CD motioned the rest to follow him into a little subdivision off to the right behind a B&B called 'The Edge'. This was made up of seven homes and the huge B&B itself.

"Right, this B&B might just be the home to troopers, ones that are not married, plenty of beds and close to everything." Rounding the corner his suspicions were justified, there before them stood four jeeps and one truck all lined up in the car park.

"We'll do this one like this, Jack, your team take the back entrance, and I'll take the front, stay close to Jack because he's got the NVG's, same with you lot behind me."

Opening the front door, Dick made his way through the reception area, dining and sitting rooms, the first room that could have been a bedroom, yielded a couple and a child in a single bed, these were swiftly dealt with. Reloading his Browning the ex-CD pulled Liz close and motioned to the third member to keep an eye out just in case anyone came out into the hallway.

Jack's team had already cleared four rooms and could also detect the sounds of Dick's suppressed Browning, eventually the two teams were facing each other, six rooms to go. Liz opened the door and Dick worked the room, Jacks offsider Lesley doing the same, all went well until one of those shot didn't die, after moving up the hallway the trooper crawled out into the hallway behind Jack and fired off two rounds from his Pindad.

"Bang … Bang." both shots found their mark, at the precise moment the two went down, Jack was entering the next room, leaving Dick's team member face to face with the crawling trooper, he hesitated, one more shot but deteriorating, the man missed.

"Bang … Bang." The sound of the unsuppressed 9mm was deafening. Dick and Liz emerged from their room to see the rear guard sitting on the floor. Still holding her Browning in the two-handed position, thinking she was hit, he went to her aid. The last room's contents spilled out into the hallway, with weapons drawn, they started firing rapidly, rounds were pinging off the walls all around. Jack shot two, leaving only one, while the ex-sniper reloaded, Liz pulled the trigger, by this time the man was nearly on top of her, the round hitting him in the head as he dropped at the kitchen hand's feet.

Thursday 26th March 2015 Team One Humbug Point

0400 hours, with Jock driving, the team of ten TRF members had successfully cleared the bulk of 'Tent City' on Humbug Point, adopting Sarge's idea of using the bayonet paid off, making the job not only safer but faster.

"Looks like another group up in front Sarge, half a dozen tents and a building of some sort" Jock was using the NVG's to navigate through the myriad tracks taking them from the top of the Point down nearly to the waterfront on the southern side.

"You three, do those two tents, Thomas, you the next two and we'll do this lot, Terri can you check out the building? Let me know what it is, if I'm right it's an ablution block put here to service the campers."

0500 hours and with all tents in the area cleared, they parked the jeep outside the toilets, which in the pre-dawn light they could see backed onto the water.

"This must be the entrance to the St Anne Bar; I wonder how the *Nancy Kay* and *Waubs Bay* are doing?"

Making their way back towards Bin Bay, Jock, instead of turning right got confused and went straight ahead, travelling for twenty-five minutes, Sarge thought they should have seen the carnage they left behind by then, but this was just a bush track, eventually descending a steep hill, the group found themselves on a main road.

"My gyro says we should turn right Sarge,"

"Reckon your right Jock, keep your eyes peeled, we will probably come across more homes, not good, now it's daylight." Winding their way into Bin Bay the first building was the B&B on the left.

"Shit vehicle coming up behind us guys, no fuck there's more than one."

"Ok it's Dick."

"You guys ok?" asked Sarge.

"No mate lost two, right here in the B&B and another earlier on, captain's wounded, what about you?"

"John's Injured and Marie rolled her ankle coming ashore, was the captain bad?"

"Shoulder wound, big hole but he should be ok, what about John?"

"Two rounds one, thigh and one the side, he'll live, hey mate we'll have to stop injuring the *Spirit* crew." The three vehicles parked at the jetty and got the word on the patients from Doc on board the *Fremantle*.

"Sit rep back on board, then sleep, food in whatever order you like."

"Same deal as yesterday troops, meeting in one hour"

0800 Thursday 26th March 2015 FCPB Fremantle at Anchor off Skeleton Cove

0900 hours, Doc welcomed them all, the seats were full of TRF members, some with bandages and some were still in the sickbay being tended by Nari.

"Before I hand the sit-rep over to Dick and Sarge we had a visitor last night, Helen, third Officer off the *Spirit* took a round in the thigh and was dropped off for some TLC, I now will leave you, while I go and assist Nari with John and Helen."

"Thanks Doc, well done team, I know it was tough to lose some of your mates, but we knew this wasn't going to be a walk in the park. You have all performed brilliantly considering the relatively short amount of training you have received, later on tonight we will hit the streets again, except this time mounted."

"Where are we headed Dick?"

"The outskirts of St Anne Thomas, Sarge will fill you in with the details." The ex-CD sat next to Patch giving her a squeeze.

"Thanks Dick, I concur with my mate here, you have nothing to be ashamed of even if we lost a few. As Dick said, we move off at 2100 hours from the jetty, pick up another two jeeps from the B&B, split up amongst them and head down the main road towards St Anne. Wallace, you stay as security for the RHIB, I know you think it's a cushy job but trust me after today there will be troops running around everywhere so potentially could be very dangerous, remember if so, withdraw back to here.

Three vehicles will stop one kilometre from St Anne at the old fish processing factory, left hand side in amongst the canal. By then, we should have a good idea how the other two crews have gone, they would have done raids last night and hopefully withdrawn to the centre of the bay to rest during the day."

"Any calls from them Sarge?"

"No, I think the satellite is in the wrong area."

"You said three vehicles Sarge, what do the other two do?"

"Oh yes, I forgot, they take the road off to the right opposite where we came out from Humbug Point this morning, this takes them to the Ansons Bay Road. If they turn right and clear whatever homes are close, say two or three clicks then turn around and head towards St Anne clearing as they go."

"And then what Sarge, we all meet up at the RSL for a cold one?"

"Something like that Jock, maybe not this time but eventually.

Remember these troops are not as soft as their NK counterparts; these are more battle hardened, especially if we come up against any of the *Korps Marinir*; and they also appear to have plenty of ammunition. Reported stocks from those we killed last night suggest on average they will be carrying 150 rounds of 5.56mm to suit their SS1-R5 Raider Assault Rifles and around sixty rounds of 9mm, and it seems not all NCOs are issued with a Pindad P2 Semi-automatic Pistol."

"How many have we killed Sarge?" Dick could see it was Terri asking the questions, pointing to his mate, Sarge let Dick take over.

"Well Terri, final tally is this-

- 240 homes cleared, just under 2000 Nationals and 126 home security.
- 196 tents cleared with no fewer than 1400 Nationals and 140 home security, or they just lived there.
- One garrison at the old B&B yielded fifty of which twenty-seven were Indonesian troopers, six of those were *Korps Marinir*.
- 293 troops, 217 SS1-R5 Raider Assault Rifles and around thirty thousand rounds of 5.56mm.
- Only 63 Pindad P2 Semi-automatic Pistols and 3,150 9mm rounds.

As a result, we will be changing our Type 68's for the smaller calibre SS1-R5 Raider Assault Rifles; we now have plenty in stock and can always top up ammunition supplies from the enemy. Sarge, Nettie, Lauren, April and Patch did a marvellous job in bringing all the weapons aboard during the night, what's that Patch? Sorry all except a stash back at the jetty."

"Right, get some sleep and we be conducting a training session on the quarterdeck, 1700 tonight, we will run you all through the SS1 Raiders and issue ammo."

1000 hours sliding into their bunk, Dick and Patch soon found something to occupy the last five minutes before drifting off to sleep. One deck below them Jack and April in the port side senior sailors' cabin, modified to sleep a couple, snuggled down already hearing Sarge snoring from over the passageway in the other senior sailor's cabin.

The sick bay was above them in the old ship's office, this had been nicely converted by the Indonesians to a well fitted out sickbay, as if they knew the importance this would be during this invasion. The rest of the TRF team was distributed in the junior sailor's cabin, this housed sixteen bunks, and the port side was partitioned off with a curtain to facilitate the females. The only space not utilised now was the old wardroom, which had been converted to a double cabin after the liaison between the doctors Rob and Margaret after the Benoa rescue mission.

1450 hours, a slight tap on the exec cabin door, Patch nudged the ex-CD who called out.

"Come in." Patch not impressed, pulled the Doonah up to cover her naked breasts and peered over the top of Dick's shoulder, it was Doc.

"Sorry Dick, Patch, bad news, John didn't make it. The thigh wound we thought was a simple sew up job ended up being a nicked femoral artery and while Nari and I worked on his gut thinking this was the more serious he bled out into the wound cavity. We had finished the gut wound, closed him up when Nari noticed his vitals going through the roof. By the time I got back in there it was too late, I've only just finished, we tried to save him mate but couldn't." Dick could see that Doc was visibly upset and told his skipper to take a break.

"Who's on watch Doc?"

"Annie and April mate."

A shower fully brought the ex-clearance diver to life, the mess was silent, so he made himself a brew, one for Patch and just then, Jack emerged from his cabin.

"Couldn't sleep Dick, and April has the afternoon watch, what's up?" Dick informed his mate of the Doc's visit, handed him a brew and reached under the counter to select a small parcel then disappeared up to the next deck.

Handing the now awake Patch a drink he tapped on the skipper's cabin door. Nari called him in, it was deja vu with Nari wearing one of Doc's tee-shirts over very little else, Doc didn't say much, Nari spoke.

"We tried Dick, too much breeding, too much." He couldn't help smiling at the South Korean's pronunciation of the word bleeding.

"It's alright Nari, Doc told me, nothing you could have done without the proper equipment, fuck me you two do a marvellous job with what you have." He handed Doc a cigar, turned and filled two tin mugs with whisky, handing one each to the pair.

"Drink this, doctors' orders, now I'm going back to get my head down for another couple of hours!"

1730 hours, Doc piped.

"Weapons training quarterdeck." Looking out over the coastline the sixty-five-year-old ENT doctor smiled. Nari, April, the Bristols and Lauren were in the galley drumming up a feast for the troops. Dick and Sarge carted the weapons to the training session while Patch and Nettie along with their personal security guard Wallace, refuelled the RHIB.

1845 hours and the mess was alive with TRF members, Doc had come and given his mate a hug, thanking him for the support, Dick even got a kiss from Nari. Sitting down to a plate of lamb stew topped off with new potatoes, the sixty-one-year-old ex-CD could detect someone approaching the table; it was one of the *Spirit* passengers from his own team.

"Err, excuse me Dick, sorry for interrupting your meal, can I put a request in for a double bed?" Looking at the twenty-five-year-old, he pointed to Doc.

"Not my part of ship Paul, you'll have to ask the skipper."

"What was all that about Dick?" asked Patch, curious as she sat down, Dick smiled and filled his wife in with the request.

"That makes sense luv, I have seen Paul up close and personal to young Nettie when she's been driving the RHIB. The ex-CD turned to see Paul talking to Doc and was not surprised when the skipper smiled and placed his arm around the twenty-five-year-old's shoulders.

2030 hours, "teams one and two to muster station aft, good luck tonight, keep your head down, oh and to make it official, Paul Gabon and Nettie Crumb have taken up residence in the old wardroom."

Chapter 27
St Anne Invasion

Tuesday 24ᵗʰ March 2015 TRF vessels Waubs Bay and Nancy Kay off Ansons Bay

2130 hours, looking to starboard, Santa could see the FCPB already slowing down preparing to drop anchor.

"Suggest we steer *176 degrees* Len." Placing the microphone back, the sixty-one-year-old ex-CD punched the setting into the auto pilot, watching as the sixty-five-foot *Conquest* automatically turned to port onto the new heading.

"How far luv?" asked Pat, knowing full well everyone else is wondering the same thing. Running the dividers against the side of the chart checking the distance.

"Sixteen miles to the turn, at our speed of twenty knots about forty-eight minutes"

2220 hours and switching the auto pilot off, Santa turned to starboard. Vert and Rose were in their cabin, Barry keeping lookout and Pat asleep in her chair. Barry watched as the *Waubs Bay* also made the turn, the seventy-foot steel cray boat slowed down and hovered mid channel, knowing full well that Santa would be negotiating the *Conquest* alongside the little jetty at the boat ramp on St Anne's Point.

"Brings back memories luv, last time we were here, the shitheads were shooting at us." Barry, back in the wheelhouse, commented.

"Sure, I remember that day Santa, you saved our bacon big time, do you reckon there's enough water to get alongside?"

"Well, it's high tide, if not we're stuffed, the *Waubs Bay* is the one with the tinny."

2300 hours and Santa swung the sixty-five-footer around to come in port side too, gingerly waiting for a prop to bottom out.

"One line amidships Barry, better wake those troops and see if they can get a vehicle." Barry, third officer Helen, deck rating Kenny and three others scarpered ashore and made their way towards the three homes at the point. Barry and Kenny wearing the NVG's approached the back door, open, phew, what a relief, with suppressed 9mm Brownings drawn they entered the first bedroom, Barry smiled 'what a way to go' he thought as he fired the 9mm into the National going hammer and tong into the female doggy style.

"Dooff ... Dooff ... Dooff." The third round missed the female who was trying to get her brain to work out why the stud on top of her had suddenly stopped mid stroke.

"Dooff." Helen approached the girl and shot her at close range in the head. Kenny was already clearing the next room; this was full of teenage kids, a miscalculation on his behalf meant he ran out of ammunition after shooting five of them. Trying to change magazines in the middle of a clearing, might seem easy but he was stressing that much, he dropped the full magazine on the bed, the girl woke up to see him groping for it and screamed.

What could he do, he knew he had to find the magazine, kill the girl and deal with whoever was left in the room, decisions decisions, still screaming, he leapt on the bed and aimed for her throat, with two hands around her neck she at least stopped screaming, next thing he knew someone is hitting him in the back. During the scuffle, he lost the NVG's and his Browning, with the punches still coming, he sat on the girl's stomach and let go of her throat long enough to belt her in the jaw.

Turning around to see another teenager hitting him in the back, he grabbed the girl, missed and tore her nightdress clean off, she managed to sit on his head continuing to belt him in the stomach. Now usually the thought of a pretty young girl sitting on his face with no clothes on would be a turn on, but tonight in all the confusion all he could think was her pubic hairs are tickling his nose, then.

"Dooff ... Dooff." She slumped onto the bed leaving only the girl underneath him. Coming too, after the jaw breaker she screamed again, this time through blood filled mouth and nose, reaching around to try and find his NVG's all he found was the Browning and belting her in the head finally got off the bed. Helen approached and handed him his NVG's, embarrassed he muttered.

"Thanks Helen, I owe you one."

"You sure do Kenny." Regaining his composure and the missing magazine he looked around at the carnage, two pretty girls, one naked, and six other children of various ages in the other beds.

Wednesday 25th March 2015 St Anne's Point Boat Ramp and Jetty

0010 hours and hearing the sound of a vehicle, Barry, Helen and Kenny crouched down behind the front retaining wall of the house.

"It's one of our guys." Barry blurted out, hopping over the wall to greet the contents; back at the jetty they reported the night's events (well not all of them) to Santa.

"Ok, next job is take the jeep and start clearing on the way into St Anne. Barry, Helen and four passengers will be enough, two sets of NVG's and two suppressed Brownings."

Spinning the sixty-five-foot *Conquest* on her nose then going out astern into deeper water Santa was much happier, reaching for the microphone he updated Len.

"Ready guys, all good, they have wheels, follow me, when we get through the bar, Len you head straight for the main wharf, first pontoon you can get on, it's a long way from shore but trust me that's good. I'll head towards the slip area and tie up there, then we'll head ashore, find vehicles and clear the houses in front of both wharves, Buck and I did them last time, but they might have moved more in since then."

0130 hours, Santa watched as Len spun the boat around, then brought the seventy-foot ex-cray boat alongside the furthest finger of the wharf. slowing the *Conquest* down, he then spun around to face the sea, coming alongside port side too.

"Weapons check team, same as before Pat, you and Rose mind the boat, you know what to do if you're approached."

"Yep, shoot the fuckers." Rose smiled thinking Pat was one funny lady. Slipping ashore, Santa made sure the vessel was held by one line amidships then gathered the team at the old slip facilities.

"Right, we'll split into three teams, you with me, Vert with you and you, Kenny you take the rest, suppressors where possible, remember if you can't see, don't go, we haven't got NVG's for everyone, but God is kind to us tonight."

"What did he mean by that Vert?"

"Full moon mate, that's all."

Wednesday 25th March 2015 Nancy Crew Stieglitz

0200 hours, Barry and team had made their way halfway between the St Anne Point boat ramp and the main road. This area years ago was made up of shacks and weekenders, as most things progress, so did this area, and why not? It was isolated from St Anne but still within twenty minutes' drive and most of the properties were either waterfront or at least could see the water from their lounge room, and those that couldn't, well they just built up until they could.

Pulling up in front of a recently finished two story house, Barry dropped half of his team off to clear the home, while he rolled fifty metres down the road to the next house.

"Helen, can you take the back while the girl and I will do the front." Up a dozen steps the thirty-year-old ex- builder nodded at the girl to open the door. He entered, Browning at the ready, two-handed stance, NVG's on. She was told to watch his back as he cleared each room, already hearing the 'Dooff' sounds coming from the back of the home, he smiled thinking 'Helen is off to a great start'.

First room was chockers, two couples and one child all snoring. 'Boy this must be fun at times' he thought, shooting each one in turn with the suppressed 9mm.

"Dooff ... Dooff ... Dooff ... Dooff ... Dooff." The next room housed just one single bed, a trooper, a common theme. As he approached the head of the bed he could see movement under the covers, it appeared he was not asleep.

Through the green tinge of the NVG's it looked like the man's crutch was moving up and down, slight moaning was coming from his mouth.

"Dooff." The 9mm hollow point round entered the left eye socket, exiting through the back of his head and hitting the bedhead with a dull thud, as he turned to leave a noise came from under the covers, at the same time, Helen appeared in the doorway and Barry put his finger to his lips, more movement so he fired.

"Dooff ... Dooff." Two rounds into the blanket, now this stopped the movement and with Helen alongside of the thirty-year-old he pulled back the covers. A woman was curled up at the bottom of the bed, the troopers right hand held his Pindad 9mm Pistol, the woman was chained to the rail of the bed.

"Well Helen, it was pretty obvious what she was doing, what I can't understand why the pistol unless he was expecting trouble, let's face it she wasn't going anywhere chained to the bed."

"Look closer Barry she's Caucasian I reckon the bastard has been keeping her as his personal sex slave."

"Dooff, well that's to make sure." Helen was disgusted with the thought and shot the trooper again not seeing that her partner had already done a good job of it.

"Might bring this up when we meet up with the others, be aware there might be others in the same situation. This is totally out of character for Indonesians, you know being strict Muslims."

"Not that strict it appears."

Wednesday 25ᵗʰ March 2015 Waubs Bay Crew St Anne

0200 hours, Len, Jill and one passenger had crept straight ahead from the main wharf, the other two teams consisted of Maurice and two passengers, with Helga and two passengers, and the last team made up of all passengers. With four prongs to the attack, it was proving economical and faster to cover the ground. A lot of the homes they entered were empty, this was obviously left over from the raid Santa and Vert had done just a couple of weeks before.

"What do you reckon Len, the Four Seasons Motel right there on the main road, close to the wharf, I think that would make great garrison accommodation, even headquarters, and well that's what I would do if I was in charge." The ex-fisherman smiled, cuddled the seventeen-year-old, kissed her hard on the lips.

"That's what I love about you Jill."

"What do you mean, is that ALL you love about me?" Ignoring the remark he continued.

"I think, to have a crack at this one we need reinforcements luv."

He knew this was not an emergency, but he needed to talk to Santa and get some advice

"Santa, Santa, got a copy?"

"This better be good Len, too dangerous to use these." The thirty-nine-year-old went on to quickly outline their idea.

"Clear the buildings over the road, we should be there in half an hour mate"

Wednesday 25th March 2015 Nancy Kay Crew St Anne Slip Yard End

0230 hours, Santa, Kenny and one passenger were finishing up when he filled Vert's team in about the radio call.

"We might just give them a hand, follow me." Dropping back onto the walking come bike track that ran all the way from the St Anne's Point Road to the town centre, was the easiest way for the six team members to move about under cover. The council had done a great job of partially hiding the track, in amongst the trees and shrubs on the roadside and with the water on the other side, it was perfect. As they crossed the bridge, Kenny grabbed Santa's arm pointing to an old fishing boat tied up alongside.

"I see it mate, a light coming from on board, looks like we have a live aboard situation or someone up to no good."

Kenny and his team made their way to the sixty-foot fishing boat and crept aboard; this aft wheelhouse designed vessel was similar to the *Waubs Bay*. The light was coming from the wheelhouse only just visible between the curtain and bulkhead, peering in gave them no clue to who was inside.

"Can't see anything" relayed one of the *Spirit* passengers as he turned the doorknob and pushed the door in, it was obvious that someone was living there by the state of the place, food and clothing lying about. Detecting sounds coming from below, they investigated further.

"Dooff ... Dooff." A body hit the deck hard, dragging the corpse back into the moonlight they could see it was just a kid and a quick search of the rest of the vessel uncovered one more, Kenny snapped the kids neck in a scuffle.

Wednesday 25th March 2015 Waubs Bay and Nancy Kay Combined Crews St Anne Garrison

0350 hours, they split into four teams, and with this motel having two stories meant a team up each fire escape either end, one in the front entrance. The other, through the kitchen, this would be a four-pronged attack. The main entrance was penetrated by Santa, Kenny and their partner. 'Nice' Santa thought, it's the main headquarters for the whole Indonesian Alliance, obvious with the office, conference room complete with wall maps of the area, prospective problem areas marked, just as he was thinking 'why is there no security?' Kenny beckoned to the front desk where the guard had just taken up his post.

"Dooff, fuck that was close mate, he must have been taking a piss?"

"Or doing rounds Kenny, anyway, let's hope he's the only one."

Wednesday 25th March 2015 Nancy Crew Main Road
St Anne's Point Road Junction

0400 hours, Barry pulled the aging M35 jeep to a halt, these were built by AM General in the USA, same as their trucks, and being pre 2000 were old technology;. with the squealing of the brake linings against drums it was a wonder they could be considered stealth.

Turning right, they stuck to the original brief, continued clearing homes until they reached the slipway, this was only about two kilometres and with homes on the left side of the road only, should not take too long.The other side of the road and between the road and the water was the bike come walking track. Taking it turnabout with each other home they had worked out a good routine, nodding at the first doorway.

"You're up this time mate." pointing to one of the *Spirit* passengers who promptly entered and started shooting, Barry could see Helen doing the same next door and he quickly backed up his partner, noises from next door alarmed the ex-builder.

"Bang ... Bang ... Bang." The sound on an unsuppressed weapon meant trouble, but he was occupied dealing with the contents of his home, he hoped Helen was ok, he had sort of become attached to the forty-four-year-old third officer, even though he had taken a shine to one of the female passengers on Dick's team. It seemed to take forever to complete the clearing, and exiting the back door, Barry couldn't wait to climb the back fence and enter the back door of Helen's home.

Confronted by a scene out of a horror show, he found Helen sitting on the passageway floor. One hand on her 9mm and the other on her leg. Alongside her were the two bodies of her partners, one man and one woman, 'shit I can't even remember their names' thought Barry. It was obvious the Indonesian Alliance trooper had shot them both with their SS1-R5 Raider Assault Rifle, the three rounds making short work of the pair or so he thought, at closer range he could see one with two bullet wounds and the other only hit in the thigh. The trooper, after being shot by Helen in the knee, had drawn his bayonet and finished the woman off by stabbing her in the stomach and then slitting her throat, the arterial blood spray was clear. Here Helen froze, with the trooper in the middle holding his knee fumbling for his weapon to finish Helen off.

"Dooff." Barry's 9mm round hit the man in the back as he crawled towards Helen.

"Fuck luv, are you alright?"

"Got me in the upper thigh mate, I don't know what happened, I just froze, it was like the world was going in slow motion, my arm was like lead, I couldn't bring my weapon to bear even though I could see he was going to either stab me or shoot me." The thirty-year-old ex-builder picked her up in one move as if she only weighed twenty kilos, moving her to the back patio to be met by the rest of his team; he placed her on the BBQ table in the moonlight.

"Mate, grab some first aid stuff if you can, or a towel." He pulled out a poultice bandage from his cargo pants.

"Something Vert taught me." He could see the quizzical look from the forty-four-year-old. Tearing her trousers to expose her thigh, he was looking for the exit wound.

"Fuck" there was none, placing the poultice on top of the relatively small wound made by the 5.56·45mm NATO round, she reached up and kissed him hard.

"Thank you, mate, you're a charmer." Embarrassed, he took the stripped sheet handed to him by his teammate and bound her leg tight to stop the bleeding.

Wednesday 25th March 2015 Waubs Bay and Nancy Kay Combined Crews St Anne Garrison

0400 hours, Len, Jill and their teammate were entering through the kitchen door, smells still lingering from the last meal. Len stopped Jill quickly, placing his hand over her mouth just before she spoke, someone was in the freezer, their partner opened the huge stainless-steel door only to be confronted to a bleary-eyed angry cook brandishing the biggest cook's knife he had seen. Too quick, the wiry young cook, probably bitching to himself, because of the early start, lunged at the *Spirit* passenger embedding the blade into the man's chest. Jill covered the man.

"Dooff, shit Len, he's dead, that fucking scared me." Searching the dining room alongside the kitchen, came up empty; Jill contacted Santa, informing him of the incident, then checked the only other rooms on the ground floor.

"Must be Officers Jill, pretty plush décor." Entering the first room found an officer snoring his head off, one quick round to the head, they exited meeting Santa in the hallway.

"Mine was a lieutenant." he declared, holding up a tunic.

"Mine too." declared Jill.

0400 hours and with both other teams entering at the end of a long hallway from the iron stairs, acting as the buildings fire escape, they were facing twenty-four rooms, twelve on each side. Vert, remembering some of the training from Sarge suggested that only two of them do the shooting. With NVG's and suppressors this made sense, another two be the door openers and magazine changers while the last pair cover their backs armed with SS1-R5 Raider Assault Rifles set on automatic fire.

Vert started one end as the shooter, Rose opening the door and holding the eight round magazines, quickly expended while Helga shot, and Maurice did the door leaving two *Spirit* passengers covering. This worked like clockwork, taking only three or four minutes to shoot everyone in each room, most of them were singles, some were bunk beds and some surprise, surprise had female company.

0500 hours, the sun was trying to peep above the horizon to the east. Everyone gathered in the foyer and judging by the officer's tunics and other NCO badges of rank, it appeared they had hit the jackpot.

"Right, back to the boats, we will meet mid bay and anchor for the day, this place will be like a hornet's nest in about half an hour."

TRF Vessel Nancy Kay

Wednesday 25th March 2015 Waubs Bay and Nancy Kay Rafted up Georges Bay

0700 hours, meeting Barry at the *Nancy Kay* carrying Helen, they strategically made their withdrawal. *Waubs Bay*, being the heavier vessel anchored, and Santa brought the sixty-five-foot *Conquest* alongside.

"Reporting on the casualties, mate, we lost two of Helen's, Helen has a nasty wound in the upper thigh, round still in there." Len reported on the man that was attacked by the cook.

"Sorry we were late, had to refuel before leaving, I reckon we will have to get Helen to the Doc, they have to get the round out ASAP, now I don't reckon she will be at Skeleton Bay until tonight, it slipped my mind about how low on fuel we were so had to refuel at the slipway. I need a couple of volunteers to come with me in the *Nancy Kay*, it's the faster vessel. We will head out of the bar tonight and meet up with the *Fremantle* around 2200 hours. Should be able to do that at twenty knots if it's not too rough and be back here by 0200 hours, not sure what the next part of the invasion is but will be guided by Dick.

"Vert, Rose and I will crew for you luv." Pat was happier to be doing something important rather than just sitting waiting at anchor.

"I'll come with you to help look after Helen." Pat winked at Rose; both women had been watching the body language between Barry and Helen.

Thursday 26th March 2015 FCPB Fremantle at Anchor Skeleton Cove

0010 hours, Santa, Pat, Rose, Vert and Barry had made good time considering the huge seas that waited for the sixty-five-foot *Conquest* outside Georges Bay, too large and uncomfortable to helm from the flying bridge, they delivered Helen at 2315 hours.

"No hurry Santa, I'll call the *Waubs Bay* on the brick phone and fill them in."

"Thanks Doc." Letting Len know they would be having a night off was a relief all round, burning the candle at both ends usually means someone makes a mistake, and at this end of the proceedings could be very dangerous. Dick, Sarge and the skipper had gone over the pitfalls of driving the teams too hard, 'after all the alliance would still be there the next day' Dick reminded them. Sarge reckoned that was right, but they might be a little angrier.

Doc, Nari and Lauren worked on the forty-four-year-old third officer, satisfied they had stopped the bleeding, Doc closed up the wound.

"She'll be ok guys?" Barry asked.

"Can I see her Doc?" detecting the passion in his voice, Doc replied.

"Sure Barry" pointing after the thirty-year-old ex-builder.

"Another shipboard romance."

"Reckon you could be right Doc." said Pat with a wink.

0600 hours, Santa pulled back on the sticks bringing the *Conquest* back to five knots and alongside the ex-Cray boat, *Waubs Bay.* Going astern to take the way off they were met by the rest of the team, Len took the amidships mooring line and made it fast.

"How's the patient Santa?" Reporting on how things went, they also reiterated the point that it was important to rest; the next part of the attack would come that night, when they hoped that the *Fremantle* would send out a two-pronged attack.

Thursday 26th March 2015 Waubs Bay and Nancy Kay

2100 hours, weighing anchor complete, Santa and Len headed their respective vessels in the direction of the St Anne wharf area. Now they were pretty sure the Indonesian Alliance would have been watching them all day and be preparing for their return. 'How could he confuse them', the sixty-one-year-old ex-CD thought as he pushed the sixty-five-foot *Conquest* ahead.

The St Anne wharf area was made up of one main off-loading jetty for fishing vessels to unload their catch, this was close to the bridge, next the fish punt then three fingers, the longest one was the first one, and this is where Santa berthed the *Nancy Kay* and last time the *Waubs Bay*. Over on the other side of the bridge was the slip yard and jetty where *Dementia* and then *Nancy Kay* berthed.

It might give them a few more minutes but it was worth a go, Len could berth *Warbs Bay* on the third finger over, this was in front of the seafood restaurant and may give them a bit more cover while Santa would bring the *Nancy Kay* into the unloading wharf. With everyone ashore they were to re-visit the headquarters in the old Four Seasons Motel, they certainly would not be expecting this.

The plan was to meet up with Dick's two jeeps coming in from Bin Bay, which just happened to come out at the motel next along the esplanade - Tidal Waters; this is where Len and crew would be clearing while Santa revisited the HQ, well that was the theory but who knows what would be waiting for them.

The fall-back plan was to just drop the raiding parties off and both vessels withdraw to the centre of the bay again, this is something that Pat loved; she hated being so vulnerable sitting alongside the wharf. Reaching for the microphone, Santa, still surveying the area, was taking it slow; with no moonlight and no navigational lights it was blacker than Hades.

"Len, if you just drop off your guys on the restaurant finger, then get Josh and one crew to take the boat back out, I'll get Pat and Rose to do the same, saves the potential of them being overrun."

"Luv if it all turns to shit, I'll contact you with the portable VHF, are you both right to come and get us, it could be a hot extraction, nothing fancy, just stick your nose where I say, don't try and come alongside."

"I reckon we could manage that, better give Rose another rub around on the Type 68, she might have to give covering fire."

2200 hours, Len was on final approach, it all looked good, no sign of activity, the skipper brought her in slow, then went astern taking all way off, the ten TRF members quickly disembarking off over the port bow. Helga counted them off, then gave Josh the signal to go astern; the seventeen-year-old feeling like a million bucks with all the new responsibility, and especially when the forty-four-year-old *Spirit* gaming supervisor slid in alongside. Spinning the eighty-five-footer around in a short round turn he headed back into night; with the assistance of his radar this would not be far, and Helga would drop the anchor.

Over on the unload wharf, Santa was doing the same, just nudging the extreme end of this wharf the ten TRF members hopped ashore, already Santa could see he had made the right choice; over to his right on the finger the *Waubs Bay* would have used, he could detect troops moving around. With everyone ashore, Pat went astern, while Rose watched for suspicious activity.

2230 hours, Len and team Whiskey (for the first letter of *Waubs Bay*) were held up behind the seafood restaurant 'The Wharf Bar and Kitchen', they too could see activity on the original finger and were glad to drop off the way they did.

"Ok team, we have about two clicks to the motel 'Tidal Waters', now most of this is along the waterfront reserve, no homes and hopefully no troops, now split up into threes, Jill and I will take two with us."

Under the cover of a timber boardwalk running the distance from the restaurant to the motel they moved, Len could see troop movements from the wharf all the way to the headquarters.

"Hope Santa can see all of this, might bring him up to speed when we get further away." Giving the seventeen-year-old a hug, the ex-fisherman waited for all his team to settle into the motel grounds, pressing transmit on the VHF.

"November, November this is Whiskey over," (November after the first letter of *Nancy Kay*)

"Receiving mate, what gives?" Len filled Santa in with all the troop movements,

"Will do mate, might give the HQ a miss if it's that busy."

2330 hours, Len and Whiskey team had reached their objective, with Maurice and two others continuing around to the right up on to the huge deck area. Off this they had access through a door into the dining room, and one into the main bar, the third was access to an area used for social gatherings. Len, Jill, one male and one female *Spirit* passenger turned left making their way to the main entrance, while the last group went all the way down to the other end of the complex and gained access through the outdoor pool area. This door was open and easily gave them access; the wing they were on, had twenty rooms top and bottom, the group immediately climbed the stairs.

The first man to stick his head up on the second floor found himself looking face to face with an Indonesian trooper, a corporal in fact, sitting on a lounge smoking; he got the bigger shock, not expecting an intruder so close to where they were billeted. The corporal was without his weapon, but this did not stop him from lunging at the TRF member, tackling him to the floor and both tumbling down the stairs, luckily the second crew team member was armed with a suppressed 9mm Browning.

"Dooff." Quickly dispatched, the corporal was dragged out of the way,

"Fuck that was close!"

2350 hours, Maurice and his two team members had no luck with the first two doors, but gained access through the third, this gave them the bar, dining room and conference and reception areas. Looking up, the thirty-eight-year-old *Spirit* bosun saw Len at the front door and unlocked it for them.

"Thanks mate, just what we needed, what have you checked?"

"Dining room and bar are all clear, haven't done the conference rooms or started the downstairs accommodation yet, although I can hear team three has started upstairs."

Friday 27th March 2015 Team November adjacent Indonesian Headquarters

0035 hours. Having elected not to enter the headquarters, Santa split his team into three, with Vert taking two *Spirit* passengers and clearing some homes in behind the newsagency, while Barry and two more did the three homes on the other side of the street that connected the main road to the Tidal Waters Motel. Santa, Kenny and two passengers made their way down the road where the old RSL club was situated.

The brief from Doc and the *Fremantle* was to clear what they could and await the arrival of Dick and Sarge's jeeps coming in from Bin Bay, this would tie up with Len's crew.

"I'll lead, you two follow." The thirty-two-year-old deck rating replied.

"I'll cover the back door, Santa."

With Santa through the doorway first, the sixty-one-year-old could sense something was not quite right. Normally a house had smells of food and sweat, well that's the way he described it, this was different, no smells 'maybe its empty' he thought, or 'maybe it's a trap'. Before he could pass on his concerns to the two following him, a door opened on his left, through the NVG's he could detect something coming out of the doorway and it wasn't a person, well it was, behind the SS1-R5 Raider Assault Rifle.

Stopping and dropping to the floor, signalling for the others to do the same, but they weren't quick enough

"Boom ... Boom ... Boom." The weapon spat out it's deadly arsenal of 5.56mm rounds, one sliced through the outer flesh of Santa's left arm, narrowly missing any vital parts, not so good for the man behind him hitting him squarely in the upper chest below the throat, as the man was trying to make it to the floor, the second and third rounds hit the last man in the torso.

Before the ex-CD could level his 9mm Browning at the offender he could see the trooper waving the weapon around trying to pick up a target. With visibility zero he had no way of seeing who was there, or even who he had hit.

"Dooff...Dooff." Santa's two rounds found their target, at only four metres he couldn't miss, hitting the trooper in the head and chest as he squared up, not knowing who was hurt behind him, Santa leant up against the passage wall and scanned the area behind him, realising both were dead, he yelled

"Kenny, men down, are you ok?" The ex-deck rating obviously hearing the gunfight was in the middle of checking his last room, turned the corner just in time to see another trooper appear from the same room.

"Dooff." One round to the head, the man fell at Santa's feet.

"Sorry Santa, had to check the last two rooms in case there was any more of the gooks."

0200 hours, Barry, after successfully clearing the three homes, met up with Vert and team, realising Santa was taking too long, they went to investigate.

"Shit Skipper, are you ok?"

"I'll live, just a scratch, how have you lot gone?"

"Slow but better than you." Kenny retrieved the two SS1-R5 Raider Assault Rifles and what ammunition he could find and also informed Santa a jeep was located out back, sending one of Barry's team in to search for the keys, they helped the now grumpy ex-CD out the back to the M35 jeep.

Friday 27th March 2015 Team Whiskey Tidal Waters Motel

0200 hours, Len gathered the crew around him, nearly losing a man was a horrendous thought, but something they all had come to terms with, he had sent Maurice and his two team members over the road to the half a dozen homes facing the motel. Satisfied they had cleared the motel they took stock of the weapons recovered. Jill had found a M35 2·-ton cargo truck fitted out as a troop carrier in the rear car park, she guessed the closest room to where it was parked would yield the keys.

"Found them!" She emerged holding them up like a trophy.

Reporting to Dick via portable VHF, Len was told the two jeeps were only a kilometre away, down near the old fish farm.

"We'll give Maurice a hand and wait for Dick and Sarge."

0300 hours and the Whiskey team were all sitting in the Light Cargo Truck when they could hear a jeep coming towards them.

"Could be trouble Len?"

"Nah Jill, there's no headlights, its TRF travelling with NVG's."

Friday 27th March 2015 Fremantle the New Teams- One, Two and Four

0300 hours, Sarge, Terri and a female passenger (team one) along with Dick, Liz and Paul, a male passenger (team four) and Thomas, one female and one male passenger (team two), having cleared all the way from the junction where the Bin Bay Road and Reid's Road met, were now approaching the old fish farm.

Jock, one female and one male passenger (team three) along with the last team (team five), Jack and two female passengers had turned off Reid's Road, this did not have many farms so would not take long to clear. When dissecting the Ansons Bay Road Jack would go right towards Priory Vineyard and clear as far as he could get in two hours, while Jock would turn left and clear towards St Anne.

0315 hours and closing in on the outskirts of St Anne, Sarge was concerned that they had encountered no Indonesian patrols or out stations.

"Maybe they are thinking the threat will come from the water like last time Sarge." The forty-eight-year-old chef trying to give her opinion, all three jeeps pulled up alongside team Whiskey in the Light Cargo Truck.

Getting Len's report and making sure everyone was well stocked in ammunition, the four drivers huddled for their next orders.

"Anyone heard from Santa?" Dick nodded to Thomas to make contact on the VHF, this he didn't want to overuse just in case the Alliance had worked the communications out and were listening.

"Well from here, it's a full on raid on their headquarters again, this time expect trouble, and we won't be going in stealth, so no suppressors and use grenades if necessary. What's that Thomas, two dead and Santa's been wounded, shit, bad, oh a scratch, right we won't mention anything to Pat or she'll kill him.

Back to the plan, jeep one, four and team Whiskey will surround the headquarters attacking it from three angles, while team November and jeep two will start clearing out towards the Ansons Bay turnoff, they will take a street each and move west.

When we think the HQ is under control and if the troops stationed at the wharf haven't joined in, we will attack them there. I'm hoping by then *Fremantle's* other two teams, jeeps three and five have made it into town, then we withdraw, we'll cover teams Whiskey and November's withdrawal onto their vessels, while we then make our way back to the *Fremantle* at Skeleton Cove, any questions?"

Friday 27ᵗʰ March 2015 Fremantle Teams Three and Five Reid's Road

0300 hours, Jack and Jock knew they didn't have a lot of time to bugger about, and with the farms a fair distance apart, they elected to not go in stealth. Using their SS1-R5 Raider Assault Rifles and switching to the Pindad 9mm pistols. was making things flow smoother, however, the two pairs of NVG's were still needed to assist. Jacks' routine was well planned, all three members would enter the front door, even if they broke it down, then split with a room each and start firing, the 5.56 rounds were just as loud as the Type 68's they were now used to, they just left a smaller hole in their victims.

"Great work guys, only a couple to go I reckon on our side anyway." Catching up with Jock at the next farm, Jack suggested he go straight to Ansons Bay Road while Jack's team would cover his farms as well as Jocks.

"Sounds good to me Jack, see you in St Anne." And with this, the jeep took off, Jack could see the brake lights come on when it hit the Ansons Bay Road. The next four farms went well, still no troopers as security forces, Jack thought they had withdrawn them to bolster numbers in town.

0350 hours, turning right, the ex-sniper had no idea how many properties were on this road, but as Dick had said, give it a couple of hours only, this would get them back into St Anne about 0630 hours, to what though he had no idea.

Same time, a bit further down the road, team three was not so lucky, clearing the first two homes was relatively easy, nothing out of the ordinary, the next one was the house from hell.

"We'll cover the back, Jock" whispered the lead passenger. The second engineer and the female passenger pushed open the front door, this brick home was just a typical farmhouse, probably three or four bedrooms, about forty years old, lots of sheds, carports etc. outside. Jock was still using his suppressed 9mm Browning but had failed to keep count of the magazines he had left.

They had not come across any security, so hadn't collected any Indonesian weapons, although had a selection of Pindad 9mm in the jeep. Clearing the first room, the second engineer started thinking 'fuck what about the sheds outside, no one's looking in them'.

"Boom … Boom … Boom … Boom." The SS1-R5 Raider Assault Rifle on automatic fire was clear, 'shit' Jock thought. The large dining room in front of the fifty-year-old then filled with Troopers, there was at least four of them, the rear door team had not seen the Indonesians come up behind them, hiding in the shed, Jock pulled the trigger on his 9mm Browning.

"Click … click shit out of ammo." His counterpart, a shapely female passenger fired her Assault Rifle but too little too late, she was cut down in the initial burst, Jock was trying to reload, but the next magazine he pulled out was for his Pindad and wouldn't fit the Browning, the last thing the second engineer heard was the scraping of the metal magazine trying to fit the butt of his Browning.

Friday 27ᵗʰ March 2015 Fremantle Team Five Ansons Bay Road

0430 hours and the Priory Vineyard was well known in the district, run by an old family who relished in their history. It was located in the small settlement of Priory close to the tourist destinations of Bin Bay and just three clicks from the town of St Anne, one of Taswegia's premium holiday destinations on the sunny East Coast.

Priory Vineyard was a boutique vineyard on twenty hectares, with ideal north facing slopes which maximised sunlight. The soil was Devonian granite, rich in mineral content, transferring a unique 'Terroir' (how the environment affects the wine.)

Formally known as Tarpot Farm, the property had been in the ownership of Julie Llewellyn's family (Reid/Clifford) for over 120 years. Julie's great grandparents settled at Priory in 1889 after migrating from England in 1880.

Before its conversion to grapes, the property was mainly used to graze sheep as an adjunct to a much larger property, grazing sheep, cattle and some cropping. Priory Vineyard has the George River as its northern boundary and the vineyard draws its water from a small dam on the property.

Jack drove the aging jeep up the curved driveway, eventually coming to a fenced off yard with a wine tasting shack on one side and a huge hay shed on the other, the main home was in front of them, the 140-year-old stone dwelling showing its age, with obvious signs of upgrades and additions in recent years.

His 2IC, a female *Spirit* passenger checked the wine tasting shed, reporting

"It's been a while since that had seen any wine tasting Jack." The ex-CD Sniper replied.

"It looks like it was a great farm in its day luv." Entering the front door, his nostrils were subjected to the pungent smell of Indonesian cooking, both girls went left towards the bedrooms while Jack checked the sitting room and more to the point the little annex bedroom that seemed all too often to be used for home security.

Friday 27th March 2015 Team November and Jeep Two West St Anne

0400 hours, Santa had drawn the main road, while Thomas was clearing along the Medeas Esplanade Road, this and the main road had about twenty small dead-end cul-de-sacs between them. The nick to his left arm had been dressed and with a renewed passion the November team pushed forward. Down to eight team members they decided to split into pairs, this would essentially get four homes done at once, the ex-CD had a shapely female passenger with him and the pair were working well together until he too, ran out of 9mm. In-between homes they took stock and reloaded their magazines with the Indonesian confiscated 9mm ammunition, although it was obvious they would not get through all the homes within the time.

0435 hours, Barry and partner were fired upon by a wiry home security trooper, a light sleeper, he heard the pair enter the home and got out of bed to see what was coming in at that hour. First shot killed the *Spirit* passenger, a woman around forty years old who was easy on the eye, 'to quote Kenny' who was a little smitten with the woman. Barry returned fire and with help from Vert and his partner from the next-door home, managed to kill the trooper.

"Fuck, I didn't see him at all Vert, he came out of nowhere." Barry obviously cut up about his partner was trembling so the ex-army sapper suggested he sit a few out in the jeep.

0435 hours, Thomas's jeep two was having a good run up the Esplanade; this road only had homes on one side, the other bordering the shallow water of the inlet and then the mud flats of the Medeas Conservation Area.

Reaching the St Anne Council yards, the only building on their left since they started, the seventy-two-year-old ex-RSM wondered how the others were going as Santa had drew the short straw, so to speak with a lot more homes to cover, but with more team members.

"We'll head down Walker Street towards the main road; let's see if we can't help the others out." With the district Pony Club grounds, numerous vacant blocks, a boat repair shop and landscape nursery all void of Indonesian Alliance, they were soon at the main road. The long street had clear vision for around one kilometre even in the slight moonlight.

"Can't see any sign of them Thomas."

Friday 27th March 2015 Team Whiskey and Jeeps One and Four St Anne Headquarters

0345 hours, the two jeeps and the Light Cargo Truck pulled up at each entrance to the Indonesian St Anne Headquarters, Dick and jeep four at the front entrance, Sarge and jeep one at the kitchen entrance while the November team used the bar entrance.

Sarge led them through the motel's industrial kitchen, this was once again occupied with early morning staff getting ready to cook breakfast, the two cooks on duty were sort of on the ball, and both had side arms on. The suppressed 9mm Brownings were good at their job, dropping the pair. Now Sarge knew Dick said they didn't have to go in stealth, but the forty-five-year-old ex-sapper loved the Browning, and well the longer they could penetrate the building without it sounding like World War Seven the better it was.

0415 hours and Dick found the guards in the foyer playing cards, he too liked the suppressed 9mm and used it effectively, dispatching the two with no noise at all. The motel's conference room supplied a surprise, four camp stretchers set up on the floor in the outer room, each with a trooper snoring, totally unaware of the danger that was to be bestowed on them, they probably were the relief guards for the front, once again four shots at close range did the job.

The small number of rooms to the right would have been the manager's residence originally, now they presumed it was officers or senior NCO's. Liz led the way with the male *Spirit* passenger following while the ex-CD covered their backs.

"Boom ... Boom ... Boom ... Boom ... Boom ... Boom ... Boom." Once again, the sound of the SS1-R5 Raider Assault Rifles could be heard from the other end of the building.

"Sounds like it's coming from upstairs Dick, I reckon Len and crew have found troopers."

0445 hours, Len had indeed found troopers, six were in the first room, all up and getting dressed, probably about to go on watch or something. The first one spun around saying something when the door opened, he probably thought it was one of his mates from the next room, well he got an eye full of Maurice, the thirty-eight-year-old Bosun, who didn't have his weapon at the ready position, a fatal mistake, even though he got his first round off killing the closest trooper to him. This took valuable time and by the time he re-aimed he was dead. Len shouldered the door open and on full-automatic gave the rest of them a burst.

This brought troopers out of the next room firing from the hip, narrowly missing the seventeen-year-old Jill, but catching the last two of the team. Jill returned fire but in turn was hit in the shoulder, the 5.56mm Raider round entering just above the joint and exiting slightly higher up.

"Shit Len, I'm hit." Not knowing whether she hit anything or not, it all happened so quickly, the seventeen-year-old collapsed to the floor in agony clutching her shoulder which felt like a truck had hit her.

Len re-emerged from the first room to see what was in front of him, Jill down, two *Spirit* passengers dead, but so were the Indonesian Alliance Troopers. Both had been cut down by Jill's SS1-R5 Raider. Grabbing the portable VHF, he transmitted

"Dick, Sarge, men down Jill injured, can you help, on the top floor suspect more troopers over."

"Len, Sarge here, we're at the top of the stairs, lay low in case we have to open up."

And that's what happened, a series of doors opening and weary eyed troopers emerging in the pre-dawn light. Len covered Jill with his body, the sound of Sarge and Terri 's SS1-R5 Raider Assault Rifles was deafening. With its thirty round box magazine and a rate of fire of 700 rounds per minute, all cooped up in the confined space of the motel's upper corridor, it sounded like a couple of freight trains roaring at you.

Sarge ran, trying to clip another magazine into the weapon, but he came across a trooper still very much alive who tried to stab the ex-sapper with his bayonet. Sarge weaponised the other end of the Assault Rifle, using it like a cricket bat, and used running momentum, along with his brute force to hit the guy fair in the head, splitting his skull sending blood and brain matter up the adjacent wall. Terri went to Jill and Len's aid, while the sounds of Sarge could be heard dispatching the cowering troopers left in their rooms, too scared to come out.

"Len are you ok mate?"

"Fucking deaf now but I think I'm ok, Jill's been hit in the shoulder, bleeding like a stuck pig, 'sorry Jill', boy was that impressive Sarge, you're a machine."

Friday 27th March 2015 Fremantle Team Five Priory Vineyard

0445 hours, an irate Indonesian National charged out of the room in front of the ex-CD sniper, the woman was brandishing a cast iron frying pan, taking a swing, the fifty-one-year-old specialist sniper ducked to avoid the iron truncheon. He turned to shoot her with his 9mm, but she was already back on her feet, she jumped on the ex-CD's back and had a go with the pan, grazing the side of his head. The other two female team members were trying to get a clear shot but didn't want to take the chance of hitting Jack, she actually succeeded with another swing and jack went down like a bag of spuds. Bringing the heavy frying pan up for its fatal blow, the female passenger fired, the round went through the woman's neck and hit the pan full flight.

Jack came too, covered with blood, he thought his time had come until learning it wasn't his blood. His head was killing him, an egg-shaped lump appeared but it wasn't over, telling the pair to clear the rest of the home, just before another National appeared, the women shot her and cleared the other rooms while the ex-CD tried to get up, no can do, he fell in a heap.

"Shit girls, I'm a bit stuffed, someone else will have to drive."

Friday 27th March 2015 Team November West St Anne Main Road

0435 hours, Santa and his female partner had cleared seven homes, the other three pairs a similar amount, his arm hurt like hell, he thought 'shit it's only a nick, glad I didn't take a full-on round'.

One of his pairs, was now only a single, Kenny's partner was shot hopping across a back fence between houses, and the poor girl got her crutch caught on one of the spear shaped fence toppers while they were under fire from a nosey Trooper across the road.

Turning around the left-hand bend in the main road meant he was now facing Thomas and his crew, with only six members left, he wondered if they would actually close the gap, the next two homes, he lost the plot, firing from the hip with his Raider Assault Rifle. This was not only deafening, but smoky, within the confines of the small units, what came next, he was surprised how much smoke came off the weapon when fired.

0510 hours and still with four or five homes between the two teams, could have been more if there were any more sets on units, something that was prevalent this side of town, the ex-CD called it quits. Whistling Thomas in, they agreed it had been a long night and decided to work their way back to the wharf for extraction.

Friday 27ᵗʰ March 2015 Team Whiskey and Jeeps One and Four St Anne Headquarters

0500 hours, they assembled in the foyer, Dick's three, Sarge's three and Len's six, including the injured Jill.

"Dick, Sarge you got a copy?"

"Receiving Santa, how's it going?"

"Mate have met up with Thomas, we're all stuffed and heading back towards you."

"Good mate, will let you know how hot the extraction will be, have you seen jeeps three and five over?"

"No nothing yet, will let you know if we see them."

Sarge sent out Terri and one of Len's passengers to reccy the wharf area; they waited ten minutes while the pair crawled aback alongside the timber walkway to the seafood restaurant and back again.

"No signs of anyone on the wharf Sarge, but we could hear shouting coming from the old police station over the road."

"Thanks guys, what do you reckon Dick, how do you want to do this?" Thinking long and hard, the ex-CD specialist commented.

"I think, to save wasting time, we call Pat and the *Nancy Kay* in to the first finger near the restaurant, get them to nose in, but count us in, we will time it to get both boat crews on the jetty at the precise time she touches, get them mounted up while we give cover fire if needed, then travel back along the Bin Bay Road."

Friday 27th March 2015 Fremantle Team Five Ansons Bay Road

0525 hours and Jack was still delirious, the *Spirit* passenger driving was not used to a manual and certainly not one of this age. The gearbox had no synchro in first gear so there was a constant grating of gears, some kangaroo hopping and general all over the road swaying. After some time, they seemed to be driving for ages; problem was the girl was only doing about thirty kilometres per hour.

"Where are we?" asks a concerned Jack trying to pull himself up to the window.

"Are we at the highway yet or have we seen jeep three?

"Sorry Jack, I'm not very good with this sort of car, wait there's the farm with jeep three outside." as they approached,

"Boom … Boom … Boom." A rapid rate of fire came from the front veranda, in the dawn light they could see two troopers running towards them, Jack leaned over and pushed his foot down on the accelerator.

"Fuck noooo I can't control it!"

The 5.56 rounds were peppering the back of the jeep. Popping his head up just in time to see the tree coming at them fast, the ex-CD sniper grabbed the wheel bringing the vehicle back into control.

"Really sorry Jack, Sal."

"Might pay you to stop now we're out of range, I'll take over, oh shit, damn fuck!" Jack had looked around at the passenger in the back seat; she was slumped forward with a hole in her back, a clean shot, a fluke right through her back into the girl's heart. Trying to console the driver as she swapped seats,

"Hell girl, that could have been me, she saved my life, I might have been sitting in the back, but I remember, she, what was her name, Sally gave me the front seat, lucky or we might have all been killed if I hadn't planted my foot on the accelerator."

Friday 27th March 2015 St Anne Wharf 0600

"Time's running out people, it's fucking daylight, we will be sitting ducks, where the fuck are the other two jeeps?"

"Maybe they didn't make it Dick."

"I find that hard to believe Sarge, and I think so do you, but they know what to do if they can't make it."

"*Nancy Kay, Nancy Kay*, are you receiving me over?"

"Got you Dick, boy we didn't think you were going to call, it's very late."

"Roger that Pat, you will do the pickup solo, repeat solo do you copy?"

"Roger that Dick, hot extraction?"

"Hotter than the bowels of hell Pat, keep your wits about you, nose touch only we will provide covering fire over."

With no anchor down Rose just slipped the amidships line, while Pat started the single V12 Caterpillar 1000 HP Turbo engine and pushed the stick ahead, the sixty-five-foot *Conquest* leapt out of the water like an excited dolphin. Rose said

"They didn't say anything about the boys Pat, I hope they are alright."

"Me too luv, me too."

Pat and Rose could see the right-hand finger coming up fast; she pulled back on the throttle allowing the nose of the vessel to come down off the plane. A light truck was negotiating the lawn between the main road and the wharf, loaded up with six of the *Nancy Kay's* crew and five of the *Waubs Bay's* crew; this was under the protection from Sarge, Paul and Dick providing covering fire.

Friday 27th March 2015 Fremantle Team Five Ansons Bay Road

It was already past 0630 hours; the road was longer than the ex-CD sniper realised

"Too late luv, we will have to turn around and make our way back to Bin Bay."

Turning the old jeep around, he barrelled back the way they had come.

"Hope we don't have to go through the horrible place where they shot at us."

"Unfortunately, we do, but that is not our biggest worry." Looking in the cracked rear vision mirror, Jack could see a Light Truck closing in behind them.

"They are not shooting at us Jack, that has to be a good thing, right?"

"Well, they probably don't know who we are, but if I'm right, they are going to find out real soon. I reckon they're picking up the troopers from the farms, so after that look out."

Whipping the antiquated army jeep around the corners on the dirt road proved to be an advantage, they soon lost sight of the truck, passing the farm where jeep three met their demise, the troopers weren't quick enough and before they could bring weapons to bear, Jack was gone.

0700 hours. All was going well until just before the turn off onto Reid's Road,

"They're coming up behind us Jack, fast."

"Boom ... Boom ... Boom." The 5.56mm rounds were flicking up the dirt road all round them as they sped towards the turn.

"Get in the back seat and get ready to fire that Raider Assault Rifle luv, when I say go, after we have made the turn, they will be vulnerable, I hope."

Backing down a gear, the aging jeep slowed around the corner, 'not enough power, you shit of a jeep' back to second gear and planted the go peddle, revving its guts out the jeep tried to get enough speed up so Jack could change into third.

"Boom ... Boom." Jack yelled.

"Now luv, let them have it on automatic." The young *Spirit* passenger aimed and pulled the trigger, the chase vehicle was halfway through the turn

"Boom ... Boom ... Boom ... Boom ... Boom ... Boom." The Light Truck came to a halt.

"Looks like you winged the driver, good shooting luv."

With an advantage of maybe three minutes while they changed drivers, Jack sent the little jeep past its desired range of operation, the speedo was on the stops most of the time. Usually confined to a sedate ninety clicks an hour, the speedo only went to 110. The dirt road was mainly straight, so Jack drove as fast as he could, the problem would come when they got to Bin Bay 'was the RHIB going to be waiting?' This truck would be hot on their tail, 'would they have time to get on the RHIB?'

"Can't see them Jack, I think you lost them."

"Oh, they will be there, luv, we can't go anywhere, and they know that, let's hope they don't have the means of radioing for backup."

"Do we?" asked a very frightened girl.

"Handheld VHF will have range when we get into Bin Bay. Let's hope it's not too late by then."

Friday 27th March 2015 St Anne Wharf 0700

The ex-CD CPO could see the *Nancy Kay* approach the jetty finger; Sarge exclaimed.

"Fuck the cavalry's here and it ain't ours!"

"Sarge was referring to the three M35 21/2 Tonne Light Cargo Trucks approaching from the St Anne Slip end of the wharf.

With Ultimax Light Machine Guns mounted above the cab, these meant business.

"Boom ... Boom ... Boom ... Boom ... Boom ... Boom ... Boom ... Boom." The automatic LMG's making a mess of everything in their paths. Len and Santa's teams were returning fire, being closer to the action. Dick's team dismounted and were seeking cover behind the restaurant wall, Sarge and Thomas's teams did the same.

"Get that RPG out Thomas; see if you can light up one of those jeeps."

The ex-RSM sighted on the first truck and pulled the trigger, the rocket propelled grenade snaked its way to the target, seeing the imminent danger they tried to avoid the smoke trail, with no hope, many jumped clear.

"Whoomph." The Light Cargo Truck disintegrated and with that diversion, Dick ordered the first group to run. Santa, Vert, Barry, Kenny and their two *Spirit* passengers were off, cowering as they ran, the industrial dumpsters were a godsend for cover. Pat nosed the sixty-five-foot *Conquest* into the end of the jetty.

Rose was armed with her Type 68 and returned fire as the team jumped aboard.

"Hit it Luv." yelled Santa, as the last man was aboard, in the wheelhouse Pat asked,

"What about the others Santa?"

"We'll attempt another run in when they are ready."

0730 hours and Sarge was hitting the last two trucks with everything he had, trying to get within throwing distance, working his way towards the public toilets, situated between the restaurant and the fisherman's unload end of the wharf.

"Look Dick more Cavalry, behind us."

The sixty-one-year-old ex-CD could see another two trucks rounding the corner from the Tidal Waters Motel.

"Fuck, not good mate, grab a couple of boys and push that dumpster over here for cover, got any more RPG's left?"

"Only two Dick, looks like we're going for a boat ride."

"Sure, does mate."

"*Nancy Kay, Nancy Kay*, are you receiving over?"

"Got you Dick, what's the plan?"

"Get ready to come in, looks like we're coming too!"

Alerting all the team, Sarge had dropped a grenade under the next truck making short work of it. They could also see reinforcements coming across the bridge on foot. Paul was blasting away at the trucks behind their position.

"Bastards think they have us stuffed Dick."

"I think they do Sarge. Thomas, on my mark, one RPG at those pricks behind us, and then next one towards the last truck left at the other end, then men, we run!"

"*Nancy Kay*, come on in!"

Thomas let rip with the first RPG, the cocky bastards didn't see it coming.

"Whoomph." The blast lifted the lighter vehicle clean off the ground

"Run, Whoomph."

The ex-Army RSM fired the last rocket then dropped the launcher and ran, Sarge, Terri, Paul and with the other *Spirit* passenger hot on their tail, were dodging rounds on the way to the end of the jetty. Santa, more confident behind the controls brought the sixty-five-footer in at ten knots, he went astern at the vinegar stroke, his men were up on deck, the 50 Calibre Machine Gun was spitting out its deafening roar. Santa held the vessel slow ahead to keep the bow against the jetty.

"Where's Dick?" yelled Sarge as he finally made the leap aboard.

"Still coming Sarge."

Dick, Liz, Paul and their team mate, now under immense fire from both ends of the wharf were halfway, concealed behind the steel dumpster.

"Get that mob there with the 50 Cal Vert, it seems to pull their heads in, then give the other end a burst, that should give Dick time."

The sixty-year-old ex-RAME engineer pulled the cocking lever back and depressed the twin thumb triggers, the 13.5mm rounds came out of the barrel at a rate of 500 rounds per minute, the belt fed machine gun had an effective range of 1800 metres and a maximum range of 7,200 metres, both targets were around 1500 metres away, so Vert had no problems in hitting his mark.

0810 hours, Dick could see his mate Vert preparing for another burst, with both his feet against the solid cowling to steady the weapon he let fly, a slight hesitation in gunfire from the enemy was all the ex-CD needed. Sending Liz, Paul and the other team member off first, he waited till Vert changed targets.

Running was never one of the ex-CDs fun things to do, as a matter of a fact he hated it with a passion, 'ah well here goes' he thought and with that, he ran like he had never ran before. Liz and Paul were aboard, a round caught the last girl, she fell on the gunwale, Vert was still blasting away at both targets in turn. Dick made the boat as Santa went astern. Nearly missing the jump, he grabbed hold of the girl's waistline as he rolled onto the deck, Ultimax LMG rounds following the ex-clearance diver aboard.

Friday 27th March 2015 Fremantle Team Five Bin Bay 0830

"*Fremantle, Fremantle* Delta Echo jeep five over."

"Jack, you old bastard, thought you were dead, where are you?"

"Approaching the extraction point Doc and well nearly could be, hot extraction repeat, hot extraction, any sign of the others, the place is crawling with Indonesian marines."

"Yeah, mate same, same in St Anne, Dick, Sarge and team had to extract with the *Nancy Kay*, they're on route as we speak, where's jeep three over?"

"Negative jeep three, all dead and we have the bastards hot on our tail over."

0845 hours and Jack could see the little jetty and the RHIB. Wallace clearly preparing to give covering fire as they stopped. Skidding to a halt the pair dismounted and ran to the waiting Patch and Nettie, Wallace had already opened fire on the approaching truck, slowly withdrawing as the spunky eighteen-year-old pulled the sticks astern then spinning the RHIB away from danger.

"Where's the rest of them Jack?" Patch already knew the answer to this before she opened her mouth 'shit that was a dumb question' she thought.

"Sorry Jack, didn't mean it like that." Putting his arm around his mate's wife he collapsed.

"He's been hit on the head with a cast iron frypan Patch!"

"Thanks, I can see the bump, but I can also see blood from under his vest, he's been shot."

Friday 27ᵗʰ March 2015 Nancy Kay and Waubs Bay St Georges Bay St Anne

0830 hours, Santa spun the sixty-five-foot *Conquest* then giving her full throttle out towards the middle of Georges Bay where the *Waubs Bay* was waiting. With no time to disperse their crew before, this was accomplished once alongside, Len, Jill and the three *Spirit* passengers were quickly made comfortable, some electing to crash on their bunks, some just wanted a cuppa. Josh and Helga very happy to have the skipper back on board. Giving his sister a huge hug, then the skipper declared,

"Great to see you guys in one piece, we were worried there for a while."

Helga hugged them both, something she never normally did but hell these were her family now.

"What now Len?" asked Josh keen to see some more action.

"Wait for orders mate." the lanky ex-fisherman hugged Jill and gave her a kiss.

"You had me worried at times, geeze I'm glad you are alright."

"Ditto luv."

0900 hours and with the *Fremantle* crew dispersed amongst the boat, Santa, Vert and Barry assumed crew positions up on the flying bridge. Santa asked

"Where's Dick, we need some direction as to what they want to do next, although I can guess, meet up with the Fremantle and transfer crew back?"

"He was sitting against the cowling up forward, poor bugger must be really stuffed, and he never said a word to me when I asked whether he wanted a cup of coffee"

Looking over the windscreen to the forecastle, Santa ran down the ladder from the flying bridge yelling.

"Buggered be stuffed, that's not like him to knock back one of his black coffees and lemon." Followed by Sarge, Jack, Pat, Rose, Barry and Vert they found the sixty-one-year-old ex-CD specialist indeed leaning against the cowling, the girl he pulled aboard alongside of him while he was slipping in and out of consciousness.

"Hi, guys, looks like she didn't make it, and I seem to have picked up a hitchhiker." And with that he rolled forward exposing a small hole in his back.

Glossary

AMPS- Advanced Mobile Phone System

Bangers- Sausages

BMND-SE- British Multi National Division South East

Bum Nuts- Eggs

CDAT- Clearance Diving Acceptance Test

CD-Clearance Divers

CDT's- Clearance Diving Teams

CDT 3-Clearance Diving Team 3

Chow- Army Food

DDG- Guided Missile Destroyer

ENT- Ear Nose and Throat

EOD- Explosive Ordnance Disposal

FCPB- Fremantle Class Patrol Boat

Heads- Toilet

HF- High Frequency

HITS- Herrings in Tomato Sauce

GSW- Gun Shot Wounds

Kai- Pronounced Kye a Thick Hot Chocolate Drink

Kip- Sleep

Local Bike- Woman of Loose Moral Standards Who Everyone Rides

MCM- Mine Counter-Measures

MHC- Mine Hunter Coastal

MIRV's- Multiple Independently Targetable Re-entry Vehicles

MTO- Maritime Tactical Operations

NK- North Korean

NVG- Night Vision Goggles

OBG(W)- Overwatch Battle Group West

Pit or Rack- Bunk, Bed

Pongos- Army (wherever the Army goes the pong goes)

Pot Mess- Scran Rustled Up Out of Whatever Could be Found in a Tin

Pussers- Royal Australian Navy

RAA- Royal Australian Army

RAE- Royal Australian Engineers

RFDS- Royal Flying Doctor Service

Roger - Received

ROV- Remote Operated Vehicles

RSL- Returned Serviceman's League

Runt-Someone of Small Stature

SAS- Special Air Service

Scran- Shit Cooked by the Royal Australian Navy

Shake- To Wake Someone Up

Slope- Derogatory term for Asian

SLR- Self Loading Rifle

Standard NATO Brew- (White with two sugars)

TAG (E) - Tactical Assault Group (East)

Tinned Cow- Condensed Milk

TPI- Totally and Permanently Incapacitated

UBDR- Underwater Battle Damage Repair

UHF- Ultra High Frequency

VHF- Very High Frequency

WM- Weapons Mechanic

Wooly Pully- The Thick Issued Navy Jumper

Weapons

Type 54 Pistols - Chinese made Tokarev batches, the 54 pistol has a 7.62mm x 25mm or 38 Calibre super rounds.

This is a knock off of the Soviet Union made TT semi auto pistol and was issued with an 8 round magazine.

Short recoil actuated locked breech, single action, and semi-automatic.

Muzzle velocity 420 m/s (1,378 ft. /s)

Effective firing range   50 m

Type 68 Assault Rifle- This is commonly called an AKM semi-automatic rifle and has a 7.62·39mm round.

With a M43 30 round magazine it fires 600 rounds a minute gas operated 350 metre effective range

Type 69 RPG - Type_69_Rocket Propelled Grenade

The Type 69 uses a 85mm rocket propelled grenade (RPG), made by Norinco, it's a Chinese variant of the Soviet RPG-7. First introduced in 1972, the Type 69 is a common individual anti-tank weapon in service with the North Korea

Effective firing range   200 m.

INDONESIAN ALLIANCE WEAPONS

Pindad P2 Semi-automatic Pistol was the standard issue sidearm, a local copy of the Browning Hi-Power. Approximately 2,000 P2s manufactured.

Firing a 9·19mm Parabellum round, It is a firearms cartridge that was designed by Georg Luger and introduced in 1902 by the German weapon's manufacturer Deutsche Waffen- und Munitionsfabriken (DWM) for their Luger semi-automatic.

The name Parabellum is derived from the Latin: Si vis pacem, para bellum, which was the motto of DWM.

'A semi-automatic pistol is a type of pistol that is semi-automatic, meaning it uses the energy of the fired cartridge to cycle the action of the firearm and advance the next available cartridge into position for firing. One cartridge is fired each time the trigger of a semi-automatic pistol is pulled; the pistol's "disconnector" ensures this behaviour.'

The SS1-R5 Raider Assault Rifles are used by the Indonesian Military. Designed for Special Forces operations such as infiltration, short distance contact in jungle, mountain, marsh, sea and urban warfare.

SS1-R5 can be attached with bayonet and various types of telescopes.

It has Safe, Single and Full Automatic firing options.

The weapon fires a 5.56·45mm NATO round and is a rimless bottlenecked intermediate cartridge family developed in the late 1970s in Belgium by FN Herstal. The 5.56·45mm NATO cartridge family was derived from, but is not identical to, the .223 Remington cartridge designed by Remington Arms in the early 1960s.

Ultimax 100

The Ultimax 100 is a Singapore-made 5.56mm x 45mm Nato rounds, light machine gun, developed by the Chartered Industries of Singapore by a team of engineers under the guidance of American firearms designer L. James Sullivan. The weapon is extremely accurate due to its constant-recoil operating system. Rate of fire 400–600 rounds/min

TASWEGIAN RESISTANCE FORCE WEAPONS

Browning 9mm Semi-Automatic Pistol - 9mm Hi Power pistols have a magazine capacity of 13 cartridges plus one in the chamber, for a total capacity of 14 cartridges. It was based on a design by American firearms inventor John Browning, firing a 7.65·21mm Parabellum round. Short recoil operated.

Rate of fire - Semi-automatic

Muzzle velocity 335 m/s (1,100 ft. /s)

Effective firing range 50 m (54.7 yd.)

Feed system: detachable box magazine; capacities 13 rounds.

9mm Glock - the Glock is a series of polymer-framed, short recoil-operated, locked-breech semi-automatic pistols designed and produced by Austrian manufacturer Glock. The firearm entered Austrian military and police service by 1982 after it was the top performer in reliability and safety tests.

Despite initial resistance from the market to accept a perceived "plastic gun" due to concerns regarding durability and reliability which proved unfounded, as well as fears that its use of a polymer frame might bypass the detection of the metal detectors in airports, also unfounded, Glock pistols have become the company's most profitable line of products as well as supplying national armed forces, security agencies, and police forces in at least 48 countries.

With an effective firing range of 50 metres, a muzzle velocity of 375 metres per second and rate of fire of between 1100 and 1200 rounds per minute this is indeed a very formidable weapon.

Rounds 9mm x 19mm Parabellum (same as the Indonesian Pindad P2 Pistol)

The Bren gun, usually called simply the Bren, is a series of light machine guns (LMG) made by Britain in the 1930s and used in various roles until 1992.

Effective firing range: 600 yd. (550 m)
Maximum firing range: 1,850 yd. (1,690 m)
Place of origin: Designed in Czechoslovakia
When the British Army adopted the 7.62 mm NATO cartridge, the Bren was re-designed to 7.62 mm calibre, fitted with a new bolt, barrel and magazine.

SLR the Australian L1A1 is also known as the "self-loading rifle" (SLR), and in fully automatic form, the "automatic rifle" (AR).

Cartridge 7.62·51mm NATO round
Action   Gas-operated, tilting breechblock
Rate of fire   Semi-automatic
Muzzle velocity   823 m/s (2,700 ft. /s)
Effective firing range   800 m (875 yds.) (Effective range)
Feed system   20- or 30-round detachable box magazine
Sights   Aperture rear sight, post front sight

F1 Sub Machine Gun- the 9·19mm Parabellum F1 was a standard Australian submachine gun manufactured by the Lithgow Small Arms Factory. First issued to Australian troops in July 1963, it replaced the Owen machine carbine. Like the Owen, the F1 had a distinctive top mounted magazine.

Sights: Offset iron sights,
Feed system: 34-round Sterling SMG compatible box magazine,
Effective firing range: 150 m
Maximum firing range: 100–200 m,
Rate of fire: 600–640 rounds/min
Calibre: 9 mm

Barrett's 50 calibre Snipers rifle- The Barrett M82a1, standardized by the U.S. military as the M107, is a recoil-operated,
The Barrett M107 is a .50 calibre, shoulder-fired, semi-automatic sniper rifle.
Like its predecessors, the rifle is said to have manageable recoil for an
effective firing range: 1,969 yd. (1,800 m)
Designer: Ronnie Barrett
Cartridge: .50 BMG .416 Barrett

The Winchester Model 70- 243 is a bolt-action sporting rifle.
Introduced in 1936 earning the moniker "The Rifleman's Rifle"
The .243 produces a velocity of 2,960 feet (902.21 m) per second with a 100-grain (6.6 gram) projectile commercially loaded, fired from a 24-inch (610 mm) barrel

12 Gauge Shotgun - A shotgun (also known as a scattergun is a firearm that is usually designed to be fired from the shoulder, which uses the energy of a fixed shell to fire several small spherical pellets called shot, or a solid projectile called a slug.
Shotguns come in a wide variety of sizes, ranging from 5.5 mm (.22 inch) bore up to 5 cm (2.0 in) bore, and in a range of firearm operating mechanisms, including breech loading, single-barrelled, double or combination gun, pump-action, bolt-, and lever-action, revolver, semi-automatic, and even fully automatic variants.

M16 Armalite - Commonly called the M16 rifle, officially designated an Assault Rifle, Calibre 5.56 mm,

M16 is a family of military rifles adapted from the Armalite AR-15 rifle for the United States military.

The original M16 rifle was a 5.56mm automatic rifle, limited twist rifling in the barrel to enable the rounds to tumble literally chopping through the jungle and with a 20-round magazine, later modifications included a 30 round curved magazine,

It had a rate of fire of 700-950 rounds per minute o and a

Muzzle velocity of 960 metres per second.

Browning .50 Calibre Machine Gun - is a heavy machine gun designed toward the end of World War I by John Browning. Cartridge .50 BMG (12.7·99mm NATO) Action Short recoil-operated, Rate of fire 450–600 rounds/min to 1,200–1,300 rounds/min (AN/M3) Muzzle velocity 2,910 ft/s (890 m/s Effective firing range1,800 m Maximum firing range 7,400 m Feed system Belt-fed (M2 or M9 links)

By the Same Author

hope you have enjoyed TOAST Book 4, Hells Retaliation. Visit my Author's page and view all of my other books. Just copy and paste this into your browser

www.rickallenbooks.com

Tales of a Saddle Tramp

The New Chinese Province

Saddlery Care and Maintenance

TOAST Book 1: **The Ride to Hell**

TOAST Book 2: **Hell's Salvation**

TOAST Book 3: **Hell's Beach**

TOAST Book 4: **Hell's Retaliation**

TOAST Book 5: **Hells Mission**

Coming soon:

TOAST Book 6: **Hells Victory**

TOAST Book 7: **Return from Hell**

Drug Runners of the Sundra Strait

TOAST BOOK 1:
The Ride to Hell

..........Emergency! Alex Brand reporting.

A force calling themselves, 'The Alliance' has landed at all major ports in Taswegia.

They are killing all the Parliamentarians on the lawns of Parliament House. They are murdering people as I speak. They are approaching my position now; I have to run ... (silence).

Dick, an ex-Navy Clearance Diver and his wife Patch looked at each other, they didn't know such a large force had survived the Nuclear Holocaust, this was not good!

What can Dick, Patch and their close friends who are now fighting for their lives against unbelievable odds do?

Find out in Rick Allen's latest book
Toast book 1: The Ride to Hell.

TOAST BOOK 2:
Hells Salvation

A danger-fraught week of travel began, with Sarge, Patch, April and Annie on horseback, and Dick and Jack travelling by road and sea.

Along the way both groups encountered Alliance troops more than once, only narrowly escaping with their lives; eventually managing to reach the relative safety of Hells Beach, where they set up camp, thinking they were well out of reach of the Alliance at last.

However, their reprieve from danger was brief; awakening one morning to find that a Fremantle Class Patrol Boat had appeared at the entrance to the bay.

Realising they were about to be discovered, they worked together to overpower the Alliance crew and take control of the patrol boat.

However, the skirmish left one of their number seriously injured, and in urgent need of medical help....

TOAST BOOK 3:
Hells Beach

Jack's idea is to search for the original pre-E1 engines that have been stored away by commercial fishermen and swap them over for the buggered E1 affected engines; a bold plan but one they know will pay off. Most professional fishermen would have kept the original engines. Sure it cost them a lot of money to change to the new E1 compliant ones, but they wouldn't have been able to see themselves just trashing the originals

or selling them back to the government for a paltry sum. Dick and Jack cooked up a plan to steal the commercial fishing vessels right out from under the Alliance noses; with Jack's knowledge in engineering and help from the others this was going to work.

"We can re-power these to form a fleet of fighting vessels; after all at the moment the Alliance has no power on the water, and from what we now know, they are not likely to get any more reinforcements."

A bold plan developed to isolate the Peninsular by opening the Sand Alley Bridge, enabling the TRF to kill all Alliance and recover the Peninsular....

TOAST BOOK 4:
Hells Retaliation

With the TRF mounting major raids at Dove, the Alliance have received another bloody nose. On the back of major defeats at Sand Alley, and after subsequentially losing control of the Peninsular, General Jun Lee is not happy.

With contact finally made with Dick and Patch's friends at High Head, they now know there is resistance north of Lawn.

Raids out of the Peninsular in their newly reengined vessels are creating havoc with the Alliance forces around the seaside towns of Purple Sands and Purple Marsh.

With the TRF coming to the aid of the West Coast inhabitants and finding Dick's old Clearance Diving mates at Wattle, ground is slowly regained against the NK Alliance.

On the East Coast the Indonesian alliance meets fierce resistance at St Anne....

TOAST BOOK 5:
Hells Mission

Welcome to the TRF update, thanks to all those billeted ashore. As you can see by the different colours I've crudely drawn on the map we have control of the following areas, which are marked in light blue:

Johnny and the peninsular TRF have the whole peninsular up as far as Oxford in the north, and Mid-Point to the west.

Mona Commander has control from Wattle in the west to Devon outskirts in the east, and just outside Brownsville in the north.

John, our newly appointed north west Commander, has secured all the north west tip as far as Devon.

Blue Bone has control all the way east from Queen to The Wall in the Wilderness.

Harold and his pirates on the *Black Ink* have control from Wood in the south to Kettle in the north, including Frog Island.

Len has from Oxford in the south to White Distillery in the north.

Santa is training the locals and *Taswegia II* passengers on Bass Island.

Buck controls the Ramat River and the northern coastline from High Head to Reed Lagoon.

Ernie's tunnel rats control High Head in the north to Earth in the south, and all the way to Scot in the east and Reed Lagoon.

TOAST BOOK 6:
Hells Victory

With the North Coast in TRF hands, the over-running of Lawn imminent, and the Indonesians reeling from a bloody nose dealt to them at Ansons Bay and Bin Bay from the vessels *Fremantle, Nancy Kay* and *Warbs Bay,* they continue to dominate the Alliance.

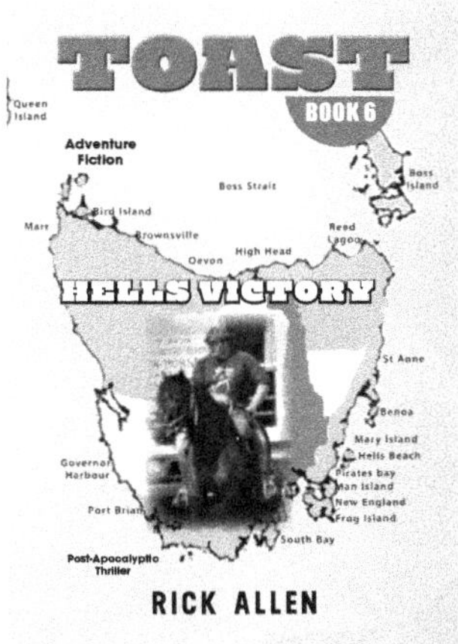

Sustaining serious injuries, the TRF are not expecting the Alliance Horse Troops to rally and are caught by surprise at Oxford. Their only option is to bring the horses out of retirement.

Bob, Zen and Tom lead a charge and are back in the thick of it. There is no other alternative than to move forward with a mounted attack towards Lakeside. Finding those still fit enough to take part is going to be a challenge.

The noose is tightening around Jun Lee's neck as the TRF move in towards Taswegia's capital. With ammunition levels at an all-time low, what will he do? Surrender, or fight to the death? ...

TOAST BOOK 7:
Return from Hell

With life on the West Coast back to normal and the Dove locals ready to move back home, the TRF start mopping up. They advance on the eastern shore, securing all the way to the Bridge.

The Alliance loses control and the General admits they have lost the northern end of the state.

Pushing west towards Kingstown, the TRF hold Queens, McKorky and East Kingstown. Kingstown is surrounded and nearing surrender, with the walls folding as the city is cut off.

After *Fremantle* sails into Kings Town Harbour the General finally meets Dick and his crew.

Governance: April draws up the PLAN. Who will be Premier? Milburn: Skipper of the *Taswegia II* and senior officers are recruited to bring back a tanker full of fuel. They find the locals affected by radiation and attacks by cannibals.

The New Taswegia: how will it work?

After much needed rain, water levels are back to 60% and power stations are back online.

What to do with the General?

The end to all the bloody killing at last! Or is it? ...

THE NEW CHINESE PROVINCE

Join Egras and Einna as they swage their way through the aftermath of what is being described as a subtle Invasion. Both are part of an Elite team gathered by a joint ASIO/CIA force. These forces, the Australian Security Intelligence Organisation and the US Central Intelligence Agency have gathered a group of ex and still serving patriotic military experts; together they will fight evil and rid their lands of the white-collar invaders. With infiltration rife amongst all levels of government and the Military ranks, they can trust no one outside their AES (Australian Elite Service).